Kit in the Serpent's Lair

A North Queensland Cadet Adventure

C.R. Cummings

Also By
CHRISTOPHER CUMMINGS

Kylie & Skip

The Boy and the Battleship

The Green Idol of Kanaka Creek

Ross River Fever

Train to Kuranda

Endeavour Island

*Kit in the Serpent's Lair

The Mudskipper Cup

Davey Jones's Locker

Fourteen

Air Cadet

Spinifex

Below Bartle Frere

Bowling Green Bay

Airship Over Atherton

Cockatoo

The Cadet Corporal

Stannary Hills

Sugar & Spice

Coast of Cape York

Kylie and the Kelly Gang

Beyond the Barrier Reef

Behind Mt. Baldy

The Cadet Sergeant Major

Cooktown Christmas

Secret in the Clouds

Mischief at Mingela

The Word of God

The Cadet Under-Officer

Through the Devil's Eye

Barbara in the Bush

The Smiley People

Barbara at her Best

Barbara's Bivouac

Kit in the Serpent's Lair

A North Queensland Cadet Adventure

C.R. Cummings

DoctorZed
Publishing
www.doctorzed.com

This 1st Edition published 2024 by DoctorZed Publishing

DoctorZed Publishing books may be ordered through booksellers or by contacting:

DoctorZed Publishing
10 Vista Ave
Skye, south Australia 5072
www.doctorzed.com

ISBN: 978-1-7636975-6-0 (sc)
ISBN: 978-1-7636975-7-7 (ebk)

A Cataloguing-in-Publication entry can be found at the National Library of Australia
www.nla.gov.au

Cover design © Scott Zarcinas
Cover image: Lava © Andre Nante | Dreamstime.com

Printed in Australia, UK & USA

DoctorZed Publishing rev. date: 18/11/2024

Dedication

This book is dedicated to the 'explorer' friends of my youth
Dr Peter Bell (Historian)
Mr Alan Broughton (Cairns Historical Society)
Mr Des Sheehan

Who helped discover and explore the lava tunnels
In the days when the world was much younger.

And

Professor David Hopley
Geography Department
of
James Cook University

Who inspired us to go and look.

Chapter 1

FAIR LADY

Thursday at school

Thirteen-year-old Christopher Walker stood nervously among the moving throng of students, his eyes focused on Diana.

Now is the time! Ask her you coward. Faint heart never won fair lady! he told himself.

Diana was also 13 and in the same Year 9 class at High School in Cairns. And she was everything Chris adored: shapely, beautiful and with lustrous black hair that gleamed in the sunlight.

And at that moment she wasn't surrounded by the Year 11 boys. *Come on weakling! Ask her now,* Chris told himself.

But fear held him—fear of being rejected, fear of failure, fear of not being good enough, fear of being rejected because he was smaller than other boys his age, fear of public embarrassment. Even not liking his name. His proper name was Christopher, but he disliked the shorter Chris, preferring the diminutive Kit.

Clenching his teeth and summoning up his courage Kit made himself start walking towards her. But Diana was on the other side of the crowded area under D Block, and he had to almost push his way through the chattering, laughing crowd of students and teachers. It was the start of the lunch break and people were moving to their usual seats.

Luckily she hasn't yet moved to her seat, Kit thought.

Like most students, Diana normally sat on the same seat with her friends. As Kit made his way towards her, she stood holding her lunch box and staring back towards the main building.

She looks like she is waiting for Fleur, he thought.

Fleur was Diana's friend and they sat together in most classes. Not wanting Fleur to be a witness, Kit glanced towards the main building. Seeing no sign of her he nerved himself to keep walking, increasing his pace slightly. Now his gaze focused on Diana and he felt his chest tighten and his heart rate shoot up.

She is just so beautiful! he thought.

He was concentrating so hard on Diana that he bumped several students as he pushed past or between them, and several made comments or shoved back.

"Watch where you are going, midget!" growled one of them.

Normally Kit would have bristled at the sneering reference to his small stature, but at that moment his whole being was concentrated on the answer to his question: will Diana go out with me?

And she was looking at him. Kit saw her head turn and her eyes focus on him. Then a slight frown creased her brow and she looked both anxious and puzzled. With his heart hammering furiously, Kit came to a stop two paces from her.

"Hello Diana," he muttered.

Now her whole forehead wrinkled into a definite puzzled frown. "Yes?" she replied.

That was not very encouraging but Kit had made his mind up, so he licked his lips and clenched his sweaty hands. "Er... Er, I wanted to ask you if you would go on a date with me," he blurted out.

The frown increased. Her eyes searched his face and finally met his. "I don't even know you," she replied.

That hurt! They had been in the same class for three months. With a shock Kit realised she had not even noticed his existence. For a few seconds his resolve faltered but then he shook his head to clear the negative thoughts and straightened up.

"I'm Chris Walker. Kit. I'm in your class," he replied.

Again her eyes searched his face. Then her face cleared and she nodded. But there was no smile. "Oh yeah! I've seen you around."

That hurt as well but now Kit was in such an emotional turmoil that he determined to go ahead. "So, will you go out with me?" he asked.

Again the frown, followed by a shake of the head. "Sorry, but I am already going with someone else," Diana replied.

Kit didn't know if that was true or not, but he felt the rejection bite deep into his now flustered emotions. He was also dimly aware that other girls had joined Diana and were looking at him. Realising he had failed, he groped in his mind for some face-saving formulae or for the magic words to make his dreams come true. But the words did not come, and he felt himself begin to blush as the humiliation of rejection began to burn.

"Thanks," he muttered.

Burning with embarrassment he turned and walked stiffly away. Hearing the other girls start to chatter and snicker only added to his hurt feelings.

She hadn't even known I existed! he thought, the hurt turning from astonishment to resentment.

Hoping that his rejection had not been noticed by too many others, Kit hurried away. His emotions by then were in turmoil as the hurt and shock took hold.

Suddenly he was grabbed from behind by the waistband of his shorts and by his shirt collar. Before he had time to react, he was lifted up, his shorts pulling tightly up into his crotch in a 'wedgie'. Then he was shoved and went sprawling on the concrete among the legs of dozens of students.

Furious and shocked, Kit rolled over and found himself looking into the mocking face of Gary Carstairs, one of the Year 10 boys. Carstairs bent down and grabbed at the front of his shirt.

"What are you doing annoying my sister, dwarf?" he queried.

Kit was even more shocked. *Carstairs, Diana's brother!* For a moment he was so stunned that he was unable to speak.

Carstairs shook him and raised his eyebrows. "Well?" he queried.

"Just talking to her. She's in my class," Kit replied.

Even as he did, he realised that Carstairs could easily check and then he despised himself for not being brave enough to speak the truth.

Carstairs curled his lip. "Well stay away from her, you runt!" he snarled. Then he shoved Kit hard and walked away.

Kit landed heavily on his bum on the concrete, before falling back to whack his head and left elbow so hard that the pain brought instant tears to his eyes. That was even more shameful, and as he rolled over to get up he burned with embarrassment, hotly aware of the watching faces, some smirking, some laughing, few sympathetic.

By then Carstairs was over talking to Diana. She did not seem happy, but Kit could not hear what she was saying. Feeling both outraged and impotent, he could only cast a glare at Carstairs before the full hurt of his humiliation swamped him. As the tears began to form, he turned and hurried away, clinging to what shreds of dignity he had left.

It was that 'runt' that really hurt. Kit was very aware that he was physically smaller than most of the boys in his year level, being a good ten centimetres shorter. And he had a slim build and narrow chest and was very self-conscious about his body and looks. Having a freckly face with pimples didn't help either!

With an effort he managed to hold the tears in, but his emotions were now so jangled he just wanted to get away. Then he noted his classmates Mervyn and Tristan coming the other way. They had not seen the incident, but Kit felt so upset that he immediately detoured and went behind F Block. The last thing he felt like doing at that moment was talking to his friends!

Then there was more anxiety, tinged with jealousy. Walking past was Andrew Collins and with him were Luke Karaku and Arthur Blake. All three were members of the same Navy Cadet unit Kit was in: T.S. *Endeavour.* Kit had been a navy cadet for nearly 6 months now but always seemed to be behind Andrew and to miss all the exciting adventures. Kit had to concede that Andrew had the advantage of being a few months older so had joined earlier the previous year and had completed his recruit training and done an annual camp, whereas he was still a recruit. But it still rankled.

And they have had some real adventures, Kit thought glumly.

The previous January, Andrew and his big sister Carmen, also a navy cadet, had been involved in some holiday adventure in Townsville during which they had helped the police capture a gang of thieves and also make a dramatic rescue that had been on TV.

Kit didn't know the details but from the bits he had heard he was jealous. What added to his envy were the rumours that during the adventure Andrew had been swimming with a very curvy blonde girl. That notion really seized his imagination as he had only reached puberty a few months before and was now very interested in girls and really wanted to know more about them. He had never seen a naked girl, other than pictures in 'Girlie' magazines and on the internet, but it was something he fervently desired.

I wish something exciting would happen in my life, he thought.

He conjured up a fantasy of rescuing a gorgeous maiden who then fell in love with him. Then he cast another sour glance at Andrew. In Kit's mind, Andrew was more handsome and better at everything than he was, and he resented it.

Feeling quite depressed, he took himself off down to the far end of the oval where he slumped down and sat with his back to a tree so that he was mostly hidden from view.

She didn't even recognise me! he thought, now shocked and wondering if Diana was really the girl for him. *And Carstairs is her big brother!*

The realisation came to him that he actually knew very little about her and her actions had certainly been a revelation about what sort of person she might be.

But she is so beautiful! he thought, brushing the niggling doubts aside.

Then misery engulfed him and the tears came. For at least ten minutes he just sat there, hunched in a ball and quietly sobbing. Which inadvertently led to more misery. Three Year 10 boys came strolling past and, as they did, one of them glanced at him. Kit had been so wrapped up in his own despair that he had not noticed them, but now he tried to hide the fact that he had been crying by looking quickly away.

To no avail. One of the Year 10s was Jack Piper, a bully who had picked on him ever since the start of Year 8. With him were Wally Dru and a vicious Filipino thug named Ricardo. As the three strolled along, Piper glanced across and noticed Kit.

"Well hello, here's little midget Shitface Walker," he commented. "Hey pygmy, what ya blubberin' about?"

Kit felt his stomach churn with fear, and he glanced around to see if there was a teacher on playground duty. But there was not even another student nearby. In response he just shrugged and looked away, hoping the bullies would just keep going and leave him alone.

No such luck. Piper's face suffused with irritation. "Hey Shitface, I asked you a question," he snarled.

To his own shame, Kit felt a surge of what he had to name as fear and he hastily scrambled to his feet. *I need to get away from here,* he thought. Without answering he began to run.

Piper at once shouted angrily to his cronies. "Hey! The gutless little turd's gunna run away. Grab him, you guys."

The three bullies also broke into a run, each going a different way. Within seconds Kit found himself cut-off against the school fence. For an instant he contemplated climbing it, but then decided it was just too high.

As Ricardo grabbed him, Kit cried out in pain. "Ouch! Let me go! I haven't done anything."

"Shut up, short arse!" Ricardo snarled. He grabbed Kit around the neck and held him from behind.

Wally Dru and Piper came to stand in front of him. Piper jabbed Kit in the stomach. "Got any fags, you skinny little runt?" he demanded.

"No. I don't smoke. Let me go," Kit cried, struggling to break free.

Ricardo just tightened his grip until Kit had trouble breathing. His eyes watered and he felt waves of fear washing through him as he wondered what pain or humiliation might come next.

"See if he's got any money," Piper ordered.

"I hav... ughh... Let me... ugh... g... go!" Kit gasped, choking and spluttering with outrage as Dru and Ricardo both felt in his pockets.

Then even greater humiliation followed. Ricardo tripped Kit and then grabbed his right ankle and lifted him up. As he came up off the ground upside down, Kit was both shocked and outraged. It did not seem possible! But it was. Ricardo was holding him upside down and only using one hand to do it!

Furious and bitterly ashamed, Kit kicked with his other leg but Ricardo just punched him in the stomach and said, "Stop squirming, squirt, or you will get really hurt."

Kit felt his other leg grabbed and saw that Dru had stepped in to grab him. To his complete shame, he was then shaken and jiggled up and down. This was done so quickly and so hard that his head seemed to shake loose, and several times it struck the ground. Luckily this was lawn, but it still hurt and made his senses swim, and he feared that his neck might be broken.

A few loose coins and pens fell out onto the grass. Piper bent and picked up the coins. "Is that all? Oh well, dump the little shit," he ordered.

Kit just had time to use his arms to protect his head and neck as he was unceremoniously dropped onto the grass. He flopped onto his back and at once curled into a protective ball. He was just in time as Dru and Ricardo both kicked him in the left thigh and stomach.

"Don't you dob, you little weed," Ricardo warned.

All the three bullies walked away, and Kit lay on his back and watched them, gasping and burning with outrage and shame. For several minutes he lay there until the waves of pain subsided. Then he began to cry again. Hunching into a ball against the nearby tree, he sobbed out his misery.

Only the appearance of several students further along the oval caused him to try to control his flood of despair. Some residual shreds of pride made him shift out of sight and then calm his heaving chest. Still seething with anger and hurt, he wiped his tears and forced himself to be calm.

Many times over the last few years he had been hurt by name calling by others, both students and teachers. Often it was quite unconscious and without obvious malice, like nicknaming him 'Shorty', but each time it stung and he ground his teeth in frustration.

And then another test was upon him. The bell to go back to classes sounded and he had to force himself to get up and walk back to the school buildings, all the while pretending he was alright and that there were no problems. Along the way he detoured to wash his face in the washroom and to have a drink. Then he made his way to his next class.

As luck would have it, this was a class Diana was in—Maths with the legendary Mr Menzies—'Old Jock' to the students who mostly held him in high regard, often awe. As Kit approached the room, he saw Diana at the port rack getting out her books. For a moment he churned inside and actually quailed at the thought of her seeing him. Images of his humiliation swirled through his mind to add to his confusion and upset. But he gritted his teeth and kept on walking.

Don't be such a bloody coward. You are going to see her every day all year, he told himself.

But then his feelings were hurt again. Diane looked around, saw him and for a fleeting moment their eyes met. Then she quickly looked away and said something to her friend Fleur who was bending over next to her. Fleur looked up and then quickly looked down again.

They are talking about me, Kit thought.

That was a worry because he had once read that when people talk about others it won't all be good. As Kit went past Fleur, she cast him another quick glance and he felt another stab of embarrassment. But he was also heartened.

Diana at least knows I exist now! he told himself.

And her having Fleur as a friend was actually another positive, he decided. Fleur was a nice person who seemed to always be concerned about other people. She had a pretty face and cascading brown curls.

But she isn't a patch on Diana.

In the room Kit sat at his usual seat near the back, next to Ed Barrow. Ed wasn't really a friend but the pair got on well enough, so the arrangement worked. From there Kit could not see either Diana or Fleur as they sat one row behind and to the left and he could only get glimpses of her when he was writing by taking quick peeks. This was a temptation he resisted.

I don't want her to think I am harassing her or that I am obsessed and chasing her, he thought.

By the end of the day Kit was very pleased to hear the final bell. *I've had enough stress for one day,* he told himself as he waited for Diana and Fleur to leave the room.

Only when they were gone from the veranda outside did he go out and pack his books. Feeling quite dejected and somewhat wrung out he walked to the bike racks to get his bike. But as he unlocked his bike he remembered that he was supposed to go to work at his father's trucking business that afternoon.

Oh man! I don't feel like working, he thought. *I just want to go home.*

His father was the owner and manager of quite a large transport business specialising in refrigerated and bulk liquid semi-trailers and heavy lift and it was generally assumed that Kit and his big brothers, Adrian and Bruce, would become involved in the running of the business as they got older. In preparation for this they were required to work after school and, unless there was some special reason, on weekends.

As he rode his bike along Mulgrave Road, Kit considered this future. It wasn't the one he really wanted but it was why he did subjects like Science and Maths. His personal desire was to do a degree in Fine Arts and to become an artist. He had a creative streak that he did not even try to suppress. His hobbies included drawing and painting. Cleaning, servicing and doing technical things to big machines he found easy but not very enjoyable.

Still brooding on his defeats and perceived defects, Kit arrived at his father's business. This was located at the end of a side street in the industrial area and was surrounded by the usual high wire fence. The whole yard was bitumen. The front part of the yard was taken up by a car park, office building and a huge shed in which the trucks were repaired and serviced. A driveway on the right led to a parking and loading area at the rear. The area at the rear was another large area bitumen and was where trucks and trailers were parked. A back gate opened onto another street.

Kit left his bike at the front and went into the office. As he did, the receptionist, Julie, looked at him and raised her eyebrows.

"What happened to you? You look like you've been in the wars," she commented.

Until then Kit hadn't been aware he had suffered any visible bruises, but her comment sparked sharp emotions as images of the day's debacles flitted across his mind.

"Nothing much," he replied. "Just the usual hurly burly of life."

Julie shrugged and gestured towards the rear of the building. "Your dad's showing some people around," she explained.

"Thanks," Chris replied gruffly.

Feeling quite upset and self-conscious he made his way down the corridor and out into the huge shed at the rear. He came out beside a prime mover that was being serviced and the pungent reek of diesel and hydraulic fluids caught briefly at the back of his nostrils. This was such a normal smell to him that it barely registered on his consciousness but what did register were loud and angry voices that were echoing around the huge shed.

What on earth is going on? he wondered.

Hurrying along between the side of the vehicle and a work bench, Kit came out into an open area and noted a number of people standing around. In the centre were his father and one of the workers.

At that moment, Kit's father snapped angrily, "You are a thief and a troublemaker, Jellman. You're fired! Now get off my property."

Jellman, a big, burly, red-faced man in faded blue overalls, raised his fists. "Don't call me a thief! You got no proof."

"No," Kit's father retorted, "Or I would be calling the police. But you are a bad driver and a troublemaker. Now get out of here."

Jellman went even redder. "I'll have you for wrongful dismissal," he shouted.

"And then I will call the police, now leave," Kit's father replied.

"You'll be sorry!" Jellman snarled, raising a fist and shaking it at Kit's father.

Kit's father was a big man and just stood his ground, contempt clear on his face. Then he turned his back and began to walk away. That enraged Jellman even more and he lunged forward, fists swinging. Kit's father heard him and tried to dodge the blow. But it struck the side of his face and obviously stunned him, and he staggered. To Kit's horror, he saw his father reel and lean on the wall and Jellman draw back his fist with the obvious intention of punching him in the head again.

Dimly aware of shouts and a scream, Kit dashed across and grabbed at Jellman's arm. It was enough to throw the man off balance, and the punch missed. Kit's father was able to step away and straighten up, his face white and showing pain.

Jellman snarled angrily and swung to face Kit. Surprise changed to puzzled recognition. Then his lip curled, and he sneered, "Keep out of this you little squirt," he growled.

"Leave my dad alone!" Kit retorted.

He had his fists up but was having trouble seeing as his vision seemed blurred from anxiety. His heart was hammering, and he was aware that he might be in for a bashing but all the pent-up emotions from the day now fuelled his determination and he stood his ground.

Jellman again curled his lip and then strode towards him, thrusting out a huge hairy hand and arm as he did.

"Get out of my way, you little runt!" he snarled.

Kit tried to jump back but the front of a truck blocked him. Jellman's hand connected and he shoved. Before Kit could recover his balance, the push sent him sprawling on his back on the concrete floor.

Oh bloody hell! Three times in one day! he thought, shame and rage mingling to raise him to a fury.

Driven by an intense desire to hit back, he rolled over and stood up. But his speed was his undoing as he miscalculated and struck his head on the front of the truck as he did. That half stunned him, and he staggered as pain lanced through his skull. He had to lean on the vehicle to keep his balance. Shaking his head to clear it, he saw Jellman striding away.

"Come back, you bloody bully!" Kit cried.

Jellman's response was an obscene gesture and then he went out of sight around another vehicle. Kit shook his head again and then glanced around. He saw his father being held up by one of the mechanics and then he noted a middle-aged man in grey trousers, white shirt and tie and next to him a girl in school uniform—his school's uniform.

Then recognition came.

Diana!

Humiliation boiled up to join the swirling mix of emotions.

Chapter 2

THE PHANTOM

For a few moments Kit gaped.

Diana! What is she doing here?

Then his attention was diverted by his father hobbling over to face him. His father reached out and took his right hand and began to shake it with both of his.

"That was very brave, my boy, very brave."

"I thought he was going to hit you again," Kit replied, embarrassed and having trouble raising his voice above a mumble.

"He was," his father agreed. "So thank you. But you shouldn't have risked yourself. A boy fighting a grown man isn't a fair fight."

His father didn't say it but from the way he glanced at the nearby mechanics Kit was sure he meant that one or more of them should have come to his aid. Then his father shook his head and took a deep breath.

"Oh, excuse my bad manners. Kit, this is Mr Carstairs and his daughter Diana. Mr Carstairs, this is my youngest son, Chris; Kit we call him."

As Kit faced Mr Carstairs, the penny dropped. *Carstairs! Diana's dad owns Carstair's Heavy Engineering,* knowledge that both scared and surprised him. He wondered how he had not made the connection before.

Mr Carstairs was a middle-aged businessman with neatly trimmed grey hair and a square face that held the same eyes as Diana and her brother. Mr Carstairs stuck out his hand.

"That was a gutsy thing to do, Kit. I hope my sons are as brave."

An image of the man's son threatening him flitted across Kit's mind and he felt a spurt of sour anger, but then a new thought came to him.

Maybe Carstairs really was just protecting his sister? Feeling even more embarrassed and slightly flustered Kit shook hands.

Mr Carstairs then indicated Diana "This is my daughter, Diana. You two obviously go to the same school. Do you know each other?" he asked.

Kit turned to face her and met her eyes then nodded. His mouth went dry and his heart rate shot up. "Yes, we are in the same class for some subjects," he replied.

Diana gave him a smile and what he thought was a slightly puzzled, quizzical look but said nothing. Again the events of the day flashed across the screen of Kit's mind, and he felt even more emotionally battered.

And his physical battering was now starting to hurt. His elbow, head and right buttock were all smarting or throbbing and he had the beginnings of a headache. He winced and his father at once became concerned.

"You hurt, son? We'd better do a bit of doctoring. You took a nasty knock on the head then."

The group made its way back into the office area and Julie and another office girl were called. Kit was seated in a chair. Cold drinks, a cold hand towel and ice pack were speedily produced. Julie began to treat his bruises, gently wiping his face and neck. In the process she stood close in front of him, and he found her breasts close to his face. The sight of them pushing out the front of her white blouse was enough to make him go red with embarrassment, even while his mind raced with teenage speculation about what they might be like under that cloth.

As this was done, Kit's father and Mr Carstairs moved to his office and continued discussing business. Diana stood in the corridor until offered a chair in the lounge by Julie.

Kit was left wondering what to do or say next. As the embarrassing silence began to stretch out, he gestured towards the workshop.

"I work here after school on Tuesdays and Thursdays and on weekends," he explained.

"Every weekend?" Diana asked.

Kit shook his head. "Not every weekend, not when I have Cadets."

As soon as he had said that he wished he hadn't. He was proud of being a cadet but had suffered a lot of grief from bullies and others about it. Being a cadet was not a trendy or popular thing to do and Kit had no idea what Diana's opinion was.

She raised a quizzical eyebrow. "Cadets? Are you one of those military morons who meet at the school on Wednesday afternoons?"

Kit blushed and felt anxious. *She doesn't like cadets,* he deduced. "No. I am a navy cadet. We meet down at the port, next to the navy base, on Friday nights and some weekends," he explained.

Diana again raised her right eyebrow but then shrugged. "Never been there," she replied in tone that indicated she was not impressed and had no intention of ever going there.

Kit blushed and felt even more flustered. For a minute or so he struggled to think of something to say. Luckily his father and Mr Carstairs returned, and his father pointed towards the front, and said, "Our guests are leaving now."

Kit nodded and stood up then followed his father, Mr Carstairs, and Diana out through the front office to the car park. A BMW limousine was parked there and Mr Carstairs went to it. Kit had noticed the car when he had arrived but had not really thought about it. Similar vehicles were often parked at the front.

Kit's father and Mr Carstairs said their goodbyes and Diana gave a weak smile and wave and made her way to the passenger seat. As he started the car, Mr Carstairs gave a friendly smile and called, "I'll be in touch, Mr Walker, but it looks like a good plan."

"Thanks," Kit's father replied.

He raised his hand to wave as the car was reversed out. Kit stood beside him, hoping Diana might wave but she just glanced at him and then turned to talk to her father as he drove the car out of the yard.

"She's a pretty one," Kit's father commented.

"Hmm!" Kit answered. He thought, but did not say, *More than that. She is beautiful.*

His father then shook his head. "And rich too," he added. "He must be one of the richest men in the city. I'm surprised she just goes to an ordinary state high school and not to some posh private college."

Kit was even more surprised and embarrassed. *I don't know anything about her at all,* he thought. And learning that she was rich instantly put him into a whirl of doubt. *She will just think I am after her for her money,* he thought.

His own family were well enough off but most of their wealth was tied up in the business. He knew that their home was mortgaged, and from what he had gathered from comments he had overheard when his parents were talking the business was having some problems.

His father nudged his elbow. "You should ask her out, son. You could do a lot worse than her," he said.

Burning images of being rejected and humiliated flashed across Kit's mind and he blushed. All he could do was mumble a reply, his mouth starting to make the claim that he already had a girlfriend but then choking up on his emotions. He was unable to utter the lie.

His father gestured towards the workshop. "Because you have been hurt you don't have to work this afternoon. You can go home. And if you don't feel up to riding your bike you can lie down until I go home."

Kit assured his father that he felt well enough. "I'll be fine, Dad," he said, even though that wasn't true either. "I'll go out and help."

His father nodded and looked pleased, so Kit collected his overalls from the change room, pulled them on over his school uniform and went through to the workshops. He found Frank Pearson, the foreman, and Darren, their mechanic, both lying under the new XRT Prime Mover.

"I told Dad I was alright, Mr Pearson," he explained. He lay down and wriggled under the front, the two men having the wheeled trolleys already. "What's the matter? I thought this one was brand new."

"It is," Mr Pearson replied. "But your good friend, Jellman, has pranged it."

"How?" Kit queried.

"Ran into a bollard or kerbing, Mr Pearson said.

Darren added. "The boys over at Casey's Warehouse reckon that he just came racing into their yard way too fast and couldn't pull up in time when he realised he couldn't make the turn. He's a bloody idiot!"

"What's the damage?" Kit asked.

Mr Pearson pointed upwards. "Bent the steering rods and put the steering out of alignment. It must have been a real struggle to get the thing back here."

Kit could see that. He was now very familiar with the mechanical side of big trucks. So they put the Prime Mover up on the hoist and set to work. Luckily, they had two steering rods of the correct size in the store so changing the steering rods was relatively simple and only took an hour.

By then Kit was very familiar with the underside of that particular vehicle, noting and pointing out other minor damage to the mudguards and some scrapes on the front guard and differential.

"He's lucky he didn't bust the diff," he commented, running his fingertip over the shallow scrape where bare metal showed through a thin film of grime.

Mr Pearson grunted and made a face then rolled out. "Out you get, and we will lower this thing and adjust the toe-in and then do a test drive," he said.

At that moment, Kit's gaze shifted to the right-hand steering arm and he frowned, then concentrated. "Hang on a sec," he called, "Come and look at this."

He pointed to a tiny hairline crack at the front edge on the steering arm. Darren rolled over and looked at it, then rubbed it with his thumb and swore. Mr Pearson rejoined them and did the same.

"Oh bloody hell! That's cracked alright. Well done, young Kit. If you hadn't noticed that we could have had a nasty accident."

Kit was pleased with the praise and went with Darren to check what parts were in their storeroom.

"Don't think we've got one in stock," Darren commented.

A check of the stock holding in the computer confirmed this and a double check of the shelves made it certain. There was no part. Phone calls were made to the local spare parts suppliers, but half an hour of calls produced only negatives. The Prime Mover was so new that none of the suppliers had one in stock.

"There may be one in Melbourne, but I suspect there isn't one in the country," Mr Pearson reported to Kit's dad, who also then swore.

"Damn! Okay, park the thing out of the way until we can get the part," he instructed.

Kit did this, under the direct supervision of Mr Pearson. Kit often drove the big rigs around inside the yard or workshop but always with one of the qualified men supervising in the cab with him. He was just big enough to see over the bonnet and to reach the pedals and gear lever. The men liked him and were polite enough to not tease him about this. Once he had parked the vehicle the cab was locked and the keys taken to the office.

Mr Walker then said, "Well done guys! Thanks for that extra effort. You will get over time for that extra hour. Now let's all get off home. Now Chris, do you want a lift?"

"No Dad," Kit replied, determined to show he was tough and independent.

He then went out to his bicycle. It was a decision he almost instantly regretted as he felt both dizzy and sore but stubborn pride triumphed and he said nothing. Half an hour later he was at home, explaining to his mother how he got the bruises and black eye.

His mother, who had also just arrived home from work, was all concern but agreed with his father. "That was very brave of you," she said. "But don't take risks like that again please."

Kit made no reply, not agreeing with her. To change the subject, he said, "Dad sacked that Jellman."

"Good!" his mother agreed. "He is a bully and a disgusting beast. Several of the girls there have complained about the language he uses and the things he says to them."

Kit could imagine. Nodding he looked around. "Have you been shopping, Mum?"

"Yes, the comics are out there on the dining room table," she replied.

Kit stood up and took his glass of cordial with him. Every Thursday afternoon his mother went to the shops and purchased some sweets and several comics that she approved of. One of these was *The Phantom* and it was Kit's favourite. He had been reading the comic adventures of the legendary superhero ever since he was a child, and the family had a huge collection of the comic books. Having a name linked to the comic added an extra gloss to his liking.

Kit picked up the comic and briefly studied the cover illustration. This showed the Phantom battling a group of 18th Century pirates.

This should be good, Kit thought.

The comic was in a plastic wrapper and he tore this open. Out fell a second *Phantom* comic, a much smaller one with a completely different layout—'landscape' instead of 'portrait'—which he instantly recognised as a reprint of one of the original *Phantom* comics of the 1940s. On its cover was a classic Phantom drawing of the 'Ghost Who Walks' slugging a burly looking thug with oafish features and a bristly crew-cut hair style.

That will be good too, Kit thought.

Picking up the main comic, he took one of the small Cadbury's Caramello chocolates that lay on the table and went to the lounge. There he unwrapped the chocolate, broke off a square and popped it into his mouth. Savouring the taste of the melting chocolate he lay down to read.

The first few pictures in the comic set the scene. There was Diana Palmer working on an archaeological site in some foreign country and the next illustration showed the Phantom settling a boundary dispute between the Llongo and the Wambesi back in Bengali.

There have to be treasure hunters or thieves in this one, Kit reasoned, remembering the cover picture.

And there were. A few scenes later, a gang of robbers appeared, skulking in the jungle and watching the archaeologists digging in the ruins of an ancient city.

"They must be digging for treasure," one of the villains suggests.

Then the local sultan or prince appeared on an elephant and with his bodyguards and his roving eye soon settled on Diana.

He is going to try to get her to marry him, Kit thought. It was a common theme in many *Phantom* stories and always provided much amusement.

Kit smiled and was sure he knew what was coming. Turning the page, he settled back to read. As he did, his big brother, Bruce, walked into the room. Tossing his school bag aside, Bruce strode across to him and without asking just snatched the *Phantom* comic out of Kit's hands.

Kit tried to grab it back. "Hey! I was reading that," he protested.

"Bite yer bum, little brother," Bruce retorted. "You know the rules, eldest first."

"So don't read it until Adrian gets home," Kit snapped back.

He knew full well that the 'rule' was just one imposed by his older siblings, not one sanctioned by his parents. But it had been the established family custom for all of his lifetime, so he accepted it. Instead he stood up and, seething with resentment, picked up his chocolate and his drink and started walking towards his bedroom.

As he did, he remembered the second *Phantom* comic. Detouring into the lounge room he picked this up and, keeping it hidden from Bruce, again headed towards his room

There he put down the drink and chocolate while thinking, *If I was bigger and stronger, my brothers wouldn't just take things off me or pick on me.*

He glanced at himself in the mirror to study his physique and appearance, and got a shock. He really did look battered with a large bruise on his left cheek, a black eye, and a scratch or gravel rash on his right temple.

Shaking his head and ruefully regretting his physique, Kit sat down on his bed. After taking a sip from his drink he flicked the comic open. And there, right on the back of the cover, was a series of pictures describing exactly his situation. It was an old advertisement for body building equipment. The first scene showed a skinny boy and a pretty girl, both in bathers at the beach and the next showed a bully demolishing the skinny boy's sandcastle, then kicking sand in his face before strolling off with the skinny boy's girl on his arm.

That's me alright! Kit thought bitterly, the hurtful memories of the day flooding back to sting his emotions again.

Despite thinking the ad was corny and untrue, he scanned it, noting how the skinny boy did all these physical exercises to build up his muscles. In the end, he was able to beat the bully in a fight and ended up with his girl back on his arm.

Kit studied the hopeful images and then gave a rueful smile. *If only!* he thought. But then he glanced at the illustrations again and clenched his fists as the humiliations and shame seared through him. *Why not?* he reasoned. *It couldn't make things worse.*

At that moment, he vowed to build up his physical strength so that he could resist the bullies. The memory that rankled the most was when Ricardo had just picked him with one hand so that he dangled upside down.

Never again! Next time he will pay for the pleasure, Kit decided.

Still feeling upset and resentful Kit lay back to read the comic but his thoughts kept coming back to the ad. He also noted the Phantom winning all of his fights.

I need to learn to fight too, he thought. Skill, he realised, was probably even more important than strength.

After finishing the comic, Kit lay back and thought hard. From thinking about how to do this his thoughts turned to wonderful daydreams of him winning fights against the bullies, then of rescuing Diana and of her being suitably grateful and then of her falling in love with him.

That would be great, he thought.

Deep in thought, Kit walked back through the house. Seeing that Bruce was still reading the big *Phantom* comic, Kit tossed the reprint on the table and took himself downstairs. Underneath their high-set 'Old Queenslander' house was an undercover area which was partly taken up by the laundry and garage and partly by a workshop and a fernery.

How strong am I? Kit wondered, thinking of the images of the Phantom climbing ropes to get up the side of big ships.

After looking around for a few moments, Kit selected an overhead beam and jumped up to grab it with both hands. The edge of the sawn timber was sharp and hard, but he ignored the pain and tried to lift himself up to do a 'chin the bar' as he had seen other students do in Physical Education at school. It was a skill he had been asked to do at school a few months before and had been embarrassed by not even being able to do one.

I'll show them, he told himself.

Mustering all his strength he moved to lift himself up so that his chin could touch the beam. To his dismay and shame, he was unable to do it. For quite a few seconds he hung there, muscles quivering but he lacked the strength and had to let go and drop to the floor.

It was such a disappointment that while he stood there with his body trembling and muscles still shivering, tears prickled in the corner so his eyes.

God, what a bloody weakling I am! he castigated himself.

Gritting his teeth with determination, Kit tried again. But within seconds he found that his muscles were already weaker and he was quite unable to lift his own weight.

Then he tried to do a push up. Once again, he felt humiliated. He had trouble even straightening his back while he held himself quivering on hands and toes.

Oh this is sad! he told himself. *The girls are never going to be impressed if I don't have a little bit of muscle.*

There and then he determined to build up his body. For the next fifteen minutes, Kit tried a variety of actions that he had been made to suffer at Phys Ed lessons: sit-ups, leg raising when lying on his back, star jumps and touching his toes. Mostly it ended quickly with quivering muscles and trembling lips. Self-pity welled up and tears prickled.

It was an unhappy boy who went to have a shower before tea.

* * *

Later in the evening, Kit took himself to his room, ostensibly to do homework but in reality he brooded. Life just seemed so unfair!

Why couldn't I be born normal! he thought, the self-pity bringing tears to prickle in the corner of his eyes.

Bad dreams of being chased by bullies did not help.

He went to school on Friday feeling quite down and nervous. Still smarting from his humiliating rebuff by Diana, he made a point of avoiding her as much as he could, although he still secretly yearned to win her affection. The actual schoolwork he found easy. But not so easy was the social stuff. There were various groups of friends who usually sat in the same seats or who went around together, but Kit did not belong to any of them.

The group he wanted to belong to was the group of Navy Cadets that included Andrew Collins, Blake and Luke Karaku. They tolerated Kit when he sat with them, but when he spoke they often did not listen or pay attention. It was all very hurtful.

After school Kit rode his bike home and then lay on his bed for a while brooding about the injustice of fate. But then he remembered his decision to build up his muscles, so he took himself downstairs and set to work with push-ups, sit-ups and a variety of other exercises. Once again, he was hotly aware of his own weakness, of not being able to do a single chin the bar properly and of only being able to do a few push-ups or sit-ups before his muscles began to quiver, causing him to cry out in pain.

He was still trying to do push-ups when his mother called him to come upstairs and have tea. "You've got Navy Cadets tonight don't forget," she added.

Kit had forgotten but now he hurried upstairs, washed and joined the others at the dining table. The main topic of conversation was again the incident at the workshop. The spare part to replace the steering arm, he learned, was still being shipped to Australia. It might be a week or more before that truck was repaired, which was bad news for the business.

Two hours later, Kit stood on the parade ground at Training Ship *Endeavour,* which wasn't a ship at all but a shore establishment adjoining the Cairns Navy Base. Kit was a 1st year cadet with the rank of Cadet Recruit. He had only a few more weeks of training to do before he could be promoted to Seaman. That rankled a bit as his rival Andrew Collins had been promoted the previous year.

The training that evening included three lessons. In the first the recruits were put in a group to keep working on their knots. While they did this, the older cadets did drill with arms in preparation for Anzac Day services. From where he sat tying bowlines, Kit could see this and he noted Andrew doing the 'Present Arms' with a 'Drill' rifle and felt another twinge of envy.

I suppose Collins will get the plum guard jobs, Kit thought resentfully.

Each year the unit provided guards for various memorial services at schools in the days leading up to Anzac Day and sometimes on the day itself. Kit really wanted to be selected to be in one of those guards but conceded he had no chance that year.

But he was still disappointed. His jealousy increased in the next lesson which was on how to furl and raise and lower flags. Often at ceremonies cadets were required as flag orderlies and Kit thought he should be able to do that. But his name was not called, and to rub salt in the wound Andrew's was.

Bloody officer's pet! Kit thought.

The whole unit, only about 30 strong, now did ten minutes of marching practice before being divided into boat's crews for a sailing activity on the Sunday. Kit was looking forward to that and he happily joined Cadet Petty Officer Crisp and cadets Toms and Hoyle in checking their boat. It was a 14' 'Corsair' and Kit had only been sailing once before and was really looking forward to the activity.

At dismissal parade they were reminded of the timings and administrative details for Sunday's activity and that got Kit even more excited.

This is going to be good! he thought.

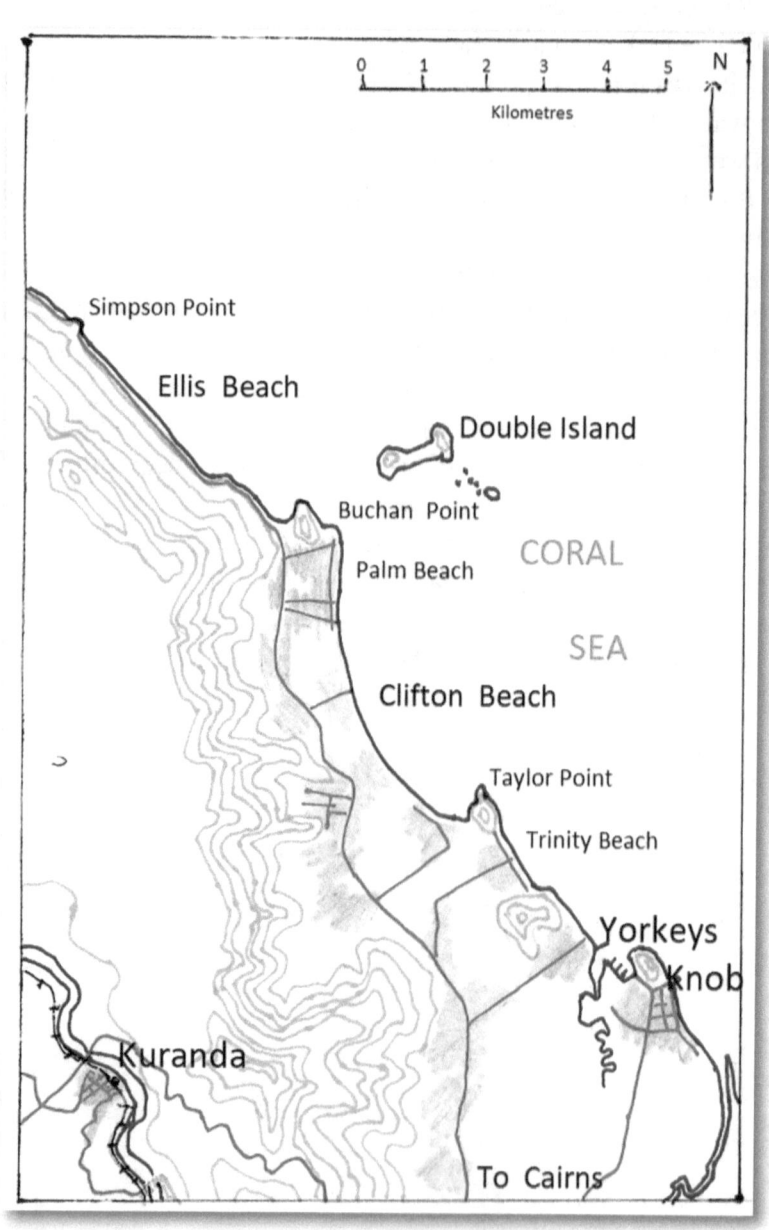

Chapter 3

SAILING RACE

And it was good.

On Sunday morning eight sail boats, one catamaran and two power boats had set out from the Yorkeys Knob Marina. Now it was afternoon and they were near the end of the race, off Ellis Beach. It was the first activity of its kind that Kit had taken part in and he was really enjoying it. He was in a Corsair commanded by Cadet Petty Officer Crisp. The other crew member was Seamen Toms, a Year 9 boy from Smithfield State High School. Kit had two jobs to do: work the jib sheet and shift his balance as required when the wind was on the beam. And he was loving every minute of it.

The activity was called a 'Treasure Hunt' but was really a test of sailing ability, with the extra challenge of having to work out what the clues meant, and to navigate from one place to the next. The clues were just messages in plastic bags that had been placed in position by the adult officers of the Navy Cadet unit.

To add spice and challenge, each clue was either in a code or was some sort of puzzle or cryptic clue. Several clues were coloured drawings of naval flags, spelling out names or distances and magnetic bearings. Others had been in Morse Code and a couple had been merely mysterious words. So far they had found eight clues. First, they had sailed north along the coast to Taylor Point, then in to Clifton Beach. Next, they had sailed along close to the shore to Palm Beach and then out to Double Island. The next leg had been in behind Buchans Point, then up to Ellis Beach, where they had stopped for lunch, being held to timings by the officers. The last leg had been out to sea to one of the motorboats. This was commanded by Lieutenant Ryan, the unit's XO, and he had two senior cadets with him.

As the boats raced along on the sparkling sea, Kit studied the other boats. To his annoyance, his boat was second and the leading boat was crewed by Andrew Collins, his big sister Carmen, and Blake. That boat was a few hundred metres ahead but apart from it the race looked to be a no-contest. The next two boats were nearly a kilometre behind and were both 'Port Watch', the closest being Petty Officer George's and the other Leading Seaman Page's. Another few hundred metres back were two more: Armstrong's and, he thought, Austin's. The last two, both 'Starboard Watch', were so far back he could not make out who was in each but he knew they were commanded by Pocock and Kent. Both safety boats were back with them.

That's because that ham-fisted lubber Kent capsized, Kit thought.

Now he turned his attention to where they were heading. About a kilometre ahead on the port bow was a rocky headland.

"Excuse me PO, what's the name of that cape?" he asked PO Crisp.

PO Crisp held up a chart, safe from spray in a plastic case, and pointed to it. "Simpson Point. It is the northern end of Ellis Beach," he answered.

Kit nodded. He knew Ellis Beach well from frequent family picnics but had never been to the north of it except by car along the Cook Highway. Twisting around to get a better look, he studied the beach and noted the three kilometres of lovely golden sand that was now on the port beam. Behind the beach he could make out the Cook Highway. It ran along the lower slopes of a range of steep mountains that rose for about 600 metres in a wall that extended north and south for many kilometres.

The next clue is on the beach just north of Simpson Point, Kit thought.

He had been the one to work out the message and he felt very pleased with his efforts and with the praise from PO Crisp. The fact that Carmen's boat was sailing an identical course also reassured him.

They must believe that is the place as well, he told himself.

He relaxed and settled to enjoy the thrill of the race and the sheer pleasure of sailing. The sun, salt spray, and sun-dappled tropical sea all added to his pleasure. His job was simple, to hold the foresheet to the jib, but he did wish they could squeeze a couple of extra knots out of the boat.

I think we are catching up, he decided.

To beat Andrew would be a fine thing, Kit decided. Andrew's perceived superiority at almost everything was a niggling sore point with him, made worse by the fact that Andrew was quite unaware of any rivalry. He was so friendly and helpful that his very niceness seemed somehow to rub salt in the wounds of pride!

Five minutes later, they tacked and began racing towards the shore,

Carmen's boat still a hundred metres ahead. Kit felt sure there must only be one or two more legs, if only because it was getting late in the day.

We still have to get the boats back to Cairns and pack up and clean up, he thought. That led to more anxious glances towards Carmen's Corsair. Kit studied it carefully and his spirits rose. *We are definitely catching up!* he told himself.

In fact, on that tack, it appeared to him that they were slowly but surely gaining, edging up a metre or so every minute. PO Crisp carefully scanned the set of the boat's sails again, then ordered Kit to ease the jib slightly.

Kit did as he was told but did wonder if it was the right tactic. He considered the angle at which they were tacking into the wind.

I wonder if we should we try for greater speed over the ground by running more off the wind rather than trying to tack as high up into the wind as we can? he thought.

But he was only a recruit and did not dare risk a rebuke for making suggestions to his superiors, so he held his tongue. PO Crisp held to their course, and Kit could only hold on and watch.

Not far to go now. If nothing goes wrong, we might just catch them at the beach, he reasoned.

He again glanced at Carmen's boat, then turned to meet PO Crisp's eye. PO Crisp nodded and said, "You be ready to jump out as soon as we run aground, Recruit Walker. Hold the bow steady and keep her facing into the wind. Leave the treasure hunt to Toms and me. Tommo, you search along to the left and I will go the other way," he instructed.

Both boys nodded, their eyes continually flicking to the pursuing boat and then back to the shore ahead of them. Another glance around got Kit worrying. Out to sea he could see masses of dark clouds with curtains of rain under them.

The weather is going to get worse soon, he told himself.

Already he was sure that the wind had become stronger, and he again looked up to check the set of the jib. The boat was really flying along now, the cadets having to lean out on the windward side to help balance her. Kit found the whole experience exhilarating. Normally the cadets only sailed in the relatively sheltered waters of Trinity Bay, or on Lake Tinaroo, so being out on the more exposed open coast was thrilling.

The waves were bigger than he was used to, but not by much. Even now he estimated they were only about 1.5 metres. That was normal for the Coral Sea inside the Great Barrier Reef. He knew that very large waves, say 10 or 15 metres, only blew up as the result of tropical cyclones, and they only occurred in Summer. Normally the wave height was kept down by the damping effect of the Great Barrier Reef, which broke up the ocean swells. Along this stretch of coast that mighty chain of reefs was about 30 kilometres offshore and the 'fetch' inside was too short to allow the building of large waves.

But the wave pattern had abruptly changed, and Kit was made uncomfortably aware of this as the Corsair suddenly pitched and rolled alarmingly, her bow butting into the crests and sending spray flying.

The water must be shallower than it looks, he decided, remembering what he had been told about the effect of water depth on wave patterns.

He looked around and noted that they were now sailing into the inshore zone where the waves began to break. Suddenly, the boat began to lurch and roll alarmingly. Kit cried out in fright and grabbed the mast to steady himself. The jib gave a couple of flaps and he hastily pulled the sheet taut again, hoping that PO Crisp hadn't noticed.

He looked around to check this and saw that PO Crisp was anxiously studying the waves. He also noted that the boat was running square on with the waves. As the next wave rolled on ahead faster than the boat, it sank down into the trough and began to roll uneasily, wind spilling from the sails as it did.

Seaman Toms looked around in alarm. "Careful! You'll have us over!" he cried. The mainsail slatted and he quickly pulled the mainsheet taut.

Kit thought so too as the boat gave several alarming rolls. *We nearly gybed then! We will look like real idiots if we capsize,* he thought, blushing with anticipatory shame and dreading the teasing that would follow. He looked around and saw that they were almost abeam of Carmen's Corsair and that it was angling away. *They are quartering the waves, not running in square with them,* he noted.

He opened his mouth to point this out to PO Crisp but again hesitated, not wanting to annoy the petty officer by trying to tell him how to sail the boat.

Seaman Toms looked around and then pointed. "They have changed tack. They are quartering the waves. We should try that."

But PO Crisp shook his head. "It is about two hundred and fifty metres to the shore, and they will have to run in square for the last twenty-five or so anyway," he said. "But they will have to sail nearly double that distance if they keep to that course. I reckon we just go straight in. You guys just make sure we don't gybe."

Kit watched the other Corsair and frowned and shook his head. To him it looked to be going much faster, and it was certainly much steadier.

If we capsize, they will beat us, he thought.

Seaman Toms wasn't happy either and didn't agree with this plan, but PO Crisp pressed his lips together and stubbornly held his course. Kit felt his stomach churn with apprehension and what he hoped was not the beginnings of sea sickness as the alarming rolls continued.

Anxiously he studied the shore they were now rapidly approaching. He saw that the northern end of Ellis Beach ended in a scatter of large rocks. The highway climbed up into a belt of dry savannah woodland as it went further inland across the end of a long spur. He noted that the bush along this section of coast was brown and dry and wondered why as he saw that it changed to dense tropical jungle on top of the range.

The foot of the spur was a mass of black rocks, some quite jagged, others large smooth boulders. Beyond them, just around the curve of the point, was a short section of beach. This was their objective. But with every passing wave Kit began to wonder if they would make it. As each wave passed them, the boat rolled and lurched and they had to struggle to keep it upright.

To make matters worse, Kit saw that Carmen's Corsair was racing away across the waves, obviously sailing at a comfortable angle. This rapidly took it off to starboard, angling inshore towards the northern end of the small beach.

They might have further to go but they are now going faster and they are much less likely to capsize, Kit thought.

Up till now Kit had admired PO Crisp and had faith in his judgement and sailing ability, but now he began to have doubts.

A few minutes later, their own boat still more than a hundred metres from the beach, Kit saw Carmen's Corsair do a rapid gybe to port about a hundred metres out from the shore. It then headed in for the beach.

They are going to beat us! he thought, his irritation growing.

At that moment, the boat gave another sickening lurch. PO Crisp cried out in alarm and slid across on his seat. As he did, he struggled to hold the tiller steady. The boat swung and rolled even more. The boom suddenly swung and Toms cried out in alarm and pulled hard at the mainsheet.

Kit knew, from several duckings during his earlier day of sail training, that the main reason for capsizing during gybes was the boom of the mainsail swinging across too quickly, upsetting the balance before they could adjust or ease the sheet. He was also acutely aware that it was the control of the tiller that was the next most important element. Having several times in the past experienced that sickening feeling of skidding around out of control while trying to gybe he now saw PO Crisp gripping the tiller hard while trying to hold it to the course he wanted.

By what seemed like a miracle the boat survived the wave and Kit let out the breath he had been holding. Shaking his head with anxiety and doubt he looked across at the other boat. It looked to be only 60 or 70 metres out from the sand. Even as he watched it did another gybe and he clearly saw Blake slide down into the hull and reach up to grip the boom to help control its swing. As soon as the boom was centred, Andrew pushed it across and began to very carefully ease out on the mainsheet.

That's how it should be done, he thought.

He itched to change places with Toms. To his dismay, he saw that Carmen's boat looked to be almost parallel to them and about the same distance out.

It's going to be close, Kit thought. He tensed ready to spring ashore. The beach was now only about 50 metres away.

Suddenly, the Corsair slid down the back of a wave and rolled wildly. Kit looked back and saw that PO Crisp was struggling to get himself upright and was having difficulty holding the tiller. Toms was pulling on the mainsheet but was leaning too far out and trying to heave himself inboard.

To add to Kit's growing concern, the boat lost way and began to wallow and roll in the trough. To his horror, he saw the next wave rear up and even as his mind raced to work out what to do it caught up and broke, white froth cascading over the transom.

Pooped! he thought as the foam and solid water gushed into the boat.

The boat wallowed even more and came to a rocking standstill, the water swirling and sloshing around inside the hull. He cried in alarm and saw anxiety on PO Crisp's face.

But before he could work out what to do, the boat broached and swung up over the next wave as it passed. There was no time to do anything before the water cascaded and sloshed around, completely upsetting what little balance remained. Before Kit could even cry out, the boat rolled. One second it was upright, the next it was over.

Kit was thrown out amid a welter of foam as the boat capsized. But even as he hit the water, his mind formed the concept of shame.

Oh no! The others will all tease us now! he thought.

He was not physically afraid. He had practised capsize drill too many times for that, but he did fear being the object of ridicule.

The water was surprisingly cold, and Kit was tumbled over and bumped on the head by the hull. He found the jib sheet tangled around his legs but still did not panic, having faith that his life jacket would bring him up. Opening his eyes, he saw the dark shape of the hull amid the swirl of bubbles and pushed away from it and then up towards the light. His head broke surface and he blinked the stinging salt water from them and looked around.

As he did, Carmen's boat went by 25 metres to starboard. Kit could see her looking at them but she made no attempt to turn.

He didn't blame her for that. *Too dangerous in this surf so close to the beach,* he told himself. It would only result in two boats being over.

Concerned about the welfare of his companions, Kit now looked around and saw both their heads showing amid the surf. PO Crisp was already clinging to the upturned hull and Toms was still holding the mainsheet. Kit quickly swam the few metres to the hull and grabbed it as well.

PO Crisp looked at him. "You okay?" he shouted.

Kit nodded, opened his mouth to reply and got a mouthful of foam. That set him spluttering and gagging but and he clung tightly on while coughing and blinking. Holding on firmly he went up and down with the boat as it sluggishly rode the waves. He noted that there was no real danger. They were only about 40 metres from the shore and the waves were only breaking about a metre high. It was just the normal sized surf he swam in when the family went to the beach.

Kit looked around to see how far it was to the beach. As he rose on a wave, he noted small rocks awash in the surf to port but also an area of more sheltered water in their lee.

If we aren't careful, the boat will be dashed on those rocks, he thought.

PO Crisp obviously throught so too. He shouted, "Get her head round into the wind. We need to get her upright so the mast doesn't break."

That took some effort. Kit had to keep a tight grip while kicking hard with his feet to help drag the bow around to face the wind. That meant that it was now stern on to the beach. Next, they had to group on the port side and put all their weight on the centre board and hull to heave the boat upright. In the waves and surf that was hard to do but after a minute or so of real effort they achieved it.

The trick then was to stop the head swinging off the wind and the boat capsizing again. PO Crisp clung to the bow and kicked with his feet.

"Keep the bows into the wind!" he shouted, the shout being cut off by a breaking wave.

This almost smothered the mostly submerged hull, but the buoyancy compartments kept it afloat.

PO Crisp came up spluttering and gasping but both angry and determined. "Toms, get aboard and pull the centreboard up so we don't damage it when we get into shallower water," he ordered.

Seaman Toms did as he was told. He then tried to bail but it was such a hopeless task that PO Crisp ordered him back into the water.

During this, Kit clung to the port bulwark, kicking hard to help hold the hull upright and facing the wind. Above his head the sails flapped and the sheets ran loose and flogged at him. The jib sheet hit him in the face and then wrapped itself around his neck. With some difficulty he hung on with one hand and managed to free himself. Then he gripped the loose end and tried to hold it so that it didn't keep hitting him.

With each wave the boat rose and rolled, and it took a real effort to keep it head to wind. Now worried about his safety, Kit looked to see how far it was to the beach. To his relief, he saw that it was only about 10 or 15 metres. He also noted that Carmen's boat was drawn up on the beach and was being pushed stern first up the beach by Carmen. Andrew and Blake were both running in different directions along the beach, obviously searching for the clue.

They haven't found it yet. We might still have a chance, Kit thought.

Then his attention was taken up with holding on to the boat as the waves suddenly grew steeper as they entered the surf zone.

Chapter 4

REAL DRAMA

K it recognised this as a moment of real danger, and he struggled to hang on while holding the boat up. In the process he got salt water in his mouth and began to cough and splutter. He felt the boat rise up on the next wave and sensed that the crisis was upon them. But he felt so weak and powerless that he knew he could do nothing but try to hang on. The boat went racing ahead in a welter of busting spray and churning white water. It was swept ashore by the next breaking wave and despite his efforts Kit lost his grip. The rope tore through his hand and he went rolling over and over in the surf. That was both humiliating and irritating as his clothes were filled with sandy water in the process. When he struggled to his knees, spitting brine and sand and gasping for air he saw that the boat was now broadside on in the backwash.

Both PO Crisp and Seaman Toms were still clinging to it, frantically hauling to try to keep it upright and to get its bow into the wind again. The sails flapped and flogged and the sheets flailed about. Kit saw what he had to do and scrambled to his feet. With water streaming off him he scurried across to shove the bow hard around. In the process he was struck by the jib sheet again, but he ignored it until he had the bow facing the wind again.

PO Crisp nodded with approval then shouted at them to lower the sails. He held the bow and Kit and Seaman Toms both moved to get the slatting sails under control. Shielding his face and eyes from the wildly flapping corner of the jib with his left hand, Kit leaned across to the base of the mast and undid the halyard from its cleat. Then he flung himself at the sail, bundling it in his arms and dragging it down the forestay.

That worked, and he was able to get the whole sail down in a bundle at the foot of the stay. Then he used the sheet to tie it into a tight mass. PO Crisp watched and then nodded.

"Not very seaman-like but it will do for the moment," he said.

Kit burned at the rebuke but then moved to help Seaman Toms as he struggled to hold the boom while working on the lift for the mainsail. Kit grabbed the boom and was amazed at the force of the wind on it. It took all his strength to hold it as it was jerked back and forth by the gusts.

Bloody hell I'm weak! he thought with dismay.

But again his efforts were rewarded as Seaman Toms was able to concentrate on lowering the mainsail. As it came down, he bundled it on the boom and then took the main sheet and wrapped it around both sail and boom, lashing it all tight.

"Drag the boat further up the beach," PO Crisp ordered.

They did, Kit now very aware that the wind was chilling him in his wet clothes. He was also uncomfortably conscious of the grit that had made its way inside his shirt and trousers. Grimacing with distaste, he tried to ignore it while he worked.

That done, PO Crisp looked around. Kit did likewise. "Too late!" he muttered.

About 50 metres away Carmen and Andrew were crouched at the base of a tree at the top of the beach and Kit could see a plastic bag containing a piece of paper taped to the tree trunk. Even as he watched, they stood up and began counting paces along the beach.

PO Crisp turned to Kit. "You stay here and look after the boat Recruit Walker," he ordered.

That rankled as Kit badly wanted to be in the treasure hunt, but he could only nod and reply, "Aye, aye."

He understood that as the lowest rank he was likely to get the odd jobs. But it was still annoying to be left while the other two went striding off to take part in the game.

So, standing at the bow and holding the forestay, Kit watched as the other two started walking along the beach. He saw Andrew count 20 paces to the base of a large boulder. Once there he bent and looked into a cleft underneath it. Almost at once he let out a cry and bent down.

"Here it is!" he called, straightening up with the next clue in his hand.

Seeing that annoyed Kit even more. *Bugger! They will win!* he thought.

Carmen hurried across to join him. Kit didn't hear what was said but saw Andrew frown and read then look around. So did Kit, wondering what the clue was. The ground in from the beach was a jumble of big boulders, and areas of exposed black rock, with clumps of grass and just enough trees on the steep slope to qualify as a forest.

Blake had run to join them, and he now pointed to a pandanus palm that grew at the top of the beach a few metres further along.

"What about that Pandanus?" he cried.

Andrew obviously agreed as Kit saw him paced out ten paces to the tree. He bent and looked around it. Almost at once he let out a cry and bent down. The strong wind made it hard for Kit to hear but he saw them do some more pacing and then begin digging with their hands.

Carmen also fell to her knees and began digging. The two boys joined her, and they quickly dug out quite a reasonable hole. As they dug, Kit struggled to hold the boat upright in the gusting wind. From time to time he looked around, wiping perspiration from his face. It had become very hot and the afternoon sun blazed down on them. He noted that clouds dropping rain were still out on the horizon, but the humidity had become truly tropical.

Might rain soon, he decided. But after studying the weather for a few seconds, he looked seaward and noted that two more boats running in, their sails spread 'wing-and-wing'. *Petty Officer George's and Leading Seaman Page's,* he noted.

The other four boats were still well out, at least a couple of kilometres away, and only one of the motorboats acting as safety boats was in sight. It was punching in through the waves towards them, throwing up bursts of white spray as it did.

Kit looked back to see how the treasure hunt was going. As he did, PO Crisp and Seaman Toms reached the diggers. Andrew let out a cry and he and Blake at once redoubled their efforts, throwing handfuls of sand in all directions. Then Andrew bent down and lifted up a grey metal box. It looked brand new and was only the size of a shoebox.

"The treasure! We win!" he cried happily.

"Open it," called Seaman Toms.

Andrew tried to but it was locked.

"We will have to wait for the officers," Carmen said.

She looked around, obviously to check how far away the motorboats were. So did Kit, and saw four civilians walking towards them along the beach: two men and two women. The sight did not surprise him as people having picnics and swims was so common. However, something about the look on the first man made Kit study them.

The first man was tubby and middle aged, with a round, red face. He wore white shorts and a bright Hawaiian shirt. On his head was a white Panama hat and he had a bag and a beach towel over his shoulder. Behind him came a tall, thin man with a sun-tanned complexion. He wore jeans but had no shirt on. His longish brown hair was tied back in a ponytail, and he had a large gold earring in his right ear. In one hand he carried a bag and in the other a spade. Both women wore straw hats and sunglasses and had beach towels over their shoulders, and both had long, bare legs which looked very attractive. One woman was a blonde and wore a shirt, half undone and tied in a knot at the front to expose her middle. She wore tight white shorts. The other woman, with a harder, more angular face, had black hair and wore a long shirt, open at the front, over a white one-piece bathing costume.

The sight was so ordinary that Kit turned his attention back to where his friends were trying to open the 'treasure chest'. Thus he was surprised when the man with the Hawaiian shirt stopped near them and spoke to them. Kit was too far away and the wind too strong to hear most of it, but he could clearly see and it was obvious that an argument had begun. To his surprise and concern, he saw the man in the Hawaiian shirt shake his head with annoyance and speak to the other man. A scuffle followed which quickly escalated into a serious incident. Andrew was struck with a shovel and then Carmen, who sprang to his defence, punched and knocked down. The man took the box. Kit was appalled, and now scared, particularly when the people all pulled out guns.

Kit had watched all this in amazement and with growing alarm. It was so unlikely and so unreal that it took his shocked mind a few moments to accept what he was seeing. He was anxious to help he but knew he had been detailed to look after the boat. So he stayed there, and it took all his strength to haul the boat higher up the beach and keep it upright and facing into the wind.

But then his shock turned to genuine fear when the tubby man cocked what looked like an automatic pistol and pointed it at Andrew.

Is that real? What the hell is going on? Kit wondered in bewilderment.

PO Crisp stepped forward and confronted the people, his actions sending up Kit's opinion of him considerably. But he was obviously threatened and warned off. Then police arrived and the younger man grabbed Carmen as a hostage. He shoved a pistol against the side of her head and then turned to yell at the police,

"Back off coppers, or this kid gets blown away!"

Until the man named Dan had grabbed Carmen, Kit had been more puzzled than anything. Now he realised that the situation was real.

I don't believe this! he thought. *Who are these people? What's going on?*

Despite feeling a bit afraid, he stayed holding the boat even though he wanted to join the group. He saw an angry Andrew step closer in a half-hearted attempt to block the black-haired woman named from picking up the grey metal box. Her response was to whip out a small automatic pistol and point it at him.

Kit was aghast, and staring at the small pistol he experienced a wave of almost paralysing fear.

Oh my God! Someone could get shot! he thought.

His goggling eyes noted how shiny the silver metal of the pistol barrel was, even as waves of cold shock coursed through him. To his relief, Andrew froze, then just stood and watched as the woman picked up the box and stepped back next to the tubby man.

He took the box off her, then shouted to the watching police, "Keep back, you coppers! Don't try to stop us or this girl gets a bullet in the head."

Kit was horrified. He stared at Carmen, apprehension welling up to grip his chest. Kit now noted that all of the police were armed, and he went cold with dread.

At that moment, one of the safety boats arrived with the CO, Lt Cdr Hazard, aboard. It surged into the small cove and rounded to, ending up facing out to sea, its engine matching the waves. An anchor was tossed over the bow and the boat began drifting in stern first.

Things will be alright now, Kit thought, relief mixing with his mounting concern.

As the adult officers waded ashore, the tubby man spoke to his gang and then the four crooks, still holding Carmen as a shield, made their way down the beach. Andrew went to follow but was restrained by Petty Officer Crisp. Kit just stood and watched, his mind racing with ideas but unable to see how he could act in such a situation. He was scared now, but also appalled by the fact that the people were taking Carmen with them. The police called out to Lt Cdr Hazard to shove off, to go away, but the sound of the waves obviously drowned out most of it and the three OOCs just looked puzzled and stood waiting as the crooks moved towards them. PO Ferguson, their adult female instructor, who had been at the wheel of the boat, remained aboard and began packing things away.

Kit watched in dismay as the crooks threatened the officers and then commandeered the motorboat. He began to hope that the crooks might let Carmen go but was appalled to see her dragged aboard despite a struggle. He was further annoyed by seeing that the crooks apparently knew how to handle a boat. His own chest was now tight with dread, and he clenched his fists and ground his teeth at his own impotence. It just didn't seem fair to him that these thugs could just climb into a strange boat and make it work! But they could and did, powering out into the waves.

By now Kit was sick with apprehension. Poor Carmen! What would they do to her? Beside him Andrew seethed with helpless rage, tears streaming down his face.

Suddenly there was a commotion in the boat. Heart in mouth with anxiety Kit saw a flurry of movement. A person fell over the side, a person in dark blue clothes and a yellow life jacket. Was it Carmen? Or PO Ferguson? He could not tell but he saw a head appear, bobbing in the wake of the motorboat.

Then another horrifying thought came to Kit as he saw two of the crooks both lean over the stern and aim their pistols.

Oh no! They are going to shoot her!

However, the tubby man turned his head and said something and no shots were fired. Kit now saw that it was PO Ferguson who was in the water. He bit his lip with anxiety lest the crooks circle back to capture her again. A couple of seconds went by, and he saw that the boat was holding its course so he decided this was not likely. It became quickly apparent that the crooks were definitely leaving her behind. By now they were nearly a hundred metres offshore.

They still have Carmen as a hostage, he reasoned. *Oh! What will happen to her?*

Chapter 5

ENVY AND CONCERN

K it stood on the beach and shivered as the cool wind blew on his wet clothes. He was feeling shocked and anxious and was hoping that somehow the other boats might save Carmen. But these hopes swiftly faded. The stolen motorboat turned slightly to port and headed north. This meant that it passed the next two sail boats at a distance of several hundred metres. This left PO Ferguson bobbing out in the waves and Kit began to worry. It was not any concern over the instructor drowning, as she wore a life jacket, but rather over the things he knew for a fact lurked in the tropical sea; sharks and jelly fish being the main ones.

Beside him a worried looking Andrew stared anxiously out to sea. "Oh I hope one of those boats sees her," he muttered.

It was Cadet PO George's boat who finally took note of the wildly waving and pointing people on the beach and turned towards PO Ferguson. As she was hauled aboard the bobbing sailboat a few minutes later, Kit sighed with relief.

Then his eyes went back to the rapidly retreating stolen motorboat. It had turned even more and was angling out to sea, but well away from the next two boats. The last two boats, and the second safety boat, were still a kilometre out to sea. Kit pinned faint hopes on that second boat, the one with Lieutenant Ryan on board, but now he shook his head sadly.

They won't even notice that the power boat punching out through the waves is our cadet boat, he thought.

The two boats passed nearly a kilometre apart, and soon after that the stolen motorboat sped into the first of the rain squalls sweeping in from out to sea. As the stolen motorboat vanished into the greyness, Kit felt his heart tighten up with concern. Andrew shook his head and he let out a little sob. Kit glanced at him and noticed tears prickling in the corners of his eyes. The sight made him uncomfortable and unsure of what to do or say. Not having a sister he could only imagine the torment Andrew might be feeling.

By this time Lt Cdr Hazard and the other OOCs had been briefed by the police and customs people on what had happened. They also stared out to sea, straining to catch sight of the stolen boat amid the drifting curtains of rain. Lt Cdr Hazard was furiously angry with the police. From where he stood Kit could only hear snatches of the argument, but it was obvious that the CO was very annoyed.

"How dare you people not warn the cadets!" he snapped angrily.

"How were we to know you lot were going to barge in to our operation!" retorted a grey-haired, grey-clad, middle-aged man, a Commonwealth Police Inspector Kit now learned.

Lt Cdr Hazard stepped closer and glared at him. "As soon as our cadets came ashore you should have moved to warn them and keep them safe," he snapped. "I don't care what long-running surveillance operation that compromised. The safety of these kids is more important than any drug bust!"

"Shh!" cautioned the equally angry inspector. "Loose lips sink ships."

Lt Cdr Hazard glared angrily back. "I'll sink your bloody ship if you don't start taking action to rescue my cadet!" he snapped. "Now get some assets moving!"

"Don't you threaten me!" blustered the inspector.

But even Kit could see he was worried. His admiration for the CO went up another notch.

Lt Cdr Hazard gave a short, bitter laugh, then said, "If it takes wrecking your bloody career to save Carmen then I will do it gladly, now act!"

"I already have," replied the inspector. "We have two cars going north along the highway; and the state police have been notified and are also sending cars to help. Even as we speak my people are contacting the navy and air force, and we hope to have helicopters in the area within half an hour or so." He pointed to where another plain clothes policeman was busy talking on a mobile phone.

"They will need to be quick," Lt Cdr Hazard replied. "It will be dark in a few hours. And any aircraft are going to need thermal imaging or infra-red surveillance equipment to work in this rain that is coming in."

Kit hadn't thought of that, and the notion of the crooks escaping with Carmen in the rain appalled him. He stared out at the rain squalls that now covered much of the eastern horizon and bit his lip. The rain didn't look heavy, and it certainly wasn't from any sort of storm, was just normal summer rain showers, but it was now spread across half the horizon and looked to be thickening up out to sea. Concern swirled in Kit making him feel anxious and slightly nauseous.

Andrew was obviously very stressed and angry, and he strode over to stand beside Lt Cdr Hazard. "Carmen is my sister. You must save her please," he said.

"We are doing all we can," replied the inspector.

"So what was in the grey box?" Andrew asked.

"I can't tell you," the inspector replied.

Kit noted the senior customs man flash a warning glance at the inspector. Andrew was plainly nettled by being told that as he said, "It was drugs or something wasn't it?"

"I can't say," the inspector repeated woodenly.

"I can!" Andrew snapped angrily.

He looked to be nearly in tears by this time and kept casting glances out to sea. Kit looked as well and noted that the stolen motorboat was no longer visible. It had vanished in the spreading rain showers.

Andrew said, "How come those crooks came here? They were looking for that box, weren't they?"

"Yes," the inspector muttered.

Lt Cdr Hazard looked puzzled. "So where was this box they took?"

Andrew pointed to the hole in the sand beside the pandanus palm. "There, sir. The note said: 'Two paces north, dig'. So we did."

"North?" Lt Cdr Hazard queried. "My note said three paces south."

"Oh no! There couldn't be two notes on the same pandanus palm!" Andrew cried.

He strode over to it and looked, then looked dismayed. There, placed under a stone at the base of the trunk, was another note. He picked it up, then fished the other note out of his pocket. At once the different handwriting was obvious. Kit studied them.

Even a different type of pen, he noted.

The inspector and the customs officer both came to look at the notes and the policeman took them off Andrew, saying they were now evidence. The inspector was then distracted by another plain clothes policeman calling him over to talk on a mobile phone.

Andrew shook his head. "But why this tree?" he muttered.

Lt Cdr Hazard made a wry face and gestured along the small beach.

"Because it is so obvious," he suggested. "It is the only pandanus palm on the whole beach."

"But why would the crooks put their drugs here?" he asked.

The customs officer just shook his head. That obviously annoyed Andrew. So was Lt Cdr Hazard. He said, "I suppose for the same reason I did. The beach is isolated, yet easy to find. The highway is just up there a hundred metres, so they could walk down from a car, then quickly drive on."

Andrew nodded, thinking it through. "That would explain why they were all dressed for a picnic on the beach. That way they wouldn't attract any attention at all."

"I think you are right," Lt Cdr Hazard said, glancing at the customs officer, who tried to keep a poker face.

"But why would they bury it here, sir?" Andrew asked. "Why wouldn't smugglers just sail in and go ashore to hand it over? I mean, it's a bit risky just leaving something very valuable."

Kit listened and agreed. It was obvious that smugglers had to be involved because of the customs involvement in the operation.

Lt Cdr Hazard looked at the customs officer and then at Andrew. "I'd guess that there are two gangs, and they are trying to arrange it so that the authorities cannot link them together."

"How, sir?"

"If the people who smuggled the drugs in by boat put them here a few days ago they could now be a thousand kilometres away and have a good alibi ready. There would be no provable link between them and the people who collected the drugs."

Kit noted a fractional nod of the customs officer's head and decided that Lt Cdr Hazard's theory was probably right.

Andrew asked, "So you think some smugglers came in from the sea and left the drugs here, sir?"

Lt Cdr Hazard nodded, then said, "Yes. They might have come off a passing freighter, come ashore in a fast boat, hidden the goods, then returned to the ship; or maybe came off a passing yacht or fishing boat. Something like that."

That made sense to Kit. Andrew nodded and said, "But there must have been communication for the crooks to know where to pick the stuff up. And how did the police know about it?"

That got him a blank stare from the customs officer. *An undercover operation maybe?* Kit speculated, having seen such things on TV.

At that moment, the next two sailboats ran ashore and Lt Cdr Hazard went hurrying down the beach to PO Ferguson. The inspector came back and also went over to see how she was. Kit stayed holding the bow of his boat, and as he did he noted that the last four sailboats, and the second safety boat, were now all only a few hundred metres offshore. They were being overtaken by drifting curtains of rain.

We will get wet in a minute, he noted with half his mind. Then he gave a wry grin, remembering that he was already soaked.

Andrew came and stood next to him and stared out to sea looking sick and miserable. Then, he sobbed and muttered, "Oh! How am I going to tell Mum!"

At that, concern and sympathy welled up in Kit and he felt guilty at having been envious of Andrew. *I must help him if I can,* he told himself. But how?

A very upset looking PO Ferguson was helped up the beach to join them. Lt Cdr Hazard took out his own mobile phone and despite a protest from the inspector, called for an ambulance and then contacted the local navy HQ. He then phoned two more OOCs who were waiting with trucks at Ellis Beach.

By then the last of the boats had run ashore. PO Crisp came over to join Kit and helped pull it higher.

"Okay Cadet Walker, you did well. You can leave the boat now and join the others," he said.

Kit did so and the cadets stood in a group discussing the incident. All of them kept turning to look out to sea in the direction that the stolen motorboat had vanished. Kit stood with them, but felt quite insignificant and lonely. Nearby stood Andrew with his friends, Luke and Blake, beside him. Blake then moved off to show the others where the clues had been. They also dug up the actual 'treasure'. This was only a carton full of chocolates in gold-coloured wrappers, but nobody felt any elation and the box was left unopened.

The rain arrived. That also went almost unnoticed by Kit and most of the others. It was warm, tropical rain and merely cooled things down nicely. Luckily it was just a steady downpour and the wind speed did not increase to any extent. Lt Cdr Hazard explained the situation to Lt Ryan and the other OOCs who had arrived on the second motorboat, then had Cadet CPO Pike, the Chief Bosuns Mate, line the cadets up. Still stunned by the shock of what had happened Kit moved to stand with the others.

The roll was checked and then Lt Cdr Hazard moved to speak to them. He told them that everything possible was being done to find Carmen and they were now to sail the boats the 2 kilometres back to Ellis Beach, where the trucks were waiting.

As Kit began moving towards his boat, he saw Andrew standing shivering in the drizzle. He was staring out to sea and looking thoroughly down. Kit felt an urge to speak to him, to offer help and comfort, but couldn't think of what to say.

As he thought this, he noted that Lt Cdr Hazard and the other adult staff were looking deeply shocked and upset and that helped. It certainly increased his liking and affection for them.

They really care, he told himself, not that he had ever doubted it.

While Kit puzzled over how to help Andrew, Lt Cdr Hazard walked over to Andrew. "Do you feel up to sailing, Andrew? You can go back in one of the police cars if you like, or in the safety boat."

Andrew glanced at them and wrinkled his nose in disgust. "No thanks, sir. I'm alright. I'll sail."

Hearing that increased Kit's admiration for Andrew and he hoped he would be able to cope as well if some similar disaster befell him.

Cadet CPO Pike was detailed to take command of Carmen's boat, and he called Andrew and Blake to be the crew. Cadet PO Crisp ordered Kit and Seaman Toms to launch their own boat. That took some doing in the wind and drizzle, but it at least got his mind off what might happen to Carmen for a few minutes.

But as they beat out over the waves, Kit saw Andrew continually glancing northwards, obviously hoping for a glimpse of the stolen motorboat. All he could see were drifting rain squalls and grey clouds. There were a couple of yachts visible right out on the horizon, but no sign of any motorboat.

The boats stayed in a group with Lt Ryan's motorboat as close escort. They tacked the boat out around Simpson Point and then sailed southwards parallel to the beach. The rain eased off and sunlight sparkled on the water, although other showers could be seen out to sea and to the north. Their course was well out to keep out of the zone where the waves were breaking. Even so, the trip to Ellis Beach only took about 20 minutes and by then Kit was recovering from the shock.

Now that the initial surprise had worn off, he was filled with concern for Carmen; and as he helped beach the boat and unrig it, half his mind was still on the sea to the north. To add to his concern was watching Andrew's reactions. His emotions were obviously in turmoil as he was shaking with anger and apprehension.

"Bastards!" Andrew muttered savagely, referring to the crooks. "If they do anything to Carmen!"

Kit thought that was just empty release. *He will never see any of them again.* Then another dismaying idea crossed his mind. *Or maybe Carmen.*

Now that was a sickening worry!

The boats were dragged ashore and unrigged then carried up the beach to a waiting truck. While they were being loaded onto it, Kit saw Andrew's parents arrive. Lt Cdr Hazard went to meet them followed by Andrew. As Kit knelt to secure the strapping holding his boat on the tray of the truck, he watched the meeting with morbid curiosity mingled with genuine sympathy. He saw Andrew start to cry as he hugged his mother and that made him wonder how he might react in similar circumstances. He found the notion uncomfortable, and he felt embarrassed seeing the family's obvious anguish.

The sound of a low flying helicopter hurrying north out to sea attracted Kit's attention. All he could do was hope the searchers were in time and that Carmen was alright.

Andrew was not allowed to return to the depot with the other cadets. Kit saw him get placed in his parent's car and it soon drove off. To his surprise, it went southwards back towards Cairns. He had expected it to go northwards to Port Douglas.

That's the way the smugglers went, he told himself.

By then the initial concern and shock had worn off the cadets were beginning to discuss what had happened and Carmen's possible fate. Kit found the speculation both stimulating and concerning.

Some of them don't care at all. They are just excited or don't like Carmen.

A few, he noted, even expressed what he considered to be ghoulish speculation at what horrible things the smugglers might do to her.

There are a few who really don't like Carmen, he thought, suspecting jealousy might be the reason. But then, he didn't particularly like Andrew either, but he did feel sorry for him.

The cadets were bundled into cars and a minibus and were driven back to the depot where they unloaded the boats and stored them. As they did, Kit was surprised to note his own parents standing talking to other parents at their car outside the fence.

They look worried, he noted. Then it occurred to him that they must know. *It must have been on the news.*

It had been. As soon as the cadets were dismissed, they hurried to meet him and his mother hugged him—much to his embarrassment.

"Aw Mum! Not in front of the other kids!" Kit muttered. But he was touched by their obvious love and concern.

"Are you alright?" his mother cried.

"Yes mum. I'm fine. I've just been sailing."

"Your clothes are all wet."

Kit made a face. "They get that way when you sail!" he replied, not wanting to mention capsizing. "And there was some rain."

They drove him straight home. Once there he was hustled out of his wet clothes, through a hot shower, and into dry clothes. By then it was 5:30 pm.

While he had been in the shower, his brothers had heard about the incident on the news and when Kit hurried out, hoping to hear some of it, they began to question him.

"What happened, Squirt?" Bruce queried.

As always, Kit resented that name. Usually his parents rebuked his brothers if they used such put downs, but they said nothing. Kit recounted the incident as he had seen it, feeling excited and concerned at the same time.

Big brother Adrian asked a few searching questions about the sea and the boats, but Bruce curled his lip. "I see the crooks didn't kidnap you."

"I was minding our boat," Kit explained, feeling guilty that had had just been a spectator to the drama.

Adrian grinned. "Maybe they are fishermen and thought he was undersize."

Bruce chortled and Kit burned. This time their father did rebuke the older boys, and Kit ended the conversation by going to his room to comb his hair. Now he resented fate that made him so small and which had also left him a mere bystander to the only really exciting thing ever to have happened in his life.

For a while Kit just lay on his bed, alternately lamenting the fate that made him undersize and worrying about what might have happened to Carmen. To help ease his concern, he made a point of joining his parents while they watched the ABC news at 7pm but there was nothing new in that bulletin.

Poor Carmen. I hope she is alright, he thought.

Dreadful images of the smugglers throwing her overboard (or, even worse, of shooting her and tossing her body into the sea), or of them possibly doing things to her (his mind briefly toyed with the concept of rape but he found the whole subject so disgusting and repellent that he quickly pushed it from his mind). Gloomily he settled in an armchair and contemplated the evil side of human nature.

I wish I could do something! he thought, a passionate desire to see the villains brought to justice mingling with the desire to be a hero.

Suddenly the telephone shrilled next to him and he jumped with fright. Quickly he snatched it up. It was Cadet PO Crisp.

"Hi Kit. I thought you might like to know. I've just heard that Carmen has been rescued. She is safe."

Kit felt a huge surge of relief. "Thanks," he replied. "Do you know any details?"

"Apparently a helicopter located the boat. It was drifting near Low Isles. The police said that a paramedic had been winched down and that everyone on board was alright. The motor has been damaged and the radio smashed, but the people are well. A Coast Guard launch has been sent to get them and should be there by now," Cadet PO Crisp explained.

Kit then had to explain all of that to his family. Adrian looked puzzled. "But didn't those smugglers still hold that girl as a hostage?" he asked.

Kit couldn't answer that. "He did not explain," he said, but he was puzzled himself.

It wasn't until the morning news the next day that he got more details. The TV people had filmed the rescue boats arriving in Port Douglas. Kit saw the images and was annoyed at the way the crowd of media people jostled and pushed for the best positions. But he did get a few fleeting glimpses of Carmen before she was shielded from the lights and cameras by her father and the police.

To his surprise, Kit saw other people being helped off the boat—a couple of adults and some young children.

Who are they and what are they doing on the boat? he wondered.

A yacht was mentioned but which yacht and why it was involved was not made clear.

Chapter 6

SCHOOL & WORK

It was not until Kit got to school the next day that he learned what had happened. Blake was the source of the information and other students crowded round to hear what he had to say.

"Those other people were off a yacht," Blake explained. "The smugglers turned into pirates on the high seas and boarded it. They put the people on our boat and then sailed away. But not before wrecking the motor and the radio."

"Pirates!" Kit exclaimed, his imagination conjuring up images of a square rigger flying the Jolly Roger, cannon smoke billowing.

Now that Carmen was safe his emotions turned to envy. He wished he had been more involved and had somehow been able to rescue her. *Or Diana,* he thought. During Period 1 he constructed a fantasy in which it was Diana who had been taken hostage and of how he rescued her.

But all he did was dream. After the previous week's bruising experiences he made no attempt to speak to her or approach her.

Carmen was not at school that day but to Kit's surprise Andrew was. He met him at morning break and was able to get more details. But these only added to his envy.

Others weren't all that impressed or happy either. Kit overheard Stephen Bell asking his friends why the smugglers hadn't sold Carmen into the white slave trade.

Donna Hendricks heard this and sniffed, her nose in the air. "Huh! They should have tossed her overboard for the sharks," she commented.

Kit was shocked. *I didn't realise so many people did not like Carmen.* He mulled this over and then decided that jealousy was the motivation. *Carmen is so good looking and so capable they must just feel jealous.*

His own feelings were mixed. And they weren't improved by overhearing Graham Kirk and Stephen boasting to his mates how he and Graham Kirk, another boy in their class, had 'jumped the rattler' and got a free ride on a goods train to the small mountain town of Kuranda on Sunday.

A tubby Year 8 boy named Roger who was accepted as part of their group frowned. "What do you mean by 'jumped the rattler?" he queried.

"Climbed on board a goods train and got a free ride. It's an expression I heard my grandad use," Stephen explained. Then he chuckled. "And Graham nearly fell and slipped off," he added.

"Was the train moving?" Roger asked.

Stephen nodded. "You bet!"

He then described how dangerous and exciting it had been. Kit listened with growing envy and frustration that he could not get a hearing to describe the drama he had been involved in.

Curious to know why, he nudged Stephen. "Why did you do that?" he queried.

"Graham wanted to try to repair his love life," Stephen exchanged.

"And did he?" Kit asked, wishing he had a love life of his own to need repair.

Stephen shook his head. "Nah! Esme has dumped him, but now he's muttering about one of the Year Eight chicks. Deslie's her name."

"Which one is she?" Kit asked.

Stephen pointed across to where a group of girls sat under D Block. "That flirty little blonde at the end."

Kit eyed Deslie and recognised her. She was new to the school, but he had noticed her. "Pretty enough," he commented.

"Yeah, but he'll be sorry," Stephen replied.

"Why?"

"She's a real flirt and a show-off," Stephen answered.

Blake had been listening to this and he now leaned over. "What was this about Tarzan? Graham was mumbling something about seeing him."

Stephen nodded and scowled. "He claims he did. Up at Stony Creek Falls."

Images of Tarzan the Naked Wildman formed in Kit's imagination. Tarzan was a notorious character who wandered the jungle and was reputed to have raped several girls. For a few seconds Kit tried to imagine what it might be like to walk around the tropical rain forest with nothing on. Having only very limited knowledge of that environment from weekend trips, he was doubtful if it would be much fun.

Too many spiky plants and thorns and too much stinging tree, he thought.

Blake spoke next. "We had more fun than that. Did you hear about Carmen Collins being kidnapped?"

Stephen nodded. "Oh yeah! What happened?"

"We were doing a sailing race, a treasure hunt, up along the coast past Ellis Beach and we got held up by these crooks with guns," Blake explained.

Kit itched to be the one to tell the story, so interjected. "Smugglers, and they became pirates later."

"Shut up, Midget! I'm telling this story," Blake snapped.

That really stung and Kit lapsed into hurt silence. He was so upset he thought of walking away but instead sat in sulky silence and listened while Blake told the tale (Poorly in his opinion!).

The story kept them going until the end of morning break. Feeling aggrieved and upset, Kit made his way to class. There his mood was not improved by seeing two Year 10 boys chatting to Diana and Fleur. That defeat still burned, so Kit made sure he avoided Diana as much as he could, taking himself to the library during the lunch break.

Otherwise it was a normal school day and, to Kit's relief, he had no encounters with any of the bullies. But he still felt down and hurt.

* * *

It was a thoroughly unhappy boy who went home that afternoon. Once again, he made himself to do a few push-ups but his morale was so low he quickly gave up and went upstairs to play computer games.

That night after going to bed he lay awake and brooded, wallowing in self-pity for a while until images of Diana edged into his consciousness. That helped him restore his mood. He began to fantasise about rescuing her. But who from?

Pirates obviously, Kit thought. But then he shrugged. *Pirates like the ones in the 'Phantom' comics don't exist anymore,* he told himself.

He knew that there were real pirates in places like the Philippines and Malacca Strait and off the Horn of Africa, but they did not fit his image of square-rigged tall ships with cannons poking out of rows of gun ports and crewed by characters with black eye patches and three-cornered hats.

But there were crooks like the smugglers who had taken Carmen hostage, and they were real enough. For the next hour or so Kit adjusted his fantasies to give himself a starring role in his own version of what might have happened. But just as he was about to take action he dropped off into a restless sleep.

Tuesday was another ordinary school day and Kit cheered up a little. After school he went to the truck depot and helped one of the mechanics remove and work on a rear axle. It was simple mechanical stuff to Kit, and he easily understood how it all fitted together and how it worked. As he did not mind getting his hands dirty, he had no problem with helping clean and grease the parts before helping to re-assemble it all. As he worked, he noted that the new Prime Mover with the cracked steering arm was still parked at the side. No spare part was available for it yet, he was told.

It was while walking to the washbasin to wash his greasy hands that Kit encountered his next challenge. The wash basins were along the side wall of the shed near the back and to reach them Kit went around the other side of the truck he was working on. As he did, he saw a person packing tools from the bench into a carry bag. Then the person glanced at Kit and there was mutual recognition.

Jellman! Kit thought. *What is he doing here? I thought dad sacked him.*

Jellman slid a wrench into the bag and stood up. A scowl crossed his face. He then picked up another spanner which he also shoved into the bag.

Kit was puzzled and also a bit scared, remembering the ugly incident the previous week. "What are you doing?" he asked. He hesitated over what to call Jellman, not sure if he should be addressed as 'mister' or not.

"Taking what's mine!" Jellman retorted. With that he reached across and picked up an electric drill.

Kit again hesitated, fear and uncertainty tying his tongue for a few seconds. Then he cried out, "Stop taking things! You need to get them through the office." To his own annoyance his voice quavered as he did.

Jellman sneered. "Get stuffed, kid! Your dad owes me and I'm takin' what I'm owed."

"You have no right to take anything," Kit replied, his voice again almost cracking with anxiety and uncertainty.

"So what are ya gunna do about it?" Jellman sneered. "Are ya gunna cry for daddy?"

That was exactly what Kit had been thinking, but the scornful tone made him again hesitate. Jellman shoved the drill into his bag and reached for a carton of drill bits at the back of the bench. That finally sparked Kit to act.

"Stop!" he cried loudly. "You have to ask. Dad! Hey Dad!"

"Shut up you little freak or you'll get hurt," Jellman snarled.

He picked up the drill bits and tried to shove them into the now overfull bag. In the process the box became stuck and he swore and pushed at it.

Kit took a step forward. "Stop!" he shouted. "Stop! Help! Help!"

"Little bastard! You'll regret that," Jellman snarled.

He grabbed a heavy wrench from the bench and hefted it, then raised it ready to strike at Kit. Instantly fear flooded through Kit. He beat a hasty retreat, bumping painfully against the truck beside him as he did.

"Help!" he shrieked, genuine fear overcoming his inhibitions.

From the other side of the truck he heard voices and footsteps and Bill, the mechanic he had been working with, called, "What's wrong? What's the problem?"

Jellman let out an oath and his face contorted with anger. But he stopped moving towards Kit and spun on his heel and began walking quickly away. Kit stopped and tried to gather his thoughts. To his shame, his heart was hammering so fast he found he was gasping for breath.

"Stop! Stop thief!" he cried.

Bill the mechanic appeared around the front of the truck behind Kit. "What is it, young fella?" he enquired.

"Jellman. He's stealing things... tools," Kit gasped, pointing to Jellman.

By then the man was striding across the large bitumen back yard past the parked trucks. Even as Kit spoke, Jellman vanished from view behind a truck.

"Jellman?" Bill queried.

"Yes. He was here, taking tools from the bench," Kit cried. "Oh quick! Stop him! He will get away."

Emboldened by the presence of the mechanic he ran forward out of the shed and across the yard. But fear of Jellman caused him to detour well away from the parked truck the man had vanished behind. Instead Kit took a route that allowed him to see clearly between the parked vehicles without going too close to them.

He was just in time to see Jellman walk out through the back gate. Kit now ran between two parked trucks to the gate to see where Jellman went next. Through eyes misted with excitement he saw Jellman climb into a small white truck that was parked in the street at the back of the yard. A second man was sitting in the driver's seat and the engine was going, and as soon as Jellman was in the vehicle pulled out and accelerated away.

As it went past the gate, Jellman turned and glared at Kit and snarled what he took to be threats. The sight made Kit shiver and he swallowed as fear swilled in his guts. Only then did he think to try to get the vehicle's number and make. The make was easy as Kit knew his trucks but by then the vehicle was at the end of the block and turning into a side street and he was only able to get the letters E and X.

Was the next letter a 'J', he wondered.

Fretting and annoyed with himself he bit his lip and turned to go back in. As he walked back across the big bitumen yard, Kit saw that several men were now standing talking to the mechanic and they were joined by his father. As Kit rejoined them in the shade of the shed, his father raised his eyebrows.

"What happened?" he asked.

Kit had to swallow to moisten his tongue and he hoped that the fear was not showing. "Jellman. He was here taking tools from that bench. He claimed they were his and that you owed him," Kit answered.

"Pigs I do!" his father growled. "I paid him out in full!" He glanced at the other workers for confirmation. Several men nodded. Then he swore again and shook his head. "The bastard was stealing. Where did he go?"

"Drove off in a white Isuzu truck with another man," Kit answered, pointing in the direction the vehicle had gone.

"Did you get his number?" his father asked.

Kit had been dreading that question and he could only shake his head and feel ashamed. "Only a bit of it," he replied crestfallen. He told his father what he remembered.

His father swore again and then looked at him. "You alright, son? Did he hurt you?"

Only my feelings! Kit thought, again experiencing a spurt of searing hurt at the 'little freak' comment. But he did not want to add to his embarrassment by explaining that in front of the other men, so he shook his head.

"No. He just threatened he would hurt me," he answered.

"He'd better not, the thieving bastard!" his father growled. He then turned to Frank the foreman. "You'd better do a check, Frank, and see what we might have lost."

Kit began to list the items he had seen and his father nodded. "Good work, son. It was good of you to confront him and stop him," he said. He shook his head and said to the men, "That might explain why we haven't been able to find some of the tools. Maybe someone has been walking in and helping themselves."

Frank the foreman nodded. "We might have to shut our back gate and keep a better watch during working hours," he commented.

Kit's father nodded but looked unhappy. "That will make truck movements awkward," he said.

"It will," Frank agreed.

Kit could only agree. Big trucks came and went several times every hour sometimes and to have to get the gate opened and then shut each time would be very annoying and slow down operations quite considerably.

"What about CCTV cameras?" he suggested.

His father frowned and looked thoughtful. "We might have to, but that is more expense and I am not sure we can afford that right now."

Frank nodded. "Might save money in the long run though boss."

Kit's father nodded and looked unhappy. "I'll look into it, get some quotes," he said.

They went back inside and began to check the tools on the bench. Kit's father went into the office to make phone calls and to get an inventory of the tools. It was all very annoying and upsetting and Kit found he was shaking with reaction. That shamed him and he made a point of keeping away from the men until he had brought his trembling muscles under control.

His father came back and said he had phoned the police. That gave Kit some satisfaction, but it also increased his anxiety.

Jellman said he'd get me, he thought, wondering if that meant the man would wait to get revenge at some other time. That was a very worrying thought: would it be at home? Or maybe at school? Then a horrible idea came to Kit: *Or on the way to or from school?*

Images of a truck knocking him down when he was riding his bike caused a frisson of fear to shiver through him.

That general fear stayed niggling at him for the remainder of the afternoon. Kit had to wait until a policeman appeared and then sat with his father to make a statement. The seriousness and legal nature of it all worried him and it was an anxious boy who finally wheeled his bike out of the front gate at half past five. Careful to look in all directions he rode home along as many quiet suburban streets as he could.

As he rode his bike home, Kit thought hard about what he might have done if Jellman had actually attacked him. Images of him trying to defend himself crowded his mind, adding to his anxiety. As he pictured Jellman swinging that wrench down in a bone crunching blow at his skull, Kit shuddered.

I could not stop that sort of a blow. I don't have the strength-or the skill, he worried.

As he did, the notion of building up his muscles and of becoming strong enough to defeat bullies returned. He resolved to get on with an exercise program and to start as soon as he got home.

But that plan immediately failed as he was met by his very worried mother who wanted to know all about the incident at the depot. Kit realised that his father had obviously phoned her, so he had to sit and relate the incident. Both Bruce and Adrian listened as well. Kit was still describing things when his father arrived home. He joined them and the whole family began to discuss the incident.

Kit's mother looked concerned. "This might explain those other things that have gone missing, the fuel and the spare parts," she said.

Kit's father nodded. "It certainly could. I've had suspicions for quite a while but had no proof until now. Now we have and we can act."

"We certainly need to tighten up security," Kit's mother commented. "We can't keep losing money like we have been."

Once again Kit spoke up. "Did you ask about CCTV cameras dad?"

His father looked annoyed. "No. I didn't have time, but I will!" he snapped irritably.

Kit knew that his father owned several truck depots and 14 Prime Movers. There were at least 30 trailers of various kinds including four big milk tankers that were operated on the Atherton Tablelands, plus six refrigerated trailers that carried things like bananas to Melbourne or prawns from Karumba to Townsville. There were also a couple of specialist heavy lift trailers.

"I'm having trouble keeping up the payments on those six new Macks," his father commented.

"The SX6s?" his mother queried.

"Yes."

Kit pictured the big new SX6s and felt a stab of concern. They were the latest and most powerful trucks available and were doing a good job and to lose them would be disastrous. They were not only very reliable they were much easier to maintain, requiring fewer services. He had worked on a couple, including the one that needed a new steering arm, and appreciated how much better they were to service.

They have a really good layout in the engine compartment, he thought. *You can get at things more easily than in the older trucks.*

The fact that they had a lot more electronics and that computers were the main tool to test the engines did not bother him. He liked computers and enjoyed doing that. But what bothered him more was that his parents rarely discussed business at home.

Things must be serious, he mused.

After a time the conversation lagged and they broke up to get ready for dinner. Kit went and worked at his homework while the food was prepared.

After the meal Kit went back to his room to finish his homework. While he worked his mind kept replaying the afternoon's incidents and images of an angry and threatening Jellman kept slipping into his mind. Kit found them both frightening and worrying. He knew that he had no real chance in any fight with the man should he catch him alone and try to bash him.

My only chance, apart from making sure I never get into that situation, is to be quicker and to have some skill, he mused. But where and how to acquire the skill?

One of Kit's hobbies was computer games and as part of his school program he was doing a Certificate II course in Computer Gaming, so he was as e-savvy as any of his peers. Using the internet was almost second nature so he then went searching to see what the experts said about exercise programs.

While he did this, it came to him again that sheer strength needed to be allied to skill so he also did a website search for local clubs. From that he selected a Judo course and also noted down when boxing was being taught at the local Police and Citizens Youth Club (PCYC). There was also reference to a fencing club and he hesitated over that, as he did over the local pistol club.

That will cost a lot more money and be much harder to do, he thought. Then he shook his head. *No. Maybe I can get to learn about pistols at cadets.*

Satisfied he had made a good start, Kit turned his attention to playing 'Ghost Recon' and for the next two hours was engrossed.

This is probably just as good a practice for snap shooting anyway, he mused.

For a few moments, fantasies of having a gun battle with desperate gangsters filled his mind. Imagining himself to be a highly skilled and super-quick pistol shot faster than Bruce Willis he quickly blasted a dozen crooks.

Which led him to a moral dilemma. *The Phantom never kills anyone,* he thought. So should he even think about it? *Yes,* he decided, accepting that the Phantom was after all a fantasy comic superhero and was not realistic, however entertaining he was to read.

Besides, I would never be a good enough shot to knock the guns out of the crook's hands. I would have to plug them.

Images from the many *Phantom* comics he had read flitted across the screen of his mind and he frowned. He doubted very much if it was possible to shoot the gun out of a person's hand without accidentally hitting their fingers or hand.

There is never anything gruesome or realistic in those comics really, he thought.

And he had always been bothered by the paradox of the Phantom never hesitating to use brute force, threats or torture to get people to talk. Torture, he decided, wasn't a concept he was comfortable with.

Never mind that. First, I have to be tough enough and good enough to win ordinary fights with bullies, he told himself. *And I am going to start tomorrow.*

Chapter 7

MORE TROUBLE

At school on Wednesday, Kit again toyed with the idea of making another approach to Diana. But every time he glanced at her, memories of his humiliating rejection made him pause. So he just watched her from afar and did not ask her. Instead, he concentrated on his schoolwork.

The day was very ordinary as he did not encounter the bullies, for which he was thankful. The only thing of interest occurred as he was making his way across past F Block towards the bike racks after school. His focus was on looking for Diana and he found himself walking behind Graham Kirk and Peter Bronsky. Kit disliked Graham. He seemed to be everything that he wasn't: fit, brave, good looking, and a spurt of jealous resentment briefly coursed through him.

The boys walked in under C Block among a milling throng of students, many of whom were now wearing army camouflage uniforms. The school was one of the few which had an army cadet unit and Kit knew that was only because Mr Conkey gave much of his spare time to organise and run it. The army cadets had their Q Store and office in two rooms under the building. Kit noted Andrew standing to one side watching. That piqued Kit's curiosity, so he detoured over to talk to him. As he did, he was teased by the army cadets that knew he was a navy cadet. Most added a few smart comments to either put down the navy cadets or to boast about how much better the army cadets were. One even suggested he transfer from the navy cadets.

Graham and Peter, both in school uniform, stopped next to Andrew and began talking to him, so Kit sheered away and then found his path blocked by a flow of army cadets. As he did, he noted Peter gesturing towards the assembling cadets. In response Graham shook his head, then walked away his face a mask of dejection. Kit saw a look of real concern on Andrew's face.

Graham joined the navy cadets at the same time as me, he remembered. *But I haven't seen him this year. I wonder what happened?*

He vaguely remembered Graham getting into some sort of trouble over the attempted sabotage of the American warships that had been visiting but he did not know the details.[1] But just knowing that Graham had also been a hero added another dollop of jealousy to Kit's dislike.

I wish I could do something heroic, he thought.

Peter watched Graham for a few moments then turned back to Andrew. "Hi Andrew! Changed your mind, have you?" he called jokingly.

Andrew smiled back. "Fat chance!" he said. Then he nodded towards Graham's departing back. "Were you trying to persuade Graham to join?"

Peter gave wry smile and nodded. "Yes, I was."

Kit did not hear the reply but was surprised. *Is Bronsky joining the army cadets?* he wondered.

At that moment, Mr Conkey appeared, now wearing his army uniform and the rank badges of a captain. He smiled at Andrew and called him over.

"Just wait till I get this show on the road," he said.

Andrew grinned. "That's what my dad said the army was like, sir," he replied. "Just like a circus, only more tents."

Captain Conkey snorted, then laughed. "Cheeky bugger! Do you want these maps or not?"

Andrew said he did. Captain Conkey again asked him to wait, gave orders to some older cadets and to a couple of teachers who were also transformed into army officers, then went into the cadet office for a while. Kit was puzzled over why Andrew might want army topographical maps, but he had no excuse to linger so he continued on towards the bike racks.

I will ask tomorrow, he thought.

He was tempted to stay and watch while the army cadets conducted their company admin parade, being interested in the differences in drill and procedures, but when he spotted the Dru brothers heading towards the bike racks he did not linger. As quickly as he could, he unlocked his bike, wheeled it out and set off along the street.

Completely forgetting about Jellman's threat until he was almost home, Kit hurried there and began his new program of physical training. To start with he decided to do just five of everything. Placing a mat on the concrete under the house, he positioned himself for a push-up. But to his dismay he had trouble even keeping his back straight and his knees began

---

[1] Read *The Boy and the Battleship* by C. R. Cummings

to sag towards the floor. Quickly he lowered himself using his arms and then tried to push back up. To his humiliation he was barely able to do it, and by the time he started a second push-up his muscles had begun to tremble.

God I'm weak! he thought.

Shame and self-pity swirled in his mind and he bit his lip and sat down. But there was a stubborn streak to his character, so he lay on his back and set himself to do five sit-ups. But he could only manage four before his stomach muscles began to quiver. Straining and gritting his teeth, he tried to lift himself up so that his elbows would touch his knees—but it was no go.

On the edge of tears from shame and frustration, Kit flopped back on the carpet and lay gasping. *Oh, what use am I?* he thought.

Next, he moved on to do some touch the toes but his body wasn't supple enough and he gave up at the top of his ankles. Even by putting his feet apart he was barely able to reach the floor and only by accepting some sharp little stabs of pain from protesting muscles.

This is hopeless! he thought. *How can I go to a Judo club when I can't even do a few sit-ups? I will be a laughingstock.*

From exercising he went to the bathroom for a shower. After he had finished, he stood in front of the mirror and studied his body while he towelled himself dry. His lack of size was obvious, but all the rest looked to be in proportion. He knew he wasn't handsome but decided he looked normal enough.

At least I look alright somewhere, he thought. Then he gave a wry smile. They weren't parts of his anatomy he could show the girls.

Because he did want to meet them. His body was now gripped by the urgent desires of puberty, and he frequently fantasised and wished for true romance while wondering what 'it' might really be like. Like all youths, he had those gnawing anxieties about whether he was normal and if, when the great moment arrived, he would be able to perform.

Then he castigated himself. *I shouldn't be thinking such thoughts about Diana. She is pure and above that sort of thing,* he told himself. *That must be true love.*

Deep down he was sure that, even if by some miracle such an opportunity came his way, he would not do anything, partly from simple morals and partly from pure fear.

None of which helped him when he experienced a particularly erotic dream and spent half the night tossing and turning. The result was that he woke up feeling drained and anxious. He still hadn't organised with his parents to go to the PCYC for the Judo lessons and did not know how to raise the subject. What he particularly did not want was his big brothers learning about it and then teasing him.

But time was running away fast and after breakfast, as soon as his brothers were out of the room, he broached the subject.

"Mum, I'd like to go to the PCYC one night," he said.

His mother paused from picking up the breakfast dishes. "Oh yes, why?" she asked.

Kit could only blush and stammer. But then he plucked up the courage to reply. "I wanted to do some self-defence lessons," he replied.

"Self-defence! Why? Are you being bullied again at school?"

"Yes," Kit admitted.

"Well, fighting won't solve it. That will just get you into more trouble," his mother said. "If you are being bullied you should tell the teachers."

"Yes, but I would still like to go. I want to do some athletics as well and build up my muscles."

His mother looked at him thoughtfully. "When is it?"

"Thursday nights," he replied.

His mother frowned. "I'm not sure I like the idea of you going on a weeknight," she replied. "Your homework is more important."

"Oh Mum!" Kit cried. "Please! I am doing well at school. A couple of hours won't hurt my studies."

His mother shook her head again. "Oh, I don't know. I will ask your father," she said, adding, "And I will speak to the school about the bullying

Silently he cursed. *Bugger! Now the bullies will really pick on me!* he reasoned.

Feeling more cast down than he wanted to admit he took himself to his room to do his homework—and to brood. Later, as he lay in bed his sore muscles cramped and he winced.

"Ouch! Well at least I can still build up my strength in case the bullies bother me again," he told himself.

And at school on Thursday he walked straight into the sort of situation he had been worrying about. Needing a pee before first lesson, Kit hurried to the toilet. It was a typical old-style schoolboy's toilet with an area near the door with hand basins and taps, and then a larger space with a long metal backed urinal and trough along one wall and five toilet cubicles along the rear wall. Quickly Kit stepped up onto the grating facing the urinal and unzipped his fly. Knowing that he was normal made this easy to do. He could stand and pee without being embarrassed or ashamed if other boys looked. Most did not and few ever made comments. This time the two Year 9 boys already there barely glanced at him.

Kit relaxed and began to pee and then heard loud voices behind him at the entrance. To his horror, Piper and his cronies came in behind him.

Wally Dru was the first to speak. "Well, well, here's little Chrissie the Sissie. How's it going, tiny boy?"

Kit flushed with shame and concentrated on what he was doing. From behind him he heard Piper call, "Has he got a tiny dick too, Wally?"

Dru stepped up beside Kit and looked down. When he answered he could not keep the surprise out of his voice: "He... Holy shit! No!"

At that, the two Year 9 boys both looked and then edged away. Kit flamed with embarrassment. This was compounded when the other two bullies both stepped up beside him, Piper on his right and Ricardo on his left. Piper bent to look. Kit was now feeling very stressed and anxious and tried to hurry what he was doing.

Piper shook his head. "It is a whopper. All his growth must have gone into it," he commented.

Ricardo chuckled and nudged Kit, leering down at him. "He probably plays with it so much it gets all the attention," he suggested.

"Hand feeds it," Piper agreed, smirking and laughing at his own crude innuendo.

Kit finished peeing. Feeling hotly self-conscious he hastily stuffed his penis back into his shorts.

At that, Piper pushed him. "Hey! We didn't say you could put it away," he snarled.

Kit could not help himself. Enraged by the humiliation and shame he retorted, "Why? Are you a queer?"

"Don't crap me, Shitface," Piper replied.

His round, childlike and chubby face went bright red and he hit at Kit and shoved him again. Kit tried to step back but found himself gripped from behind by Ricardo. A blow struck him in the side, Dru getting in a punch. Then Piper hit him in the stomach, and he doubled up.

"I put him in piss trough, eh?" Ricardo suggested.

"Yeah, good idea," Piper agreed, punching Kit again in the chest.

Oh bloody hell, no! Kit thought as he felt himself picked up.

The trough of the urinal was a-swim with stinking yellow urine and had cigarette butts and other filth in it. He began to struggle violently to try to avoid such a humiliating fate.

Suddenly, a voice called loudly from behind them. "Stop that! Let him go, Ricardo."

It was Andrew Collins. Kit turned his head to look, his feet still scrabbling to keep himself upright and away from the urinal. With Andrew were his friends, Blake and Luke.

Piper turned and glared. "Mind yer own business, Collins," he replied. But he held back his next punch. Ricardo still held Kit firmly, but he desisted from trying to push him over into the trough.

Andrew came to a halt a couple of paces from Piper. "It is my business. I stand by my friends," he replied coolly.

Luke Karaku, big and very black, stepped up close to Ricardo. "You let him go," he said quietly.

Ricardo did, but in the process he gave Kit a hard shove. Kit lost his balance and instinctively put out his hand to break his fall. Even so he would have crashed hard into the trough if Luke hadn't grabbed his arm and held him half upright. As it was, Kit's left hand smacked against the wet stainless steel and slid down into the trough. Disgust and dismay were added to his sense of outrage.

Luke hauled him upright and then squared up to Ricardo. Ricardo was bigger but Kit now saw the muscles rippling in Luke's arms and massive shoulders and he noted an anxious look flit across Ricardo's face. Ricardo held up his hands in a placating gesture and stepped aside, then scuttled towards the door. Piper and Wally Dru followed.

At the door, Wally turned. "You wait, Walker, we'll get you when your friends aren't around."

"And you'll regret it if you do," Andrew called.

The bullies vanished amid a crowd of a dozen other boys crowded in, attracted by the prospect of a fight. Luke steadied Kit.

"You alright, bro?" he queried.

Kit nodded. "Yes thanks. Just a couple of bumps."

"Do you want to tell the teachers?" Andrew asked.

That was exactly what Kit's mother had told him to do but Kit was reluctant. *If I do the bullies will get back at me when there are no teachers or witnesses around,* he thought. So he shook his head and despised himself at the same time.

"I'll be okay. Thanks for helping," he croaked.

Andrew smiled and shrugged. "It's okay. You are one of us. We aren't going to let a member of our unit get bullied without lifting a finger to help."

"That's right!" Blake added, clapping Kit on the back. "Us navy cadets stick together."

Kit was embarrassed but grateful. *Navy cadets,* he thought, deeply touched by the idea. But perversely he also felt resentment at having had to be rescued by the others. *If I wasn't so small I could stand up for myself,* he told himself bitterly.

To his annoyance, he found himself resenting Andrew even more. But he hid this and tried to be friendly and openly grateful.

They were only trying to help, he told himself.

Now reaction set in, and he began to tremble. But rather than let anyone see this he strode briskly over to a wash basin.

"Get out of my way, you Year Eight warts," he gruffly commanded a group of boys who were clustered there.

To his surprise, the boys addressed quickly moved aside although a few smirked and made hurtful comments about having fallen in the poo while he washed his hands.

Andrew and his friends shooed the other boys out. "Show's over," Luke said and the younger boys at once obeyed his directions to leave.

Soon after that the bell went and a still shaken Kit made his way to class. The lesson was Science, for which he was grateful as Diana did not do that subject.

It will allow me time to get over it, he thought, amazed at how much his body had reacted and how long the emotions and physical manifestations lasted.

The day then went on its usual routine. During the breaks Kit kept a very wary eye out for the bullies and even though it made him despise himself for being a coward, he stayed close to his friends. And as the day wore on so did his apprehension grow at the thought of what might happen when the bullies caught him alone.

He became so anxious he felt quite nauseous and found he was trembling. The boil of emotions was another reason for him to pour scorn on his own image and to deride himself.

Some Phantom you would make! he thought bitterly.

After school, as Kit rode his bike to the truck depot, his mind now moved to worrying about Jellman and his threats. But nothing happened and he began to feel silly.

I'm getting paranoid. Why would someone like Jellman risk going to jail over someone as insignificant as me? he told himself.

Even so he kept an eye open to check that no-one was in the transport yard who had no right to be there. In reality there were two hours of work washing trucks and he soon forgot about the man.

He was pleased to see that his father had three new CCTV cameras installed, but when he went into the office to check with Julie how they looked on the newly installed TV monitors she shook her head.

"They are good, but I don't know how we are going to pay for them, not with two Prime Movers out of commission."

The idea that the business was in such financial trouble was very worrying and he spent the next hour working hard to help get the second Prime Mover fixed. The spare part for the first still had not arrived, much to his father's annoyance.

It was nearly 6pm before Kit arrived home. There was just time for a quick shower and change before tea. And during tea he was again hurt. This time it was by his brother.

His mother started it when she said to him, "Chris, I heard you had some trouble with bullies at school. What happened?"

Kit groaned mentally as he saw his brothers watching. *Oh blast! How did mum find out?*

But seeing the look on his brothers' faces told him. Obviously school gossip had reached them and one had told her.

"And did you tell a teacher?" his mother asked.

Kit shook his head. "No Mum."

"Why not? I spoke to the Deputy on the phone and he said he would look into things," she answered.

"Because… because the teachers can't do anything, and besides, if I dob and the bullies get into trouble they will just take it out on me later," he said.

"Oh rot! You have to take action. Next time you tell," his mother snapped.

"Yes Mum," he replied. He felt so miserable he had trouble keeping the quaver out of his voice. "That's why I wanted to go to the PCYC," he added.

Bruce at once questioned why he wanted to go there. Before Kit could think of a face-saving answer his mother spoke.

"To learn some self-defence," she explained.

"Self-defence!" Bruce retorted in a voice laden with scorn and derision. "Waste of time. The little toad should concentrate on running."

Adrian laughed but did look a bit sympathetic. "He should be able to hide easily he is so small," he added.

"Stop teasing your brother and go and do your homework!" their mother snapped.

That's right! Kit thought.

But he was stung yet again by his brother's obvious lack of respect and support. And now the anxiety began to swamp him and he started to tremble, wishing he could change his mind but lacking the courage to back out.

His father heard all of this but said nothing, which upset Kit even more. But his mother was adamant.

"You are not going to learn fighting. I will not have my children learning violence. So just tell the teachers."

"Yes Mum."

Kit did not agree and vowed he would learn to defend himself. Giving his brothers a resentful look he left the room. In his own room he again vowed to get strong and to able to look after himself. But a glance in his mirror defeated him and his face twisted into a mask of self-pity.

Oh why couldn't I just grow up normal!

Chapter 8

PCYC

When he went to school on Friday, Kit felt physically wrung out and sore. Worse, he was scared. Fear of the bullies almost made him ask his mother if he could stay home. But scorn at his own cowardice drove him to act. Reluctantly he rode his bike to school and, even as he locked his bike into the bike racks, he looked anxiously around for any sign of the bullies. To his relief, there were none to be seen. Almost slinking from building to building, Kit made his way to his own area. He did this while trying to act nonchalant and relaxed but inside his heart was hammering and his mouth was dry.

He found it a relief to go into class. Relief then turned to a queer mixture of pleasure and pain as he studied Diana's beauty while remembering her hurtful rejection. But at least the schoolwork was easy. The day slid by with few problems. During the breaks Kit again kept an eye open for the bullies and he only went to the toilet when a group of his classmates also went. The whole situation humiliated him and made him resentful of the lot fate had cast him.

Friday night was Cadets, and the main topic of conversation was the incident with the smugglers the previous weekend. Kit listened but contributed very little while secretly wishing he had done more. Through his mind he replayed the scenes, searching for any time when he might have been able to play the hero. But there were none, or none that made sense to him.

Not without taking stupid risks and putting other people at risk, he told himself.

So he concentrated on the marching practice for Anzac Day and the seamanship lesson, in this case learning about navigation buoys and lights. The last forty minutes were taken up with cleaning and re-stowing the boat they had used the previous weekend and that brought back all the memories in a vivid rush. Once again Kit fantasised about being a hero, this time rescuing Diana from the crooks.

On Saturday, Kit and his brothers worked at the truck depot. He found that a bit of drag, wishing he was out sailing or doing something more exciting. But at least it was money.

I will be able to afford to take Diana on a proper date, he told himself with satisfaction, aware that he had amassed quite a sum over the last two years.

The most encouraging thing that day was learning that his mother had spoken to his father and reluctantly agreed to allow him to go to Judo lessons at the PCYC. It was arranged to start on the next Thursday evening.

The next morning was chores around the house and, while he was mowing the lawn, the notion of building up his muscles and becoming strong enough to defeat bullies returned. As soon as he was able, Kit took himself under the house and, after making sure his brothers weren't around, began trying again to do the chin the bars, push ups and press ups he had been unable to do the previous day. To his surprise, he experienced a few sharp twinges from these previously under employed muscles, but he gritted his teeth and persevered.

And he overdid it, so that next day he had some very sore muscles and suffered a few cramps.

I need to plan an exercise regime, he thought, remembering the jargon his PE teacher had used.

Even so, he made himself do a limited number of the exercises and then did a few other stretches and tests to use other muscles.

School resumed on Monday with all the anxieties of watching for Jellman while riding to school and of avoiding the bullies. These added a tenseness to the day that he wished was not there. There was also more cause for jealousy as he sat in line waiting for the school assembly to begin. He was on the end of the line and listened to the conversations going on around him. One of these was between Stephen and Lorna, who sat in the line in front. It was about what they had done on the weekend. Kit was astonished to learn that Graham and Stephen had ridden their bicycles all the way to Kuranda. That was thirty or forty kilometres and across a mountain range, and Kit was sure he would not be able to do that.

Maybe I would try that hard if it was to meet Diana, he mused.

But knowing that was unlikely to happen just added to his feelings of inadequacy and dejection.

The jealousy came from overhearing comments that suggested that Graham, Stephen Bell, Lorna, and a couple of other girls had gone 'skinny dipping' near Kuranda. Images of naked girls flashed across his mind and Kit found himself both very aroused and very jealous. The idea of swimming naked with girls like Lorna was intensely appealing. For the next few minutes he sat there with a mind full of erotic fantasies and envy, his thoughts intensified by Lorna's giggling. She was rumoured to be a 'goer', but Kit could not imagine how he might ever persuade her to take her clothes off for him.

She would just laugh at me or sneer, he thought unhappily.

Monday mornings often meant a whole school assembly in the school hall. Normally Kit just sat there bored, but that morning there was one item that got his attention. As usual, the Deputy Principal, Mr Fitzgerald, read notices which were information and reminders to various students and classes. Then Mr Fitzgerald moved away and the principal, Mr Crosswell, took his place at the microphone.

"This is a reminder about the school fete in eight weeks' time. As you know, the fete is a major event for this school, and I am asking for your help and co-operation to make it a success. Not only does the fete bring us in much needed funds for the Parents and Citizen's Committee, but it also showcases the school to the parents and community."

Mr Crosswell paused and then went on: "A major part of this is to be the school dance. Usually this is just a dance but this year we are making it into a fancy-dress ball open to the parents and selected local dignitaries. Everyone is asked to come in costume and to make a big effort to ensure the fete is a success. We are telling you now to give you time to prepare costumes."

A fancy-dress ball! Kit thought, his imagination fired by the concept. *Great idea!* But what could he come as? Even as he puzzled over this, the image formed in his head. *I will come as the Phantom.*

But then he bit his lip and experienced a spurt of anxiety. *People might laugh at me because of my physique,* he thought. But then another idea came to him. *I could wear an overcoat and hat and dark glasses and be The Ghost Who Walks.*

Considering this kept him thinking through the remainder of the assembly. As he sat there another idea came to him.

Maybe I could ask Diana to come with me?

But would she? He glanced anxiously at her and saw that she was deep in whispered conversation with Elise. Uncertainty and fear of another humiliating rejection swirled in Kit's mind, making him feel almost nauseous.

I can only try, he decided.

But he didn't ask her that day. There never seemed to be an opportunity. Most of the time she was with a group of her friends, and he did not think it good tactics to ask her in such a public way.

It might be embarrassing for her too, he told himself.

And then he despised himself for not acting. He wrestled with his thoughts, wondering if he was a coward. Was it really concern for her feelings, or was it just him being scared of being rejected again?

It was all very stressful.

Nor did he ask her on Tuesday. Instead he concentrated on his schoolwork, and after school he hurried home and began his new program of physical training. Realising he had been overdoing it, he decided to go back to doing just five of everything. After placing a mat on the concrete under the house he positioned himself and began to do push-ups. To his relief, he was able to do a couple of good ones before his back and his knees began to sag towards the floor. Gritting his teeth, he forced himself to straighten up and to complete the five.

Panting from the effort, he lowered himself using his arms and then tried to push back up a sixth time. To his humiliation and dismay, he was barely able to do it and by the time he was up his muscles had begun to tremble.

God I'm weak! he thought.

Shame and self-pity swirled in his mind, and he bit his lip and sat down. But there was a stubborn streak to his character, so he lay on his back and set himself to do five sit-ups. But he could only manage four before his stomach muscles began to quiver. Straining and gritting his teeth he tried to lift himself up so that his elbows would touch his knees, but it was painful. With difficulty he managed it then lay back and felt like bursting into tears.

Wednesday at school was a very ordinary day. Much of Kit's attention was taken up with completing assignments and he spent the breaks in the library with no incidents. But Thursday was stressful, and the stress built as the day went on. Knowing that he was to go to the PCYC that evening filled him with dread. The fear was fuelled by worrying about being sneered at or teased because of his small size and the anxiety became so great that he felt quite ill by the afternoon.

This is going to be painful and humiliating, he brooded.

That evening his mother drove him to the PCYC and dropped him near the front door. And now the anxiety began to swamp him and he started to tremble, wishing he could change his mind but lacking the courage to back out.

Twenty minutes later he was still standing outside the large hall and trying hard to stop himself physically trembling.

Go in, you coward! he told himself.

For several more minutes he hesitated, hotly aware of other people giving him curious looks as they moved past him. Then he took a deep breath and forced himself to move.

If I don't do this I will despise myself for ever, he reasoned.

So, almost shaking with anxiety, he walked stiffly to the doorway and in through it. Once inside he was almost overwhelmed by the barrage of new impressions—the sheer size of the hall, the noises, the focused groups of people engaged in a dozen different activities, the strangeness of the place.

In an attempt to regain control of his rapid breathing and blurred vision, Kit stood and deliberately focused his eyes to study the layout.

Which group do I join? Where do I go? he wondered, noting nearby people in loose white costumes moving quickly in pairs in obvious fighting attitudes.

Into his vision swam a young woman, also dressed in white—the same loose top and baggy long pants the others wore, belted at the waist by a black sash. She had an attractive face framed by short dark hair. Dark brown eyes sparkled merrily in her smiling face.

She is pretty, he thought, noting with disappointment that she appeared to be quite a few years older. *In her early twenties,* he estimated.

"Can I help you?" she asked.

Kit nodded and gaped. "Yes... Er, yes. I'm Kit, I mean Chris, and I'm here to start Judo training," he explained, embarrassed that his voice sounded nervous and unsure.

"Oh hi! I'm Sally and I am a Judo instructor. I will just check the enrolments. If you would come with me," she answered.

Sally smiled again and led Kit over to a small office at the side of the hall. Here she picked up a clipboard and ran her fingers down a list of names and then nodded.

"Yes, Chris Walker, is it? Good. And your fee has been paid. Okay, come with me and I will introduce you to the others. Do they call you Chris or Kit?"

"Chris usually, but I prefer Kit," he replied.

Feeling very nervous, Kit walked with her towards the group of white clad people. Just looking at them increased his anxiety. They looked so competent and fit. He mentally cringed and braced himself to endure scorn and teasing.

It wasn't as bad as that. Sally led him over to where a group of white-clad young people were doing breakfalls and tumbles. When she stopped the group for a moment to introduce him some just glanced and then ignored him and others smiled a friendly greeting. Only a few gave what Kit took to be critical looks as they assessed his size and physique.

Sally said, "Gang, this is Kit. He's joining the group."

One of the boys, about the same age as Kit but at least 20 centimetres taller, curled his lip and said, "Are we recruiting midgets now?"

Some of the others laughed and Kit blushed and stared hard at the youth. The youth had that superior, arrogant look that Kit so hated.

Sally stepped forward. "There's no call for comments like that, Carl," she snapped. Then she turned to another boy. "Kit, this is Cory, and this girl here is Jessica."

"Hello," Kit replied, noting that Cory looked years younger but was bigger than him and that the girl looked to be only Year 6 or 7.

Another boy was introduced as Wallis, and he smiled and stepped forward then offered his hand. Blushing with embarrassment, Kit took it and shook. Then another boy joined the group and was named as Theo. He was the same size and age as Carl and merely nodded. The last member of the group was another young girl: Emma. She had freckles and a very friendly smile but also stood as tall as him.

Sally clapped her hands. "Okay people, back to work!" The others resumed their practice and Sally turned to Kit. "Now Kit, what do you know and where do we start?"

Blushing Kit shook his head. "I don't know anything. You'll have to start at the very beginning."

Sally nodded and looked thoughtful. "Okay, that's fine. I will start you off with safety and then on some exercises and then move onto falls so that you don't get hurt. First, we will get you dressed."

Kit was led back to the side area and from out of a locker Sally produced some of the baggy white costumes and pointed to where the male change rooms were. He was allocated a locker and signed for the key and then Sally hurried back to her class. Feeling even more anxious and self-conscious, Kit made his way into the change room. But what he feared did not happen. There was no-one else there. Anxious not to be the object of pity or derision, he quickly stripped off and changed into the white costume. The sash belt baffled him for a moment as he was unsure what knot to use. In the end he settled for a large bow. After placing his clothes in the locker and locking it, he turned to face the door. Then, after taking a deep breath to calm his fluttering stomach, he made his way back out into the hall.

To his own surprise, he felt instantly better. At least he no longer felt so conspicuous, and he felt he could pretend that he was an experienced veteran rather than the newest rookie!

Sally saw him coming and moved to meet him. She took him to one side where they had a mat they could use, and she briefed him on the safety procedures and then set him to do some simple flexing and stretching exercises. After watching him for a minute or so, she told him to continue and then turned to watch the other members of her class. Kit kept on with the exercises, hotly aware that he was already starting to hurt and thinking that he must look ridiculous.

After about ten minutes, Sally demonstrated a throw to the others and set them to practise and then came over to Kit and watched. He forced a grin but felt very inadequate. She smiled but shook her head as she watched.

"You aren't very fit, are you?" she commented.

A spurt of hurt, followed instantly by resentment and anger surged through Kit. "No, but I'm working on it!" he retorted.

Sally looked a bit taken aback by his abrupt reply, but she smiled. "We will work on it together. That's what I'm here for. Now, you need to be able to fall down without hurting yourself or breaking bones," she explained. "I will show you some simple techniques to break your fall which will prevent or minimise injury. Watch."

She then demonstrated a simple 'break fall'. "Okay, you have a go," she instructed, gesturing to the safety mat.

Kit felt very apprehensive but after taking a deep breath he made himself do it. To his surprise, he found it didn't hurt at all. The look of astonishment on his face made Sally grin.

"See," she said. "It works. Now do fifty of them."

His confidence somewhat restored, Kit did as he was told. Five more falls went without a hitch, and he began to secretly wish the others were watching. But then he got overconfident and landed slightly wrong. That gave him a bruising thump on his left shoulder, and he had to bite back a cry of pain and then pretend he was not hurting. Forcing a grin and hoping nobody actually had been looking, he got to his feet and made himself fall again.

This time he got it right and he felt relieved. He stood up and did three more. By then he was starting to feel his muscles and had broken into a sweat.

This is harder than I thought, he told himself.

By the end of the two-hour session Kit was feeling quite battered and sore. But he was also feeling satisfied. He had mastered the simple breakfall and could now move on to more difficult training.

Sally was very pleased with his efforts. "You have tried very hard and are doing well. Will I see you next week?"

"You bet!" Kit replied.

"Good."

For a moment their eyes locked and Kit felt quite drawn to her. *Pity she is too old,* he thought.

Feeling sore but happy he made his way out to meet his mother. During the drive home he described the training and his mother was pleased. But Kit was still anxious about being teased by his brothers.

Chapter 9

ANXIETY

A nd he was.
As soon as he went inside, still dressed in the white costume, Bruce curled his lip and said, "Well, well! The Karate Kid!"

Kit clenched his teeth and wished he had showered and changed at the PCYC. He was about to retort when his mother cut in.

"That's enough teasing thank you Bruce. It's a pity you don't try to do some self-improvement. Have you finished your homework?"

Bruce scowled. "Nearly," he replied.

"Then go and do it now!" their mother snapped. "Now Chris, put that costume in the wash and come and tell me about it. Do you want supper?"

"Yes Mum," Kit answered.

He felt a spurt of malicious glee at his brother's chastisement but carefully hid this to ease future confrontations.

As Kit placed his Judo costume in the washing basket, his mother said, "I see in the school newsletter that there is to be a fancy-dress ball at the fete. Are you planning to go to that?"

"Yes Mum," Kit replied. Silently he berated himself for not raising the topic sooner.

"What as?" she asked.

Kit had been dreading this moment, which was the main reason he had put it off, but before he could open his mouth Bruce called from the lounge room, "He could go as one of the Seven Dwarfs!"

His laughter burned and Kit gritted his teeth. His mother was not amused. "That will do, Bruce! You stop saying horrible things to your brother. He can't help it if he hasn't grown quite as fast as you. Just you be thankful you are normal," she snapped.

Which means I'm not! Kit thought bitterly. But he kept his feelings hidden and summoned up his courage to answer.

"I was thinking of going as the Phantom," he said.

That brought more laughter from Bruce. "The Phantom!" he hooted, derision clear in his voice. "You'd be better off going as one of the Bandar Pygmy People! Hah! Ha! Ha!"

"Bruce!" snapped their mother.

Bruce lapsed into almost silent sniggers which further hurt Kit's feelings. More determined than ever, Kit replied, "I was thinking more of being The Ghost Who Walks with an overcoat, hat, and dark glasses over the Phantom costume," he explained.

"That will be very hot, won't it?" his mother queried.

Before Kit could answer that it would be May by then and therefore cooler, Bruce again interjected. "Then he needs a pet wolf, and they might not let him in with that! Ha! Ha!"

"Bruce, that's enough! Go to your room and finish your homework," their mother cried angrily.

"I've done it," Bruce replied sulkily.

"I don't care! Go to your room!"

Bruce did, although Kit half expected him to defy their mother. She then turned back to Kit. "So we need to see about a costume."

"I think you can hire Phantom costumes," Kit answered. He had seen one in a Party and Costume shop a few months before.

"I will look into it. Now you have your supper and go and do your homework as well," his mother said.

After supper, Kit went to his room and did his homework. Then he took himself to bed. But he was feeling so emotionally confused that he had difficulty falling asleep. Every little hurtful jibe and taunt from his brothers and various bullies rose to the front of his mind and made him mentally squirm with shame and distress. By midnight was feeling very dejected. His sense of self-worth sank even lower.

Friday morning found Kit feeling very sore and tender in places. The muscles he had overused all hurt and when he moved suddenly small pains lanced through him. Wincing and muttering to himself, he flexed his arms and hands and then massaged his arms before swinging them around to loosen the muscles more.

At least I've got some muscles to get sore, he consoled himself.

Memories of the previous night came back to give him very mixed feelings. He was glad he had gone and pleased he had mastered something new and useful, but he still felt inferior to the others in the club.

But there was nothing he could do about that, so he showered, had his breakfast, and got ready for school. As he rode his bicycle to school, he was assailed by anxieties about being bullied. Several times he considered turning around and going home, but despite his fear he clenched his jaw and continued on.

And his fears were all for nothing. The bullies did not bother him all day and he only saw the Dru brothers once, and then from a distance.

It was in a Modern History class with Mr Conkey that he was given real food for thought. The class was starting a study of the French Revolution and were being introduced to the ideas of the Enlightenment. Mr Conkey gave them a number of ideas that became important at that time, like the concept of all men being born free and equal.

Then he faced the class and smiled. "It was the same philosopher I think, Voltaire, or maybe it was Jean Jacques Rousseau, who said: 'Many terrible things have worried me in my life—and a few of them even happened.' What he was saying is that often things are never as bad as we imagine them to be; that fear of what might happen is one of the human race's big mental issues."

It was as though a light had come on in Kit's brain. *That's me,* he thought. There and then he resolved to face up to his fears and to keep trying.

That afternoon at home he did. Regardless of the jibes of his brother, he continued with his muscle strengthening exercises. To his immense satisfaction he found he could do two complete press-ups and was able to lift his whole body off the ground with his arms. But he could not lift himself high enough to get his chin to the bar or to lift his feet up to touch it.

"Never mind. I'm getting better," he told himself. "I will get there."

Friday night meant cadets, and most of the evening was taken up with preparations for Anzac Day and the school ceremonies that preceded it. This meant lots of drill—marching practice and the like and also a lesson on Saluting and Compliments to make sure they knew when to salute and who. On hearing that some cadets would be needed to be Flag Orderlies to raise the Australian Flag at school ceremonies, Kit became very interested. Ever hopeful, he paid close attention to the instructor. When he at last got a turn at the flag halyards he tried his very hardest to do it right.

I hope I get picked! he thought.

Being a Flag Orderly was his best chance of doing something special, as he knew he had no hope of being selected to be one of the cadets who were to be cenotaph guards. Kit learned that the unit had been asked to provide cenotaph guards at several ceremonies and he also learned that these cadets would be doing this with rifles. The new term 'catafalque party' entered his lexicon, and as he watched the older cadets who had been selected to be members of the guard practising he was smitten by jealousy and then by a fierce desire to one day perform that duty.

And there was more jealousy. During the break between lessons, Kit overheard Andrew being asked what he was doing during the next school holidays. Andrew shrugged and replied, "Going to a place called Endeavour Island camping for a week."

"Where's that?" Anthony Simmonds asked.

"Off Cardwell," Andrew replied.

As Kit tried to mentally place the location and to wonder what camping on an island might be like, Percy Parsons said, "Who are you going with?"

To Kit's surprise, he saw Andrew blush. Andrew shrugged and then said, "Oh, my sister and a family from Townsville."

At that, Blake chuckled. "Is that the big blonde who likes to go naked?" he asked.

Andrew blushed even more and again shrugged. "That's the family, but there will also be some other navy cadets from Townsville."

"Oh yeah? Who?" Percy queried.

Andrew named a couple of names, but Kit barely noted them. His mind was seized by images of a naked blonde with big breasts, and he became both aroused and very envious. Andrew meanwhile became all flustered and defensive and kept insisting that there was nothing improper in it as her parents would be there and also his sister and another female navy cadet named Anne.

Blake summed up Kit's thoughts when he concluded, "Still, it's a situation you might get a few opportunities out of."

That night in bed Kit lay and fantasised about that situation. Picturing several scenarios involving moonlight, pretty girls and beaches he became very aroused and had trouble getting to sleep. What added to his envy was the knowledge that for him the two weeks of the Easter holidays just meant days of work at the truck depot.

Saturday was spent working at the truck depot and Kit came home tired and grimy and feeling a bit depressed and sore. Then, with a discipline he was proud of, he even made himself do his exercise program when he was home alone. And he held each move to only five—although he still could not really do even one chest heave or chin the bar properly.

He repeated this on Sunday and felt better, certain it was becoming easier.

I did those sit-ups with no problem at all, he told himself.

Monday brought more jealousy. While sitting to one side at school pretending he was happy, Kit overheard Stephen boasting about a party he and Graham Kirk had been to at a place called Myola on Saturday. They had taken the train to Kuranda again and spent the weekend there.

"Where is Graham?" Roger Dunning asked, looking around.

"Off seeing his little girlfriend, I suppose," Stephen said, also looking around.

Stephen then boasted that he had gone swimming in the nuddy with three girls at Barron Falls on the Sunday.

"What three?" Blake demanded to know.

Stephen pointed across the quadrangle. "Lorna and that skinny ginger-hair Heather and Deslie in Year 8."

Blake raised his eyebrows. "How did Kirk like that? Isn't he taking that Deslie out?"

"He wasn't happy," Stephen replied with a grin. "But he missed out because he went to the police station to report that Tarzan guy and arrived too late."

Then Kit learned that Graham claimed to have seen 'Tarzan' again. That gave him a bit of a jolt as he had heard on the radio that Tarzan had raped a Swedish tourist at Crystal Cascades on Saturday, and now Graham claimed to have seen the man at a place called Glacier Rock when he and Stephen were on the train going up to Kuranda.

It was when he heard Graham explaining that he and Stephen, their friends Peter and Roger, were going to hike to Kuranda in the first week of the holidays that Kit was again stung by dejection and envy.

Everyone else seems to be going somewhere for their holidays and to be planning to be with girls—and I will just be at home or greasing bloody trucks!

The day then proceeded normally, the bullies leaving Kit alone most of the time. All he encountered were a couple of sneering glances from Ricardo as he passed him and a shouldering aside from Wally Dru. The schoolwork was easy and even the first of the exams, Physics, was no real challenge. After school, Kit made his way home and before his brothers arrived did his push-ups, sit-ups and chin the bars. To his satisfaction, he was able to manage all five each except the chin the bar. Here he struggled to do even one correctly but consoled himself by noting that he could lift higher and hold on longer, even if there was a bit of a struggle to do that last lift.

This set the pattern for the week: exams each day, assignments to hand in, minor bullying—and jealousy over what others were doing during the holidays. Tuesday and Wednesday slid past and Thursday arrived. As this was the last day of term, the Friday being Good Friday, there were no real lessons as at least half the students were away. This thankfully included the bullies. Diana was not in class and her brother was nowhere to be seen. Kit began to relax a little, at least until Thursday lunch time when anxiety about the bullies began to build.

Fearing that he might encounter the bullies again the next term, Kit made sure of doing his exercises that afternoon. He managed seven push-ups and sit-ups and again almost got his chin to the bar. Knowing he could be humiliated again brought up the temptation to do more but he sternly disciplined himself.

You will only pull a muscle and then you will look even sillier, he warned himself.

Kit found walking into the PCYC hall that evening even more nerve wracking than the first time. Now he was all in a fluster about having to join the others and about what Sally might think. He wasn't sure if she would be there or even if she would be the class instructor as he knew there were others. But he hoped she would be.

And she was. As he walked in, he saw her speaking to a group over near the counter. He walked over and gave her a nervous smile. To his relief, she smiled back.

"Hi Kit! I'm glad you came again," she said.

So was Kit after a welcome like that! Feeling greatly boosted he made his way to the changeroom and changed. After locking his clothes into the locker allocated to him, he made his way out to where Sally and some others now stood at the mats.

Sally got them all to practice some break falls after limbering up and for once Kit wasn't too humiliated when he did a couple of push-ups as part of the preparation.

Sally then called them all together and said, "We will practice simple throws. Watch while I demonstrate." She then called over Carl and used him to show how it was done.

It looked easy enough, but Kit wondered who he was to team up with. The two young girls were an obvious pair and so were Cory and Wallis and the two older boys.

Sally solved this by saying: "Carl, you team up with Chris for a moment and Theo can practice with me."

Carl looked at Kit and sneered, then stepped closer. A moment later, Kit found himself flying through the air upside down. He crashed to the mat hard. Only a quick, almost instinctive break fall saved him from a really bruising landing. As it was, it really hurt and Kit was momentarily stunned.

Carl looked down and prodded him with his toe. "That's how it's done, midget."

Kit was both hurt and angry. It had been so quick and unexpected. Masking his hurt, he stood up and moved to face Carl.

"How do I do it?" he asked.

"Like this," Carl replied.

He suddenly reached out, stepped forward and placed his right leg behind Kit's right ankle and then effortlessly tossed him over his hip. Again Kit crashed to the mat.

You bastard! Kit thought. *That hurt.* Wincing at the pain in his right shoulder he got up. This time he let his anger show.

"I meant explain it to me, not bully me," he snapped.

"No-one's bullying you, you little runt" Carl retorted.

Sally stepped between them. "That's enough. Theo, you partner with Carl, and I will show Kit what to do."

She led Kit to one side. He was hotly aware of the contemptuous looks on both Carl's and Theo's faces, but he determined to ignore them.

I need to learn this. Then I can set them on their arses, he told himself.

Then he got another surprise that he wasn't ready for—the soft touch of a girl's hands. Sally took his and then instructed him on where to put his hands and feet. He found it very nice to be so close to a girl, and when he had to put his hips against hers he got a shock. As he pulled Sally backwards over his hip, his right arm went across her front and he distinctly felt her breasts through the loose cloth.

Anxious that he might get into trouble for inappropriately touching her, he muttered, "Sorry. I didn't mean to touch you like that."

Sally stood up and shook her head. "It's okay. But that's why we usually don't have boys and girls together."

Kit nodded. "You can team me up with another boy," he suggested.

Sally nodded. "I will. You take turns with Cory and Wallis," she replied.

Kit would have preferred to keep doing it with Sally, but could only agree. So he did a practice throw of Wallis and then Wallis did the same to him. Three more times they did it before Sally was satisfied. Then they both swapped and Kit had three throws with Cory. As he did the last throw, Kit saw Carl sneering at him. That hurt but Kit just hid his feelings and concentrated on practicing until he was sure he had the throw right.

After that there was some competition throws and Carl won every time. Pairs faced up to each other and then tried to get in first. Kit again faced up to Carl but, to his chagrin, the contest only lasted seconds before he was thrown hard to the floor. He resented the apparent ease with which Carl had done it, but at least had the satisfaction of throwing Cory and even of making it hard for Theo. Then Carl stepped forward and again managed to catch him off guard and throw him hard to the floor. It hurt and both shame and a desire for revenge welled up.

You bastard! Kit thought, resentment burning through him.

He itched to get the chance to throw Carl. Sally made no comment, but Kit saw her eyes narrow and her lips purse and she then stepped forward, feinted and then grabbed Carl in a different hold and threw him hard to the floor.

Serves the bastard right! Kit thought.

But it was his physical appearance that became an issue when they were sent to shower and change at the end of the session. Kit had brought a towel with that in mind but was now reluctant to do that. For a few seconds he contemplated just changing back into his clothes or even going home in his Judo costume, but he did not want to look different so he reluctantly walked with the other boys to the male changeroom.

And as he feared he was picked on by Carl and Theo. They waited until he had gone into a shower cubicle and was standing under the shower before they came to annoy him. The first warning for Kit was when the shower curtain was pulled aside.

It was Theo. He had an evil grin on his face and wore only a towel around his waist. "G'day midget! Let's see what sort of a boy you are," he said, his eyes flicking down Kit's body.

Kit felt very self-conscious being seen naked. "Go away!" he growled, bracing for more trouble and turning his back as he heard Carl's footsteps approach.

Carl pulled the shower curtain further aside and leaned in to look, a sneer on his face. Kit met his look with a defiant stare.

I won't put up with being bullied, he told himself. He decided the pain of being bashed was a lesser price to pay.

Carl reached in and grabbed at him. "Give us a look little boy," he ordered.

Kit defied him and remained with his back to them. "Go away!" he repeated.

Carl's response was to reach across and flick on the taps so that Kit was suddenly deluged with cold water.

"Hey! Stop that, you big bully!" he cried.

Carl laughed and sneered, then pushed at him. "Oh yeah! And who's gunna make me?" he retorted.

Gritting his teeth and trying to block out the embarrassment and shame, Kit prepared to fight him. He 'squared up' with fists raised. He was hotly conscious of his nudity and aware that several other boys were watching.

Luckily at that moment, one of the instructors came in. "Stop that you pair!" he called.

At that, Carl curled his lip at Kit and turned away. Kit moved quickly back into the shower and pulled the curtain across. For many seconds he stood there, breathing hard and flexing his fingers in angry frustration. Then he became aware of the cold shower and turned it off. Still embarrassed, he towelled himself and moved out to dry himself and to change.

To his surprise, he found both Wallis and Cory there. Wallis moved to stand next to him. "You okay, Kit? Did he hit you?" he asked.

Kit shook his head. "No. He just turned the cold water on."

"He and Theo are always doing things like that. And they come to look at us when we've got no clothes on."

Cory nodded vigorously. "Yeah, they do that all the time. It makes you wonder if they are gay or something," he said.

Kit hadn't thought of that, and it gave him and uneasy feeling. Then he realised that he was standing with just the towel on. Quickly he dressed, feeling sick and ashamed.

There was another testing moment as he went to leave. Sally stopped Kit. "Are you alright? Did something happen in the shower?" she asked.

Kit blushed again. "Carl and Theo turned on the cold water and wouldn't leave me alone," he replied. He felt anxious doing that, fearing the bullies would then hurt him more.

"I will speak to them," Sally promised. "Please don't be put off. You are doing well. I hope you are coming next term."

"Yes," Kit replied emphatically. He was now determined to become a master of Martial Arts.

"Good for you," Sally said, "And just watch that you aren't alone with Carl and Theo. There have been a few rumours about them."

"I will," Kit agreed.

Maybe they are queers? he thought.

The incident left Kit quite shaken and embarrassed. But he was now very determined not to give up.

No matter what, they are not going to win, he vowed.

Chapter 10

HOLIDAYS

That night Kit lay in bed with tears of self-pity streaming down his cheeks.

I'm useless. I'm a freak, a midget. I'll never be good at anything and I won't ever get a girlfriend.

And thinking about girls did not help. Memories of Stephen's stories about naked girls and of feeling Sally's breasts through the cloth got him fantasising and aroused. It was all very frustrating and stressful!

The following morning Kit slept in. Then he lay in bed for a while. Even though it was Good Friday and he had been baptised a Christian, he had very little interest in religion. His mother occasionally went to church, his father never and both of his older brothers professed to be sceptics. Kit was inclined to think the same way, finding the brutal, egotistical God of the Old Testament hard to believe in, let alone worship.

Except maybe out of fear, he mused. Definitely not a being to love!

Kit rarely thought about death and the hereafter. He had never witnessed death except on the TV News, and so far had never had any experience that came close to it. So instead he focused on the here and now. That led his thoughts to the fact that many boys he knew were off on holidays—holidays in which girls seemed to figure large. Again jealousy crawled in his mind and then erotic thoughts as he began to fantasise, until he thought of Diana. Then guilt made him try to push such disloyal thoughts away and he made himself get up and have a cold shower.

As his brothers and father were apparently still in bed, Kit dressed and went downstairs and made himself do his exercise regime, one ear cocked for any sound of movement upstairs. He did not want to be caught in the act and ridiculed again! It had been raining heavily when he got up and the rain continued. There were minor flood warnings on the radio so no chance of going anywhere.

After that the day crawled, with computer games and reading in attempt to stave off loneliness and boredom. Saturday morning was the same and Kit began to feel real pangs of self-pity and loneliness.

Despite the continuing rain, his father and two brothers took themselves off fishing during the afternoon, but Kit had discovered that he disliked sitting in smelly mangrove swamps in an equally smelly boat in the rain or hot sun while being annoyed by sandflies and mosquitoes while trying to lure some unfortunate fish to its doom. He did not enjoy catching and killing them.

Easter Sunday was a nice family day with all the usual chocolate Easter eggs, but they did not go on the traditional picnic as the rain continued. Monday was spent at the truck depot, even though it was a public holiday. There was so much work to be done but their father explained that the business could not afford to pay the regular workers overtime. It was a long day, and Kit was glad to help pull down the roller doors to the workshops and to lock up. As they did, he noted that the Prime Mover with the defective steering arm was now the only one parked out in the yard. They were still waiting for that spare part!

When they got home, Kit did his exercises while he waited his turn for the shower and then revelled in the hot water and feeling of cleanliness. It was as he came out to the lounge room after dressing that his interest and jealousy was sparked by hearing his father calling to his mother that they had caught 'That bastard Tarzan'. Curious to learn more, Kit went to watch the TV news, something he rarely did. He was astounded to learn that the notorious rapist had fallen to his death after being shot by a policeman on a cliff top in the Barron Gorge. There was a garbled mention of teenagers being saved and of a fight, but the details were not given.

These were forthcoming as headlines in the morning paper the next day. When Kit came out for breakfast his father was busy reading *The Cairns Post* and the headlines at once caught his interest, and then sparked his envy:

HERO TEENAGER SAVES GIRL FROM NAKED MADMAN

But it was what was under it that was the real cause of the jealousy. He read that Graham Kirk, a 13-year-old student at Cairns High, had been the hero of the hour. First, he saved a group of Girl Guides from rising floodwaters at Kamerunga at great risk to himself. Then he helped rescue a mentally disturbed man from the floods before climbing up to the Kuranda Railway and stopping a train from driving onto a bridge damaged by a landslide. He then helped save a teenage girl who was being attacked by that notorious madman nicknamed 'Tarzan'.

Kit read with jealous amazement how Graham had grappled with Tarzan at a place called The Devils Cauldron Lookout to save a girl (unnamed) and how, during the ensuing struggle Graham was twice thrown over the cliff by the man. The first time Graham had climbed back up and again grappled the madman, who had been busy bashing Graham's friend Peter Bronsky. Graham had then been pushed over the cliff again but had managed to cling to a tree root, being saved by the arrival of the police who shot Tarzan just as he was about to smash Graham's head in with a rock.

Bloody Kirk! Always being the hero. He will be insufferable now, Kit thought. But then he tried to imagine hanging over a sheer drop by a tree root and shuddered. *Would I be strong enough to hang on until help came?* he wondered. It was a very sobering thought and made him even more determined to stick to his exercise program. *Particularly those chin the bars,* he told himself.

The incident became the main topic of conversation, especially when his parents learned that Graham and Peter were at their school and Peter was in Kit's class.

"I'll bet the girl was that Deslie that Graham was going to see," he said, and explained what he knew and almost itched with curiosity to find out the real story.[2]

Tuesday also meant work and because of the wet weather Kit and his brothers went with their father in his car. Kit spent all day under one of the big Mack trucks helping Frank the Foreman check the steering. By late afternoon he was well educated on steering arms, connecting rods and 'toe-in'. He also had another check on the damaged one that was still waiting for a part. Knowing that while it sat there it still had to be paid for and that was hurting his parents made him resent Jellman and people like him.

That night Kit had trouble sleeping again as he had seemingly continual dreams of being with girls—frustrating dreams where they were going to let him do things but something always got in the way, so he never did.

---

[2] Read *Train to Kuranda* by C. R. Cummings

He was woken by hearing the home phone ringing. Kit heard his father groan and get up then pad along the corridor to answer it. He then heard comments like: "You are sure?" and "Anything taken?"

A few minutes later the phone call ended, and Kit heard his father almost stamp back to the master bedroom. There was loud muttering from his parents and then Kit heard his mother cry, "Stolen! The new Prime Mover?"

"Yes, XRT," his father replied. "Stolen."

That got Kit fully awake. He tossed his bedclothes aside and was sitting up when his father appeared at the doorway.

"Get dressed. The workshop has been broken in to and the new Prime Mover has been stolen."

Kit did as he was told, feeling distinctly distressed as he sensed this was serious for the business. His brothers were roused and they all adjourned to the kitchen, joined by their mother who had hastily dressed. A check of the clock showed it was only 5am and not yet daylight.

"Have a quick drink and something to eat and we will get down to the workshop," their father said. "God, this is going to set us back!"

It was an unhappy and upset family that got out of the car at the business office half an hour later. The workshop manager, Mr Simpson, was already there with a policeman and Frank Pearson, the foreman, arrived as they were about to go and look.

"Has the office been broken in to?" Kit's father asked.

Mr Simpson nodded his head. "No. And the key cabinet hasn't been forced open. But they broke into the workshop. Whoever did it just cut off the padlocks with bolt cutters. Same on the back gate."

"Anything on the security cameras?" their father asked.

The manager shook his head. "Nothing. The two at the back were blocked with spray paint by someone who knew exactly how to approach them without being on camera."

The policeman frowned. "An inside job?" he suggested.

Instantly a name sprang into Kit's mind. *Jellman!* he thought. He was about to blurt it out but then stopped himself. *It might not have been, and I don't have the right to cast suspicion on someone without proof.*

He knew the police would look for evidence like fingerprints, so he decided to wait.

His father shook his head. "What about the alarms?"

"They worked. That's how we knew," the manager replied. "But whoever it was, was quick. They were gone within five minutes."

"And they took XRT?" Kit's father queried.

The manager shrugged. "Must have. It's not in the workshop or in the yard."

Kit saw a look of anguish cross his father's face and felt a surge of sympathy.

This is really serious, he decided.

"So how did they do that without a key?"

There was much shaking of heads and discussion of the ways a modern vehicle might be started without the keys. But there were no answers, and there wasn't much more they could do. The police wanted to check the premises properly and did not want people there while they did so. After a few moments discussion, it was decided that the manager would stay and that the family would come back at 8am. In almost complete silence the family drove home.

A sombre breakfast followed. From what he overheard, Kit gathered that the business, while appearing to be going well, was actually teetering on the edge of failure.

"We owe more than we are now earning," his father explained. "And we will still have to pay for that stolen Prime Mover."

Kit was appalled. "But you haven't got it!" he cried.

"Sorry son, but that is how the world works. The bank loaned me money in good faith, and I owe them. It all looks pretty bleak."

Kit's mother looked to be almost on the edge of tears and that distressed Kit even more. She said, "The insurance will cover some of it," she said.

Kit's father nodded but grunted. "If they assess our security as having been reasonable," he replied.

It was all very sobering. The family returned to the business after breakfast, and when the police had finished they set to work to tidy up. Not that there was much.

Mr Walker made a wry face and said, "Whoever they were they knew exactly what they wanted."

"Yes, it could have been worse. They could have trashed the place," Bruce added.

That was also sobering food for thought and added to the gloomy view Kit already held of much of the human race. His mood was not improved by being set to work for the remainder of the day to wash and clean another truck and its refrigerated trailer. They had to work twice as hard to get it ready to go back on the road a day ahead of schedule.

During the remainder of the holidays, Kit and his brothers worked hard in the truck workshop. Kit did not really mind as he was aware that the business was in some sort of financial difficulty, and while there he again heard mention of the trailer that had been stolen a few months earlier. He spent many hours helping overhaul another truck, helping to take out axles and dismantle differentials and brake drums until it seemed he knew every tiny part of the huge machines.

And each afternoon at home he persisted with his exercises, lifting his totals to six and then to seven and eight. By the time school resumed he could do five chin the bars and could easily lift himself off the floor the first time. It was some satisfaction. What wasn't so satisfying was the frustrating state of his love life. He daydreamed about Diana and even fantasised that it was him saving Diana from the madman on top of a cliff.

As soon as we get back to school, I will ask her again for a date, he told himself.

But he didn't. On the first Monday back it wasn't his love life but his emotions that were stirred. Again this was by envy. And it wasn't over Graham Kirk's exploits but instead those of Carmen and Andrew Collins. As he joined a group of friends ready for morning assembly, Chris was astonished to learn that Andrew and his sister Carmen had been involved in real drama at sea and on the island they had been camping on.

To Kit's amazement, he learned that Andrew and Carmen had been involved a real drama with smugglers dressed as pirates. There had been gun fights, knife fights, and a yacht burned to the water line. The arrival of a rescue helicopter and the police had saved them all from a violent or watery end. It all sounded so thrilling and adventurous that Kit was smitten by jealousy.[3]

Real pirates! Oh, I wish I'd been there! he thought.

His jealousy was then sparked some by hints that somehow naked girls had figured in the holiday. Blake asked, "What were you doing on the beach in the middle of the night, Andrew?"

---

[3] Read *Endeavour Island* by C. R. Cummings

Andrew blushed bright red and just shrugged and this had at once been seized on as proof that he had been with a girl. Blake cackled with mirth and nudged him.

"Some hanky panky, eh? So how is the luscious Letitia?" he teased.

Which made Andrew even more flustered and embarrassed and Kit even more envious. To add a sharp little twist to his jealousy, he also believed that Andrew was a profoundly moral boy who would also not harm any innocent person.

Then the bell went for assembly and those thoughts were driven out by seeing Diana and then by what the principal had to say. Kit was sitting admiring Diana and wishing he could somehow impress her when Mr Crosswell took the microphone.

"You are reminded that in four weeks we are having the school fete. To help with the fundraising each class has been allocated a stand to run and we are also asking for volunteer groups to set up their own stands. The list of stands will be in the newsletter on Wednesday."

Mr Crosswell paused and then went on: "And another reminder about the fancy-dress ball that is part of the fete. You will remember we asked everyone to come in costume to help make a big effort to ensure the fete is a success. I am asking again. If you haven't thought about it you still have a few weeks to organise your costume. There will be a number of prizes for Best Costume and so on. The details will be in the Newsletter."

The fancy-dress ball! Kit thought. He had forgotten about it. He remembered his idea of coming as The Ghost Who Walks, wearing an overcoat over the Phantom costume. *If wear a hat and dark glasses, it should be alright.* But he experienced a real spurt of anxiety. *Is that a good idea? People might laugh at me,* he thought. And would Diana be impressed?

That worry got him thinking about what other costumes he might wear. In quick succession he rejected dressing as a pirate or a sailor. Considering these options kept him thinking through the remainder of the assembly. As he sat there, another idea came to him.

Should I risk it and ask Diana to come with me?

But would she? He glanced anxiously at her and the humiliating memory of that first meeting sent a chill through him. Fear of another humiliating rejection swirled in Kit's mind, making him feel almost nauseous.

Maybe I should impress her first, then ask? he decided.

But that decision rankled too. Deep down Kit felt he had made it because he was being cowardly and that hurt. Again he despised himself for not acting.

Then school and ordinary life swept out most such thoughts. Classes went on and Kit did the schoolwork without any real effort. He even found it less stressful when he was at classes that Diana wasn't in.

Even the bullies seemed to have forgotten him, but he still kept a wary eye for them and made a point of avoiding the places they frequented. But that hurt his pride too and helped fuel his determination to learn to fight and to be strong.

After school he rode home and after having afternoon tea did his exercises. To his satisfaction, he found he was able to do seven proper push-ups before starting to weaken and he was able to do the five sit-ups he had on his plan. Better still, he was able to lift his weight off the floor and even got his chin right up to the bar.

It is working! he told himself.

But his love life wasn't, and while he lay in his bed that night he brooded over this and then fantasised over having a girlfriend. This included dreaming that he was rescuing Diana. But when it came to any suggestions of sex, he found difficulty.

She isn't like that. She is too nice, he thought. So in his mind he substituted another girl from school, Sandra in Year 10.

Tuesday and Wednesday were virtual repeats. The only thing of note was having to dodge the Dru brothers during morning break. That afternoon, Kit again worked at the truck depot and then he went home and did his exercises, managing seven of everything and barely noticing the effort.

Thursday came around and, remembering how easily he had done them the previous day, he made sure of doing his exercises that afternoon. He managed eight push-ups and sit-ups and again easily got his chin to the bar twice and almost managed five lifts. Worrying that he could be humiliated again at school brought up the temptation to do more but he disciplined himself to leave it at that.

Kit found walking into the PCYC hall that evening even more nerve wracking than the first times. He hoped Sally would be the class instructor but knew there were other adult staff. To his relief, she was. As he walked in, he saw her speaking to another staff member over near the counter. He walked over and gave her a nervous smile. To his relief, she smiled back. "

Hi Kit! I'm glad you were brave enough to come again," she said.

Kit glowed at the praise. Feeling greatly boosted he made his way to the changeroom and changed. As he did, he kept glancing anxiously around for any sign of Carl or Theo, but they did not appear. After locking his clothes into the locker, he made his way out to where Sally and some others stood at the matts.

The lesson began and still there was no sign of Carl or Theo. Kit began to relax and enjoy himself and then to feel slightly foolish. When Carl and Theo did not appear, Kit thought, *Mr Conkey was right—or rather that French philosopher fellow was—I was afraid for nothing.*

It was a good lesson in life and Kit went home feeling much better.

Friday was also a good day with no complications with bullies. Kit was pleased to learn that he had done very well in most of his exams and that boosted him even more. So did pushing his exercises to nine and being able to lift himself up and hang from his hands for the count of fifty.

In case I have to hold on over a cliff, he thought.

That afternoon he particularly enjoyed the *Phantom* comic which was all about how The Ghost Who Walks beat a huge giant in a wrestling match. That got Kit fantasising, and he realised he knew next to nothing about wrestling.

I will learn that too, he decided.

At Navy Cadets there was more preparation for Anzac Day and school ceremonies. The CO, Lt Cdr Hazard, informed them that he had approval for them to wear their uniforms to school ceremonies. That news left Kit feeling quite anxious. He wasn't sure if he wanted to be seen in front of the school in his cadet uniform.

It will just give the bullies something else to tease me over, he thought unhappily.

Then the CO put up a list of who was in the other guards. There were two of these, one at the Stratford Dawn Service and one to be part of a vigil at the cenotaph on the Esplanade. As he expected, Kit was not in either of them, but nor were Andrew or any of his friends. Carmen was in the Stratford guard but that was all.

I'd still like to be a Flag Orderly, Kit thought.

But he knew that was unlikely too. He was too low a rank and too new a recruit. His attention was then focused on making sure he had a uniform that fitted (It was a bit too big) and on being able to march in step.

Saturday and Sunday passed quickly—chores on Saturday and visiting relatives in Innisfail on Sunday. Kit made sure he found the time to do his exercises and felt immense satisfaction at being able to push his totals up to ten.

I am definitely getting stronger. Now I just need to learn how to fight, he thought.

He broke into a furious pretend bout of fisticuffs against some imaginary thugs. It was a good dream but led to more teasing by Bruce who came into the downstairs area while he was doing it.

"What's wrong with you little brother? You suffering from St Vitus' dance or something?" he jeered.

Kit flamed with embarrassment and scowled but held his tongue, thinking, *Not yet, but I will show you one day big brother!*

But he did stop his exercise and went upstairs to shower, his sense of general grievance at having drawn one of life's short straws gnawing at him.

Monday at school was just an ordinary day with no whole school assembly. The reason was that there was to be a whole school assembly on the Friday for an Anzac Ceremony and the thought of that again sent Kit's stomach into little nervous knots and twitches. When the Form Teacher read a notice informing all students who were cadets to be in the Assembly Hall for practice on Thursday, he became even more anxious.

I am just a new recruit. I could just stay out of it, Kit thought.

But he did not feel good about even thinking like that. Not only would Andrew, Blake, Luke, and the other navy cadets know but he knew he would despise himself for being a coward.

The next three days seemed to go by in a blur of schoolwork, frustration and anxiety. There were no incidents with the bullies, other than an odd 'put-down' comment or shove and no progress with his love life. He was still unable to summon the courage to again ask Diana and he felt it was disloyal to even think about any other girl, although he did admire them.

Every afternoon after work, regardless of the jibes of his brother, he continued with his muscle strengthening exercises. To his immense satisfaction he found he could do twelve complete press-ups and was able to lift his whole body off the ground with his arms. But he could not lift himself with one arm as he had seen done and he still had trouble with the chin the bars.

"Never mind. I'm getting better," he told himself. "I will get there."

Thursday morning brought a challenge of a different sort—a mixture of fear and jealousy. An intercom message from the principal directed all students who were cadets were assembled in the hall at the start of first period after lunch. Even though he had been expecting it, Kit was amazed out how anxious he quickly became.

Will I go? he wondered, the fear churning in him.

Chapter 11

ANZAC CEREMONIES

To his shame, Kit knew he was being a coward.

Don't be so gutless! he castigated himself. *The bullies will pick on me anyway because of my size. It won't really make it worse.*

So he took a deep breath and started walking towards the hall. Within minutes he was glad he had plucked up the courage to act as he encountered other navy cadets also walking that way.

Andrew and Blake and Luke all know I am a navy cadet. If I chicken out, they will lose respect for me, he told himself.

So he mingled with the growing group of army, navy and air cadets and made his way to the hall. Inside, Mr Conkey took charge, seating them in three groups by service, navy on the right, then army and air cadets on the left.

"This is protocol," Mr Conkey explained. "By tradition the navy is the senior service and always stands on the right during parades or leads any march. So, navy cadets move over there and sit down."

As he moved to the right-hand end of the milling throng, Kit experienced a little spurt of pride. He was pleased to learn that the navy, as the 'Senior Service', always paraded on the right of any parade, or led any march. But he was a bit disappointed at the disparity in numbers.

There aren't many of us navy cadets, he thought after doing a quick count. In fact, there were only eight navy cadets. *Not many from a school with more than a thousand students,* Kit decided as he sat down.

Then he watched as the army and air cadets were directed where to sit. Looking around from the comparative security of his group, Kit was surprised at how many cadets there were and felt a little better about being one. From where he was seated, he leaned forward to count and noted that there were at least 25 army cadets and ten air cadets.

We don't even have as many as the air cadets, he thought resentfully. It didn't seem right or fair somehow.

His resentment then increased when Mr Conkey called out the senior cadets from each service to allocated jobs. This led to Kit experiencing another spurt of jealousy. For some jobs there was no debate about who got them. The school army cadet unit had four Cadet Under-Officers, the highest rank that any cadet could reach, and they all had to have important jobs. This left the navy cadets out as they had no student at the school with the equivalent rank of Cadet Midshipmen.

I will get to be a Cadet Midshipman, Kit thought, picturing his unit's only Cadet Midshipman, Bob Armstrong, as he did.

There was no AAFC CUO at their school either so four army cadet CUOs were tasked to command the catafalque party, make a speech and deliver the Ode, lay a wreath and to command the formed body of cadets who would parade along the side of the hall. The senior cadet from each service was chosen to lay a wreath each and that meant that Petty Officer Ken George from the navy cadets was chosen, CUO Hansen from the army cadets and a Flight Sergeant named Davis, a Year 11 student, from the AAFC. Kit had no problem with the wreath layers. They were all higher ranks, and he had not expected to be selected for such a job.

It was with the other duties that Kit had issues. For the navy cadets, Carmen Collins was called out to be one of the catafalque party that would comprise the cenotaph guard. She was the only navy cadet in the guard and seeing her walk over to join the other four caused Kit a real stab of genuine jealousy.

I will do that one year, he told himself, although he was very aware he had not been trained at the drill.

The cenotaph guard commander was CUO Grant from the army cadets, a Year 12 student and House Captain for Flinders House, so Kit had no quibble with that. In fact, he thought CUO Grant looked very handsome and capable.

The other members of the catafalque party were two army cadets, both sergeants in Year 11, and an air cadet sergeant, also in Year 11. Then the Flag Orderlies were chosen, one from each service. To Kit's chagrin, he was not selected. Instead, the navy cadet position went to AB Carthew, a Year 10 student.

He's just a favourite who gets all the plums. And he gets to do it at Stratford on Anzac Day. It isn't fair! Kit thought.

Kit knew he was jealous and that did not help as he thought of himself as a good person. But it still hurt, and he quietly simmered with frustrated resentment.

It's only because I am so small, he told himself.

He studied the other students who had been nominated. One of the army cadet sergeants in the catafalque party was a male, Ken Cleland from Year 11, but the other was a most attractive female Year 11 student, Anastasia Mitrovitch. Just looking at her got Kit's heart rate pulsing up. Anastasia was the heartthrob of half the school and just studying her sultry beauty got him aroused.

I wish I could get a girlfriend like her, he thought. And then he felt guilty for having disloyal thoughts about Diana.

The other army cadet nominated as a Flag Orderly did not stir his emotions as much, even though she was a very attractive Year 10 girl name Loretta. Loretta was so bright and so beautiful that Kit just felt in awe of her.

The cenotaph guard, flag orderlies and wreath layers were sent off to rehearse while Mr Conkey organised the remainder into their groups. Kit knew he would not be chosen to stand at the front of the navy cadets but still felt hard done by. Cadet Leading Seaman Tom Pocock from Year 11 got that job. Another army cadet CUO got to stand in front of the army cadet detachment, and a CUO was also appointed to be the commander of the whole cadet group. An Air Cadet sergeant, Jason Branch, another Year 10, was made commander of the AAFC detachment.

Everyone was now told to stand, and they were moved a group at a time into the places where they would stand the next day. Yet again Kit's feelings were ruffled when he was not chosen to be the 'Right Marker' of the ANC group. That position went to Blake. Kit ended up in the middle of the single rank with Tina Babcock on his right and Grace Raishbrook on his left.

Tina was also in Year 9 and Kit thought she was very attractive, noting her large bosom out of the corner of his eye. But then he felt quite guilty. He actually liked Tina. She was a 1st Year cadet like him and also only a Recruit like himself, and she was a very friendly and likeable person. For a few seconds Kit tried to imagine her as his girlfriend, but then he remembered Diana and felt guilty.

I just wish I had a girlfriend, he thought.

Grace was only a Year 8 and another Recruit, but there was no friendship between them. She was cool towards Kit and he did not particularly like her, so he ignored her.

For the next half hour they were talked through the ceremony by Mr Conkey. The cadet group just stood and watched most of the time as the catafalque party slow marched into position around the improvised memorial constructed in the left front corner of the hall. The School Captains practised being the Masters of Ceremony and giving speeches and the wreath layers laid practice wreaths. Only during the *Last Post* and minute's silence did the main group of cadets get called to attention and again for the National Anthem. They were then sent back to their classes with instructions to bring their best ceremonial uniforms the following day.

That meant an hour of polishing and ironing that evening. As he prepared his uniform, Kit felt his stomach churning a bit with anxiety as he was afraid of being teased by other students at school. 'Cadets' was not 'cool' or popular, and students who were cadets were often picked on by students who were not.

That stomach churning anxiety returned with redoubled force on the Friday morning. Images of the bullies taunting him filled Kit's mind and he shivered with apprehension.

Maybe I should stay home? he thought.

For some time Kit sat in his bedroom feeling worse by the minute. His apprehension grew until he actually did feel sick. But in his heart he knew he was just being a coward.

I would have to lie to Mum, he thought miserably.

Shame made him feel worse. And then the moment of decision arrived. His mother came to the door to collect his uniform. She was taking it to school in her car, so it did not get crumpled or soiled.

"Ready?" she asked.

Kit took a deep breath and nodded. "Yes Mum," he said.

Knowing that whatever he did might end up hurting he stood up and forced his limbs to move. Feeling a bit like what he thought a condemned man might feel, he handed her the white uniform on its coat hanger.

The anxiety remained as he rode his bicycle to school, and when he arrived he again had shameful thoughts of not putting the uniform on or of not going to the ceremony in the hall.

But when the time came he collected his uniform from the office where it had been placed along with all the other cadet uniforms and he then joined the other boys in the toilets to change. Once he was dressed, he wished he had a full-length mirror to check his appearance but all he could do was hope. He did not want to ask one of the others.

As always, Kit felt very self-conscious and a little bit embarrassed in his sailor's uniform, but he was proud too and the mix of emotions helped to steel his nerves. It was the Ceremonial Whites, and it was the first time he had worn that order of dress. Wearing it did give him a measure of genuine pride—along with the fear. To divert his thoughts, he studied the uniforms of the other services with a degree of fascination.

Watching the other boys get changed and then fiddle and check their uniforms made him both anxious and interested. The differences in uniforms and badges between the three services Kit found fascinating, but when he watched the army cadet sergeants putting on and adjusting their scarlet sashes he was quite envious.

There was also envy as he watched the male army Cadet Under-Officers put on and adjust their Sam Browne belts. Seeing those shining leather symbols of officer status made Kit quite jealous.

I will get to be a Cadet Midshipman, he vowed.

Kit's unit had positions for only two of these, and some years they had only one or even none. Kit knew his chances of making that rank were not good, but he was determined to try. With his mind set on this, he made his way to the door along with other cadets who were also ready.

And, as he had feared, there was teasing. On his way to the hall Kit walked with several other cadets, feeling very conspicuous and self-conscious as he did. And on the way he met Piper, the Dru brothers, and Ricardo.

"Well, hello sailor!" called Piper in a jeering voice.

Kit tried to ignore him, but the bullies fell into step on either side of him. Wally Dru sneered at him. "What are you, runt?" he asked.

"A naval cadet," Kit managed to reply, even though his mouth had gone dry with fear.

"Huh!" jeered Ernie Dru. "Anal cadet more like."

"That's right!" Piper cried. "My dad said the navy are all homos."

That brought a sneer and taunting laugh from Wally Dru. "That's right. Remember the old sailing ship motto of 'Rum, Sodomy and the Lash'!"

Kit bristled and burned with embarrassment and resentment, but bit back an angry retort, fearing it would make the teasing worse.

The bullies kept up their teasing. Ernie Dru called an obscene joke to his friends. Kit flamed with shame and resentment but made no reply. Ernie Dru jostled him.

"Don't you think that's funny, you little squirt? So what about the homosexual sailor who fell overboard. He was found clinging to a buoy. Hah! Hah! Ya get it? Clinging to a boy!"

To Kit's amusement, neither Wally nor Ricardo 'got it' and Ernie had to explain the play on words, laboriously explaining the difference in spelling between a buoy and a boy.

"What's a buoy?" Wally queried, thus secretly giving Kit more satisfaction and amusement, which he carefully hid.

Ernie explained and the group then finally gave up as more navy cadets arrived to join the group. From then on there were only some general jibes called from a distance and sneering looks and the occasional shouted "Atten—shun!" and so on. It made Kit feel more angry than hurt, and he just wished he could somehow lash out or get back at them.

But he remembered what Mr Conkey (Captain Conkey now he was in his army cadet uniform) had said: "They will tease you because they are jealous and a lot of them, in their hearts, doubt if they are good enough."

They aren't either, Kit told himself as he walked with the other cadets to the hall.

During the second period there was a full rehearsal which involved more than a hundred students and five or six teachers including the Deputy Principal. The school orchestra was there and also the choir plus school captains and students who were helping teachers to provide sound systems and the videoing of the ceremony. The Deputy Principal controlled the rehearsal and Capt Conkey made sure the cadets did the right thing at the right time. He was now in his army cadet uniform and wore medals and a Sam Browne. Seeing that row of medals reminded Kit that Capt Conkey wasn't just a boring old History and Geography teacher. As a young soldier he had fought in the Makassang campaign and was a decorated war veteran.

I will earn medals when I join the navy, Kit thought.

At the end of the rehearsal, the cadets were told to have a drink and go to the toilet and, to his shame, Kit felt a real need to have a nervous pee. By the time he had done this and come out of the toilet, the bell had gone and classes were moving to the hall under the supervision of their teachers. Still feeling very conspicuous in his white sailor suit, Kit made his way back to re-join the other navy cadets.

When all the classes were present the ceremony began. The principal and a group of VIPs arrived in the hall and Kit stared at them with interest. They included a navy lieutenant commander in dress whites, obviously regular RAN.

From HMAS Cairns, Kit deduced.

There was also an army major in a khaki ceremonial uniform and a number of politicians and community and school leaders. The group took their seats on the right front of the hall quite near the navy cadet detachment and then the School Captains took over and conducted the ceremony.

The catafalque party slow marched in, and Kit watched in silent envy. But he had to grudgingly admit they did it well. Once the guard was in position the speeches began. The usual prayers, hymns, and poetry readings were done and then the wreath laying. During this, Kit stood at ease with the other cadets and scanned the audience looking for Diana. But his class were on the other side of the hall and he could not see her. So Kit shifted his attention to the Year 10s and noted that there were some other very pretty girls. For several minutes he admired and studied them.

I wish I had a girlfriend, he thought, the emotional and physical frustration making him fidget in his uniform.

Another hymn began and the wreath layers were called. Once again Kit experienced little stabs of jealousy mingled with admiration as he watched the wreath layers do their duties. As the three straightened up, stepped back, and saluted, Kit was struck by the three different ways each service saluted.

The guard was then called to 'Attention' and did a 'Present Arms' with their innocuous Steyrs. Next the army cadet CUO at the front of the cadet group called them to attention. Kit obeyed but had to smile as he was used to the navy 'Ho!', not the army 'Atten.... shun!'

But the smile was gone, and he stood rigid and respectful during the playing of the *Last Post*. At the end of the bugle tune, the guard came back to the 'attention' and the leaders stopped saluting and everyone stood in respectful silence for the minute. 'Rous' followed and then the School Captain instructed the audience to remain standing for the National Anthem. The guard was called to the 'Present' and the cadet leaders out the front saluted again. Kit stiffened with pride and as he looked around at the white, green camouflage, and blue uniforms and at the red, white, and blue flag now hoisted to the top of the indoor pole he felt very proud to be an Australian and to be a navy cadet.

The Guard came down from the 'Present', did an inwards turn and marched off in 'Quick Time'. Then the ceremony was concluded. The cadets were fallen out and, as he marched off, Kit was gripped by a sudden urge to have Dianna see him in his best uniform. To that end he hurried across the crowded hall, his eyes questing to locate her.

As he threaded his way through the dispersing throng of students, Kit noted many students looking at him, some with blank faces, others with surprised recognition, and a few with contemptuous or sneering expressions. But nobody spoke to him, and he ignored them. His eyes kept scanning for a sign of Diana, but he was disappointed. There was no sign of her and all he could do was make his way to the toilets to change back into his school uniform.

Kit did not see Diana again that day and the effort of walking around the school looking for her during the lunch break left him feeling frustrated and let down. The only good thing was that the bullies ignored him.

Friday night meant more cadets and that meant practicing for Anzac Day. The dress was the usual mottled blue and grey DPNU and Kit was glad of that. Once again there were rehearsals for guards and flag raising and again Kit experienced spurts of jealousy. Marching practice followed and that did not go very well. Many of the cadets had trouble marching in step and Kit feared they would look bad.

Particularly compared to the Air Cadets and Army Cadets, he thought.

Then there were more rehearsals, the catafalque parties and flag orderlies busy perfecting their drill while the others did more marching. Seeing the catafalque parties stirred Kit's jealousy again and he began to nurse a grudge about not being selected for any of the guards the following day. He also developed a strong desire to be part of the city parade. This desire began to gnaw at him and then grew into anxiety lest he not be able to take part. Finally, when his mother took him home, he asked her if he could go to the parade on Sunday.

"Of course," his mother replied. "We always go to Anzac Day. You know that. Now, are you planning to go in uniform?"

"Yes Mum," Kit replied.

"Then you'd better get the one you wore this morning washed and ironed," she said.

Sighing with relief, Kit hurried to his room and collected his whites and took them down to the laundry. Feeling much better, he took himself off to bed.

On Saturday morning after breakfast, Kit hurried down to the laundry. Having started the washing machine going he sat on the back steps and polished his black parade boots until they had a mirror finish on the toecaps. Then he carefully whitened the brim of his cap which had begun to show some staining from being touched or held too many times.

That done, he did his exercises, managing to do 13 push-ups and sit-ups and seven chin the bars. For good measure he did a few stretches and star jumps and some muscle exercises. Then he did his other chores—sweeping out downstairs, weeding and watering in the garden, hanging the washing out to dry. Later he did his homework and, when his brothers weren't around, more physical exercises. He found to his great satisfaction that he could actually do fourteen push-ups and sit-ups and was able to lift his chin up to the bar six times.

I am getting stronger, he told himself.

Even so, he was careful not to overdo it and stuck to his program of slowly increasing the number of exercises each day.

Late in the afternoon he unpegged the washing and took it upstairs. Very carefully he ironed his white uniform ready for the next day. It was a task his mother insisted he do.

"If you are old enough to be a navy cadet you are old enough to care for your uniform," she had said. And Kit was proud to do so.

I hope Anzac Day goes well, he thought.

Chapter 12

A MOMENT OF SHAME

His parents had obviously discussed the program for the following day because at dinner time Kit's father asked Adrian and Bruce if they wanted to go to the Anzac Parade. Neither did.

Bruce curled his lip. "I don't want to go to the parade. I don't think Anzac Day should happen. It celebrates war."

Kit bridled and tried to marshal his thoughts to refute this, but his father got in first. "It is a commemoration, not a celebration. It's a way of honouring and thanking those who sacrificed themselves for our country. So you don't have to come but we will be going. Now, Chris, you get to bed because reveille with be at 6am if we have to be there by 8am."

Pleased that their father held such strong views on the importance of Anzac Day, Kit stood up, gave Bruce a reproachful look, then hurried off to clean his teeth.

At 07:45am the next morning, Kit climbed out of the family car where it was parked on the side street near Munro Martin Park.

"We will walk. It will be too hard to find a park closer than this on a day like today," his father explained.

As he self-consciously put on his cap and adjusted it, Kit had to agree as many other cars were arriving and people were moving in small groups and singly in the direction of the Esplanade.

He took a minute to straighten his collar and then followed his parents towards the gathering crowd. The number of people who had risen early for the ceremony was a real surprise for Kit.

There are hundreds! he noted. *I didn't expect that many.*

The parade was to form up near the Casino and that was five blocks to walk in the hot sun. Kit began to sweat and wished they had parked closer, but looking at the already full parking spaces and steadily growing crowds he had to concede they did not have many other options.

At Lake Street his father gestured. "We will make our way to the RSL. You are big enough to go on your own now. Do you know where the parade is forming up?"

"Yes Dad," Kit replied, pleased at the show of confidence.

After making arrangements to meet his parents after the ceremony, he left them and headed east along Lake Street and into the CBD. He felt very conspicuous and self-conscious in his navy cadet uniform but also very proud. Determined to do his best, he hurried on.

As he got closer, he looked anxiously to see if any other navy cadets were there. At first all he could see were civilians of all ages and a few old veterans in suit and tie and with jingling medals pinned to their coats. Then he glimpsed white uniforms and felt a surge of relief.

There they are, he told himself.

At the end of the Esplanade, thousands of people were now milling around. Kit saw that as well as the cadet units there was a detachment of soldiers from the army and numerous other community and school groups. He noted Scouts and Guides, St John Ambulance, nurses and police, firemen, and numerous school groups.

Right at the front were the veterans, most in coat and tie with medals. Kit eyed them with wary respect and wondered if would be brave enough if he ever had to fight for his country. Behind them were the uniformed services. The Navy led this group and were standing in three ranks in their white ceremonial uniforms. Kit studied the 'regulars' and was very impressed because the officers carried drawn swords and the sailors had rifles. Many had medals from active service in the Middle East or South Pacific and he thought they looked very good.

That is what I want to be, he told himself, now gripped by severe insecurity mingled with determination to try his hardest. He did not want to let down the cadets in front of the adult regulars.

Behind the Royal Australian Navy detachment came a detachment from the army, mostly the 51st Battalion, Far North Queensland Regiment. There were no adult RAAF personnel, so behind the army were the cadet units in their order of seniority. Finding the navy cadets was easy. In the bright tropical sunshine the white uniforms really stood out.

But then there was a small dose of humiliation as the unit were formed into three ranks and Kit found himself placed in the middle rank and in the centre of the unit, along with all the other smaller cadets. Unhappily Kit had to concede that he was the smallest person in the unit. All he could do was smile and shrug and accept it.

I will grow one day, he consoled himself.

Then there was the problem of the drink bottles. Lt Ryan, the XO, came along and told them all to hand over their drink bottles. By this time Kit was feeling quite thirsty and he wished he had brought one with him. But all he could do was lick his lips and watch as those who had quickly drained theirs and gave it to the Admin Officer when she came past with a large cardboard box.

"Collect them after the ceremony," she said.

The parade began. It was 9am by then and the sun was right up and the heat quite stifling. Even so, thousands of people had now arrived to line the Esplanade. Marching between the throngs of clapping people gave Kit a real boost and he straightened his back with pride. He had always enjoyed Anzac Day and felt that all Australians should take part. It irritated him that many people just took it as another day off.

Once the marchers arrived at the cenotaph in front of the RSL they were lined up in tightly packed groups and then stood at ease. There was some confusion as the groups were marshalled into position and Kit thought it could all have been a bit better organised.

And a venue with more shade mightn't be a bad idea, he decided.

This notion was because he and the other cadets, along with most of the audience, were now standing in the blazing sun. And the navy cap gave no protection at all, the sun being so bright he had to squint and keep blinking and wiping perspiration from his brow to stop it trickling into his eyes.

There were so many people, and the Navy Cadets were so far back, that Kit could only just glimpse the top of the cenotaph 50 metres away with occasional glimpses of the dignitaries conducing the ceremony.

The ceremony began. To Kit, standing in the sun and unable to hear or see most of it, it all became a bit of a drag. He started to feel bored and to fidget. A wave of tiredness seemed to engulf him and, as he fought it off by conscious effort, he suddenly realised he was dizzy.

I nearly fell over then, he thought. *Oh, how shameful that would be!*

So he made an effort to stand still and to pay attention. Except that now he felt very thirsty. Blinking and licking dry lips Kit now regretted not having drunk more at home.

I am dehydrated, he realised.

Movement next to him made him look and he saw it was another young First Year cadet who had sat down on the grass. The words 'Bloody weakling' formed in Kit's mind but then he shook his head and knew he was being unfair. Instead, he became anxious lest he also faint.

Several more cadets sat down and couple fell out and were taken to the rear by the adult staff. This all made Kit feel superior and he was even more pleased when he saw some of the soldiers and even regular navy people falling out.

It is certainly hot! he thought.

After what seemed like hours, the speeches were finished and the wreath laying finally over. The MC called the parade to attention—with the usual confusion as most soldiers and cadets waited for their own commanders to give the order.

Last Post. I must stand to attention and not move, Kit told himself as the bugle tune rang out.

With a conscious effort, he stood as straight as he could, ignoring but disapproving of any movement around him. Then the minute's silence began and Kit remained stiffly at attention. Sweat trickled down his forehead and the middle of his back and he knew his shirt was soaked with perspiration. Under his armpits felt very sticky.

This is a silly cap to be wearing in the tropical sun, he thought, then felt disloyal to the navy by having such critical notions.

Suddenly, Kit blinked and staggered. He realised he had taken a step forward.

Bloody hell! I nearly fainted then, he thought.

The shame of that was something he really did not want so he refocused his mind and tried to relax his body. Around him the crowd stood in silence and the seconds seemed to drag on.

Oh hurry up! Kit cried in his mind, aware that he was feeling nauseous and concerned that his now trembling muscles might cramp.

To his enormous relief the bugle rang out with the 'Rous'.

Won't be long now, Kit told himself.

Then, to his dismay, his stomach heaved and he tasted bile in the back of his throat. With an effort he held it down but then several sharp pains bit through his stomach and he found he was gripping it.

Bloody hell! I nearly spewed then, he thought.

And then his stomach heaved again and he doubled up and vomited. It wasn't much of an ejection—he hadn't drunk enough for that—but at least a mouthful of sticky, sour tasting liquid spurted and then trickled out. Dribbling, sticky streamers of vomit fell down and stuck to his mouth and then broke off. Embarrassment surged hotly and he tried to straighten up but then his stomach churned again, and he coughed and spat several more sticky drops.

A hissed, "Bloody weakie!" from Davidson added to the sense of shame. Kit burned with embarrassment. With his eyes misting from the pain and humiliation, he made an effort to straighten up.

I need to stand to attention for the National Anthem, he told himself.

Wiping his mouth with the back of his hand he forced his body upright just as the music started.

A hand gripped his arm. "Are you alright, Seaman Walker?" he was asked. It was Sub Lt Mullion.

Kit nodded and kept himself at attention. "Yes Ma'am," he croaked.

But he wasn't really. He felt ashamed. But there was no way he was going to fall out. Gritting his teeth, he held himself steady until the parade was ordered to stand at ease.

At last! he thought. But oh, how he wished he hadn't disgraced himself! *What shame!* he thought.

The parade was dismissed and Kit braced himself for more teasing. But to his surprise nobody said anything.

They either didn't notice, or they are just being polite, Kit thought.

On the edge of tears he quickly pushed his way through the crowd so that he did not have to face them. Glancing down he saw that there were dribbles of damp on the front of his uniform and he did not want anyone noticing that either. In his mind, the moment of weakness seemed to undo all his good efforts.

His parents didn't help. They were full of praise and clearly had not seen him vomit. Nor did they appear to notice the marks on his uniform. His mother handed him a drink and Kit took it gratefully and drank. He really wanted to swill his mouth out, but the cold fruit juice was still very refreshing.

His father patted him on the shoulder. "Well done, son! We are really proud of you," he said.

Kit glowed at the praise and wondered if he should mention being sick. But he was not game, so he just nodded and mumbled his thanks.

Then it was home and lunch. After lunch, Kit lay down to rest. His emotions were very mixed. Some of the time he brooded on having been sick and some of the time he glowed with satisfaction for having taken part in the march and ceremony. But the memory of that public humiliation certainly hurt and spoiled things. He found it all very distressing! Still feeling very mixed emotions, he dropped off to sleep and slept for a couple of hours.

In the evening he watched TV with his parents and read the latest *Phantom* comic. Both his brothers went out to parties and that made Kit jealous as well.

Monday morning meant school and that presented something of a challenge. What was worrying him was being teased because he had worn his cadet uniform to the school Anzac service.

The bullies will probably pick on me, he fretted.

But it was a challenge of a different sort that he faced during morning assembly. Once again, the Principal stood up on the dais and reminded the school about the fete and fancy-dress ball.

"It is now only three weeks away," Mr Crosswell reminded them. "And if you are going you do need to get your costumes organised. There will be a reminder to parents in the school newsletter that goes out today. Also a list showing the allocation of classes to run various stalls is to be in it and will also be put up on the main noticeboard. Form teachers are to discuss this with their students and are to start getting names of volunteers to help run the stalls."

The fancy-dress ball! Kit thought.

He had tried to push it out of his mind. He remembered his idea of going as The Ghost Who Walks wearing an overcoat over the Phantom costume. A spurt of anxiety made him regret having ever suggested it.

I wonder if I can just forget about it? he thought.

Then school and ordinary life swept out most such thoughts. Classes went on and Kit did the schoolwork without any real effort. The only interesting thing was reading the list of class stalls allocated for the fete. Kit's Form Class had been allotted the 'Magnetic Fish' stall and seeing that caused him to wrinkle his nose.

That is a real little kid's stand, he thought.

Despite this, he took a pencil and wrote his name in one of the spaces on the roster attached to the class list.

Even the bullies seemed to have forgotten him, but he still kept a wary eye open for them and made a point of avoiding the places they frequented. But doing that hurt his pride too and helped fuel his determination to learn to fight and to be strong.

After school, he rode home and after having afternoon tea did his exercises. To his satisfaction, he found he was able to do fifteen proper push-ups before starting to weaken and he was able to do the twenty sit-ups he had on his plan. Better still he was able to lift his weight off the floor and get his chin up to the bar six times.

It is working! he told himself.

Later that evening at home, his mother said while he was washing up, "I see in the school newsletter a reminder about the fancy-dress ball at the fete. Are you still planning to go to that?"

"Yes Mum," Kit replied.

His anxiety level at once shot up and he braced himself for hurtful comments from his brothers who were in the lounge room.

"Are you still planning to go as the Phantom?" she asked.

"Yes Mum, but as The Ghost Who Walks rather than the Phantom."

This drew a guffaw from Bruce. "Ghost Who Walks! Hah! Hah! Going as one of the Bandar Pygmy People would be better!" Then he burst into chuckles and Adrian joined in.

Their laughter burned and Kit gritted his teeth. His mother immediately reacted. "That will do Bruce! You stop teasing your brother. It is just cruel bullying, and I won't have it. I want my children to have some compassion and decency in their attitudes and behaviour. And anyway, what are you planning to go as?"

Bruce went red, then shrugged and curled his lip. "I wasn't planning to go. Dressing up is just little kid stuff."

"Oh is it!" their mother snapped. "Well it is for a good cause, so you make a choice as you are going to help make the fete a success as well. You are not just going to torment your little brother and not help. So you think of a costume fast and we will get it organised."

She turned back to Kit. "So who's this Ghost Who Walks? What sort of costume is that?"

Kit was astonished. "Mum! That's the Phantom when he goes to town in disguise. Look, I'll show you."

He hurried into the lounge room and picked up a *Phantom* comic, just managing to reach it before Bruce could lean over and snatch it away. Back in the kitchen he showed his mother.

She studied the pictures and nodded. "I see. But you still need the Phantom costume underneath."

Kit nodded. "Yes, but we also need an overcoat, hat and dark glasses over the Phantom costume," he explained.

His mother nodded and looked thoughtful. "So we need to see about a costume. We will go to a costume hire place on Saturday morning before you go to work. Now go and finish your homework."

Chapter 13

BULLIES

School the next day led to more complications. During the Lunch Break Kit noted Diana sitting with her friends under D Block, and as he walked towards them he shook his head in admiration for her beauty.

She is just so wonderful! How can I get her to like me? he wondered.

And then his eyes met those of her brother. Carstairs and two of his cronies were coming the other way. A spasm of near panic caused Kit to instantly change course. Not wanting a confrontation, he looked around for a way out of the potential trouble. Along the side of the next building he glimpsed the library.

I will hide there. They won't do anything in the library.

So he hurried along past C Block and towards the library, all the time feeling both scared and ashamed. Knowing in his heart that he was running away added to his sense of self-contempt.

It is all very well for people to say that discretion is the better part of valour and that those who run away live to fight another day, he thought. But he still felt ashamed and thought he was being cowardly.

He reached the library and hurried inside then paused and glanced back. To his relief, there was no sign of the bullies.

Maybe they didn't see me come in here? he decided.

But he was still anxious, so he walked to the far corner of the library looking for somewhere to hide. There was a row of carrels with computers in them but only the end one was unoccupied, so he slid down into the seat. Now mostly hidden he peeked towards the door. Then he noted a girl at the next carrel giving him quizzical glances, so he pretended to be using the computer.

From that he became genuinely interested and decided to use the time to do some research for his next History assignment. That kept him going until some people came and stood close around him. Kit saw their legs and shoes and glanced anxiously up. It was Carstairs and two of his Year 10 cronies: Springer and Watson.

Bugger! I forgot to keep watch, Kit thought.

Before he could open his mouth, Carstairs clipped him hard on the back of the head.

"Don't even look at my sister, you little creep!" he snarled.

Kit was about to retort that he would do what he liked, when the girl next to him suddenly spoke.

"Stop hitting boys smaller than yourself, you bully," she said.

Carstairs turned to face her. "Shut up, Fuzz Face!" he hissed.

Kit tried to turn and get up. *He is a real pig!* he thought.

Determined to act, he decided that a bit of a thumping would be worth it if he could get Carstairs into trouble with the librarian and witnesses. But Kit was held by Springer and both cuffed and pinched.

The girl flushed with anger and embarrassment. "Don't you use crude, filthy names to me!" she snapped, "Or I will report you to the office."

"Then mind your own business," Carstairs snarled, bunching his fists on his hips. He then turned back to Kit. "You got the message, midget?"

Kit could only swallow and glare back, again ashamed at not acting. He looked around, hoping to see one of the teachers. To his relief, he saw that the librarian, Mr Millard, was watching them from the other side of the room.

Good, that should end it! he thought.

It did. Watson nudged Carstairs and indicated the teacher. The three bullies then turned and walked out. Kit seethed with impotence and distress.

One day! he thought.

Turning to the girl he said, "Sorry about them."

"They are just foul-mouthed pigs," the girl replied.

Jocelyn, Year 10. She lives in my street, Kit remembered. She was fairly plain and had freckles but she also had a nice smile. To his dismay, she said, "Do you fancy Diana Carstairs?"

That really embarrassed Kit. All he could do was go red, shrug and mumble, "She's in my class."

"I know," Jocelyn replied. "I think she is very pretty, so it doesn't surprise me you admire her."

Kit blushed even more and struggled for words. "Thanks for speaking out," he said.

Jocelyn shrugged. "I hate bullies who pick on people smaller than themselves," she replied.

That caused Kit to burn more. *She is only in Year 10 but she is much bigger than me,* he noted.

Then his gaze quickly roved over her. He realised he had often seen her but never really paid her any attention. He liked the way her bosom rounded out the front of her shirt.

She met his eyes and smiled. "What are you studying?" she asked.

"History," Kit replied. "How the Ancient Egyptians built the pyramids. What about you?"

"Science—Biology," Jocelyn answered.

At that moment, the bell went and Kit felt a stab of disappointment. He was about to say, 'See you again' when she said exactly that.

Kit could only nod. He stood up and walked with her to the door. There he gave what he hoped looked like a casual nod and went off towards his own class.

There he was able to surreptitiously study and admire Diana, but he found his thoughts wandering to Jocelyn. And again that night as he lay in bed to fantasise he found he was picturing Jocelyn and he did not have any pangs of guilt at imagining her in passionate scenes.

She seemed friendly, Kit thought.

It was with her in mind that he went to the library at lunch time the following day. To his own surprise, he found he was feeling quite anxious.

She might not even be there, he told himself. Or worse, she might just give him the brush off as most girls seemed to!

But she was there, and when she saw him she smiled. With his heart skipping happy little beats, Kit walked across the room to where she sat at the same computer as the previous day. Luckily the one next to her was vacant, so Kit 'casually' sat down.

"Hi!" he muttered.

"Hello! Any trouble with the bullies today?" Jocelyn asked.

Kit shook his head and replied, "No."

But then he was stuck with what to say next. His tongue seemed to lock up and all he could think of doing was opening the computer programs and pretending to study. Jocelyn did not keep talking but turned back to her own computer.

So he worked there quite happily, and it was only later in class when he was studying Diana that he felt a twinge of guilt.

I am being disloyal by thinking about other girls, he told himself. *Diana is the one.*

But thinking that Jocelyn might actually like him lifted his morale and he went home much happier. He even did one more push-up than his plan required and being able to do that lifted his spirits even more.

On Thursday, Kit deliberately went looking for Jocelyn. To his disappointment, she was not in the library; and when he went walking around the school looking for her, he got chased by the bullies.

Nor did he get a chance to see her after school. He was rostered to work, and it was a very frustrated and grumpy boy who rode his bike to the workshops. There he was set to work helping change a battery in a new Prime Mover.

I'm getting sick of this truck! Kit thought.

It felt to him like he had cleaned or fixed almost every part of it. That thought made him smile and he rubbed a small scratch he had accidentally made in the back of the cab.

Next, he was told to help tidy up the workshop. That put him in an even grumpier mood as it meant finding and sorting all the loose tools that lazy people had not put back on the peg boards and then dusting and wiping the work benches and finally sweeping the concrete floor. He was glad to finish at 5:30pm and head off home.

Thursday afternoon brought its own anxieties as well. Memories of the unpleasant incident in the showers at the PCYC the previous week made Kit wonder if he should go to Judo. But then he despised himself for even considering that. His father's advice was not to run away from such situations but to face them, and Kit knew in his heart that it was sound advice.

Another option was to avoid the changerooms and showers completely, but that notion also stuck in his craw and he determined to go. As a result, there was another, even more dramatic incident. It happened after the training session during which they had learned several new throws and holds. Almost dripping with sweat, Kit made his way to the changeroom with the other boys and then faced up to stripping to have a shower. Reluctantly, Kit undressed, keeping his back to the others as he did. Then he wrapped his towel around himself and waited.

As usual, Carl and Theo pushed the smaller boys aside and were first into the showers. There were five showers but two were occupied by boys from another team, so only Wallis and Cory could go in. Kit sat on the long bench that the bags and clothes were placed on. Several other boys came in and also sat or stood. They chatted among themselves and ignored Kit. He made a point of not looking at them as they undressed.

Then Carl came out of the cubicle and began dressing. To Kit, he appeared to be a bit of an exhibitionist, allowing other boys to see him naked. The situation made Kit feel uneasy, so he looked away. Pretending not to notice, he stood up and moved towards the now vacant shower cubicle.

As he passed Carl, the bully suddenly snatched Kit's towel away and began flicking him with it. The blows stung and the bully's jeering laughter added to Kit's unhappiness. Then Theo joined in. Kit called on them to stop but they kept hitting him. Hurting and afraid, Kit turned and bolted out the door into the hall, snatching up a spare towel and wrapping it around him as he did.

The shouting had attracted the adult staff and Kit almost collided with a male instructor and Sally just outside. By then Kit was so upset he burst into tears. He was already feeling ashamed at having run away, and now he was even more embarrassed at Sally seeing him cry and also seeing what he believed was a very scrawny physique. He was sobbing so much he had trouble explaining.

Carl and Thoe followed him out and at once accused Kit of having started the incident. Kit was stunned at the blatant lie and denied it. He was now so upset he had difficulty in controlling his voice and keeping back more tears. Pride helped. Luckily, several other boys corroborated Kit's version of events and Carl and Theo were given warnings by the manager.

"No more fighting here," he said. "Martial Arts are to learn restraint and self-discipline, not to let out aggression. Now get on your way."

That was all very unsatisfactory to Kit, and he seethed with indignation. As he watched Carl and Theo leave, he shook his head.

"It isn't fair," he muttered to Sally, who was now standing next to him. "They started it. But thank you for listening," he said. Then he blushed with embarrassment, "And sorry for causing you trouble," he added.

"You didn't. I am sure those two were the real troublemakers. Now, I think we will arrange for you and them to be in different groups and maybe to come on different nights," Sally replied.

And that was how it was arranged. Kit was told to come on Tuesday nights if he could. He was able to confirm that almost at once as his mother came in, wondering why he was delayed. When told of the incident she became really angry and concerned. Kit did not want to go into the details as he found them all too embarrassing, but his mother fussed and looked at a bruise forming on the left side of his face.

"Tell those other boys I will take it to the police if they do anything else to hurt my son," she threatened the manager.

"So Tuesday nights then?" Sally checked.

"Yes," Kit's mother replied.

But will that be the end of it? Kit wondered.

He pictured Carl and Theo waiting for him and bashing him in revenge. From that he considered giving up the PCYC altogether. But stubborn pride held his mouth shut and he again told himself not to be a coward.

Going to school next day took courage. Fear of encountering the bullies there made him almost so ill he thought of telling his mother he was sick. But then stubborn pride drove him to go. And then he did not even see the bullies until he glimpsed them at morning break. By sitting with his friends he avoided any sort of confrontation, and the bullies did not seem to notice him.

Friday slid by—Kit avoiding the bullies by sitting in the library next to Jocelyn. Being Friday there was Cadets that evening. It was a normal 'Home Training' activity with work on seamanship, knots, signalling, and navigation. Kit enjoyed all of that, but it was on the first parade that he got the biggest boost.

The CO made a special speech of thanks to those who had taken part in the guards and in the Anzac march and ceremony.

"We got a lot of praise for our good drill and presentation," he said. "So thank you."

Kit glowed and felt very proud of himself. *And maybe next year I will be selected to be a flag orderly or to be in one of the guards*, he thought.

During the canteen break, Kit noted a group clustered at the notice board so he went over to enquire.

"What is it?" he asked.

Blake was closest and answered. "The nominations for the Specialist Courses and a week-long camp in the June school holidays," he replied.

Kit read the notice and was interested to note that the camp would be held in Townsville and would include sailing activities. It would also provide him with the opportunity to complete his Recruit Training and be promoted to Seaman.

I hope I am allowed to go, he thought, worried that he might have to work all of the holidays.

A Joining Instruction for a weekend activity in four weeks' time was handed out at dismissal parade. The cadets were reminded to get the information to their parents about the June camp as quickly as possible as the food and transport cost had to be paid in advance.

"We want the money within the next two weeks," Lt Ryan told them. "That's because we have to book coaches and order bulk food."

That got Kit anxious too, even though he felt sure his parents would pay. As soon as he was in the car, Kit asked his father about being allowed to do the two activities. To his relief, his father just nodded and asked for a few details. Anxiously Kit told his father what the XO had said.

At home his mother also appeared happy for him to do the activities. "Especially during the June holidays. Your father and I will both be at work all day and Adrian will be at work too, so you are better off at cadets," she commented.

"What's Bruce doing?" Kit asked.

"He is going to work at the business," his father answered. "You can too if you want."

Kit shook his head. The choice between earning more money by being at the workshop and inside all day did not rate against the image of sailing on the tropical ocean among palm studded islands.

There might even be pretty girls, he thought.

Chapter 14

MORE EMBARRASSMENT

S aturday morning was taken up with household chores and then with going to the shop with his mother.

"We need to see about a costume for this fancy-dress ball," she said.

That idea got Kit all anxious and he was very nervous as he walked into the Party Hire shop with her an hour later. His mother made the request to the lady behind the counter. The lady glanced at Kit.

"Is it for this boy?" she asked.

"Yes," his mother replied.

The lady nodded, and even though she said nothing the absence of comment hurt. "We do have one in stock, but I think it is for younger boys," she replied.

She went into a back room and re-emerged a few minutes later carrying a purple Phantom suit on a coat hanger.

To Kit, the costume looked ridiculously small. "I don't think that will fit me," he commented.

"It's Lycra. It will stretch," the lady explained.

Kit looked at it dubiously, not wanting to put himself in a humiliating situation. But his mother now took charge.

"Well, we are here so you can try it on anyway," she insisted.

Blushing with anxious anticipation, Kit took the costume and was directed to a changeroom nearby. It only had a curtain across the front and contained a full-length mirror. Now feeling very self-conscious Kit took off his shoes and then his shirt.

I am going to look ridiculous in this! he thought.

He was reluctant to take off his shorts but eventually did so and then stood in his underpants and studied his gawky physique in the mirror. Wishing fervently he had not suggested such a costume, he set to work to put it on.

The lady was right, it did stretch—but it was very tight. It took such a struggle he became very anxious lest he rip the stitching or ladder the Lycra. His mother didn't help by calling to hurry up.

"We have other shopping to do," she said.

So Kit twisted and stretched and finally got his arms into the upper part of the costume and then looked down to adjust the legs and torso. As he did, he was shocked to notice how scrawny and rude he looked in the thin, stretch material.

Oh bloody hell! I can't wear anything as revealing as this, he thought. Anxiously he studied himself in the mirror and was appalled. *This is so embarrassing!* he thought.

He was about to call out that it was no good when his mother called, "Have you got it on?"

"Yes Mum, but it's very tight. I don't think it's suitable," Kit replied, burning with anticipatory shame.

"Let me look," his mother called.

With that she swept the curtain aside and peered in. Kit saw the shop lady standing with her and he burned with shame. His mother looked him up and down, her gaze seeming to linger on his lower regions. Kit blushed furiously with embarrassment.

And the shop lady's eyes also seemed to stare. Her eyes flicked up to his and then back down again and then up.

"It is a bit tight," she commented.

Kit burned even more, humiliation searing his pride.

His mother made it worse by saying, "Yes, it is a bit revealing. But you planned to wear an overcoat, didn't you?"

Kit nodded, aware that he was red in the face with shame and embarrassment. "Yes," he croaked, "And trousers, a hat and dark glasses."

I'll want those dark glasses! he thought.

His mother nodded and then said, "It will have to do. We don't have time to arrange anything else." She turned to the shop lady. "How long will it take to order a bigger one in?" she asked.

The shop lady shrugged. "Probably about two weeks," she replied.

"When is this fete?" Kit's mother queried.

"Two weeks," he replied.

To make it worse, the shop lady kept glancing down at him. She said, "I can't guarantee that," she said.

Kit's mother pursed her lips. "Well, I don't have time to make one, even if I had the material. It will have to do. We will take it thanks," she said.

Kit had been about to suggest he wear another costume, to go as a pirate or something, and was shocked to hear that. But, to his own shame, he did not speak up to overrule his mother.

She turned to him. "It will have to do. Okay Chris, get changed," she instructed.

Kit nodded, too embarrassed to speak. With a shaking hand he pulled the curtain across and then turned his back in case his mother pulled the curtain aside again. Nervously, he peeled off the tight costume and hastily dressed in his own clothes. He then found he was so embarrassed that he did not want to leave the change cubicle. But he had to, so he took a deep breath and pulled the curtain aside. As he placed the costume on the counter, his eyes met the lady's and he blushed even more. He wasn't sure if it was smirk on her face over his size or because she had noticed his shame, but either way it hurt.

I don't have to go the fancy-dress ball, he told himself. *Or I can go as something else.*

Over the next few hours Kit experienced steadily rising anxiety. Memories of what he had looked like in the costume rose to set his heart palpitating. There was the problem of an overcoat for the 'Ghost Who Walks' to wear.

His mother shook her head and muttered, "Finding a full-length heavy overcoat in a tropical place like Cairns is not going to be easy."

And it wasn't. During the remainder of the morning they visited the 'Op Shops' and St Vincent De Paul and 'Lifeline' shops but all they could find was a dressing gown with a blue and red chequered pattern on it.

When she held it up for Kit to see, he was appalled. "Oh Mum! Fair go! That will look even sillier," he cried.

"I will take off the cord and add a proper belt and I will sew a few buttons on it," she answered.

Kit did not like that idea either, but his mother got stubborn and went ahead and purchased the dressing gown. That got Kit feeling even more anxious.

I wish I'd never mentioned going as the Phantom! he thought unhappily. But still he could not summon the courage to argue for a change of costume.

The long trousers and leather shoes were no problem. Kit already had them. An old felt hat was purchased and then some dark glasses. Kit was not really satisfied and still felt sure he was going to make a fool of himself.

Bruce didn't help with his sarcastic comments when they got home. "What about 'Devil'?" he queried.

"I don't need him," Kit replied.

"Yes, you do! The Ghost Who Walks always has his dog with him."

"Devil is a wolf," Kit retorted.

Bruce coloured. "Smart arse!" he snorted. "We will buy you a stuffed toy dog on wheels for you to drag around then." With that he chortled with malicious glee and kept teasing until their mother told him to stop.

Kit squirmed with embarrassment and wished the fancy-dress ball had never been suggested.

"What about you? What are you going as?" he snapped angrily.

"I'm not going. That's all just silly little kid stuff," Bruce replied, sneering as he did.

Their mother then weighed in. "Oh yes you are! This is to raise money for the school and you can do your bit."

Kit could not restrain himself. A smirk gladdened his face and he let out a chuckle. "You can go as King Kong the gorilla. You won't even need a costume," he called.

Bruce went red and jumped up. "You'll need a new face after I mash it!" he snarled.

Once again their mother intervened. "That will do! Chris, there was no need for that. Go to your room and do your homework. You too, Bruce; and I don't want to hear any trouble from you two again. Now go!"

Kit went, still gleefully enjoying his brief moment of revenge.

But Bruce got his own back next morning. Kit woke up by Bruce calling loudly and shaking him.

"Get up, you little slug!" Bruce said.

As he did, he began to haul at the bedclothes. That sent an instant spasm of alarm through Kit. As he jerked into wakefulness, he became aware that all he wore were thin, cotton pyjama shorts.

"Let go! Leave me alone!" he cried, grabbing at the bedclothes and trying to keep himself covered.

By then Bruce had half uncovered Kit, to the extent that he could see he wore no pyjama top. "Hoh, ho! Sleeping in the nuddy eh, Mister Ghost Who Walks!" he yelled. With that he hauled even harder.

Now blinking awake and aware that the door to his bedroom was wide open, Kit clung frantically to the bedclothes, blushing with anticipatory shame and fearing any possible embarrassment to come.

And it did come. Bruce chortled with glee and turned to drag Kit off the bed, bedclothes and all. Bruce let out a whoop of triumph and reefed the bedclothes away so that Kit went sprawling naked on the floor.

Now furiously angry as well as embarrassed, Kit rolled over to try to get up, hotly aware of his lack of clothing.

"Leave me alone!" he shouted.

Then he gulped and swallowed. Standing in the doorway staring at him was his mother! And standing behind her with a wide-eyed and shocked look on her face was a middle-aged woman with a very large bosom and a string of pearls on her cleavage. Kit recognised her as being the secretary of some church charity his mother was involved in.

For a frozen second or two, Kit crouched there before he made a frantic effort to cover himself. Using both hands he tried to cover himself with the bedclothes, curling up as he did. A fiery flush of shame began to surge through him.

But Bruce had not yet registered their mother's presence and kept trying to drag the bundle of bedclothes away. Kit clung on with both hands, struggling to stay covered.

Whack!

Kit accidentally hit his head on the bedstead and was momentarily stunned. Squirming in the tangle of bedclothes and seeing stars from the blow, he struggled to stay covered, hotly aware that both his mother and the lady were obviously staring.

Flaming with embarrassment, Kit curled up and dragged the bedclothes over him. Tears began and waves of smarting pain lanced through his skull as the effect of the blow began to make itself felt.

"Ow! That hurt! Go away, Bruce, and leave me alone!" he cried.

Their mother now stepped into the room and Bruce became aware of her presence. His mouth dropped open, and he gobbled as she turned angrily to snap at him.

"Leave your little brother alone, Bruce! Go to your room! I will speak to you later. And stop bullying Chris!"

Bruce fled, his neck and face mottling with embarrassment as he did. Kit stayed curled up, now thankfully covered but hotly aware of his condition. It was so shameful! He wished the floor would open to swallow him. Sobbing, he rubbed at the back of his head.

His mother didn't help by coming to kneel beside him. "Are you alright, Chris?" she asked, reaching to examine the back of his head.

Kit could only nod, hotly aware that the church lady was still staring in the doorway. *I wish she'd go away!* he thought as more waves of shame and embarrassment pulsed through him.

"Yes Mum," he managed to mutter.

"Well go and have a shower and get dressed and then come and have breakfast. I will speak to Bruce," his mother said.

"Yes Mum," Kit replied, more shivers of shame passing through him.

To his relief, his mother stood up and left the room. As she closed the door, Kit heard her apologising to the church lady. For several minutes Kit lay there, sobbing and ashamed. As his emotions subsided and the pain lessened, he got up and untangled himself from his bedclothes.

And he did not want to go out through that doorway to face more embarrassment. Burning with shame he adjusted his shorts and found a top and slid it on. Then he tossed the bundle of bedclothes onto the badly rumpled bed and then stood there, tears of mortification and self-pity streaming down his cheeks.

For more than five minutes he just stood there, his emotions in turmoil as he battled with his pride and courage. Sadly he knew that he must pluck up the courage to go out and face the embarrassment—but it was so shameful!

At last he mustered the nerve and opened the door and made his way along the corridor to the bathroom. As he did, he heard his mother's voice coming from Bruce's bedroom and that caused him both more waves of embarrassment amid small spurts of satisfaction.

After showering and dressing, Kit made his way back to his bedroom—to find Bruce in there remaking his bed.

"Sorry little brother," Bruce mumbled, although he did not sound very sincere to Kit.

"Thanks," Kit muttered, not entirely satisfied but aware the apology was probably as good as he was going to get.

After tossing his PJs into the corner, he took a deep breath and headed for the kitchen. His mother was there preparing breakfast and the sight of her and the memory of what she had seen caused him to blush again.

She turned to face him. "Feeling better?" she queried.

"Yes Mum," Kit muttered, so ashamed he felt he was burning up.

A glance around showed no sign of the church lady, which was a small relief.

"Oh it's alright boy! I'm your mother," she cried. "It is only natural, and I see your father with no clothes on all the time. I know what men are like."

That was an embarrassing concept too and caused Kit to blush even more. He had never seen his father naked and, while he intellectually understood that his father and mother must have made love more than once to have three children, he found it a slightly disturbing concept.

"Yes Mum," was all he could reply.

A very trying week followed, during which Kit kept avoiding the bullies at school and becoming more friendly with Jocelyn during the lunch breaks. He kept on his physical training program and was confident he was steadily becoming stronger.

But not growing any bigger! he thought unhappily after he had yet again measured himself against the ruler on the wall and weighed himself on the bathroom scales.

On Tuesday evening he plucked up the courage to go to the PCYC. And, once again, he found that all his anxieties were for nothing. Sally put him in a nice group of three boys: Jason, Fred, and Harry. They were all a year older but were very friendly and quickly set about making him feel welcome and teaching him new skills. Kit went home feeling much happier and satisfied with having mastered yet another throw.

The remainder of the week slid by without any serious incidents. The only thing that stuck in his mind afterwards was after work on Thursday when he asked if the stolen truck had been located and he was told no.

Darren, who seemed to know about such things, said, "Usually when big trucks or top-of-the-range luxury cars are stolen, they are for a buyer who has already made all the arrangements. That Prime Mover would have been south of the Queensland border within 24 hours, probably before we even realised it was gone. Then it would have been 're-birthed' with a new VIN and paint job and number plates and paperwork and so on."

Which was depressing to think about—that were people in the world who were so immoral, so evil.

Chapter 15

THE FETE

All day Friday Kit was in a state of anxious excitement. All he could think about was the fancy-dress ball and how he might get out of it with dignity. At the back of his consciousness nagged tiny doubts over loyalty to Diana because he was constructing fantasies about Jocelyn.

As it was Friday night Kit got ready for Cadets, had a shower and his tea and his father drove him to the depot. It was a very ordinary night with lessons on how to splice and whip the ends of ropes to stop them fraying and on First Aid—bleeding.

Saturday was the 1st of May. Saturday night and Sunday passed in a general mood of dejection. Monday, being May Day, was a public holiday and Kit spent it at home. Then on Tuesday his mood had the added frisson of anxiety added to it when he sat on school assembly and the principal reminded them that the fete started on the next Friday.

Only five days, no six, to the fancy-dress ball on Saturday, Kit thought. *And I still don't have anyone to go with.*

Despite this he still could not bring himself to risk another rebuff from Diana and none of the other girls in his class were that attractive to him. Several times he toyed with asking Jocelyn, but again he did not want to risk a rebuff.

Besides, she is Year Ten and I am only Year Nine. She won't want her friends teasing her for having a younger boyfriend.

So there were bullies to avoid, peers to be rejected by and to be jealous of, and family worries to wear him down.

I don't think I will go to this fancy-dress ball, he thought.

That was an easy out, but he wasn't sure if his mother would allow it and just thinking such thoughts made him feel uncomfortable.

So after school Kit went to the business and Frank the foreman got him to sort and check lots of tools: spanners and wrenches and grease guns and so on. Afterwards at home, when his brothers weren't around, he did his heaves, sit-ups and push-ups, managing 21 and 22 easily. He was able to do five chin-the-bars easily.

At least I'm getting stronger, he consoled himself.

Wednesday was a virtual repeat of Tuesday with the exception that Kit had to run away and hide when the bullies began taunting him at lunch time. That did not help his self-esteem. And Jocelyn was not in the library, and when he did glimpse her and got a chance to speak she told him she was doing a practical assignment in the kitchen, cooking a sponge cake.

On Thursday there was a change of mood. The whole school was suddenly gripped by fete fever and several periods were devoted to making craft objects and to preparing to set up stalls. The tension and personal anxiety were added to by Kit's mother bringing home his Phantom costume after work.

Kit stared at the package aghast, memories of his embarrassment at the shop flooding his mind.

I can't possibly go wearing that, he thought. But he did not know how to avoid the situation. *Maybe I will just hide and not go,* he mused.

The only consolation was that she had found a brown plastic raincoat with a collar and belt that at least looked like the Phantom's greatcoat.

Friday arrived and Kit still had not formulated a sufficiently plausible plan or excuse. Feeling quite tense he took himself to school. That did not help as classes only took up the morning session and after that all efforts were devoted to preparing for the fete. His feelings weren't helped by the cheerful enthusiasm of most of those around him.

The fete was a major event in the school calendar. Its main purpose was to raise money for the school, but it was also a good time for the school to show itself off to the parents and community. It was also an excellent opportunity for students to be given responsible tasks and leadership roles. The fete ran for two nights. Friday night was a practice run. The event really got under way on Saturday afternoon and the main activities were on Saturday night, culminating in the school dance. That dance, this year the fancy-dress ball, now loomed massively on Kit's mind.

Virtually the whole school was roped into taking some part. There were the usual stalls with knock-em-downs, darts, archery, mini-golf, roundabouts, and rides for the small children, 'Fishing', 'Dunking' of teachers and so on. As well numerous food and drink stalls were set up: hot dogs, hamburgers, hot chips, a coffee shop, ice cream and soft drink stalls; plus the usual chocolate wheels and raffles. There were also several big displays. There was a large HO scale model railway which Kirk, Bronsky, and their tubby Year 8 mate, Roger, helped set up. There was a large Art and Craft display, and a model display.

Kit glanced at the models of aircraft, tanks, ships and 1:35 scale soldiers and warriors and was instantly jealous as there were some superb examples of craftsmanship on display.

Various school groups also had displays: Folk music, Drama Club, Bushwalking Club, Environment Club, Marine Studies, Music and various academic, and the Army Cadets. The Army Cadets had a stall where they displayed photos and army equipment. There was a science display that took a lot of preparation and setting up and Kit knew he should have been happy and looking forward to the event.

I would be if I wasn't so dejected over Diana. He had not seen her all afternoon, but she had been constantly in his thoughts. *Bloody fete! How can I get out of this?* he thought.

And there she was, with her friend, Fleur. Seeing Diana and Fleur happily wandering around socializing amid the preparations did nothing to ease his emotions. He was hotly aware that he had failed in his plan to have her as his partner at the ball.

At least I don't have to come tonight, he consoled himself. Friday night meant Navy Cadets.

But Cadets wasn't very interesting. Quite a number of cadets were absent, being students at his school and apparently having opted to attend the fete as well. Hearing that was painful as Kit found he really wanted to see Diana; and he fretted over whether she might be there. Instead, he found himself in the Boat Store checking the inventory for a Corsair and then checking ropes and splicing or whipping ones that needed attention.

Bedtime brought little rest. Jealousy began to gnaw at him as he fretted over who Diana might be going out with. To his surprise, the jealousy extended to Jocelyn.

He woke on Saturday morning feeling drained out and anxious. Breakfast and his morning routine were difficult but luckily there were then the usual chores. These took up most of the morning but even during them Kit continued to brood.

How can I get out of this? he fretted as each minute brought the fancy-dress ball closer.

But no plan came to mind and after a hasty lunch he took himself downstairs and did his physical exercises. They were easy and he managed 22 and 23 push-ups and sit-ups and even a dozen heaves and felt sure he could have done more.

Finally the moment he had been dreading arrived. At 11am his mother called, "Time for you boys to get ready to go to the fete."

To Kit's surprise, it was Bruce who began to object. "Aw Mum! I don't want to go," he grumbled.

Kit badly wanted to add his voice to the appeal but was also curious to see how his brother fared, so he remained silent and watched. His mother shook her head and pursed her lips.

"You are all going! This is a charity event, and you can't just pay all that money and not turn up. The tickets cost me $25 each and you will all donate and also buy some raffle tickets."

"Aw Mum!"

"No! You are going! Now go and have a shower and get dressed," their mother snapped.

So after lunch Kit showered and dressed, then carefully placed the costume he was going to wear to the dance in a large carry bag. With the felt hat and overcoat it made quiet a bundle, and he felt very self-conscious as he carried it out to the car. His mother drove him and Bruce to school at 1pm. His father was already there, in charge of the Magnetic Fishing Lucky Dip. As soon as he arrived, Kit placed his costume in the classroom being operated as a cloak room by 10C then had a quick look around.

To Kit's intense disappointment, there was no sign of Diana. Instead, there was an unpleasant moment when he saw three of the Year 12 bullies: Burford, Harvey, and Macnamara, lounging about with a group of loutish youths. He avoided them by hiding in the crowd and kept walking. The last thing he wanted was trouble.

After twenty minutes he found Andrew at the army cadet display, yarning to some of the army cadets who were in their disruptive pattern camouflage cadet uniforms.

"G'day Kit. How's tricks?" Andrew asked.

"Fine. You here to spy on the opposition?" Kit replied.

Andrew snorted. "Opposition! This lot! We can beat them any day. We don't need to spy on them," he replied loudly.

At once all the army cadets within hearing reacted. "Oy oy!" called a big sergeant. "You mind your manners, Collins. Any cheek and you belly button cadets will be out on your ear."

"Belly button cadets?" Kit echoed, and immediately wished he hadn't.

The army cadet sergeant chortled and then grinned. To Kit's added mystification, he suddenly swung his right hand across his waist and then back in an obvious saluting movement.

"Navel cadets, ya get it?" he explained in an insulting tone.

A dozen army cadets burst into laughter and Kit saw Andrew purse his lips and glance at him with annoyance. In an attempt to make a suitable riposte, Kit gave what he hoped looked like a contemptuous shrug and said, "My grandad told me that when World War Two broke out, his father and an uncle both decided to join up. His uncle said that he had half a mind to join the army, to which his dad replied, 'That's all you'll need!'

Andrew grinned and nodded approval and a few of the army cadets also smiled. A few were obviously annoyed and one growled back to "Watch it!"

Unable to think of any more smart comments, Kit turned and took himself away. He continued with his quest to find Diana. But he was disappointed. There was a large crowd, growing larger by the minute and many were girls but there was no sign of her.

Feeling distinctly down and very lonely, he went on a slow tour of all the exhibits. This took him through rooms full of displays of student work, science experiments, paintings, sculptures, photographs, and a video display. For a while he sat at the back of the many rows of chairs which had been placed on the grass quadrangle and watched dancing displays on the main stage: Scottish, Irish, Modern, and Tap. He enjoyed looking at the girls but seeing their beautiful shapes just made him even more conscious that he did not have a girlfriend.

An hour was then spent helping run the Magnetic Fishing stall during the times he had volunteered for. While doing that, Kit noted two young girls, Year 8s by the look of them, wandering by wearing puppy dog costumes. One wore a brown dog suit and the other a white one with black spots on it.

'Spot' or 'Snoopy', Kit thought.

Then he sneered, thinking it was silly to walk around in costume before the fancy-dress ball. But that certainly reminded him that the time to change was fast approaching, and he felt his stomach churn with an anxiety he did not want to name as fear.

Once again, he cast around for some plan to avoid the ball but then he saw his mother in the distance. She was talking to another lady, but the sight sent his hopes sinking. He knew that the plan was for everyone in costume to do a 'Grand Parade' so that the parents and visitors could see them and so they could vote on the best costumes.

And then it was time. *Oh no! I'll hide and not go,* he thought.

But he knew there was no honourable way out, so he steeled himself for more humiliation and made his unhappy way to the cloak room to retrieve his costume. Feeling like a French aristocrat on the way to the guillotine, he walked to the changerooms.

Here he had miscalculated—as had many others. Time became the problem. There weren't enough change booths in the room allocated for it, and many male students were busy just changing out in the main room. There was absolutely no way Kit was going to try to wriggle into that Phantom costume with everyone watching, so he waited. Then a booth became available but as he walked towards it a Year 11 boy just strode across and pushed him back.

"You wait your turn, scrawny," the youth said, which really hurt.

Finally, with only fifteen minutes to the start time for the 'Grand Parade', Kit got into a booth. By then he was in a lather of anxiety, and the perspiration made it even harder to pull the Lycra on over his damp skin. He tugged and struggled and became quickly very upset. But he did get the suit on. But one glance in the full-length mirror against the wall convinced him he must keep that greatcoat on!

Oh my God! I do look really scrawny! he thought.

Tears of misery formed and he contemplated taking the suit back off and slinking away into the night. But a stubborn streak held him there and after a few minutes of silent self-pity he tugged the long trousers and greatcoat on. That looked a bit better. Only then did it occur to him that he could have worn a long-sleeved shirt and tie. Blushing with shame at his own error, he shrugged and moved to pull up the Lycra hood. Pulling the mask and head covering on had a peculiar feel that did not help his emotions. And the stretch mask over his eyes made it hard to see and he felt foolish. But the hat and sunglasses then added anonymity. And it was five minutes to!

Almost hyperventilating with anxiety, Kit packed his other clothes in his bag and hurried out to deposit them with the students in charge. By then the room was almost empty, just a few boys still hurrying to change. Luckily there were none from his class and nobody made any comment. Almost running he hurried downstairs and along to the hall. As he did, he put on the dark glasses and immediately slowed down. The dark glasses made it even harder to see in the areas of shadow. For a few moments he considered taking them off again but then decided they helped give him some sort of anonymity.

The Grand Parade was forming up outside the hall and Kit was astounded at the number of people and the noise. Clearly the fancy dress theme was very popular and a big success. Everywhere he looked there were different costumes. Many were so good he could not recognise the wearers. And there were teachers in costume as well as students. Dozens of parents, including his own, were standing talking and watching. Kit became even more flustered as a loudspeaker announced the start of the parade.

Oh! Where is my class? he thought.

Real anxiety began to grip him.

Chapter 16

THE FANCY-DRESS BALL

K it found his path blocked and he came to a gasping standstill. For a moment his vision went blurry and he stood there with his chest heaving, torn by near panic and misery.

Oh, why have I done this to myself? he thought.

Then he steadied himself, took off his dark glasses and stood studying the scene. He knew from briefings that the parade was arranged in year levels and by classes, but there were so many people milling around it was hard to work out the pattern. Then Kit remembered that the parade was to form up in reverse order, the Year 7s lining both sides near the door, then the Year 8s and so on. That way the younger students would get to see the entire parade go past them.

And there was Mr Ritter, Kit's Maths B teacher, now dressed as the Emperor Julius Ceasar complete with toga and laurel wreath, but with a clipboard and loud hailer.

"Year 8D, move here," he instructed.

Knowing that his class—9A—would be next and on the other side, Kit put the dark glasses back on and pushed his way through the throng. This earned him a few scowls and shoves from bigger students, but he got a glimpse of a face he knew: Graham Kirk from 9B. Graham was dressed as a Napoleonic Wars 'redcoat' with long-sleeved red shirt with a dozen horizontal gold ribbons sewn across the front, long blue trousers with red stipes sewn down each side and, on his head, a shiny black 'Shako' made of painted cardboard with a red plume and gold badge and braiding.

Next to him was Andrew, dressed Kit realised as Captain Cook—or an 18th Century naval officer—white longs, white shirt and a blue coat with gold buttons and adornments. The blue bicorne hat with gold braiding looked particularly good until Kit got close. Then he saw that it was only painted cardboard. But it was still good enough to make Kit jealous and to wish he had come as a pirate.

That wish was instantly reinforced when he joined the group and Stephen, dressed as a French artist with beret and false moustache, said,

"What are you supposed to be, Kit? Are you Al Capone or some American gangster?"

Kit blushed and shook his head. "I'm the Ghost Who Walks," he said.

"Who?" a cowboy—Blake it was—asked.

"The Phantom, you know, when he's in his town clothes. The Ghost Who Walks," Kit explained.

A clown standing next to them burst out laughing. "The Phantom! The bloody Ghost Who walks! You! You look more like one of those old winos who sleeps on park benches!"

The insult burned! Kit pursed his lips to endure the laughter. He turned to move away and blundered into a very thin girl dressed as a fairy. Both nearly tripped and they clung to each other to regain their balance.

"Sorry!" Kit blurted, still having trouble seeing through the dark glasses and the tears misting his eyes.

It was Elise, a skinny wisp of a girl in his class. She had the fairest of fair hair, braided in two long plaits, and wore a pale green pastel-shaded dress of some sort of gauze. Green plastic wings with yellow and light green patterns on them completed the look.

"Are you alright?" she queried, holding tightly to his left arm.

Kit nodded and, for something to say in his confusion asked, "Are you an elf or a pixie?"

"I'm Tinker Belle, the fairy," she said.

There was a loud laugh next to them and Kit looked to see a Jedi Knight—he thought it was Nolan from 9C—who sneered under his plastic Darth Vadar mask and said, "Then Walker is with the right group. He's a fairy."

That hurt too. Kit went to reply but Elise tugged his sleeve and pulled him away. "Leave them," she hissed. "Just ignore them."

Easier said than done! But the classes were being marshalled quickly. Another teacher came long, ordering them into lines: Miss Tate, their Maths A teacher, dressed as 'Wonder Woman'.

And very much looking the part, Kit thought, admiring her very shapely female form. She was a very attractive young woman in her twenties, nicknamed 'Miss Tart' because of stories about her behaviour.

Tina, dressed as a French 'matelot': white sailor cap with a red pompom, in a white sailor suit, moved to stand beside him on his left. Beyond her was Gareth dressed as Frankenstein's Monster.

Kit overheard Vincent, dressed as a doctor, say to him, "You didn't even need a costume mate!"

I wish I could think of witty things like that to say, Kit thought.

As things settled into orderly rows of students stretching off into the school yard, Kit was able to relax, look around and to take note of details. He had been initially overwhelmed by all the cowboys and pirates but now saw that there were enough 'Imperial Storm Troopers' and robots to provide the 'extras' for a Star Wars movie.

Stepping slightly forward, Kit scanned his own class and was amazed and very pleased. Of the thirty in the class at least twenty were present. And they had made a big effort with their costumes. Peter Bronsky had come as a Cossack (That figures!), Harriet, a very tall girl, as a basketballer (Which she is!), Yin Foo as Ming the Merciless or Ghengis Khan, Angus as a Scotsman (Which he was) in kilt and plaid, Rhonda as a nurse, Merv as Batman, and Louise as Cat Woman.

And Gwen Copeland is a Princess, he noted.

Gwen was a natural for the part. With her golden hair now crowned with a tiara, her shapely figure displayed in a pale blue dress with gold belt and with gold sandals on her feet she looked just so good!

Then Kit saw Rowena, the beautiful Rowena, and he sucked his breath in. She was Cleopatra.

And she is beautiful!

Then he sucked his breath in again with shock and then envy. Burrows had come as Tarzan, wearing only a sort of loin cloth and sandals and necklace of some sort of animal teeth. It was the brevity of his costume that surprised him but the broad chest and rippling muscles that elicited the jealousy.

And there were more daring costumes. Elise pulled at his sleeve and pointed. "Oh look at them! The teachers must order them to get dressed!"

The couple in question were Lorna, wearing only the skimpiest of bikinis and a cloth wrap, and Naomi who was an Arab Harem Girl with a tiny bra barely covering her splendid bosom and the usual see-through baggy pants. But they weren't told to cover up, although Kit noted a few raised eyebrows and frowns among the teachers and parents. Lorna, Kit now learned, was acting as Stephen's artist's model. Naomi teamed up with a Year 11 boy dressed as an Arab Prince or Indian Rajah with turban and equally baggy pants held in place by a broad blue silk cummerbund.

Mr Page, their Geography teacher, dressed as a 19th Century explorer with 'solar topee' and leather leggings, came to check they were ready. And then the procession began. It was led by the principal, dressed in his academic gown and 'mortar board' cap. He so looked the part of an old-fashioned headmaster that a wave of spontaneous applause broke out.

He was followed by several teachers and then the Year 12s. Only then did Kit realise that Elise was still clinging to his arm. He blushed but then shrugged. Her class nickname was 'The Stick Insect', but it was still nice to have someone who liked him! He gave his attention to the passing parade.

That passing parade then provided both entertainment and amazement. Among the Year 12s, Kit recognised (sometimes with some difficulty) two of the army cadet CUOs: Mike Masters as Napoleon and Sheila Sherry as Marie Antoinette; and the other two as a Roman tribune in golden armour and Coralie Bates as a Roman lady.

Then Kit gasped and gaped. Anastasia, the most beautiful of all the Year 12 girls (in the general opinion of the male student body) was dressed (only just) as a Tahitian dancer—grass skirt, two coconut shells over her breasts held on by a piece of rope, a lei around her neck and flowers in her hair. She was smiling and wiggling and obviously enjoying the attention. Kit was instantly smitten by lust and jealousy.

Oh! If only!

She was followed by a Year 11 boy dressed as a gorilla and the contrast was such as to cause a ripple of laughter and the usual comments about not needing a costume. There was then a succession of astronauts, Goths, Count Dracula's, cowboys, pirates, and various superheroes.

The Year 10s began filing past and Kit got another shock. Diana was there on the arm of her brother. She was dressed in a very pale blue, long gauzy dress and carried a tiny silver bow and arrow, and it was only when Peter Bronsky muttered that she might be Diana the Huntress, he recognised her from the ancient Greek myths. To Kit she looked just so beautiful, and he sighed—but she did not even glance in his direction, leaving him feeling hurt yet again.

But then he got a bit of satisfaction. Piper came along dressed all in black as a Nazi SS officer and the Dru Brothers beside him as German Waffen SS. They were stopped by Mr Ritter who pointed to the Swastika armband on Piper's left sleeve.

"Take that off," Mr Ritter ordered.

"Why? It's part of my costume," Piper replied defiantly, a slight hint of insolence in his voice.

Mr Ritter leaned closer, anger showing on his face. "Because it is against the law, that's why! And cover up all those badges with swastikas on them." He pointed to the eagle badges on their jackets and helmets.

"How will we do that?" Piper retorted.

"Tape, band-aids, I don't care, but do not go in until that is done," Mr Ritter snapped.

Muttering with bad grace, the trio turned and pushed through the crowd. As they did, Kit grinned with delight, only to find Ricardo—a pirate—right in his face.

"Wot you grinnin' about, midget? Eh? We might pulp ya, ya little turd." Ricardo then shoved past him, nearly knocking him over as he did.

Elise steadied Kit and he gave her a grateful grin, which she returned. But then Mr Ritter started 9A moving. Kit watched Year 8 Willy Williams, an Air Cadet, dressed as a World War 1 pilot, take the hand of his girlfriend, a Year 7 named Marjorie, who was dressed as a gypsy fortune teller. Marjorie was a pudgy girl and freckles and scraggly hair, but the sight still made Kit envious.

I wish I had a girlfriend.

And then his class was moving and he found he was holding Elise by the hand—but was not sure if he took her hand or she his. He found his heart rate rapidly increasing and this shot up even higher as they went through the doorway into the hall. He was enveloped by the environment of sparkling lights from a mirror ball and the sound of march music.

Kit began to enjoy himself. The sound and spectacle were both inspiring and he smiled and even chuckled. He even kept hold of Elise's hand and returned her smile from time to time. The long snake of costumed people circled around past the stage where the musicians were busy, and then past a series of tables where four VIPs sat: the Deputy Principal, Mrs Massey (dressed as Matron), and an elderly couple in old-fashioned 'evening dress'.

"They are the judges," Peter said, waving as they went past.

Kit nodded. He had guessed that but also knew that the parents could vote as well using ballot boxes and voting slips that were placed around the room.

The procession was so long that the Year 8s and Year 7s had not come in the door before the head of the parade was passing the judges again. Miss Tate took over leading them and guided them inside so that the head of the 'snake' went inside and began to curl on itself. That way Kit and his class walked around the room twice before the last Year 7 (another pixie) had walked past the judges.

The marching music then stopped and the MC—Don from Year 11, dressed as Elvis—told them all to dance with their current partner and the music changed immediately. Kit danced with Elise, getting quite hot in his greatcoat as he did. When the music stopped, he was left wondering what to do as Elise was standing looking hopefully at him. Luckily, the entire audience format dissolved as people moved into friendship and social groups and everyone shifted to the sides of the hall, leaving the centre of the hall empty as a dance floor. Kit walked towards his friends. To his mild annoyance, Elise moved with him.

Kit stayed with a group which included Andrew, Blake, and Peter. Cordial and soft drinks were available, but what Kit really wanted to do was dance with Diana. So he stood there looking hopefully around. The next dance began—another fast and modern (The program was to alternate with slower 'traditional' dances as well, these still being taught during PE).

While he stood there watching, people kept asking Kit who he was supposed to be. Most suggested an American gangster of the 1930s which he found annoying. Several times he took off his hat, sunglasses and scarf to show them the head and mask part of his costume. And he was sweating. That was unpleasant and he began to worry that the Lycra might smell as he perspired.

The MC then called for a drum roll and once it had ensured silence informed them that the winners of the prizes for the best costumes would now be announced. The Deputy Principal, Mr Fitzgerald, dressed as he usually was, made the announcements. They were:

Yr 7 Robin Hood & Rainbow Fairy
Yr 8 Mr Squiggle & Snow White
Yr 9 Cleopatra (Rowena) & Genghis Khan
Yr 10, Captain Hook & Little Red Riding Hood
Yr 11 Crusader Knight & Nurse
Yr 12 Napoleon & Marie Antoinette

Teachers Miss Tait & Mr Ritter

Best Overall—Rowena as Cleopatra & Mike Masters as Napoleon

Lucky colour Blue—Gwen Copeland

Lucky door Couple (Yr 8s—Teletubbies)

Another dance was announced, a progressive barn dance. Kit liked that idea. He had been taught in PE how to do it.

And I get to meet a lot of girls in a very short time, he told himself.

So he led Elise out and then danced. And he did briefly meet a lot of girls—but mostly it was not a rewarding experience. Most were taller than him and plainly were not interested in him. Many of his attempts to strike up a conversation just ended in faltering embarrassment.

That dance ended and the dancers ebbed to the sides again. The MC called for 'gentlemen to select their partners for the next dance' implying it was to be a slow dance. At that moment, Kit saw Diana standing on her own not far away.

Now is my chance, he thought.

Taking a few deep breaths he plucked up his courage and started walking towards her. As he did, his vision narrowed down to just her and he barely noticed the people he dodged around or walked past.

When he was only a few paces away from Diana, she turned and noticed him. He saw her eyes widen and a frown form on her brow. Only when he stopped a couple of paces from her did her mouth open.

"Oh! Oh hello. Kit, isn't it?"

That hurt. *She still isn't sure who I am!* he thought.

Kit nodded. "Yes, I..." he started to say.

But before he could open his mouth to get the next word out Carstairs pushed between them and shoved Kit back.

"What do you want, midget?" he snarled.

"To speak to your sister, thank you!" Kit replied as frostily as he could.

Carstairs sneered and looked him up and down. Kit was aware of others moving to stand beside Carstairs—people in black.

"Well ya can't! I told ya to stay away from her."

"She can talk to who she likes!" Kit retorted.

He was rewarded by Diana pushing between her brother and the person in black; Piper in his SS uniform Kit now recognised.

"That's right!" Diana snapped. "I do my own choosing, thank you!"

Carstairs curled his lip. "Suit yerself, sis, but I reckon you shouldn't talk to this dwarf."

Kit went to speak but Piper beat him to it, calling loudly, "What are you supposed to be anyway, Walker? A drunk who sleeps on park benches?"

Kit burned at the insults and swallowed. "I'm the Phantom," he croaked. He started to undo the buttons on the front of the greatcoat.

"The what?" Carstairs cried in disbelief.

Deeply angered, Kit almost shouted back, "The Phantom! You know, the Ghost Who Walks." As he did, he undid the last of the buttons, meaning to open the greatcoat to give a brief glimpse of the purple Phantom costume underneath.

As he started to open the coat, Piper laughed and called, "Don't look, Diana! He's probably one of those dirty old men who flash at little girls down at the park."

That really hurt! But Kit had pulled the coat open by then. Carstairs looked him up and down and then sneered and bellowed with laughter.

"Ghost Who Walks! You, you weedy little runt! You aren't a superhero! You are just a freak of a midget!"

Kit glared back in a red mist of hurt, dimly aware of a fleeting look of sympathy on Diana's face.

Then Carstairs stepped forward and pushed at him. "Clear off, Creep Who Walks, and stay away from my sister!"

Kit tried to keep his balance but staggered and then went over backwards. He landed hard on his bum, his arms going out into a 'breakfall' to protect spine and head. But he still landed hard on his back and it winded him. The coat billowed open, and Kit was aware of purple legs and shiny black Lycra boots waving in the air. He was also very aware of the great shout of laughter that went up from those watching.

Burning with embarrassment, Kit squirmed on his back, trying to close the coat while at the same time rolling onto his front to get up. A feeling of total humiliation scorched his self-esteem as he realised that what looked like half the school was watching, and many of them laughing!

Chapter 17

HUMILIATION AND SATISFACTION

Kit was so mortified he could barely see. Tears blurred his already obscured vision, and he felt so ashamed he just wished the floor would open up and swallow him. He could never remember being so humiliated in front of so many in his life. For a few seconds he just lay there on the dance floor, half-winded by the fall but even more stunned psychologically.

Burning with embarrassment, he rolled over onto his front, horribly conscious that tears were now springing from his eyes. A total hush had fallen on the crowd, and people who had not witnessed the original scene now turned to look. Some stepped back so as not to be involved, leaving him even more isolated and obvious.

There were raised voices but what they were saying Kit did not care. His mind was now a mush of hurt emotions and shame. But there was just a residual spark of pride that made him realise that the costume hat and glasses had come off and were lying on the floor. He got to his knees and reached out to pick them up.

As he did, Piper pushed him with his boot. Kit was sent crashing on his side. He heard another gust of laughter, which scarified his soul. More loud voices and shouts. Kit clutched his glasses and hat and rolled away and got to his feet. For a moment he stood there, shaking his head and blinking and feeling like a mouse surrounded by cats.

And there, just visible through the mist of tears, was Piper, reaching out to push him again.

"Clear out, Walker!" he snarled.

And there was that hand and arm, just as Sally had demonstrated in Judo. Letting go of both glasses and hat, Kit reached out and just did what he had been taught. A look of astonishment and then agony appeared on Piper's face as Kit twisted him around. Without really thinking about it, Kit lifted Piper over his hip and down he went.

There was a moment of stunned silence and then a loud cheer went up. Kit found himself staring into Diana's eyes. She looked astonished, and then he thought he glimpsed a little smile before she shook her head and turned away.

Teachers appeared: Mr Page, the Geography teacher, Mr Conkey, Miss McLeod. They at once took control and moved Kit and Piper apart. Kit was moved off to the side of the hall by Mr Conkey and Miss McLeod and told to calm down. What Kit really wanted to do was to just run away. He was so upset he could barely hold his emotions in check.

Mr Conkey stood between him and most of the crowd. "What was that all about, Chris?" he asked.

Kit didn't really want to say as that might mean repeating the horrible words that still burned into the very core of his very being. He shrugged and then muttered, "They were teasing me, sir."

"I guessed that," Mr Conkey said, nodding and looking grim. "I presume they were making unkind comments on your size."

Kit nodded. "Yes sir, and about my costume," he agreed.

Miss McLeod now spoke, "What exactly is it?"

Mr Conkey gave her a surprised look. "Why the Phantom of course."

"The Phantom?" Miss McLeod queried.

Mr Conkey smiled. "Miss McLeod! Your education has been sadly neglected. Have you never read a *Phantom* comic, the famous 'Ghost Who Walks'?"

It was as though a lightbulb had come on in Miss McLeod's head. "Oh yes! My brothers used to read them, and my dad."

Kit was somewhat relieved and also mildly amused, which calmed him down. Mr Conkey then said, "I actually saw Carstairs push you over, so what followed with him and Piper was just you defending yourself."

"It was, sir. I didn't hit him," Kit said, anxious to avoid the suspensions and expulsions that sometimes followed for people fighting.

"I note that. He tried to shove you, and you pushed him away and he fell over," Mr Conkey answered.

Kit was about to shake his head and explain the throw and then it dawned on him that Mr Conkey was actually telling him the words to use if the matter went further. A little glow of gratitude warmed him.

"Thank you, sir. Can I go now?" he asked.

"Yes, just stay away from those bullies if you can," Mr Conkey said.

Kit nodded. He would certainly try to do that, but it was very hard in the school environment. He was about to turn away when Elise stepped in front of him and held out his hat and costume glasses. She had a small, shy smile and was looking at him in what he thought might be a hopeful way.

He did not really want to encourage her, was in fact afraid he might be teased for associating with her, but he was also grateful, so he took the hat and glasses and put them on.

"Thanks," he said. Then he turned to go.

"Are you leaving?" Elise queried, walking beside him.

All Kit really wanted to do was sneak away and hide, to lick his mental wounds in private, to somehow escape the public humiliation. But now he had to rethink that.

People will really think I am a coward if I just slink away, he thought.

But he felt he needed to be honest with her. "I was thinking of doing that," he agreed.

Elise shook her head. "Don't. Don't let the bullies win. They were really horrible, and I hope they get expelled. They pick on all us… us… little kids all the time," she explained.

That brought Kit to a standstill. They were near a table loaded with paper cups and cordial jugs, so he gestured to them and said, "Want a drink?"

"Yes please."

So he stayed. To his mixed annoyance and pleasure, Elise stayed with him. He was joined by Andrew and Blake.

"Bloody good throw that, Kit," Andrew said.

Blake nodded. "The jungle trembles when the Phantom is angry," he added, using one of the famous quotes from the comics.

That surprised Kit as he did not think Blake was the sort of person to read *Phantom* comics. But he did manage a smile.

More people arrived to join the group: Graham Kirk, Peter, Stephen, and Roger and several girls. Graham also shook his hand and congratulated him.

"It was bloody good to see that mongrel Piper get thrown on his arse."

Peter nodded agreement. "Do you do Judo or something, Kit?" he asked.

That embarrassed Kit too as it was something he had wanted to keep secret, but he managed a nod. He fancied he noted a tiny flicker of respect on some faces as he did.

"The Ghost Who Walks has many skills," he managed to say in a casual tone.

That provoked a small gale of laughter, mostly friendly in its tone. Elise gave his left hand a squeeze and only then did he realise he was holding hers. He did not remember taking it but somehow it felt good, and he kept holding it.

That led to him actually dancing with her and then spending the remainder of the evening with her. As he did, he noted a few unfriendly faces and Piper and his cronies scowling at him. Carstairs also sneered at him, but it was his sister that Kit was really interested in and she was nowhere to be seen.

Thus he was stung by jealousy when he saw Diana walk back into the hall a few minutes later with one of the Year 12 boys.

Has she been outside with Metcalfe? he thought.

He pictured her and Metcalfe walking out on the oval in the darkness— or worse smooching and cuddling. Knowing that was exactly what he wanted to do added another dimension to his emotions.

To add a fine touch of irony was the feel of Elise still holding his hand and transmitting through her face, eyes and body language that she would almost certainly be glad for him to take her for a walk in the moonlight! It all made him very confused, and he continued to experience very mixed emotions all night. Shame, embarrassment, humiliation, satisfaction, jealousy and even the first stirrings of affection and lust all swirled in him. It was a very mixed-up boy who mumbled a goodnight to Elise at midnight. He was sure she wanted him to say something more and he even suspected, from her hopeful look, that she might like a kiss.

He was driven home by his parents, who had not witnessed any of the incident. Kit did not want to mention it either, so he steered the conversation to the costumes. Personally he thought that 'Buzz Lightyear' in Year 8 should have won the prize for that year level.

Alone in his bed he replayed the evening in his mind and found that the memories gave him a mixture of embarrassment and satisfaction. To his surprise, the image that kept forming in his mind was of Elise and he wondered how he had never noticed her before.

Sunday was a 'down' day emotionally. Failure to impress Diana combined with shame over his very public humiliation was coupled with doubts over Elise. Now he regretted encouraging her, fearing to be teased over that as well. But he had to admit that he did like her, and he had certainly appreciated her support the night before. The day was taken up with a late breakfast and then chores: mowing the lawn, washing the dog, washing the Phantom costume so his mother could return it; finishing a homework assignment, helping weed the garden and cleaning up his room.

That night he was in something of an emotional ferment. Mostly this had to do with anxiety about what might happen at school the next day, but there was also a worrying degree of arousal and fantasising about girls—his thoughts now dominated by hopes over Diana but including some more realistic imaginings about him and Elise.

Worry about what the day might bring flooded his mind when he woke on Monday morning. The fears grew until he felt quite ill. With an effort he hid this from the other family members. There was a temptation to tell his mother he was sick so he could stay home, but even forming such notions made him feel even worse. In his heart he knew he would despise himself as a coward if he did, so he 'sucked it up' and put on a bold face.

And at school there was teasing. But there were also a few compliments, some genuine and some backhanded. One such was from Jocelyn. She stopped him in the playground at Little Lunch and said, "I thought you said you were going to come to the fancy-dress ball as one of the Bandar Pygmy People."

That allusion to an incident after school a few weeks before caused Kit to blush with shame and regret. It also hurt as it was what his brother had unkindly suggested.

All he could do was shrug and say, "No, I decided to go as the Ghost Who Walks." Seeing a blank look on her face he added, "That is what the Phantom is called when he puts on ordinary clothes and comes into town in disguise."

Jocely nodded but he still wasn't sure if she had understood. But she then grinned and said, "It was really good to see you put that bully, Piper, on the deck. He's a really cruel mongrel and deserved it."

Kit agreed with that, but it also reminded him that Piper might be the sort of person who would want revenge. So he spent the remainder of the day keeping a good lookout and sticking close to his friends. In fact he did not see Piper or his cronies all day and that was almost as worrying.

Nor did he see Piper or any of the bullies the next day. Keeping a good lookout, Kit found tiring but he made the effort. Instead, he spent much of the day chatting to Elise, who attached herself to the group and stayed around, despite several fairly unkind and blunt hints from others that she was not wanted. And when the others realised that she was obviously interested in Kit, there were a steady flow of teasing comments. To this she turned up her nose and snapped back, but Kit burned with shame as some of the hurtful comments implied that she was all he could manage to get as a girlfriend.

But he did note that she was actually quite pretty, and a bit shapely. He also realised she was courageous and that she had a strong personality.

And very kind eyes, he decided.

But the day left him wondering how to get her to lose interest, and then ashamed of such ungracious and ungrateful thoughts.

That afternoon he went to work at the truck depot and then in the evening he did his exercises, easily managing 27 push-ups, sit-ups and 20 chest heaves and chin the bars. To his intense satisfaction, he noted not only that he was growing stronger but that he was also developing some obvious arm and chest muscles. A tape measure informed him that his chest had grown by at least a centimetre, so that it was actually bigger than his waist—65cm against 64.

Encouraged, he measured himself against the wall chart and was even more pleased to note that he had grown almost a centimetre in the previous two months.

155cm, he thought, but then he remembered that most of his male peers stood 165cm and some even 170cm. *I might end up normal,* he thought hopefully.

And then Wednesday brought disaster. Morning lessons went as usual and Kit saw no sign of the bullies at morning break. Nor did he see Elise. When lunch break came around, he still had not seen her and realised he was starting to enjoy her company. So he went walking around the school looking for her. First, he visited the library but the only girl there he knew was Jocelyn. To his own mild surprise he found he did not want to sit with her. So he walked out into the main central part of the school— straight into trouble.

He was standing in the middle of the main open area looking around when he was suddenly grabbed by his right ear. This was twisted painfully and he tried to pull away, only to be whacked by an open hand on the other side of his head.

"Stand still, shitface!" a boy snarled.

It was Ricardo. He twisted the ear some more and Kit cried out in pain, putting his own hands up to grip Ricardo's to ease the pain.

"Ow! Stop it! That hurts!" he cried.

"Oh it hurts! Of course it does, ya stupid twit!" Ricardo taunted.

Jeering, mocking laughter came from Piper and the Dru Brothers who were with him. Their sneering faces filled Kit's vision.

By now he was both scared and angry. Once again, he was being painfully humiliated in public and there was no teacher in sight to stop it. And he was aware of other students watching and he burned with embarrassment. Which quickly turned to anger and then to furious rage. And now he had both hands gripping Ricardo's right hand and wrist.

The temptation was too much. Again a Judo lesson flashed across his mind, and he acted on it. He pulled at Ricardo's little finger, making the bully cry out and let go. But even as he did, Kit gripped tightly and then swung down and under, swinging himself around as he did. Ricardo was caught by surprise and a second later he was facing back towards his cronies with his right arm twisted up behind him.

"Hey! Ouch! Hey!" Ricardo cried, half in anger but mostly in surprise.

Kit did not wait. Seeing the shocked and surprised looks on the bullies' faces he let go and shoved as hard as he could. Ricardo stumbled forward, cannoning into Wally Dru and Piper. They let out cries of alarm and also stumbled. Piper fell flat on his back and Ricardo and Wally Dru both staggered and just managed to avoid a fall. Only Ernie Dru was left standing and he just gaped and blinked with surprise through his glasses.

Kit knew he should run, that he had made the bullies really angry. But his own surprise at putting a 'Half-Nelson' on Ricardo was also being replaced with a mixture of satisfaction and anger.

"Bastards! Leave me alone!" he shouted.

By then Ricardo had recovered his balance and was obviously furious. "Little shit! You pay for dat!" he shouted. He sprang forward.

Once again Kit thought of running but he did not think he could get away, so he did the unexpected. He jumped forward, grabbing Ricardo's shirt front with both hands. Ricardo began punching at his head with both hands, a veritable rain of blows, screaming while he did.

Kit was half stunned but stayed sufficiently in control of his thoughts to act on them. Bending his left leg, he slammed his right shoe up into Ricardo's stomach and at the same time he threw himself backwards, keeping a tight grip as he did. The move caught Ricardo completely by surprise, and the next moment Kit was also surprised, mostly that his move had succeed and partly at how easy it had been. He went down on his back and catapulted Ricardo over his head. The bully went flying through the air in a tumbling somersault so that he crashed onto the pavers on his back a couple of metres from Kit.

Kit rolled over and sprang to his feet, fists raised, in time to see Ricardo rolling around on his back and gasping for breath. The fall had obviously winded him. A feeling of intense satisfaction flooded through Kit for a few seconds. It was fine revenge for when Ricardo had picked him up by one hand and shaken his money out! Fear then took its place, and he went to run before Ricardo got to his feet.

But before he could, hands grabbed him from behind and a punch whacked into his kidneys. Piper had his left arm and was hitting with his right fist and Ernie Dru had hold of his right arm. Wally Dru appeared, fists raised. Kit braced for a beating, dimly aware that hundreds of students were now watching.

"Stop that! Stop that fighting!" shouted a teacher. Mr Collier, one of the Manual Arts teachers appeared.

Ernie Dru shook his head. "We aren't fighting, sir. We are stopping Walker from kicking our friend."

Kit nearly choked at the injustice of the statement. "That's not true… aaargh!" he began to say, but Piper twisted his arm. "Ow! You are hurting me!" Kit cried.

"Let him go!" Mr Collier snapped. Both Piper and Ernie Dru did so, but not before Ernie Dru gave him a sharp pinch. "He came up and started calling us names, sir," he said.

"I did not!" Kit cried, stung by the false accusation.

He looked angrily around and saw that Ricardo was now on his feet, glaring at him. And the look in his eyes and the expression on his face boded no good for Kit.

I have hurt his pride, he thought, both regretting doing so but pleased he had thrown the bully. *And I am in trouble now if there aren't any witnesses game to tell the truth.*

Chapter 18

SUSPENDED

A surge of self-pity began to well up in Kit, starting low down in his stomach. But a burst of cheering and hand clapping interrupted it. Kit blinked and looked around—and then gaped. He had been dimly aware that other students had been watching the fight but to his astonishment he now saw that there were hundreds. They were standing in solid masses on all sides, and they were looking at him and clapping.

It dawned on him in a burst of emotion like a starburst of joy that they were actually applauding him! He saw Andrew grinning, and he called out, "Well done, Kit! That showed the bullies who's best!"

Kit gaped and shook his head in disbelief. *They are cheering me!* he thought.

A warm glow of pride now mingled with the satisfaction of having thrown the bullies—and anxiety over what might now happen. He knew well that fighting was against the school rules and that there were nearly always serious consequences.

To his added surprise and embarrassment, he was now joined by Elise and she began walking beside him. Part of him wanted her to go away but the other part was touched, and he managed a sickly smile. But he still had a feeling of impending doom overlaying this.

They walked in silence to the main office, the bullies following and hissing threats and murmured insults the whole way, making Kit dread the future. To make things worse, the bullies hurried on ahead and were the first to be interviewed by the Deputy, Mr Fitzgerald.

When Mr Fitzgerald looked out of his office a look of surprise showed on his face when he glanced at Kit. Kit had never been in trouble at the office and was ashamed to be there now. Mr Fitzgerald took the note Mr Collier had written and read it, frowning as he did.

"Alright, Piper, you and your mates sit over there. Walker, sit on the other side."

He then looked at Elise. "And why are you here girl?"

"I'm a witness, sir," Elise replied, moving to sit beside Kit.

Mr Fitzgerald's eyebrows went up fractionally and he nodded. "Maybe, but you sit out on the veranda."

As he said this, Wally Dru burst out. "Oh, sir! She's his girlfriend! She will tell lies to get him off."

Mr Fitzgerald frowned. "Slandering people won't help anyone's case. So keep your insults to yourself, thank you. And what do you lot want?" This to another group of students who were coming up the main stairs.

It was Andrew, Blake, Luke, and Peter Bronksy. Andrew answered, "We are witnesses too, sir," he said.

"Okay, wait out there," Mr Fitzgerald. "Ricardo, you come first and tell me your version of what happened."

Ricardo stood and walked towards the doorway, curling his lip at Kit as he did. "Walker came up behind me and tripped me, sir," he said as he went in.

Kit boiled. "Oooh! You bloody liar!" he muttered.

The false accusation not only made him angry it made him feel sick in the stomach, suspecting that all the gang would lie.

They probably did, but he did not get to hear their testimony. Instead he sat and felt worse by the minute. This increased when the bell for classes went and he was left there alone, passing students staring at him and whispering behind their hands. He did not know if Elise and his other witnesses had stayed but could only fret and wait. Ricardo came out and sat with his cronies, giving Kit a malicious sneer as he did. Piper went in. Ten minutes later he came out and Ernie Dru was called in. Then Wally Dru.

Finally it was his turn, and he braced himself and tried to explain as clearly as he could what had happened. When he had finished he was near to tears.

"They do it all the time, sir. They pick on me and call me horrible names. I hate it!"

To his shame, he sniffled and his eyes watered. Mr Fitzgerald bent to write notes then looked up. "There was a similar fight at the dance last Saturday night. What was that about?"

Kit flamed with embarrassment and forced himself to try to explain, without really giving the shameful details. He was then told to go back out and wait. Mr Fitzgerald then walked past and called for the next person. Kit was both pleased and relieved to see that Elsie and the others were still waiting on the veranda. She gave him a little smile as she stood up and walked past and he felt a glow of gratitude. But he still felt defeated and miserable.

His mood hardly improved as the witnesses left one by one, most giving him a grin or a thumbs-up as they did. That cheered him a bit—but then his father appeared at the top of the stairs and his heart sank.

The school has called Dad from work! They must think it is really serious! he thought.

Mr Fitzgerald came out to meet him and Kit was told to join them. As he did, he saw that Ricardo was looking at his dad with some apprehension. Mr Walker was dressed in shirt and tie and Kit suspected that Ricardo thought he looked like he might be someone official. That cheered Kit a bit. Mr Fitzgerald ushed them to a chair and called Mrs Brown through from the next room. She was introduced and sat at the side.

Mr Fitzgerald looked at his notes and then at Kit's dad. "You son has been in a fight, several in fact. I have to say that he did not start them. He was being bullied and provoked."

Kit's dad gestured towards the closed door. "By that pack of ugly looking thugs out there, I assume," he commented.

Mr Fitzgerald did not reply to that but went on, "A group of students have been picking on him. It seems in both cases the bullying was unprovoked. In this case another boy came up behind him and began twisting his ear."

Kit's dad turned to him. "Are you hurt, son?"

Kit shrugged. "Only a few bumps and bruises," he replied, not caring to mention his hurt pride and public humiliations.

Kit's dad went on, "Have you told the teachers about this, Chris?"

Kit was now on the edge of tears again and desperately struggled against it, not wanting the shame for him and his father of crying in public. Again he shrugged.

"Yes Dad," he mumbled, aware he had not made a big issue of it.

Kit's dad fumed. "So what is the school doing about it?"

Mr Fitzgerald looked embarrassed. "We are aware of the incident on Saturday night."

"Oh! What was that?" Kit's dad queried, turning his attention on him.

Kit had to again describe in outline what had happened. His father was annoyed. "You didn't say anything to us on the way home," he said.

"Didn't want to make too much of it, Dad," Kit replied. "I thought if I did the bullies would get into trouble and then pick on me even more."

That sent the focus back onto Mr Fitzgerald. "The Education Department is very strong against bullying. We have policies and procedures to deal with it."

At that, Kit's dad curled his lip. "That is a good political statement but I'm sorry, it doesn't cut it. If there are no consequences that really hurt, there is no effective deterrent."

"Appropriate action will be taken," Mr Fitzgerald replied, a blush mottling his face.

"So what? What happens to Kit?"

Mr Fitzgerald looked uncomfortable. "He has been fighting. There must be a consequence."

"Defending himself! You can't expect a person to just stand and be hit, hoping a teacher might come along," Kit's dad reported angrily.

Mr Fitzgerald looked even more uncomfortable and shrugged. Kit suspected that he agreed with his dad. "Even so, both parties are going to be suspended. Kit for two days and the same for some of the others."

"So he not only gets beaten up, he gets a school punishment for trying to defend himself!" his dad exploded.

Mr Fitzgerald gave a thin smile. "I gather he did a bit better than that. He twice threw the main bully to the ground."

Kit's dad turned to him and grinned. "Did you, son? Well, well! So those Judo lessons are paying off after all?"

Kit felt a spurt of pride and affection. "Yes Dad," he agreed.

Mr Fitzgerald went on. "The main perpetrator is now being considered for exclusion."

"Good!"

That was good news to Kit, but also got him worrying about how Piper and the Dru Brothers might get back at him.

Mr Fitzgearld went on, "But Chris will still have to be suspended for two days."

"I'm not happy! I think that policy stinks," Kit's dad retorted.

Mr Fitzgerald stood up, ending the interview. Kit and his father made their way out. As he went through the doorway Kit looked but none of the bullies was there. He was surprised to discover that it was nearly 4pm and that the school was empty.

They collected Kit's school bag from outside his classroom and then made their way downstairs and out to where Kit's bicycle was standing alone in the racks. Kit unlocked it and pushed it to where his father had his car parked.

"Get in and tell me the whole story," his father said.

So Kit did, still leaving out the more embarrassing and humiliating bits. But he did describe how he had thrown Ricardo each time. His father reached across and thumped his shoulder.

"Well done, young man! Well done!" he said.

"Sorry Dad," Kit replied.

"Don't be! I despise the modern world's view of justice. It seems to punish the innocent more than the mongrels, and they are encouraged by that. Worse still, their friends see nothing happen to them, so they are then tempted to do something similar. And they have to go one better to show off. It is an escalating situation. Never mind. I'm glad you stood up for yourself."

Kit glowed at that and stayed positive till they got home. But then he had to face his mother. She wasn't so forgiving but was also very angry with the school policies.

She shook her head. "Maybe he should go to a private school?"

Kit was dismayed. He knew his parents could afford it, but it wasn't what he wanted. "Mum! No please! All my friends are here."

"Oh well, we will think about it and make some enquiries," she replied. "In the meantime you can work at home for Thursday and Friday."

But Kit's father shook his head. "I have a better idea. I am driving that engine part to Karumba tomorrow. Chris could come with me. A change of scene might do him good. What do you think of that, Chris?"

"Oh yes please, Dad!" Kit cried.

It was some months since he had been on a long drive with his father, and he had always found them enjoyable. He knew that even though his father owned the trucking business he liked to do frequent jobs to keep in touch with the conditions, so he understood his driver's problems and road conditions.

His mother wasn't all that keen but gave in. So it was agreed—Kit would go on a four-day road trip to Karumba and be back in time for school on Monday.

"But only if you have all your homework and assignments done!"

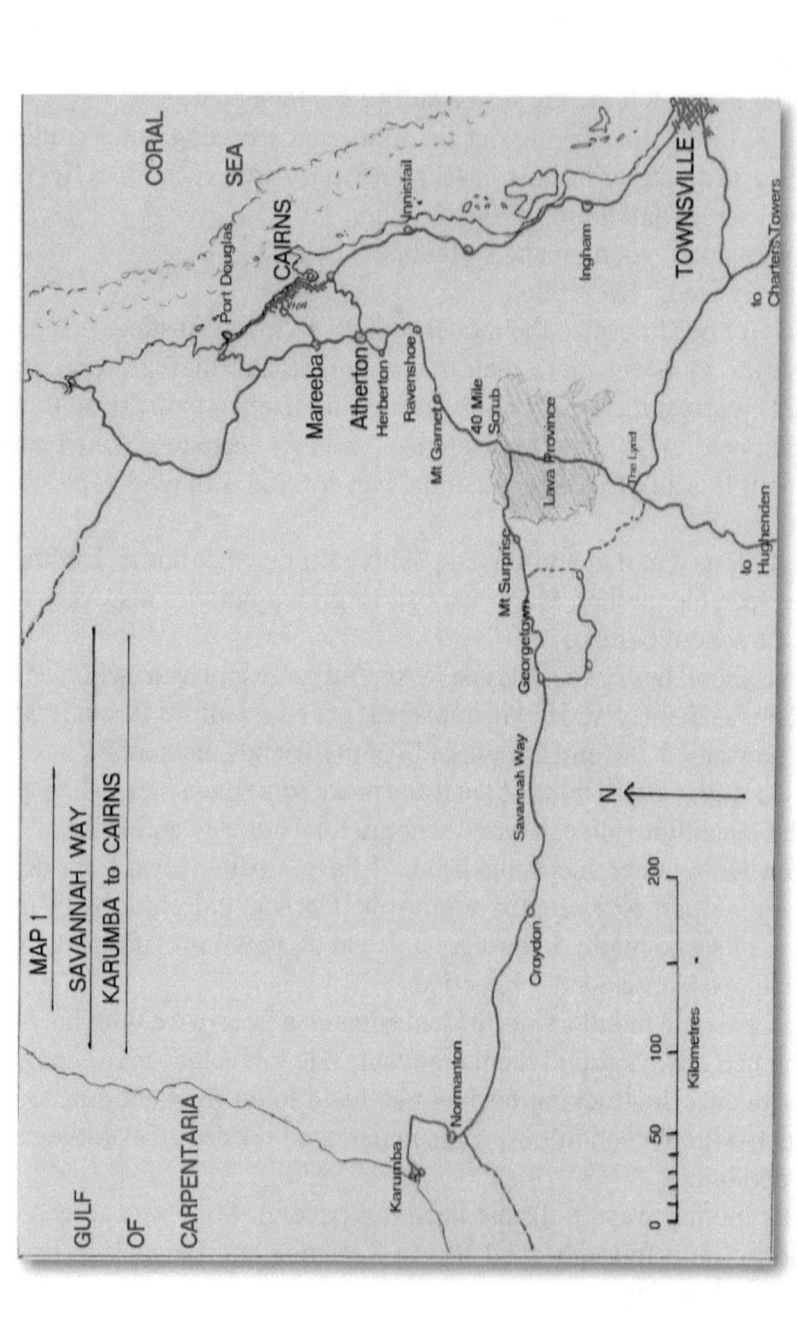

Chapter 19

TO THE GULF COUNTRY

That is how at 08:30am next day Kit was seated in a prime mover beside his dad as they set out from the depot. Behind them was a 50-ton 'low bed' trailer on which the massive engine part was secured. As they accelerated along Mulgrave Road, Kit turned to his dad.

"What is this thing, Dad?"

His father grunted and kept his eyes on the three lanes of traffic they were now in. "It's an impeller pump with a swivelling attachment," he replied. "The mining company sends the ore from their Mt Egbert Mine in a slurry—a mix of water and crushed ore, for hundreds of kilometres through a pipeline to the sea, at Karumba."

That sounded quite incredible to Kit, but he could only nod. "What happens then?"

"It is stockpiled and then loaded into a small ship—I say small, but I believe it can carry thousands of tons. It is small compared to the giant ore carriers that transport the ore to overseas refineries—in Japan, I think. This pump system is needed to transfer the ore, to pump it up from the small ship, to the big one."

"How much does it weigh?" Kit asked, remembering how carefully his father had checked the chains securing the load before they started.

"About forty tons. So, with the trailer and the prime mover our all-up weight is about eighty tons."

Kit knew that his father had been responsible for heavy lifts where the total moving weight had been nearly 150 tons, so could only shrug.

"So why are they sending it by road and not by sea? Isn't sea transport cheaper?" he queried.

He was well aware of the geography of North Queensland and had even been to Karumba, the small port on the west coast of Cape York Peninsula where the pump was needed.

His father did not answer for a minute or so as he manoeuvred to go around the corner into Sheridan Street. "Because they want it in a hurry and the barge that services Weipa and Karumba isn't due back in

Cairns for another four days. Then it would be another week before it was loaded and moved."

That made sense. Kit checked the load in his rear vision mirror as they swung wide and then settled in the centre lane heading north.

"We don't need an escort vehicle or anything?" he asked.

His father shook his head. "No. The load is heavy, not large, and certainly not oversize. We will be fine. And I can fit a container on to help pay for the return trip."

That was good news. Kit was well aware of the cost of keeping trucks on the road and clearly understood that running empty was bad news.

"What will the cargo be?" he asked.

"Prawns, in a refrigerated container," his father answered.

By then they were approaching the high school and Kit studied students he could see who were walking to school. He hoped to see his friends and realised he was actually hoping to see Elise—before he remembered he was supposed to be interested in Diana. He saw a couple of people in his class but none of his friends. As the vehicle made its way past the school, Kit stared at it and experienced regret that he was suspended. But then he remembered how he had thrown Ricardo and managed to stand up to the bullies and he experienced a fierce surge of satisfaction and pride.

I did it! I managed to beat one of the bullies! he told himself. It was something to savour, even if there was going to be more pain down the track.

By then they were past the buildings, and he concentrated on his dad's driving in heavy traffic, most of which was heading into Cairns from the beach suburbs to the north.

Kit did not need to have the route explained. He had a good memory for roads and geography, and he also had a good map. He knew it was much shorter to have gone south along Mulgrave Road and the Bruce Highway to Gordonvale and then up the Gillies Highway to the Atherton Tablelands. But he also knew that the Gillies was 16 kilometres of winding mountain road going up nearly a thousand metres while the road they were heading for, the Kennedy Highway up over the Kuranda range, was only 8 kilometres of uphill winding mountain road and about 400 metres in altitude. The difference in altitude would be made up gradually over 50 kilometres.

The Kuranda Range was no novelty to Kit. He had been up it dozens of times but usually in the family car at a much higher speed. This time the rig crawled up in low gear, frequently pulling over into the slow lane to let the impatient drivers go by. Kit enjoyed the scenery. He loved the jungle covered mountains around Cairns and was glad he lived in such an interesting place.

After crossing the Kuranda Range and the big bridge over the Barron River at Kuranda, the route led southwest for 50 kilometres through small ranges of hills and into progressively drier country. The coastal mountains caused a 'rain shadow' effect so by the time they re-crossed the Barron at Mareeba they were in fairly dry savannah country. There were lots of farms interspersed with patches of bush, all of it familiar to Kit.

From Mareeba the highway went due south, straight as can be for nearly 10 kilometres, then wound its way up a small range onto the next level of the 'Tablelands' at Walkamin. It was 10:00am when they stopped in the small town of Tolga for a toilet break and refreshments. Comforted by a hot pie and a vanilla slice, Kit settled for the next stage.

This took them through the picturesque 'Tolga Scrub', a belt of rainforest, all that remained of the vast area of 'scrub' that once covered the Tablelands. Then it was through the town of Atherton in a cold drizzle. From there they went on up a steep range for another 10 kilometres to Herberton. They could have followed the Kennedy Highway which ran up a long ridge further east, but Kit's dad disliked it because it was much narrower and had many more sharp bends.

It was 11:00am by then so they enjoyed another short break and more refreshments before continuing. Kit was glad to get back into the cab as the mountain air had a real chill to it.

The road went on to rejoin the Kennedy Highway and then through more lovely rain forest country on the Evelyn Tableland before reaching the small town of Ravenshoe. They did not go into the town but stopped at a service station on the highway to refuel and to have lunch. Kit was given the task of refuelling and, as always, found his fingers starting to cramp from holding the pump for the length of time it took to fill the four huge 100-litre fuel tanks.

"Thirsty buggers in the mountains," he muttered, knowing that fuel costs were among the biggest problem for the business.

But they were out of the mountains then and on a long downhill run with a few hills as they ran out past the last of the forested hills and back into dry savannah country. Kit knew it would stay that way all the way across to 'The Gulf'. He settled down to enjoy the trip, keeping track of their progress on his map. He had done the trip several times before but not often enough to know it well or to be bored by it.

There were not many real features that stuck in his mind, just miles and miles of bush and an occasional creek or side road. A few rocky hills showed in the distance from time to time. Apart from the small towns of Innot Hot Springs and Mt Garnet the first area that actually caught his attention was after about an hour's drive when they entered an area of very dense, dry bush. This was on both sides of the road and looked to be a really thick tangle.

"That looks a bit thick," he commented.

"It's called the Forty Mile Scrub," his father answered.

"Is it forty miles across or forty miles from somewhere?" Kit queried.

His father shrugged. "Couldn't tell you. Maybe from Mt Garnet?"

Twenty minutes later they came out of the 'Scrub' into ordinary bush and reached a rest area with a toilet at a major road junction. After a short toilet break and a few minutes of checking all the tyres and chains they continued on. At the road junction they turned right along the 'Savannah Way'. The other highway went on south towards Charters Towers or Hughenden.

Now the country subtly changed. It was still savannah woodland but was much flatter—very gentle rolling rises and all studded with basalt rocks the size of footballs. From a previous visit with family the year before Kit remembered it was called the Kinrara Basalt Province. He knew it was a vast area of what had been ancient lava flows and remembered that he had been told there was almost no surface water as it mostly flowed underground.

In lava tunnels, he thought.

The truck roared past the turnoff to the Undara Lava Tubes Tourist Resort. The family had spent four days there, two of them looking through the massive and spectacular natural lava tunnels with rangers to guide and provide information. He had found it all fascinating and he remembered the visit fondly.

Another hour of driving had them at the tiny town of Mount Surprise.

The family had also visited it two years before and they had stayed at the Bedrock Caravan Park in a cabin and spent two days fossicking for topaz at the remote O'Brien's Creek Gem Field. Kit had actually found a couple of nice pieces of clear quartz and some small pieces of topaz but had not been gripped by the experience. He had actually enjoyed more seeing the small silver 'rail motor' called the 'Savannahlander' when it had rattled past one morning, Mount Surprise being on the old railway that ran from Mareeba to the even tinier and more remote town of Forsayth.

It was 4:00pm by then and his father had to take a mandatory rest break. The truck was parked near the police station and they both lay down on the bunks in the space up behind the driver. Normally only one person used the space, but a second bunk could be swung up and clipped in position and Kit got this. It was cramped but saved many hundreds of dollars in accommodation costs. The cab also contained a tiny toilet and wash area, and they were also useful.

Kit did not think he would sleep and considered going for a walk but after a while he dozed. His father actually slept soundly and after hearing his snores Kit did not dare move or risk disturbing him. So he lay there and again drifted into a restless slumber.

At 6:00pm his father woke to an alarm and they both freshened up and then walked to the hotel. In the Dining Room they ordered meals, Chicken Kyiv and Chips for Kit, and his dad phoned his mum. After reassuring her they were both well and that the trip was going well they ate a big meal. They then strolled the length of the single main street and then watched the TV news and a current affairs program in the hotel lounge. During this they both had a soft drink, Kit knowing that his father never drank alcohol during driving jobs.

By 9:00pm they were settled into their bunks. Once again Kit did not think he would sleep, but when he lay there fantasising about rescuing Diana from pirates he found she kept turning into Elise and then he was sound asleep.

They were awake at 04:30am. Kit made his way to the nearby public toilet while his father heated water and shaved, then also went to the toilet and changed into clean clothes.

"Always do your morning routine as a drill, son," he advised as he combed his hair.

Kit was more interested in food but no café was open, so they did another check of the wheels and chains. And there were a lot of them. A normal trailer on a 'semi' is supported at the front by the dual wheels at the rear of the Prime Mover but this was a heavy lift trailer and had its own front set of eight wheels (two dual sets), just back from the 'goose neck' which was then attached to the towing pintle. It took nearly half an hour with Kit crawling underneath to check the inside wheels.

They set out at 06:00am, driving westward along the highway. There was very little traffic, and the sun came up behind them so it was easy driving. A few sections of single lane bitumen needed care but otherwise there were no problems. There was half an hour of low gear grinding up a small range of bare, stony mountains—the Newcastle Range the map said—and then down the other side. Kit enjoyed that as the view in the morning light was spectacular.

"You can just see for ever!" he cried, staring at the vast expanse of mostly flat country that extended seemingly to the horizon.

It was borne upon his consciousness that Australia was a very big place. *And very empty,* he added, as they had not passed a single building for an hour or more.

By 07:45am they were at the very pleasant little town of Georgetown. After crossing the long bridge across the wide, sandy bed of the Etheridge River they pulled left into the main street and pulled up. As they did, Kit's father laughed and pointed.

"Well, we are in the bush now!" he cried.

Kit looked and could not believe his eyes. Waddling slowly across the bitumen street was a large goanna. It seemed to look back over its shoulder and sniff disdainfully at them before continuing on to vanish in long grass in an empty allotment between a shop and a house.

The rig was parked along another empty allotment and Kit was handed a tyre pressure gauge.

"Check them all please, son," his father instructed.

Kit really wanted breakfast but could only comply. He was already glad that he was on the trip as the change of scene and tasks had taken his brooding thoughts off the bullies and the situation at school. He had never been afraid of the hard work or grime involved in looking after trucks, so he now started at the near side front wheels and then systematically worked his way back, crawling in underneath on the bitumen to locate the valves and do the checks on the inside tyres of the sets of duals under the prime mover and trailer. As he did, his father again checked the chains and then wrote up his logbook.

They cleaned up and made their way to the nearby café and roadhouse and enjoyed a feed. For both of them this was the full breakfast: cereal with milk, sausages, bacon and fried eggs on toast with coffee. Kit wasn't really keen on coffee, but the café did not have any hot chocolate or Milo.

Feeling much better they set off again at 09:00am. The rig was driven around the block to get back to the main highway. In the process it passed the Georgetown Terrestrial Centre. As they drove past, Kit's father pointed to it.

"I must bring you guys out here to see that. It has a really fantastic collection of minerals and gems: world class."

Kit liked the idea of another family expedition but was worried lest the plan now conflict with a Navy Cadet camp or course.

"When Dad?" he asked.

"Next school holidays maybe?" his father suggested. "We could combine it with a few days at Cobbold Gorge. You enjoyed our trip there, didn't you?"

Kit had. He had seen plenty of tourist images of the place before they went and had not been all that keen, but once he was there he realised it was a really impressive place. The trip had been very informative and enjoyable. He had been glad his father had thought it was worth a visit.

"We could do another couple of days fossicking at Agate Creek too."

"We could," his father agreed.

"What's agate?" Kit asked as the rig swung back onto the highway.

"Agate is another type of gemstone," his father explained.

He went on to talk about volcanic 'bombs', a place called Crystal Hill, and of various types of crystal that they might find.

The discussion kept them talking until they were well out of town, again heading west along the Savannah Way. This next section for a couple of hours Kit did find a bit boring. It was mostly through fairly flat savannah woodland. Only a few small ranges of hills and an occasional change of vegetation type gave variety. Now they were in that roughly defined region known as 'The Gulf Country', that vast swathe of flat, swampy land that borders the Gulf of Carpentaria.

By 11:00am they were in Croydon, another small town with a square grid pattern layout. There were lots of empty allotments, but looked quite neat and prosperous. Kit had been there on a previous trip to Normanton and Karumba with the family, and he really liked the place. Lunch was purchased at the roadhouse on the eastern edge of town, and they stretched their legs and checked tyres and ties.

Then it was on, the only change to the flat savannah woodland being that they had a railway on their left for an hour or so, and then on their right after crossing it. Kit knew it was only a tourist line, kept open for a single railmotor called the 'Gulflander' which ran a couple of times a week in the tourist season. He had seen it at the historic railway station in Croydon and again at the equally historic station in Normanton.

By 02:00pm they were in Normanton but they only stopped for ten minutes to refuel, check oil and water and tyres, and then on. The road was good bitumen, mostly straight and two lane and almost completely flat as they were now close to the actual Gulf. Mangroves and tidal saltwater indicated how close to the sea they were.

Then 3:30pm found them rolling into Karumba. Having been there before Kit knew what to expect but he still studied the place with interest. He was fascinated by how other people made their living, by how local economies worked. Karumba is really two towns: the main town along the bank of the Norman River and the smaller tourist town at Karumba Point. The pump was required at the main wharves, so the rig rolled on past the turn-off to Karumba Point. After passing the Golf Club and through a small 'suburb' of normal houses, they crossed an open area of swamp and turned into the town proper.

The town really has only one main street and a couple of short back streets. At the T-junction with the school on the right and a petrol station on the left they turned left and drove along past the shops, fishing lodges, some old buildings and light industry. Then it was past the hotel and fish and prawn processing plant and freezers, more shops on the left and then a large caravan park—mostly empty as it was still too hot and early in the year for the tourists.

Beyond that there were only swamps on the left and, on the right, various industrial and transport yards. These lined the riverbank behind loading 'hards' or wharves. At the far end of the road Kit knew there was a modern museum and more ordinary houses, but before then his father swung the rig into a large open yard on the right.

They had arrived.

Chapter 20

KARUMBA

They were expected. A group of men was waiting outside a demountable building that was obviously an office. Kit knew his father had been on the phone several times advising of progress so was not surprised. The men, nearly a dozen, mostly wore the usual Hi Vis yellow work shirts, dark blue longs with reflective bands on them, work boots, and 'hard hats', but two wore white long-sleeved shirts and ties.

Management, Kit assumed.

As his father braked the big rig to a stop, he nodded through the front. "I thought this job might be really important. That looks like the boss man himself," he said.

"Who?" Kit asked, looking at the two men in white shirts.

"Mister Rod MacGregor, mining magnate and multi-billionaire, the one on the left. He owns MacGregor Enterprises, which owns the Mt Egbert Mine," his father answered as he switched off the motor. He unclipped his seat belt and opened the door. "Well, come and meet him, son," he said, indicating the fit looking man of about 35 or 40 years of age.

Kit was a bit diffident about that. He was used to being introduced to the local business-people and civic leaders in Cairns, but Rod MacGregor was a national figure. Feeling quite nervous, he undid his seat belt and climbed down. As he moved to join his father who was shaking hands with the great man himself, Kit felt very conscious of his small stature compared to the bulk of most of the workers who seemed to be all big, burly men.

His father turned to gesture him forward. "My youngest son, Kit," he said.

Kit found his hand being shaken and himself looking into a pair of very bright eyes which seemed to scan him in a single appraising glance.

"Hello sir," he said.

Mr MacGregor smiled and said, "You look a bit young to be truck driving, young Kit," he said.

"Yes sir. I'm still at school," he replied.

Mr MacGregor raised an eyebrow. "Isn't today a school day? Taking a couple of days off for work experience then are you?"

Kit blushed, aware everyone was watching and listening. He was also aware he did not want to shame his dad. For an instant Kit was tempted to lie or give an evasive answer. Then it came to him that Mr MacGregor must be a very bright man to manage such vast mining companies.

"No sir. I was suspended for fighting."

Mr MacGregor's eyebrows went up again. "Fighting, eh? I hope it was in good cause."

"I was being bullied, sir," Kit replied, a stubborn streak of defiance welling up.

"He was bigger than you?" Mr MacGregor queried.

"Yes sir, and there were four of them," Kit answered. He bit his lip, unsure how to go on.

His father helped him. "They are. I saw them when I was called to the school," he said. "One of them is as big as this bloke," he said, gesturing to one of the workers. "I'm told Kit put him on his arse twice."

At that Mr MacGregor nodded and smiled. "Good for you. So you chose to fight instead of running away."

Kit nodded, not sure if he was being teased or mocked. "Yes sir."

"Good man!" Mr MacGregor said. "There are times to run, but also there are also times to fight. Self-respect is more important than getting thumped. The pain of a beating only lasts a day or so but hurt pride damages you for years. But if you were the victim, why were you suspended?"

Kit did not know how to answer but his father did. "Stupid bloody policy against fighting. A person can't even defend himself."

Mr MacGregor nodded. He said to Kit, "So you go to a state high school?"

"Yes sir, Cairns State High."

Mr MacGregor nodded again. "My eldest daughter, Rose, goes to a boarding school: the Northern Goldfields College in Charters Towers."

Kit nodded. "Never been there sir."

"You must try go to there," Mr MacGregor replied. "Charters Towers is certainly worth a visit. Anyway, good to meet you. Now, we'd better get this pump unloaded and fitted. It is costing a heap of money."

Kit nodded and stepped back out of the way. He knew from things he had heard that ships cost many thousands of dollars to run every day. His father obviously had the same thought.

"I hope you haven't got a ship waiting out there for a cargo," he said. "If you have, I apologise for any delay. I could have left Kit at home and brought a second driver and we would have been here yesterday."

Mr MacGregor shook his head. "No, the time given in the contract was today. We have a bulk carrier arriving tomorrow afternoon, but the pump should be fitted by then. Now, I am going to leave these men to get on with their work and go on a sunset cruise with my family for a couple of hours. Would you like to come, young Kit? Is that alright Mr Walker? He can help look after my little Ball of Busyness."

"Sunset cruise, sir?" Kit stammered, unsure. "Ball of Busyness?"

Mr MacGregor chuckled. "A nickname for my 15 month-old daughter. You can help her mother mind her. It is on a tourist launch I have hired so she can see a crocodile."

At the mention of crocodiles, Kit hesitated. He knew that tourists came to Karumba to do just that, and to do fishing cruises. He looked at his father who smiled.

"Go on son. You go and enjoy a boat trip." He looked at Mr MacGregor, "And if he gives any trouble, just chuck him overboard."

Both men laughed. Mr MacGregor looked concerned. "You alright in boats, Kit?"

"Oh, yes sir." Kit replied, not wanting to boast.

"He's a Navy Cadet," his father added.

"Navy cadet, eh?" Mr MacGregor commented, approval clear in his voice. "My daughter, Rose, is an army cadet. She loves it. Now, come away and let these people do their job."

He led Kit across towards a white 4WD parked near the office. As he did, the other man in the white shirt began explaining to Kit's father where he wanted the load moved to. As Mr MacGregor unlocked the vehicle and got in, he glanced at the men and said, "They don't need the big boss standing there watching their every move. That makes people nervous and they don't do their best work then. You remember that if you get to be a leader. Explain clearly and then trust them. If you have chosen well, the job will be well done by people proud of their skill. Now hop in."

Kit did so, deciding that he really liked Mr MacGregor. He did not fit any of his preconceived ideas on how very rich people might be. Mr MacGregor concentrated on driving until they were out on the main road. Then he gestured out the window.

"Have you been to Karumba before, Kit?"

"Yes sir. We did a fishing trip here last year," Kit answered.

He had not really enjoyed that as it had been hot and the mangroves had been full of sand flies and mosquitoes. And there had been crocodiles.

"And how long have you been a Navy Cadet?"

Kit blushed and wished he could boast of many years of experience but just stuck to facts. He sensed that not telling the truth to this man would not be a good thing to do.

"I've done nearly a year now, sir. I hope to be promoted from Recruit to Seaman soon."

"That's good. Every little step is important in life—and the first one particularly so," Mr MacGregor replied. "My girl, Rose, is a second year and a cadet corporal. Do the Navy Cadets have corporals?"

Kit's mind raced to calculate relative ranks. He shook his head. "No sir. That would be a Cadet Leading Seaman."

As they talked, Mr MacGregor drove along the main street and stopped at the hotel. Kit was told to hop out and wait. Mr MacGregor went in and a few minutes later came out with a pretty but chubby woman carrying an equally chubby toddler. Mr MacGregor introduced his wife as Mrs MacGregor and then chuckled and pointed to the toddler.

"This is Belinda, our little Bundle of Mischief. Belinda, this is Kit."

Belinda looked at him, giving him a very searching study. She had bright, twinkling eyes and certainly looked like she could be mischievous.

"I Bub-O Busy Bee," she corrected.

There were more chuckles and she was placed in the baby seat in the back. Kit got in beside her in the back. Mr MacGregor and his wife sat in the front. They set out and Kit set himself to chat to Belinda. To his relief, she responded, her head flicking from side to side as she took in the sights.

Mr MacGregor drove back out of town and past the Golf Club to the turn-off to Karumba Point. As they did, Belinda kept looking from side to side and pointing and calling out. Her words were not very well formed but her meaning was clear.

"Kangywoo! Kangywoo!" she cried, pointing to some wallabies on the Golf Course.

By the time they arrived at the houses, motel and shops at Karumba Point she was happily chatting to Kit, who tried to respond.

Certainly a busy bee! he thought.

The vehicle was parked in a large bitumen car park right at the tip of the point beside a large boat ramp. Belinda was taken out and stood beside the car and immediately, to Kit's surprise, put her hand up for him to hold. He glanced at her mother and she nodded and smiled.

"Just walk her down onto the beach but keep her away from the water," she said.

Feeling very self-conscious, Kit walked hand in hand with Miss Busy Bee across the hot bitumen to the edge of the beach. This sloped down for 50 paces to the water. A tourist boat with a front-loading ramp was beached there waiting. At that point the river mouth was about half a kilometre wide, the far side being a wide strip or grey mud and a long wall of mangroves. The open sea was too his right.

But Belinda immediately put up both arms to be picked up. Embarrassed and somewhat diffidently, Kit did so. But almost immediately she jerked and twisted and he nearly dropped her.

"Big birds!" she cried.

Bloody seagulls! Kit thought, noting half a dozen arriving to circle and land.

Then Belinda squirmed and wanted to be put down to chase the seagulls. That game didn't last long as she tripped and fell on the soft sand and began to cry. Her mother picked her up, dusted her off and handed her back to Kit.

"Hold her while we get under way," she requested.

He made his way down to the boat, which he now saw was a flat-bottomed, flat-nosed tourist barge with a small ramp that enabled passengers to walk on board safe and dry. Mr MacGregor led the way and the couple, a middle-aged man and middle-aged lady who were the crew, noted their names and ushered them aboard. There were already a few other passengers and Kit nodded at them when he got eye contact.

His problem then was to keep hold of Belinda as she wriggled and squirmed continually. This went on for the next two hours until he was feeling exasperated and exhausted. Every time a bird flew by—which was often as the crew of the barge put out small fish to attract hawks and eagles—she pointed and cried out and twisted around to look.

As the boat motored back up the river, Belinda had to be restrained from leaning over the side and had to be held firmly when she looked at where a big fish had jumped.

"Big fish are being chased by an even bigger fish," he said, but while both parents nodded she just struggled to break free.

And there was a crocodile. A four metre 'salty' was lying on the mud on the far bank and the boat was steered as close as it was safe without running aground so people could see and photograph it. Belinda just glanced at it and did not seem interested. But Kit was, and he stared at the creature with respect and anxiety as it slowly crawled into the water and vanished from view.

To Kit's surprise, the boat made its way back up the river to Karumba and then pulled into a small wharf below the old Qantas Flying Boat base and lodges.

"Built in the 1930s," the tour guide explained.

Kit knew that from their previous visit, and he also noted the memorial up on the bank to the RAAF Catalina crews from World War 2. He found it hard to imagine how such a tiny, apparently out-of-the-way backwater like Karumba could once have been an important link in an international air route.

Belinda was getting restless by then, but she did subject four more tourists who were embarking to very searching scrutiny. Then she went back to wriggling and squirming to look at the swooping eagles and hawks. The launch pulled out and headed up river beside the town.

Kit found that more interesting, especially when they slowly passed a large blue-hulled ship which was the 'lighter' which transferred the ore out to the big ships. Mr MacGregor pointed out to his wife the pump that was even then being lowered into position on top of the superstructure by a large mobile crane. Kit looked for his father among the cluster of workers up on the ship but did not see him.

He will be refuelling the truck ready for tomorrow, he reasoned.

There were other boats and ships to hold his interest, a large landing barge used for resupplying islands in the Gulf, launches and trawlers and small boats. Belinda wasn't very interested but was distracted by the lady handing her a plastic tumbler of cordial. Kit was offered soft drink and he opted for lemon squash. Then Belinda wanted some but after the first sip she pulled a sour face and pushed it away. Luckily she returned to her cordial and that kept her busy for a few minutes.

The tour took them across the river to the mangroves and then downstream through a dozen moored yachts and launches. Then it was on around the wide curve past where the crocodile had been. Kit kept eyeing the grey, muddy water anxiously, worrying that the croc might suddenly surge up out of the water and grab someone (Him!).

The boat made its way out along a marked shipping channel to a large sand island exposed by the falling tide. By then the adults were drinking champagne and beer. When the boat beached and the bow ramp was lowered everyone walked ashore. As they did, Belinda struggled to get put down so Kit hurried across the ramp and did so. Luckily the sand was damp and firm. Belinda began to run around, picking up sea shells and pieces of driftwood and then chasing tiny crabs that scuttled down holes or into the water.

With crocodiles at the front of his mind, Kit quickly restrained Belinda. She let out several frustrated wails and Kit glanced anxiously at her parents. But they just smiled and strolled up to the highest point of the sand island. Beyond them the sun was setting in a orb of red in a haze of smoke or dust. Belinda ran up to them and Kit hurried after her.

"Certainly a ball of energy," he commented.

Her mother smiled. "You will wear out before she does," she commented.

But she scooped Belinda up and, when she reached out for her champagne glass, allowed her a sip. Belinda's face at once puckered up and she pulled back crying, "Yuk! Yuk!"

Her mother let her slip to the ground again and she went racing off to try to catch a seagull that had landed nearby. It simply flew further off. Belinda ran after it and Kit had to follow. After ten minutes of this he was winded and getting tired of the game.

During that time the sun sank into the sea to the west—a novelty to Kit because in Cairns it rose from the sea and set behind mountains. Dusk set in and the lights of the boat were turned on. The skipper called them all back and Kit managed to grab Belinda and lift her up.

Belinda had seen a crab and kept reaching down for it while wailing, "Want! Want!"

Ignoring this, Kit carried her quickly back to the boat. Once on board he thankfully handed her back to her father who held out his arms for her. Belinda almost leapt into them and proceeded to explain in baby talk all that she had seen. The boat reversed back into deeper water, turned and began making its way back towards the line of bright lights in the distance that marked Karumba Point. Kit sat and tried to relax, his gaze drawn alternately to the red glow of the western sky and the bright lights on the water beside him.

School and bullies and all their problems seemed very far away!

Chapter 21

HEADED HOME

An hour later, Kit was seated in the hotel dining room with his father. His father had insisted they have a good night's rest and proper food so they were booked into the hotel. Mr MacGregor had driven them all there as he and his family were also booked in. Belinda had been whisked off by her mother to have a bath. Kit had found his room and also enjoyed a shower and change of clothes. Now he sat sipping water and waiting.

To his surprise, Mr MacGregor had asked if they would join them for dinner and a table had been arranged. The hotel staff had instantly agreed and organised a table. Kit looked around. The dining room was fairly ordinary but was air-conditioned and much quieter than the nearby public bar.

"I suppose if you are that rich you can get whatever you want," he suggested to his father.

His father grunted and nodded. "Son, if you had as much money as this man you could not just buy the hotel, you could buy a whole chain of hotels and not even blink."

"I suppose so," Kit agreed. "But he seems a nice enough guy."

"I think he is. His employees are very happy to work for him and speak highly of him. He certainly doesn't give himself airs and graces."

"He sends his daughter to a boarding school in Charters Towers and he says her friends don't know who she is. She's a corporal in the Army Cadets," Kit said.

"Here they come now," his father said.

He stood up as Mrs MacGregor, Belinda in her arms, arrived with Mr MacGregor. Introductions were made and as they did Belinda began leaning across with her arms out towards Kit.

"Tit! Tit!" she cried.

Kit blushed and hoped Mrs MacGregor had not heard that, but he did smile back at Belinda and at a nod from Mrs MacGregor took her.

She grinned. "She likes you! That's unusual. Normally she is very stand-offish with strangers."

"She is a real little cutie!" Kit replied.

At that Belinda bristled. "I not little! I big girl now! Daddy say so," she insisted.

"You are too, especially when I have to carry you," Kit agreed.

He then helped put her into a highchair that a waiter suddenly appeared with. Belinda didn't want that but her mother spoke quietly and firmly and she subsided into sulky obedience.

Their orders were taken by a waitress, who made much of Belinda. As she did, Kit noted that everyone else had to go up to the bar to place their orders and pay. But he couldn't help liking Mr MacGregor.

He seems a pretty nice bloke, he decided.

A very nice meal followed. Kit enjoyed Chicken Kyiv and chips and saw that Belinda was given chicken nuggets and chips. She also ate some carrot and beetroot. During the meal the talk was general, mostly about the Sunset Cruise and the crocodile. Kit drank fruit juice and felt relaxed and happy. Then he saw that Belinda's head was nodding. Her mother noticed as well, and she stood and wiped the toddler's mouth and face and then lifted her up.

"I suppose you will be gone early tomorrow?" she said to Kit's father.

"Yes. We will be on the road by seven at the latest," his father agreed.

"Well, it was nice to meet you. Now Belinda Busy Bee, you say goodnight to the nice people."

Belinda looked and gave a little wave. Looking straight at Kit she called, "Goo ni!"

Kit smiled back and waved. "Goodnight Busy Bee," he called. As he did, he thought he had never seen a nicer baby.

If I ever have a daughter, I hope she is just like her, he thought.

Mother and daughter made their way out and Mr MacGregor turned to Kit's father. "Tell me, Mr Walker, have there been any problems with trucks being stolen in the Cairns area recently?"

"Why yes," Kit's father agreed. "I have lost three prime movers in the last year and two had trailers attached. One was a refrigerated trailer."

"Hmmm. Well, I have lost four prime movers between Mt Egbert, that's near Kajabbi, Cloncurry and Mount Isa, in the last six months. The thieves did not take the trailers—they were all ore carriers, so pretty specialised, but the rigs were brand new and very good quality," Mr MacGregor said.

Kit was shocked. "That's a lot of trucks, sir," he said. "What do the thieves do with them?"

As he said the word 'thieves', Jellman's face floated into his mind.

Kit's father answered that. "They re-birth them, son. They hide them somewhere and give them a new paint job and logos and so on and also try to give them a new VIN and so on."

Kit new that the VIN was the Vehicle Identification Number and that it was stamped or engraved onto key components by the manufacturer.

"New number plates I suppose?" he suggested.

"That is the least of their worries. It is providing the forged documents a vehicle needs that is now one of their problems. With all the state Transport Departments and police linked by computers if they are pulled up they are easy to detect."

Kit's father nodded. "Sometimes they just copy the details of another vehicle of a similar make and hope that the system doesn't note that there is another vehicle with the same details somewhere in another state at that moment."

Mr MacGregor chuckled. "That would be tricky to explain away," he said.

"Have you tried satellite tracking?" Kit's father queried.

Mr MacGregor nodded. "We have, but the crooks are onto that and have either turned them off or blocked them somehow."

"Inside jobs then?"

"Possibly, "Mr MacGregor agreed.

"Jellman," Kit commented.

"Eh?" Mr MacGregor asked.

Kit's father answered. "Just a fellow I had to fire and who we believe stole our newest prime mover a few days later."

"But these people must need some sort of workshop to do this stuff in surely?" Kit asked.

Mr MacGregor nodded. "They must. And there aren't many large sheds in Northwest Queensland or the Gulf Country, and the police have searched all they can find. It really puzzles us because it is hard to steal a big truck in an isolated place like this as they have to drive for many hours to get to the next town, and the police have plenty of time to set up roadblocks and so on."

"Yes, it is much easier down in Southeast Queensland where there are towns every hour or so and lots of farms and big sheds," Kit's father agreed.

Mr MacGregor nodded. "You are right. We even had one stolen hauling ore on a dirt road near Forsayth a few weeks ago. The trailers were just left beside the road but there was no sign of the prime mover or the driver. There were reports of possible sightings on nearby dirt roads but then nothing. It was very puzzling. The police are still looking."

Kit's father glanced at his watch. "I hate to be unsociable, sir, but we need to be on the road early tomorrow, so we need to take ourselves off to bed."

Mr MacGregor smiled and stood up, holding out his hand. "Of course. Well, it has been a pleasure doing business with you, Mr Walker. If we have another job in this part of the world we will certainly keep you in mind."

"Thank you, sir," Kit's father replied, shaking his hand.

Mr MacGregor then held his hand out to Kit. "And you, young Kit, you keep on with doing the right thing. And good luck with the Navy Cadets. Well, I'd better get up to read Miss Bundle of Mischief a bedtime story or I will be in trouble," he said.

Kit had to grin at that and the notion of a multi billionaire reading to his baby daughter really made him feel he was a very nice man. "Thank you sir," was all he could manage. He felt humbled and privileged to have been trusted with Belinda and again hoped he might one day have a daughter like her.

Mr MacGregor left them at the stairs and father and son made their way to their room. Within half an hour both were sound asleep.

* * *

At 07:45am the next morning they were well on their way towards Normanton. On the trailer was a refrigerated container full of fresh prawns from the Gulf Fishery. As they had left the hotel, Kit had looked around, hoping to say goodbye to Belinda and her dad but he saw no sign of her. Now he stared out at the dry, flat plains dotted with cattle and pondered life and his future. Knowing that it was Saturday, and that it would be back to school in about 48 hours, added a sharp little niggle to his thoughts.

Will I have trouble with the bullies? he fretted. But he also decided it would not be all that bad. *I do have friends there too, and there are girls.* But when he thought of them it was not Diana but Elise who came to mind.

By 08:00am they were in Normanton, but they just drove straight through and on south until they came to the junction of the Savannah Way and turned left, heading for home. Two hours later they were in Croydon and enjoying a break and refuelling. Then it was on again, heading eastwards at a hundred kilometres per hour. The road was straight and good and they had no problems.

They were in Georgetown and enjoying lunch by 12:30pm. Half an hour later it was on again, grinding up over the Castlereagh Range and then east again through the rolling savannah country.

Mount Surprise was the next stop at 2:40pm. Kit knew his dad was hoping to reach at least Mt Garnet for the night so as to get home earlier on Sunday.

As they pulled up on the verge near the tiny timber railway station, Kit's father said, "I need to go to the toilet. While I am doing that I want you to do a tyre pressure check. And I mean right in underneath."

Kit did not really want to do that as it meant crawling under the trailer and getting dirty while checking each tyre with the pressure gauge. But he understood it was important. So far they had been lucky and had no punctures or blowouts. His father pulled out the keys and held them up.

"I will have them in my pocket and the brakes are on. You will be safe," he said.

Kit had a drink from a water bottle and then climbed down. His father walked past and vanished into the nearby public toilet. Grumbling and muttering a bit Kit walked to the nearside front of the trailer and first checked the electrical connection to the freezer unit. The refrigeration seemed to be working fine, as loud as usual, so he turned to the tyres. He knelt to start testing the tyre pressures. He was hoping there were no problem because then he would have to get out and set up the air compressor to pump a tyre up.

Or, worse still, take the bloody thing off and change it! he thought.

At the rear of the trailer there were six sets of dual tyres. To check the inside ones he had to crawl right in underneath, squirming on his side and back and taking care not to hit his head or soil his clothes on the many oily, greasy parts. But it was something he had done hundreds of times so it was no novelty and he quickly worked his way forward. He was just thankful he was wearing loose long blue trousers and a long-sleeved blue work shirt. It was something his father insisted on when driving, to protect the skin from being in the sun all day and from dirt and grease.

Once the rear tyres on the trailer were checked, he chose to crawl forward under the trailer to check the four forward tyres on the inside of the dual sets. Because it was a low-bed, heavy lift trailer, it had a second set of its own wheels at the front, the trailer being attached by a swivelling 'goose-neck' extension which went up and forward to rest on the towing pintle of the prime mover, which also had two sets of rear dual wheels as well. In all there were 32 tyres to check.

I will do the inside tyres first and then I will do the outside ones, Kit told himself.

Quickly he checked both inside tyres, and that put him right under the front of the trailer near the towing extension. Rather than squirm backwards to start the outside ones, he opted to go on forward to check the rear wheels of the prime mover. He was just crawling past the forward set of dual wheels when above the noise of the fridge unit he heard the crunch of boots coming across the bitumen road towards the prime mover.

Wondering who that could be, he paused and turned his head to look. But all he saw were boots and lower legs encased in dark blue work trousers. To Kit's surprise, the person stepped straight up onto the prime mover and opened the driver's door. Kit's first reaction was annoyance and then he assumed the person was looking for his father.

But then the person climbed into the cab and from the movement of the vehicle Kit deduced he had seated himself in the driver's seat. That puzzled him as he was sure his father was still in the toilet. But then the starter motor whirred and the engine burst into life!

"Hey! Hey, I'm under here!" Kit shouted.

But just as he did the engine was revved and the noise, along with that of the refrigerator unit, drowned him out. He opened his mouth to shout again but the clash of gears being engaged warned him and near panic surged.

Christ! He is going to drive over me! he thought.

Fear of being squashed or dragged surged. Just behind him were all those sets of dual wheels and he understood that if the driver pulled the vehicle out onto the road at a sharp angle they might just roll over him!

Even as that notion flashed across his brain, the motor roared and the vehicle began to move!

I'm in trouble! Kit thought.

He let out another yell—but as he did he reached up to the front of the trailer and grabbed it, dropping the pressure gauge and banging his face as he did. He was only just in time as the motor roared even louder and the vehicle and trailer lurched and accelerated. Kit found his boots dragging along the gravel. Right beside him, only centimetres away, was one of the trailer wheels and just ahead of him the rear wheels of the prime mover.

For a second or so he considered letting go in the hope that the huge trailer would pass over him without any of the wheels hitting or crushing him. But he lacked the courage and clung on, literally for dear life, as the heels of his boots scraped out onto bitumen.

As they did, another ghastly notion came to him. The prime mover had turned slightly to the right to get out onto the road, but he saw that if even a small turn to the left was made the steel tray and goose neck would grind his hands and he would then drop hard.

And by then we will probably be going much faster. I will really get hurt!

The only option he could think of was to drag himself up and somehow get up on the trailer or prime mover. But to do that he could only use his hands!

Desperation welled, fuelled by fear. Kit blinked to clear the grit that was getting in his eyes from the swirling dust and studied what he could grab. There were several projections and steel flanges. But to reach up to them he would have to let go with one hand!

Oh God, give me strength! he thought.

Gritting his teeth, he hauled himself forward and looked up. He saw that the huge steel towing goose neck was only a few centimetres from his hands. And the tray was hard to get a grip on once he reached above the steel bar used for tie downs. But there looked to be no other choice and he was horribly aware that the truck was accelerating every second and was now really racing along the highway. A glance sideways showed him they were passing the caravan park on the edge of town.

There is a curve to the left before the bridge on the edge of town. I must be up before then.

A sob of near despair escaped him, and he again gritted his teeth and nerved himself to let go with his left hand and reach up. He did it with a convulsive jerk. His hand closed on a steel rod. What it was he wasn't quite sure but all he could do was hope it wasn't some handle that moved. With a huge heave he hauled himself up so that his heels were now only tapping the bitumen occasionally.

To his great relief, he found he was gripping the refrigerated container. Quickly looking around, he let go with his right hand and whipped it up to grab the container's steel bracing higher up. With another heave he lifted himself until his waist was level with the towing goose neck. And that towing pintle was just there and grinding dangerously close to him as the prime mover made slight turns. It was obvious to him that a sharp turn would bring the rear of the prime mover and the front of the trailer together in a shearing action that would mangle his body or legs and either crush him to death or cut him in half. Driven by a mix of fear and desperation, he quickly hauled himself higher up.

Thank God for all those chest heaves I've been doing, Kit told himself.

He was sharply aware that without the strength he had built up he would have fallen off by now. And now he could see what to do. He reached higher up, clinging on with one hand but confident he could do it. Then he lifted his other hand and himself, just as the truck began to turn left and the trailer moved over so that there was no safe space. Gasping with effort and fear, he lifted his knees out of the way and scrambled up another couple of metres, clinging to the narrow steel frames with just his fingertips. But then he was able to brace his boots against the frame of the container. That was an instant and enormous relief.

"Made it!" he gasped.

But almost immediately he realised he hadn't. The grip of his fingertips was so tenuous on the narrow steel flanges that he almost slipped and lost his grip as the prime mover bounced across a bump in the bitumen. Only having his boots braced saved him. He broke into a cold sweat and looked over his shoulder and down.

By then the vehicle was moving at full speed and he knew he would suffer serious, probably fatal injuries if he fell. A glance over his shoulder told him he had to take another terrifying risk.

I have to get onto the back of the cab, or I am a goner! he thought.

That meant crossing the steel gooseneck extension of the low-loader trailer, which was swivelling on the pintle but which had no protrusions he could grab. It looked to be just smooth steel which narrowed from about two metres to one.

Another series of bumps from potholes or badly laid bitumen sent more stabs of fear through Kit. He knew he could not hesitate. Any lurch or bump could send him plummeting to his death! After picking where to grab, he half turned and then hunched before springing backwards. It was an awkward jump but it took him across the gap. The whole time he kept his gaze fixed on the small steel rungs that gave access to the roof of the cab. Sobbing with exertion and fright he clawed at the chosen one.

His right hand closed on the horizontal steel bar, only about 20 centimetres across. As it did, he slammed against the back of the cab—or rather against the pipes, boxes, and fittings that were fastened there. The shock of the impact half stunned him and he felt a stinging blow to his left shoulder. But his fingers closed on the bar. For an instant he fell and he felt his grip slipping from sweat. But his leap had succeeded. His boots thudded onto the rim that ran across the rear of the cab and he scrabbled to grab something with his left hand.

He succeeded. What it was he did not know till he later looked—to find it was a hydraulic cable—but it was just enough. His body swung out and then back to slam hard against the protrusions and steel pieces on the back of the cab again. This time he changed his grip to another rung of the ladder and then braced his boots on the rim between two steel boxes.

Safe this time, he told himself.

Gasping with exertion and relief he looked around, noting the bitumen whizzing by below and the bush they were passing at high speed as almost a blur. For a minute or so he clung there, steadying his thoughts and his breathing. He was trembling with shock and only slowly did he start to consider what to do next.

Chapter 22

TIME TO GET OFF

K it clung on as the vehicle lurched and bumped along. For a minute or so he was so bewildered and shocked by what had happened that all he could do was cling on. But as the adrenaline wore off, he shook his head and took a deliberate grip on his very frightened emotions.

Now, what the hell is going on? Who is driving this truck? And where are we going? he thought. Of one thing he was sure—his father was not driving the vehicle! *That person came from the other side of the road. Dad was still in the dunny over the other way. But how did the person start the engine?*

Kit was sure his father had taken the keys with him, mainly as a safety precaution while he was underneath. Into his mind came a clear image of his father pulling out the ignition key and holding it up to show him.

So how?

Kit knew that motors could be started in many types of older vehicles without a key. "But not this one," he muttered.

And there had not been time. The person had just climbed up into the cab and started the motor almost immediately.

Driven by anxious curiosity, Kit studied the back of the cab to ensure he had plenty of safe handholds and that his boots would be firmly wedged on the narrow platform which held the tool boxes and other fittings. Then he carefully moved across, one limb at a time, until he was just at the right hand side of the streamlining screen that was part of the rear of the cab. Then he cautiously peeked around the outside edge and forward. As he did, he squinted to protect his eyes from the rush of air.

Because he knew what he was doing, he was instantly able to get a reflected image of the driver's face in the rear vision mirror.

"Jellman!" he gasped, immediately pulling back out of sight. Now it was clear.

Jellman must have made duplicate keys of our vehicles while he was working for Dad. The low, thieving bastard!

For the next few minutes Kit clung on behind the screen, mulling over what he now knew. Jellman had obviously stolen the vehicle and trailer. But where was he taking it?

That was a real puzzle. *There is just this one bitumen road until you get to that junction with the Lynd Highway near the 40 Mile Scrub,* he thought.

There were a couple of side roads to properties, and he had noted the sign for the alternate Savannah Way that came down through the bush from Almaden up to the north.

How can Jellman hope to get this big truck and trailer out of the area before the police are alerted and set up roadblocks?

That was the puzzle. He knew it was a couple of hours drive to the nearest town to the north—Mt Garnet, and even further to the next ones to the south.

Greenvale, he thought, was at least two or three hours as well, and the bigger towns that way after the Lynd Junction: Charters Towers and Hughenden, were four or five hours away. In between was nothing but huge stretches of bush and a few cattle stations. He remembered the conversation between his father and Mr MacGregor about the truck thefts in the Cloncurry area.

So how does Jellman think he can possibly get away? Kit wondered.

But then he was almost immediately answered by the truck suddenly slowing down and swinging hard off the highway onto a gravel road. The turn was so sudden Kit nearly lost his grip and had to cling on, one boot slipping off. He swore and scrabbled to get his footing again while looking out to see where he was. But this was difficult to do as the slipstream was now sucking in dust and leaves and throwing grit in his eyes.

The big rig suddenly slowed and brakes squealed. Dust caught up making Kit very aware that they had turned off onto a gravel road. Fear gushed through him as he looked around for the reason for the slowing down. If it was a gate, he decided, he might get a chance to jump off while Jellman opened it. With that in mind, he looked to the left to see if there was any cover in the open savannah woodland beside the road.

To his disappointment, there was very little and he was considering having to lie flat in the grass when the engine was again revved. The rig began to accelerate and then bumped across a steel cattle grid.

No gate! he thought. *So no safe chance to jump off.*

He was sure the truck was still moving too fast for him to safely take that risk.

The trailer rumbled across the grid and then the truck accelerated even more and sped on along the dirt road, bumping and swaying and sucking up a huge trail of reddish dust. On both sides of the road was just fairly open and flat savannah bushland. The yellow-brown grass appeared to be studded with football sized rocks. Now he had to squint and blink continually as the slipstream eddies sucked a real cloud of dust into the swirling turbulence between the prime mover and the container.

Kit then tried to determine the direction of travel and finally decided it was south. The road deteriorated to just two wheel ruts in the long grass, and to Kit it seemed that Jellman was driving at quite an unsafe speed. This was reinforced a few minutes later when the truck suddenly slewed to the right and Kit was nearly thrown off. Gasping with fright he clung on and looked out, noting that the trailer was canting sharply over as it followed the prime mover rapidly around what felt like a right-angled bend.

As they went around, way too fast for Kit's liking, he glanced to the left and again gasped in fright. Right beside them was a steep drop down a rock-studded grassy slope to a creek line.

Bloody hell! If we go over here I could be killed, Kit thought, breaking instantly into a cold sweat as the nearside wheels were very clearly crushing the long grass beside the road.

The wheels even struck a few rocks in the long grass, but by then Kit was clinging on grimly and he was not thrown off. The rig settled back onto its wheels and slowed slightly as Jellman steered it back onto the road. The trailer looked for a second or two that it was going to roll but it then followed and also fell back onto its wheels with a shuddering crash.

Strewth! That was close, Kit told himself.

He licked suddenly dry lips and then looked out, trying to see ahead on the left without his face being reflected in the rear vision mirror. Now he knew he had to get off at the first opportunity. It would mean a long walk—he wasn't sure how far and now wished he'd paid more attention to the time and the distance travelled—but he was so scared that getting off was at the top of his thoughts.

I must get off before Jellman stops, he reasoned worrying that Jellman might have cronies.

Suddenly, the vehicle slowed again and Kit tensed ready to spring off if it slowed any more. But it suddenly went up a steep little slope, and through his watering eyes Kit noted that the road was crossing a sharp little ridge of black rocks. These extended off into the bush as far as he could see. As the rocks definitely offered some places to hide, he changed his grip and nerved himself to spring off—to no avail!

The prime mover suddenly bounced across several rocks and at the same moment changed to going steeply downhill. Kit's boots were bounced off the steel rim they were braced on and he fell sharply.

The drop was so sudden and the pain of his shins banging and scraping against a steel rim so acute that he cried out aloud, before clamping his mouth shut as he realised his mistake. Luckily, his hands had convulsively grasped the steel pipes and he hung there for a couple of seconds as the prime mover rumbled and growled down the small rise, the heavy trailer lurching and banging behind, the container only centimetres from his head.

Hang on! Get up! Kit commanded himself.

Fear helped and he hauled himself back up with his arms and blindly groped with his boots to jam them firmly against something. He managed this just in time as the vehicle was back on flat ground and accelerating again. To Kit's dismay, he saw the ridge of stones receding rapidly.

Just as suddenly, Jellman swung the vehicle to the right. Once again Kit was nearly thrown off, but he clung grimly on and gasped in fright. Out of his blinking vision he noted a dirt vehicle track continue on and then that the truck was moving onto a large clearing which was mostly just dust.

I have to get off soon. If there is anyone else here they won't be friendly, Kit thought, assuming that anyone Jellman knew was liable to be a crook. *I don't want to meet them.*

But he did! All too soon the truck slowed and, as Kit looked out to try to pick some cover to dismount into, he noted that he was now in the middle of a wide, dusty flat with no cover at all. Worse still, there were two men there. That sight sent Kit's heart leaping into his mouth and he stared in alarm. He was sure that the two men would be cronies of Jellman's and that being discovered on the truck would not be good!

One of the men held up his hands and pointed and the semi slowed and began to turn to the left. That allowed Kit a clear view through the widening gap on the right between cab and container—and what he saw dismayed him. He glimpsed the steel rails and fences of a set of cattle yards and then a large, open-fronted, steel shed. This was set back against the side of the stony ridge which here became a real hill. The large rocks on it made the word 'Tors' spring to mind. Amid the rocks and along the ridge, obviously a continuation of the same one the truck had just crossed, were clumps of dark green bushes and more gum trees.

The truck kept turning until it was facing back the way it had come. Dust swirled and brakes squealed. But Kit did not dare move. The two men were back there somewhere. Now the vehicle shuddered to a stop and Kit was enveloped in the trailing dust.

Is this my chance? Do I jump off and run for it in the dust? he wondered.

But even as he thought this, he shook his head as the dust was already blowing clear and was not dense enough to hide in. And there was no cover out in that dusty clearing!

To Kit's surprise, Jellman began reversing the trailer and rig.

What's going on now? he wondered.

The shed he had glimpsed did not look nearly big enough to take the prime mover and trailer. One of his thoughts was that the vehicle was stolen and Jellman would need to hide it. Curiosity warred with terror and it took and effort of willpower to risk a peek. And what he saw dismayed him even more. Then the rig came to a stop and Kit tensed, ready to jump off.

But he didn't. One of the men started walking towards the cab.

He looks a mean bastard, Kit decided.

The man was tall and lean with a hard, hawk-like face, his lower face covered with stubble and the top of the head a woolly mop of untidy black curls. The man wore only a crumpled, long-sleeved, khaki work shirt and soiled and grimy blue jeans and riding boots. But even at a glance his face was not forgiving.

Oh shit! I'm in trouble here! Kit thought.

All Kit could do was stand still, braced against the back of the cab, hoping that he wasn't seen. His heart was already hammering and now it pounded. His eyes went blurry with anxiety and his breath came in rasping gasps. As the thud of the man's boots sounded above the rumble of the motor and refrigerator, the fear shot up another notch.

And there was the man! He came into view right beside the trailer. Kit froze and tensed, ready to spring off on the other side. But the man was focused on the cab and did not turn his head or glance between the cab and the container. He vanished from view and Kit heard his boots thud on the steel treads as he sprang up to the driver's window.

"Bloody hell, Jello! What's this?" the man shouted above the engine noises.

Jellman obviously had his window down and shouted back, "It's one of Walker's trucks. I just nicked it," he replied.

"Just nicked it! When? Where? How long ago?" the man shouted.

"In Mount Surprise about half an hour ago," Jellman answered. He sounded to Kit quite defensive.

"Nicked it! You bloody idiot!" shouted the man. "Why did you do that? Did the boss tell you to?"

"No," Jellman replied. "I was just sittin' in the pub and it pulled up just across the road. Walker himself was drivin' it and he got out and went off to the public dunny over near the railway line. I dunno what came over me but it seemed too good an opportunity to miss."

Hearing this sent Kit's eyebrows up. *He didn't see me!* he thought. That gave him a spurt of hope.

"So how did you steal it? Did he leave the keys in it?" the man snarled.

"Nah, I got me own set of all Walker's keys. I made 'em when I worked there," Jellman replied.

"So why did ya take this bloody thing?" the man shouted.

"Aw, sorry Snake. I just couldn't resist. That bastard abused me and sacked me for no good reason. I hate the mongrel and he owes me," Jellman replied.

Hearing that about his father annoyed Kit, and the injustice rankled. Despite wanting to hear more, he wondered if he could now get off the other side while the two men talked but did not know where the second man was and was afraid to move lest that attract attention. And he really was curious. So he stayed pressed against the back of the cab and listened.

'Snake' obviously was not happy. "So you just nicked this thing on an impulse?" he said.

Kit only heard half of Jellman's answer but it was clear from that that Jellman had just acted on an impulse and that 'Snake', whoever he was, was very angry about it.

191

"You bloody fool! This could land us all in the shit!" he shouted. "By now the cops will be looking for it and there aren't many roads to block or search in this part of the world. What are we gunna do with it eh?" Snake snarled.

"Put it with the others," Jellman suggested.

"Bloody hell! I suppose we will have to, but that means shifting a few things around to make room. Bugger you, Jello! Now you've given us a real problem—and the boss is not gunna be happy. Now switch that thing off and come and help us move the others to make room," Snake ordered.

Jellman immediately obeyed and the engine shuddered to silence. Only the hum of the refrigeration unit running on its battery still broke the relative silence. Kit tensed, wondering if this might give him a chance to get away. He heard Snake climb down and then the driver's door open. There was the thud of Snake's boots in the dust and then Jellman climbed down as well.

Then Snake appeared right beside Kit. His face looked furiously angry, but he was concentrating on somewhere behind the trailer and he strode back out of Kit's view, muttering and swearing. Kit heaved a mental sigh of relief and then tensed again as Jellman walked into view.

Jellman was looking quite annoyed and was shaking his head as he followed Snake. Kit stared down at him, willing him not to look around, sweat now beading his brow and hands.

And then Jellman turned his head and looked up just as he was passing. His eyes went wide with astonishment as he saw Kit and he stopped in his stride. Then he turned and put his clenched fists on his hips and a cruel grin spread across his ugly face.

"Well, well! Look what we have here!" he said.

Oh bloody hell! Sprung! Kit thought.

Chapter 23

CUNNING!

Kit was aghast. He stared back at Jellman, frozen with fear. His next thought was:

Run!

And he acted on it. He turned to jump off the other side of truck but awareness of the hot exhaust pipe was his undoing and his left boot slipped. His leg dropped sharply and he was only saved from falling right down by the strength of his grip on the ladder. But as he frantically scrambled to haul himself back up and get a better stance, his shin struck something and stabs of intense pain shot up his leg. Awareness of his peril was added to by Jellman's loud yells and that sparked Kit to ignore the pain and to spring off.

But his haste caused his right boot to slip on the smooth steel as he leapt off. Instead of the controlled spring he wanted, he went out awkwardly in a sideways leap like a startled frog. So he landed awkwardly. Another sharp pain shot up his right leg and he went rolling in the dust. As he scrambled to his feet and the weight came on his right ankle, it was immediately apparent that he had hurt it somehow. How badly he did not know, but fear got him running and he gritted his teeth and tried to ignore the stabs of pain that shot up his leg at every second step.

A quick glance showed the third man, a middle-aged man with grey hair, a workman of some sort by his grey overalls, was standing and gaping near a steel gate. Thinking he could easily outrun the man, Kit started sprinting towards the ridge of rocks a hundred metres away. But then a shout from Snake started the workman running towards him. A quick glance and an even quicker mental calculation told Kit that the workman—Jones apparently—had slightly shorter distance to travel and would possibly catch up with him before he reached the rocks. So he changed direction to angle away from him.

This gave him the dilemma of shortening the distance Jellman and Snake had to cover coming around the front of the truck. And there they both were! A glance over his right shoulder showed Kit that both men were now racing hard on his heels. And his short legs, injured ankle, and relative unfitness did not help! Within 50 paces Kit was starting to feel winded, and after another 20 strides was gasping. Now he was running directly towards the narrow gap in the rocky ridge through which the dirt road came. For no logical reason it seemed to offer hope, but his rational mind told him that was not so.

Another terrified glance showed that Snake was fast catching up—from being 100 paces behind was now only 50. It was very obvious that Snake was fitter and faster, even in the work boots he was wearing. And Kit could now hear those boots thudding in the dust close behind him.

"Oh help!" he croaked—but it was with despair, and he could see that there was no help anywhere. All around was just bush.

And then Snake was behind him, swearing and panting as he ran.

"Come here, ya little shit!" he snarled.

And then Kit felt the man's hand touch his shirt.

He immediately jinked and managed to avoid the man's grasp. But Snake skidded and swerved in a cloud of dust. He swore and came pounding after Kit and lunged again, grabbing at him. Kit tried to break free and then tripped in a rut and went rolling in the dust. Snake skidded to a stop and hit at him, a sharp blow that only partly connected with Kit's shoulder. Kit shook his body and struggled as Snake got a grip on his forearm.

And there was a hand—just where Sally had trained him to act. Almost without conscious thought Kit stepped forward, obviously catching Snake by surprise.

He thought I was going to try to pull away, Kit reasoned.

He gripped Snake's wrist with both of his and then swung himself quickly around and under. Snake was so taken off guard that he was spun around in an instant. And then it was a simple matter for Kit to use his right leg to sweep Snake's left leg sideways and then, as he lost his balance, to push. Snake cried out in alarm and went sprawling face down in the dust.

Once again Kit broke into a frantic sprint, thinking that Snake would now be very angry. And he was. His furious shouts and swearing and threats made that very clear. A quick glance told Kit that his supposition was correct. Snake's face was a mask of fury. His eyes glittered and his mouth was set in a rictus of apparent hate. And Snake was now up and running.

And once again Kit's short legs and unfit body and lungs quickly led to Snake catching him up again. By the time he did, Kit was nearly 200 paces from the trucks and the gap in the ridge looked to be only about 50 metres ahead. But there was to be no repeat performance. Snake was now obviously wary and instead of grabbing at Kit just struck him hard in the back of the head with his fist, sending him cartwheeling head over heels in the dirt.

As Kit rolled aside and tried to get to his feet, Snake dashed in and kicked him hard in the lower body. The kick both winded him and caused him to double up in pain. Despair and agony mixed as he tried to roll away. But it was no good. This time when Snake grabbed him he grabbed his upper arm and twisted it hard up behind his back.

"Get up you little mongrel!" Snake snarled, hauling him painfully to his feet.

Dazed and winded, Kit could only stand there trembling and gasping. He spat dust from his tongue and blinked to clear grit from his eyes. Fear flooded him so that he could barely move. Snake now shook him roughly.

"Who are you? Where the hell did you spring from?" he demanded to know.

Despite his fear, Kit had to suppress a sarcastic retort that it must be pretty obvious where he had sprung from. Something about the man who was now shoving him roughly back towards the truck made that seem unwise.

"I'm Kit Walker. My dad owns that truck," he managed to croak.

"Walker! What were you doing on the truck?" Snake asked, astonishment clear in his voice.

By then they were rapidly approaching Jellman and Jones who were hurrying from the other direction. Snake didn't wait for Kit to answer but instead began shouting at Jellman.

"You stupid bastard, Jello! How come this kid has ended up here? Why did you bring him?"

Kit and Snake came to a stop facing the other pair in the middle of the dusty open area. Jellman first looked annoyed and then anxious. Spreading his hands and shrugging he said, "I didn't know he was on board. I never seen him."

Snake shook Kit and glared down at him. "Where were you, kid? How did you hide? Were you in the bunk or something?"

On hearing that Kit shook his head but kept his mouth shut. This earned him an instant clip under the ear from Snake who put his face close to his and yelled at him.

"Answer me kid! Tell me how you came to be on that truck!"

To Kit's shame, fear seemed to engulf him and for a few seconds he was unable to speak. Another whack to the side of his head sent his senses reeling but loosened his tongue.

"I... I was on a trip with my dad," he managed to croak.

"Yeah, but how come you were on the truck when Jello nicked it?" Snake snarled.

"I was underneath the trailer checking the tyres when Jellman here walked across and got into the cab," Kit explained, darting a resentful glance at Jellman as he did. "Then, when he started the motor, I thought I was going to be run over so I hauled myself up onto the back of the cab."

Snake swore and Jellman looked surprised. "Why didn't ya just get outa the way?" he queried.

"Because by the time I managed to climb up the truck was going too fast. I thought I would be hurt if I jumped off," Kit explained.

Snake made a face and nodded and Jellman looked sheepish and shrugged. Snake then shook his head and swore again.

"So why didn't ya jump off when you turned off the highway?"

Kit couldn't help himself. "Because Jellman is a very bad driver and was going way too fast. It's lucky he didn't turn the whole rig over at that sharp bend back there," he said, curling his lip at the man as he did.

Jellman went red and stepped forward with raised fists. "Why you cheeky little bastard!" he shouted.

Before Kit could duck, a fist slammed into his face. He was just in time to half turn his head but being held by Snake meant he could not duck completely. The blow stunned him and he tasted blood. Through eyes that were now blurred he saw Jellman draw his fast back.

He went to punch Kit again but Snake swung Kit aside and fended off the blow. "Stop it, Jello, you bloody drongo! We have enough of a problem already now that the kid is here."

"Yeah, well, what ya gunna do about him?" Jellman snarled, clearly angry and annoyed.

He stood there, his chest heaving and fists clenching and unclenching, the image sending shudders of anxiety through Kit.

Yes, he thought, *what are they going to do with me?*

Through his mind flashed a series of ideas, among which was the terrifying notion that he now knew too much so the crooks might want to dispose of him permanently! Anxiety moved up several notches to bowel-watering fear.

Snake gripped Kit firmly and stared at him, worry obvious on his face. "I dunno. I'd better ask the boss. This is a different level of problem. Bugger you, Jello! You should have seen the kid and then none of this would have happened."

"Well I didn't!" Jellman retorted angrily. "I came out of the pub and that was across the road in front of the truck. I saw Walker go around the front and off to the dunny and could see there was no-one else in the cab. I never seen this little shit at all. Bloody little trouble-maker. It was him what got me sacked."

Snake looked hard at Jellman. "Are you drunk?" he queried.

"Aw! I had a few," Jellman replied, obviously put on the spot. "Never mind me! What ya gunna do about the kid?"

"Yeah well, I better ask the boss what he wants," Snake said.

"Just bump the little turd off and hide his body in the back of the caves," Jellman suggested.

Which was exactly what Kit had been fearing, and which sent his anxiety level up to dread. To his relief, Snake shook his head.

"No way, not unless the boss says so. You've given us enough of a problem as it is. Now we got this rig to hide, and we'd better be quick about it. The coppers will be lookin' for it by now."

"Just stick it down in the cave," Jellman said, pointing behind him towards the steel shed.

Kit looked that way but all he could see were a series of steel cattle yards and the open-fronted, steel shed built over near the rocky hill on the long, rock ridge. A smaller shed stood to one side and there was also a typical outdoor 'dunny'. The shed looked to be just a typical 4-bay shed with a back wall and two side walls but open at the front with some boxes and stuff in the left-hand bay on the concrete floor. A work vehicle, a dusty looking 4WD, was parked in the right-hand bay.

Cave? Kit wondered.

At that the older man in the grey overalls looked annoyed and shook his head. "Oh, easy for you to say! We'll have to move both those rigs down there before we can fit this one in."

Snake nodded. "That's right. And we need to move it fast because if the cops come lookin' and we haven't got things out of sight and squared away the whole set-up will go down the tubes—and the boss won't be happy with that. Now move, Jello!"

That made Jellman appear to blanch, which gave Kit a tiny spurt of malicious satisfaction but then his attention was diverted back to his own worries when Snake shook him.

"We better tie this little shit up first. Let's see what we got to do that with."

With that he began half pushing, half dragging kit towards the yards and shed. The other two men hurried along with them and Kit noted that the older man, Jones, kept glancing around at the sky.

Is he worried about the police using an aircraft or helicopter? he thought. Hope briefly flared.

He was hustled in through the open gate and across a smaller dusty yard to a second gate. This was opened and the group continued on to the left side of the shed. Snake stopped at the left hand steel post and held Kit against it.

"Find some rope or somethin', you pair," he snapped.

This took a few minutes. Kit stood and sweated, both from the heat and fear. He noted that Jones went to a small store room or annex in the far back corner of the shed and vanished through a door. Jellman went to the parked vehicle and looked in the back of it. He groped around and then held up some dusty old pieces of rope.

"This might do," he suggested.

Kit mentally agreed but Snake was dubious. "Looks a bit old and rotten," he commented.

That caused Jellman to take a length of the rope in both hands and pull at it. Dust came out but it held, even after Jellman gave it a few sharp tugs. Kit's hopes sank. Snake shoved Kit forward.

"Tie his hands and leave enough to tie his feet," he ordered.

Jellman grunted assent and then shoved Kit hard. "Turn around, ya little shit, so I can tie yer hands," he snarled.

Kit did as he was told, aware that there might be a chance to run if

Snake moved away. But he didn't. Instead he moved to grip Kit's right arm and to hold his hands behind his back. Jellman began fumbling with the rope.

"Cross yer wrists, shitface," he growled.

Feeling Jellman's movements with the rope Kit experienced a torrent of ideas from everything he had read or heard about holding his hands to make it easier to get free when an opportunity offered. He tried to hold them far apart and well up his arms but after Jellman finally got a knot of some sort around Kit's left wrist he began wrapping it around both arms, dragging the dusty rope through the V of Kit's arms in a way that rubbed grit on his tender skin and made him wince with pain.

Jellman saw this and laughed. "Hurts does it, eh? Good! Serves ya right."

He gave the resulting big knot a sharp tug to tighten it. He knelt and started to wrap the rope around Kit's ankles.

Snake pointed and said, "What ya doin'?"

"Tyin' his feet like you said," Jellman replied.

"What, you gunna carry him down into the tunnel are ya? Leave all that end. We will use it to tie his legs after he's walked down."

Kit saw Jellman look foolish and then angry but nodded and stood up. Snake gestured and said, "Just hold him while I go and help Jonesy and open up."

He turned and walked across the shed to the storeroom in the far corner. Jellman glowered after him and then glared at Kit. Kit deduced that Jellman was both angry and aware that he could outrun him so he held him hard against the corner post and passed the end of the rope around it.

Snake went through the same door as Jones and the door closed. There was then a wait of a minute or so before a grinding noise in the concrete and the whirring of distant machinery made Kit stiffen from anxious curiosity. Before his astonished eyes the whole centre section of the concrete floor began lifting at the outer edge. Kit could only gape in surprise as the whole floor tilted up, obviously hinged at the back. Into view, pushing the end of the floor up, came two shiny stainless steel telescoping rods or tubes. To Kit they looked like the mechanisms used on big tip trucks. And where the floor had been was a steep, sloping ramp, angling down into blackness.

Jellman unwrapped the rope from the steel post and jerked him to move towards the top of this ramp.

"Come on ya little weasel, let's get outa sight," he said.

With that he shoved Kit so hard he nearly fell flat on his face. Only by running a few steps—until pulled up with a jerk by the rope held by Jellman—did Kit manage to avoid a nasty fall. Jellman laughed and pushed him again but he was ready for it and managed to keep his balance.

By then they were at the top of the steep ramp and Kit stared down in surprise. He found he was looking at what he half expected to see—ever since a cave had been mentioned—a lava tunnel. Having toured three of them the previous year during the school holiday trip with his family, Kit was ready for the scene. But this lava tunnel looked even larger than even the biggest he had seen the year before. It was huge! It was larger in diameter than a double track railway tunnel and seemed to be crammed with vehicles—prime movers and trailers. The whole scene below was brightly illuminated by electric lights for what looked like half a football field in length. Then it shaded into blackness at a gentle bend.

For a few seconds he gaped and looked around and then had to look down and concentrate on keeping his footing as they started walking down the steep ramp. This, he now saw, was covered with a layer of rough concrete and was made of rocks and gravel. As he and Jellman made their way down, Snake passed them coming up.

"I'll just move those cattle across to cover your tracks. Dump this little troublemaker at the bottom and get back ready to move that rig you pinched," he ordered.

Then a vehicle engine roaring into life ahead of him attracted Kit's attention. He saw that Jones had climbed into the first of three prime movers that were parked one behind the other in the middle of the tunnel. There were a couple of trailers parked over beyond them and further back in the tunnel.

Looking to his right from halfway down the ramp, Kit noted a steel ladder coming down from under the far side of the shed—which explained where Jones and Snake had gone. The ladder led down to a brightly lit workshop area with several benches and an assortment of tools: drills, lathes and the like. Next to it, just visible beyond the parked vehicles was a small kitchen and then a table and chairs and beyond that a couple of bunks.

Then it came to Kit. *This is where the stolen trucks are brought to be worked on. The cunning bastards!*

By then they were at the bottom of the ramp. Jellman staggered and seemed unsteady on his feet. Jones noted this and leaned out of the cab of the nearby prime mover.

"Tie that little bugger up and leave him over there out of the way and go and get ready to back that stolen rig down in here," he shouted, pointing to the wall on Kit's left.

So Jellman did. He just tripped Kit and rolled him over against the wall of the cave near the bottom of the ramp. Then he quickly wrapped the rope around Kit's lower legs and tied a knot.

"Just stay there kid or you'll regret it," he threatened.

Then he walked slowly back up the ramp, leaving a terrified Kit to dread what might be ahead.

Chapter 24

IN THE SERPENT'S LAIR

As Jellman puffed his way back up the ramp, Jones revved the engine of the prime mover and then drove it right over near Kit. For a few seconds Kit was afraid he was going to be crushed under the huge front wheels, but then Jones swung the steering wheel and pointed the front up the ramp. As soon as Jellman vanished over the top, Jones engaged low gear and slowly drove the prime mover up and then out of sight.

Kit watched it go and noted that the prime mover had a few strips of chrome and some shiny new paint, but it looked very familiar.

I wonder if that is Dad's XRT with new number plates and detailing?

Jones obviously parked the prime mover somewhere out in front of the shed as he came walking back down a minute or so later. As he reached the bottom, he scowled at Kit.

"You little mongrel! Now you've given us a real problem," he said.

"You could always just let me go and start running," Kit retorted.

He was scared but reckoned that the worst he might get was a bit of a kicking. *If I'm going to die I may as well say what I like,* he told himself.

Jones made his way to the next prime mover in line and started it up. It was moved forward but to the left over closer to the workbench. It was edged so far up on the other side of the ramp that it blocked Kit's view of the workbench area. Then Jones switched that motor off and walked back to climb into the cab of a parked semi-trailer. This was also driven forward to close behind the prime mover on the other side of the tunnel.

By now the tunnel was filled with exhaust fumes and Kit began to cough and feel sick. Jones switched off the motor and climbed down. Once again he went back and moved the last semi-trailer forward and across. This left a lane clear on the side of the tunnel closest to Kit. Jones then walked past, casting Kit another malevolent glance as he did, and made his way up the ramp again.

Realising he was now alone, Kit at once began testing his bonds to see if he could get free. But it was no good. The bindings seemed to have too many turns and felt too tight. Luckily they were not so tight that they cut off the circulation in his hands and he was able to wriggle his fingers. Temporarily defeated, he lay back, his consciousness a squirming mess of anxiety.

There was then a delay of at least half an hour. During that time he heard motors start up and vehicles move but he could not work out what was being done. There was then a period of silence during which the only sound he was conscious of was the distant throb of a motor somewhere outside that he decided was a diesel generator providing electrical power to the set up.

Then engines started again outside and a sudden blocking of sunlight above him warned Kit that the men were coming back. A prime mover appeared, reversing down the ramp, being guided by Snake who walked along after it using hand signals to help the driver. This told Kit that the prime mover was an older one that did not have a good reversing camera. As it got closer and then scrunched down onto the gravel next to him, Kit studied the vehicle and saw that Jellman was driving it.

That is Dad's truck, the one Jellman just stole, Kit noted, wondering why it had been unhooked from the trailer.

Jellman glanced down at him as he passed, giving a sneer. He continued reversing back along the tunnel and, to Kit's surprise, went on for about 75 metres, almost to the bend. As he did, the truck's reversing lights lit up the tunnel and Kit was able to study the curved structure of the rock, the bands of strata and streaks of dark and white that he knew denoted places where water had seeped or trickled down, or were salts or dried bird or bat dung. It was only as he thought about it that the smells registered in his olfactory sense above the stench of diesel fumes and various oils.

Jellman stayed in the prime mover with its engine going and lights on. Snake went striding back up the ramp, giving Kit a hostile look as he did. There was another delay of a couple of minutes and then the light was again blocked, causing Kit to curl his neck back to look up. He saw the back of the refrigerated container was coming down. It was so large the top of the container was almost scraping the roof and then only just cleared the back of the hinged concrete floor above him. The front of the container also looked as though it might hit the roof, but it slid past the end of the floor with a few centimetres to spare and then the prime mover followed.

There was a lot of hissing of compressed air as brakes were continually applied and the grinding of wheels on the rough concrete and then on gravel and more fumes engulfed Kit, causing another coughing spasm and his eyes to water. The heavy lift trailer reached the bottom of the ramp and began to lift as the prime mover moved backwards onto the ramp. The whole rig was eased down slowly in reverse until the prime mover was also down off the ramp.

Snake was half way down the ramp by then and he used his hands to signal 'switch off'. The engines of both prime movers shuddered to silence and their lights were turned off. Snake started to shout instructions and then suddenly stopped and cupped his hands to his ears. A look of alarm crossed his face and he suddenly turned and sprinted back up the ramp and looked out. Then he shouted down into the tunnel.

"A chopper! It might be the cops. Quick! Close the ramp cover. I'll go up and pretend to be looking after the cattle. Move!"

He went running up and out of sight. Jones swore and came clambering down out of the cab near Kit. Without glancing at him, he went running around the front of the prime mover and over towards the workshop area. As he did, Kit clearly heard the distinctive vibration of helicopter rotors. His hopes went shooting up.

If it's the police I might be saved, he thought.

Then the depressing idea that the crooks might use him as a hostage came to him and he could only hope and pray.

There was a loud hiss nearby and Kit flinched and then saw that the concrete floor, braced underneath he now noted by a criss-cross of steel beams, had started to move. The hydraulic ram near the top of the ramp on his side was where the noise had come from and it was visibly shrinking. Fascinated in spite of the situation, Kit watched the shiny, stainless-steel rod sliding back into its cylinder. The same thing was happening to the ram on the far side near the ladder.

The helicopter noise grew louder and Kit fancied he could even see dust blowing in from the rotor downdraft.

Oh, hurry up and land! he thought as he watched the gap between the concrete floor and the top of the ramp getting smaller by the second. *If they don't hurry it will be closed and they won't see that it is more than just an empty shed.*

But it was not to be, and as the bar of daylight grew less and less, and then abruptly ended, Kit's hopes slumped as well. Torn by anxiety and frustration, he struggled with his bonds and then considered yelling. But he didn't as his rational mind told him it would not be likely to be heard above the helicopter's engine noise.

And the men will probably gag me if I do. Instead he decided to act small and scared—not that that took much acting! *I will try to get them to think I am no threat and stay as inconspicuous as possible and watch for a chance to escape.*

Once again he struggled with his bonds, alternately bending to look at the ropes around his lower legs and out towards where the men were. The crunch of boots on stones caused him to freeze and he looked around. It was Jellman walking towards him from where he had parked his father's stolen prime mover. Jellman made his way over to near him and bent to look then grunted and gave Kit a painful kick in the left thigh.

"Little mongrel! You've spoiled everything," Jellman snarled.

Kit braced for more kicks but, to his relief, the man just turned and walked out of sight around the front of the prime mover near Kit.

There was then another wait of ten or fifteen minutes. During that time there was only the distant vibration of the generator and the occasional mutter or men's voices. This was ended by the clang of steel on steel, and Kit twitched and looked up to see where the sound had come from. He saw that a trapdoor had been opened at the top of the ladder. Boots and then legs appeared and Snake came into view climbing down.

Kit braced himself for whatever might be his fate, dread almost crippling his muscles and emotions. Snake went down out of view and there were voices then the crunch of boots. Around the front of the prime mover came the three men. They came to a standstill looking down at Kit.

He managed to moisten his dry throat and croaked, "Was that a police helicopter?"

To his surprise, Snake answered. "Dunno. Might have been one they hired. It was just one of them little mustering choppers."

"Did it land?" Kit asked.

Snake shook his head. "Nah. I was on me horse moving a few cattle across the vehicle tracks and the beasts started to scatter and I shook my fist at 'em and they just looked into the shed and then flew away. Hey! I'm the one asking the questions."

There was a moment of silence and Kit wondered what his policy should be. But he could not see any point in not answering any questions.

They will probably torture me if I don't answer, he decided. Then he shrugged. *Besides, I haven't got any secrets to give away.*

It was Jones who spoke first. "What's in the container on the back of that trailer? It's a fridge unit."

"Frozen prawns. We got them in Karumba this morning," Kit replied.

"Bugger! They'll be worth a quid or two. I better get power to them," he said.

Snake spoke next. "What were you doin' in Karumba? I thought your dad lived in Cairns."

Kit nodded. "He does. He had to take a big part for a pump on a ship."

Snake frowned. "But he's the big boss. Why was he drivin' a truck?"

"Because he likes to keep his hand in and likes to know what his driver's problems are," Kit replied, experiencing a little glow of pride in his father.

Snake nodded and was about to speak when Jellman cut in. "He's just like all the bosses, a greedy, sneaky bastard who cheats and sweats the workers."

"Stow it!" Snake snapped. "Save yer 'workers-of-the world-unite' shit for later. You are half pissed yer nong so go and sleep it off. You might have to drive later if the boss wants this load shifted and there's no point in having a good set of false papers and a truck with new plates and VIN if the cops book ya for being over the limit."

Jellman looked truculent. "And what are you gunna do?"

"I'm goin' to drive to Mount Surprise to use a public phone to ask the boss what he wants. You be ready when I get back. Jonesy, go and hook some power onto that trailer full of prawns and then get to work and get some false plates put on it."

Kit now spoke. "Can I have a drink please?"

Kit expected Snake to answer but it was Jellman who did. "No!" he snapped emphatically.

"Well, can I go to the toilet please? I need to do a pee."

Jellman curled his lip and then laughed. "No. Do it yer pants, ya little runt."

Snake now spoke. "Come on. Get moving you blokes," he ordered.

Jones nodded and made his way back towards the workshop. Jellman scowled at Kit and followed him. Snake stood there and shook his head then bent to look at the bindings around Kit's legs and arms, half rolling him over to check his hands. After rolling Kit roughly back onto his side, he shook his head again and grunted before also making his way back towards the workshop area. There were more voices and Kit heard Snake's voice raised in anger.

"I said go and sleep it off, Jellman! You might be drivin' all night. Now go!"

Snake then appeared climbing the ladder. Kit watched him with a mixture of trepidation and hope.

He is going to ask the big boss what to do with me, he told himself. But as Snake vanished through the trapdoor, the notion came to Kit that Snake was the really dangerous one. *And he will be gone for a couple of hours. Can I get away?*

As he resumed feeling around his bindings, a dragging noise accompanied by the thud of boots sounded, and then the sound of something being thrown. Jones appeared. He also bent to glance at Kit, who now realised he was lying in a patch of shadow cast by the vehicle next to him. Jones grunted and made his way along the side of the vehicle and bent to pick something up. Kit saw it was a long length of orange-coloured electrical wiring which he had tossed across under the trailer. Jones began unrolling it towards the back of the refrigerator unit. The end of the cord was plugged in and Jones then went back out of sight. A minute later the motor of the fridge unit began to hum. Jones reappeared and checked that it was going and then moved around the trailer with a torch, noting things and tapping at various objects. Kit decided he was a mechanic rather than a driver, and that he was the one in the gang who 'rebirthed' the stolen vehicles mechanically.

As soon as Jones had vanished around the far side of the trailer, Kit resumed testing his bonds. When Jellman had first appeared with the rope, Kit had been dismayed by its thickness but now he realised that the diameter was favourable to him. The rope was so thick that it not only did not cut off his circulation but it made the knots difficult to pull tight. By even a little careful examination, Kit appreciated that the outer bindings were slightly loose.

Being a naval cadet and already trained at basic knots, he also understood how knots worked. He looked around for something to help him tug at the coils of rope. Near him were the wheels of the prime mover but the vehicle did not really offer hope. To get a better look up at it, Kit rolled onto his back, until brought to a stop by a rock.

That got him looking around and he noted that dozens of rocks were protruding from the layer of mud and silt that formed the otherwise relatively smooth floor of the tunnel. Several rocks along the tunnel wall looked quite sharp, so Kit began wriggling towards the nearest. That was a painful thing to do but he gritted his teeth and persevered, reasoning that his life might be at stake, so a few scratches and bruises were neither here nor there.

The rock he chose had a pointed end poking up about 15 centimetres and he was able to lie beside it and, by rolling half on his front, was able to get his wrists up over it. To his intense satisfaction, he felt the rock snag at the coils of rope and he then began to carefully move the ropes until he was sure that the one around his right wrist was the one that was caught. Then he began to slowly work that piece of rope backwards and forwards.

Minutes went by and soon Kit was gasping and sweating. Then he heard the crunch and thud of boots and Kit lay still. Jones came into sight around the front of the prime mover next to him. A torch beam was turned on Kit who lay and pretended he was asleep.

I hope he doesn't notice I moved a couple of metres, he fretted.

To his relief, Jones just grunted and went back the way he had come.

Kit waited until he heard the sound of metal on metal over in the workshop area before starting to work on his bindings again. The specific place he was interested in was where Jellman had first tied the end of the rope around his right wrist. To Kit that had felt like just a simple knot.

Like a thumb knot, just once around itself, not a clove hitch or anything like that.

And he was right. The knot suddenly came undone and Kit's already low opinion of Jellman went down another notch.

Useless mongrel! he thought as a surge of intense satisfaction pulsed through him.

Feeling that loose end got him struggling and squirming frantically until he found he was sobbing and gasping and his muscles were hurting.

Slow down you idiot! he told himself.

He began to systematically test and feel and then discovered that if he pushed against it the outer rope binding bulged up loose. A coil of this was hooked onto the sharp little rock outcrop and Kit then gently rolled away to tug at it. The coils became even looser. More squirming and pushing soon had several coils quite loose and he experimented and found he could move his right forearm up and down. Another couple of minutes of careful testing and moving and he was able to slide his right arm free of the ropes.

Elated, he lay there for a few seconds listening, then quickly set to work with trembling fingers to free his left arm.

Now my legs, he told himself.

His ears still tuned to detect any sound of the men approaching, he sat up and reached down to his legs. That also gave him a surge of intense satisfaction.

If I hadn't done all those sit-ups, I would never have been able to do this, he thought.

And then he was free. He kicked and shook the coils of rope off his legs and then rolled on his front and lay looking around and listening.

I'm free! Now, how do I get out of this place?

Chapter 25

INTO THE DARKNESS

K it lay on his front listening and staring intently around. The thudding of his heart made it hard to hear, and the pools of shadow made it hard to see but his mind was now racing.

I must get out. How do I do that? he thought.

His first hope was up the ramp, but it was immediately obvious that was no option, not while the concrete floor was in place. But could he hide until it was raised and then somehow slip out or even run?

Next, Kit studied the side of the ramp up from where he lay against the wall of the cave. He saw that a narrow space led in beside it, the sides braced and rivetted with steel and timber, but an overhead light left very little shadow in it.

No chance of hiding there, he decided.

The shine of polished steel showed him that the hydraulic ram that raised that side of the floor was positioned there, and no place to hide.

Carefully, Kit looked to his left, to where he could just see above the front of the prime mover the top end of the ladder and the trapdoor. The other ram was also there, but both were in a space that looked brightly lit and were past the area where he could hear someone (Jones?) at work with some grinding machine on steel. There was obviously no chance of sneaking past there and up to the trapdoor.

Kit shook his head and then looked under the prime mover. Through the gaps between all the intervening wheels he could just make out the office and kitchen area and but the lights over them were switched off.

That got him considering if he could hide under or in one of the vehicles until the men were back along the tunnel searching. To test that, he rose to his hands and knees and crawled over under the prime mover near him. Crawling under trucks was no novelty to Kit, and he was able to get right forward where he could peer around the nearside front wheel. The familiar smell of rubber and oils was a comfort to him. From there he could see the start of the office and workshop area, and it was even more obvious he could not sneak past to get to the ladder.

Silently cursing, he half-rolled to move back. As he did, he reached up to grasp a steering rod for leverage. A sharp little sting in the palm of his right hand caused him to let go and draw it away.

Ow! What the bloody hell was that? he thought.

Hunching around he looked up. There was just enough light to see the steering rods and arms. His trained eye quickly detected a small hairline crack in the steel. Rubbing his finger tips very gently on this he found a very small piece of steel protruding. Then it came to him.

This is dad's XRT, the one we were working on when it got stolen. It hasn't been repaired.

He remembered the story of how Jellman had accidentally run the vehicle into a bollard.

That idiot has driven this rig here and ignored the warning we gave him.

Shaking his head in disbelief Kit was about to crawl back under the rear of the prime mover when he heard the crunch of boots coming towards him from the workshop.

Someone coming!

Panic surged and he gasped and quickly rolled back out from under the truck. For a second or two he dithered, wondering if he should start running. But where to?

He will be coming to check on me, Kit assumed.

So bluff seemed the best ploy. With that idea Kit scuttled back to where he had been lying. Snatching up the tangle of ropes, he quickly sat and wrapped several coils loosely around his ankles and then lay on his side and pulled the other end up behind him and around his crossed arms. He knew that his subterfuge would not last a second if Jones actually bent to study the ropes, but he hoped that the pool of shadow would be just enough.

And there was Jones! He came to the front of the prime mover and then stopped. A torch beam was shone on Kit but he just shut his eyes and lay there, heart hammering while hope surged up and down. To his intense relief, Jones did not walk any closer. The torch was turned off and Kit heard his boots receding. He sighed with relief and lay there trembling and sucking in deep breaths.

As soon as Jones was back in the workshop area, Kit pulled the ropes off. But this time he arranged them more neatly so he could pull them back around his legs in a more convincing way if he needed to. Then he went back to thinking hard about how to escape. Once again, he considered hiding in or under one of the vehicles but after a few minutes he shook his head.

These men know all about vehicles like these. They will find me for sure and next time I won't be able to untie the knots.

That seemed to leave only one option—back along the tunnel. Kit had been shying away from that out of fear of what that might entail. But now he thought about the visit to the Undara Lave Tubes the previous year.

They were lava tunnels just like this. And two of them we walked in at one place and then continued on and came out at another place where the roof had collapsed.

So, was there a second entrance to this tunnel? With a sinking heart, now gripped by growing fear, he knew that the only way to find out was to go back along the tunnel—into all that darkness!

It took Kit another minute to summon the courage to start. With a sort of sob of anxiety he stood up, chest heaving, and stared back along the tunnel. The first bit was well lit by reflected light—there were no overhead lights even as far back as the last vehicle. But after that it became steadily more gloomy until the gentle bend in the tunnel which prevented seeing what was further along.

It took another sucking up of courage for Kit to make himself start walking. He understood very clearly that if there was no way out he would be trapped as soon as the men realised he was free. So anxious was he that he found it hard to keep his balance, trembling and sucking in deep breaths. It took another conscious effort to calm himself.

As carefully and quietly as he could, he walked slowly back along between the refrigerated container and the wall of the cave. There was so little room between them and so many small rocks and bumps that he had to put his left hand on the rock wall and to grip the steel of the trailer with his right to keep his balance. At the back of the trailer he paused and looked across to the other side of the tunnel. It was mostly in shadows— but enough light to make out a camp stretcher with a lumpy form on it—a lumpy form that snored.

Jellman! Asleep! Kit noted, his anxiety level shooting up again.

Then he nerved himself and tiptoed across the gap to the rear prime mover. He increased speed past it but then had to slow down as it became steadily darker. As he walked, Kit's mind went back to the visit to Undara the previous year and what he had learned about lava tubes.

They came in all sizes and lengths he remembered. There were also several theories about how they formed. Information that he had learned in Geography lessons at school with Captain Conkey (Mr Conkey really, but Kit always mentally gave him his army cadet title) told him that there were two types of volcanoes: scoria cones and shield volcanoes. The scoria cones were formed by volcanoes which blew out large quantities of dust, ash, cinders, and pumice—that ultra-light grey rock full of gas bubbles.

They make the perfect cones, like Mt Fuji, Kit thought. *And they also make up all those little hills on the Atherton Tablelands.*

Images from a Geography field trip came to him of The Seven Sisters near Yungaburra, Mt Quincan and the hills beside the Kennedy Highway at Wongabel south of Atherton.

But he knew this tunnel must be in the massive shield volcano that was formed by the Kinrara Lava Province. Captain Conkey had shown the class a 1:250 000 scale map of the area with the main contours 'layer tinted' and even from the back of the classroom the lava dome had stood out like a giant fried egg. Kit did not remember the exact details, but he did remember that it was a vast area, half the size of a European country, well over a hundred kilometres across.

It had lots of active craters over a very long time, he remembered.

Some of the lava flows had spread vast distances. Several had flowed east to partially block the distant Burdekin River, forming the swamps and lakes of the 'Valley of Lagoons'. If he had not seen lava flows on TV in places like Iceland and Hawaii, Kit would have had trouble believing it possible.

But here is actual proof, he mused, knowing that some of the discovered lava tubes were thirty or forty kilometres long. Now that was a daunting notion!

As he walked, Kit kept looking up and around. He noted that the walls were streaked with horizontal layers of colours, presumably from different rock types. But there were also lots of vertical streaks and lines caused by salts deposited by water leaking from above. There were also moss and lichens, but these got less the further he got from the 'daylight' near the entrance. A few tree roots hung from the roof or grew down the sides, reminding Kit that the 'roof' of the tunnels was often only a thin layer of rock a few metres thick. It was that knowledge that was giving him hope because the entrance to this one was almost certainly like the entrances to the tunnels he had visited at Undara—caused by a collapse of the roof so that access was possible down the resulting pile of rocks.

Some tunnels were just formed by the magma, the molten rock that is lava at the surface, when it forced its way along fractures in the rock or even melted one layer of rock but not the ones above or below, he remembered.

Images from TV nature programs showing the molten magma streaming across small gaps in cooling black lava—underground rivers of molten material—came to him. But he also had to consider the theory that some of these tunnels were formed when magma reached the surface and then flowed down the existing stream lines and valleys, filling them up but then cooling on top while still flowing molten underneath; to be finally blown clear by steam and gas when the magma pressure eased.

This tunnel certainly looks like it might have been made that way, Kit considered, looking at how smooth the walls were. *It is just below ground level.*

But then his eyes detected other things in the gloom and his thoughts shifted back to nervous anxiety. First he noted a few small creatures he thought might be cockroaches scuttling around among the rocks along the side of the tunnel. Then he saw several toads, and several toad or frog skeletons.

Living creatures live in these tunnels, bats and snakes and things, he thought—and then wished he hadn't.

By then he was rounding the bend and ahead of him was nothing but darkness. His steps faltered and he came to a standstill, his courage temporarily failing him. Tiny bats flitting around his head did not help his composure. He could feel the terror rising and with it the first stirrings of panic clutched at his throat. He had been hoping to see a glimmer of daylight somewhere ahead but instead it was just absolute blackness.

For a minute or so he stood there, breathing heavily and shivering while he considered turning back and again trying to get out somehow. But all his previous observations still seemed valid and he could only stand and shake his head. Then another emotion began to take hold—anger at himself—and shame.

Don't be a coward! he told himself.

That stung his pride and got him moving. Not for anything did he want to be named a coward, not even by himself. So he resumed a steady walk into the darkness—until he tripped on a protruding rock. The stumble slowed him down and worried him.

If I get injured, I will get caught, he reasoned.

So he carefully made his way across to the nearest side of the tunnel—the right as it happened. There was still just enough light for him to pick out the main features and he paused, leaning on the cool and gritty rock wall. Once he looked back and immediately regretted it. Just visible around the bend was a faint glow outlining the shape of the tunnel. The temptation to turn and hurry back to the area of light rose up to almost choke him with emotion.

It took another conscious effort to make himself start feeling his way into the darkness—only to come to a stop after only a few steps.

Water!

Aghast, he realised he was starting to wade into shallow water. It was just visible as a different type of blackness, a few tiny flickers of light perhaps reflecting the distant dimness as his movements sent out tiny ripples. Water, but how deep was it, and how far did it extend? And what might lurk in it?

Fear again brought Kit to a standstill.

Chapter 26

TERROR IN THE TUNNEL

His muscles rigid with fear, Kit stood there in the darkness and debated with himself—go on or go back? Once again he tried to tell himself that many lava tubes had two entrances because part of the roof had collapsed. But did this one? Not knowing added immensely to his anxiety. Once again he thought about trying to somehow sneak past the men to the trapdoor.

But then he clearly heard the clang of someone (Jones presumably), hammering steel on steel.

That might wake Jellman. He will check and find me gone, Kit thought, adding to the swill of fear in his churning stomach. But then he experienced a wave of shame. Once again he berated himself for being a coward. *Come on weakling! Go on,* he told himself.

He gave a little sob and made the effort to summon up his courage. Tears of self-pity sprang into his eyes as he forced his trembling legs to start wading into the darkness. To his relief, the bottom felt like firm sand and the black water was not deep, so he was able to keep moving. But then he nearly tripped on a rock and only just managed to save himself from a fall.

I need to stay next to the wall, he reasoned.

So he splashed slowly across until his outstretched hands encountered slimy, cold rock. Turning left, he resumed slowly wading. By a conscious effort that cost him in emotional stress, he managed to keep wading with frequent stops. Painfully conscious that he needed a pee, he paused to relieve himself. Then he moved on. He was now moving in total darkness. It was so dark that he could not see his hand in front of his face. He tried it and experienced another stab of fear.

But then his imagination became his worst enemy as the water was now halfway up his calves.

Could crocodiles live in this tunnel? he worried.

Urban myths about alligators in the sewers of Chicago eating the sanitation workers flitted across his mind, even though he tried to be rational and tell himself they were just stupid stories. He also tried to tell himself that even if there were crocodiles, they could only be little freshwater ones, like the ones he had seen in the Cobbold Gorge on the family holiday.

But then he remembered what his father had cautioned, about the saltwater crocodiles.

'*Crocodilius porosis,*' he had warned, '*live in all the rivers in the region, even in freshwater hundreds of kilometres from the sea.*'

Into Kit's mind sprang the image of the croc he had seen on the mudflat at Karumba and with that came paralysing fear.

For a few minutes he stood there in knee-deep water, sobbing and terrified. But nothing moved, no other sounds came to his straining ears and his rational mind tried to say such ideas were rubbish as a croc in the tunnel would have nothing to eat. But his mind was filled with horrifying images from TV wildlife programs and holiday trips of lunging Saurians, and he stood, rooted to the spot and trembling.

It took another conscious effort to force his muscles to move and he resumed wading. He was spurred on by again hearing muffled and distant sounds from back where the trucks were.

Have they discovered my escape? Kit wondered.

Anxiety again clutched at his throat and chest. And, to his dismay, the water was slowly getting deeper, now up to his thighs. Worse still, there seemed to be more rocks littering the bottom and the bottom was beginning to have patches of soft mud.

Kit found it all but impossible to estimate how far he had travelled, or the passage of time. But he did think he had gone at least another hundred paces since his shameful bout of fear. But his apprehension increased as the depth of the water did. After another 50 steps he found he was wading in waist deep water and having difficulty in keeping his balance. To add to his woes, he realised he had developed a headache. This was so unusual for him that he shook his head several times and tried to ignore it.

Suddenly, he stubbed the toe of his boot on a larger rock and the next moment he tripped and fell.

Splash!

His head went under and he floundered. Shock and terror flooded his emotions. Not being able to see anything was the worst of all. Only his hands and feet touching bottom gave him any clue as to which way was up. The total darkness underwater he found completely unbearable. Driven by a pulse of sheer terror, he pushed himself up, scrabbling to find the wall and to keep his balance. But he was on a pile of loose rocks and several shifted, depositing him back into the water.

Kit cried out in absolute fear as he fell. Despite his frantic efforts to keep his balance, he again went under, tasting horrible, slimy water. He came up, gasping and spluttering. Once again he floundered and scrabbled to get back up. Using his arms he pushed himself up, water cascading off him, the sounds echoing around the confined space. Luckily this time his right hand encountered the cave wall and he was able to stay on his feet.

Sobbing and gasping he stood there while the water drained off, his heart hammering and his entire body tingling. For a minute or so he just stood there trembling until his nerves settled.

Oh God! he mentally wailed. *Get me out of this! I just want it to stop.*

But he knew the situation would not just go away. It was reality and he took several deep breaths and then instantly regretted licking his lips as the slime went into his mouth.

"Oh yuk! Well, at least thirst won't be a problem," he muttered.

But he knew he had to make himself move. Nobody else was coming to help him.

The only people likely to come are the men and they will probably kill me to shut me up, he reasoned.

The notion that the men could then dispose of his body here in the black, slimy water added another dimension of dread to his already jangled emotions.

That fear over-rode the fear of the darkness and what might lurk in it and got him moving again. He slowly and carefully shifted each foot in turn while keeping his hand sliding along the wall. Another 20 steps were taken without too much trouble, except that the water was now up to his lower chest. And he was having trouble thinking and several times took deep breaths and shook his head.

And then it quickly got much worse. Within ten paces Kit found he was chest deep and he paused for a moment to calm himself before continuing slowly on. And it got deeper. Soon he was neck deep and wondering if he was going to have to swim. The idea of swimming in that absolute total darkness was almost more than he could face.

Suddenly he felt a stinging pain in the back of his right hand. The shock was stunning and fear and adrenaline streaked through his being. He tried to snatch his hand away but, to his total horror, found it was held by whatever it was that had latched onto him.

"Aaargh! Oh my God! What's got me?" Kit screamed.

He again jerked violently back to try to free his hand and then horror was added to horror as he felt a thing—a something—a slithery, moving something, descend onto his forearm and start gripping him. In that darkness he almost fainted with fright.

But a tiny portion of his brain was working at self-preservation and told him what had him—a snake!

Snake! Oh my God!

And not just a snake—a big snake!

Screaming in mortal terror, Kit jerked back and this time fell over, immediately submerging in the slimy water. And to his horror the snake came with him and he felt what might be a coil go around his arm. Driven by primeval fear and the will to live, Kit struggled and fought blindly back. Luckily his boots found the bottom and he was able to push up and get a breath. It was not a very good breath and he swallowed as much water as air and began gagging and coughing.

And then he fell again, the water surging up his nostrils as he felt the snake's body, coil after coil, touching the front of his body and his arm. Utter panic gripped him at the feel of that reptilian touch. And the creature still had its teeth into his hand!

Again his frantic struggles helped. He slammed against the wall of the tunnel underwater, his elbow taking the shock. But that helped him get oriented and he was able to use his legs to push himself up. Once again water cascaded off him and he gasped and then used his left hand to grab at the snake at its neck. Again a glimmer of sense penetrated the almost complete funk that he was in. It told him that the snake must be a python.

Not a poisonous snake. They just strike and stick their fangs in and then withdraw, he thought.

But the bite was hurting and terrified him and he tried to pull the snake's jaws from their grip, only to cause more searing stabs of pain and then to smell blood—his own blood! The snake tightened its grip and then a coil slid around his right arm. Then part of a coil—the tail?—

slithered up and started to go around his neck. Knowing that pythons were constrictors sent another spurt of fear through Kit.

They kill by constricting, by suffocation, he thought. *I mustn't let it get a coil around my neck or chest.*

Letting go with his left hand, he reached up and grabbed at that terrifying, moving tail and heaved the whole coil back up over his head. As he did, he got a better measure of the size of the reptile. It was actually only about as thick as his arm. That was a relief. He had seen pythons ten or more metres long and as thick as his legs at the zoo. He knew that he would not have been able to fight off a creature that big.

His left hand again groped and found the snake's head and neck. For the next couple of minutes he struggled with it, sobbing with desperation. Terror added strength but the serpent was stronger and he could not break its grip. Then he fell again and was under water in that terrifying total darkness.

Frantic to live, he again felt the bottom, got onto his knees and then managed to get his feet under him. He struggled up but overbalanced and bumped his head on the side of tunnel. For a few seconds he stood there, half stunned and in mortal dread. But that gave him desperate idea. He started banging the snake's head against the rock wall. After the third desperate blow, the jaws suddenly let go and Kit held it off with his left hand. Feeling it twitching and uncoiling he cast the head away from him, hearing it land in the water with a splash.

The rest of the reptile fell off and Kit found that almost as terrifying. The creature was just there somewhere but he could not see it! And his own struggles were making so much noise he could not hear it. Desperate to get away, Kit turned and started to flounder on along the tunnel, even into neck deep water. Then there was no bottom and had to swim! Knowing that the python was swimming somewhere near him and might attack again at any second sent frissons of fear pulsing through him.

Terror again almost paralysed Kit. But he had to keep his muscles moving to swim—a gasping sidestroke. And then he slammed into the wall of the tunnel. Just in time his hands felt the rock, so his face did not hit the wall. Gasping and disoriented, he dogpaddled and then his boots touched bottom. Sobbing with relief he stood up. Feeling totally disoriented and afraid, Kit could only stand and shake for a minute or so.

All that time his ears were straining for any clue as to the whereabouts of the snake. He found that the fear of the unknown was much more potent than actually confronting the creature. Slowly he calmed down, consciously now controlling his breathing. A bout of dizziness made him almost faint, and he feared he had struck his head too hard on the rock wall.

I must keep moving, he told himself.

Very carefully he leaned on the wall and began feeling with his boots so as not to trip into deep water again. After a dozen steps, he stopped and let out a sob, part exasperation, part annoyance.

I am using my left hand to lean on the wall, he told himself. *I am going the wrong way! I am going back towards the men.*

Thinking hard he agreed that was so. It seemed to take an enormous effort to reason it out but finally he was sure. So he turned around and put his right hand on the rock wall. That hand hurt, throbbing with pain—and he hoped not with poison—and seeping blood from the tooth incisions and scratches. But he had nothing to bandage it with so he just rinsed it off and shrugged, then started walking again.

But every step took a measure of courage. Into his mind had come a memory of that previous visit to the lava tunnels. One of the rangers had shone a torch up and in its beam Kit had seen a small, very pale snake hanging from the side of the tunnel.

'They live in cracks and fissures,' the ranger had explained. *'To hunt they get a firm grip in a crack in the rock with their tail and then hang down and wait for a bat to fly close.'*

The idea of trying to catch food like that had struck Kit as amusing and not very believable at the time, even after learning that many snakes did not use their eyes in the dark but actually had infra-red sensing. But there was nothing amusing about the situation now, and he had to suck in deep breaths and summon up will power to move his hand along the cave wall and to take every step.

The water grew deeper again until he could just keep his chin above water. He found he was coughing and sobbing and wondered if he was reaching the end of his nerves.

Is there no end to this bloody tunnel? he fretted.

All he wanted to do now was sit somewhere dry and recover his composure. But there was more water, slightly shallower—between chest and waist deep—and that was a help, except that there were slippery patches of mud.

By sheer willpower he forced himself to go on. Prickling anxiety about the possibility of the snake attacking again kept bothering him, but after looking behind a few times he just felt foolish as he could see absolutely nothing. And then the water began to get shallower and abruptly ended at a jumble of rocks. The change was so abrupt that Kit stumbled and almost fell forward, his hands breaking his fall by landing on and gripping slimy rocks which blocked his path. Kit paused, chest heaving with emotion and rapid breathing.

Is this the end of it? Is this a rock fall where the roof of the tunnel has collapsed?

Chapter 27

COURAGE TESTED

For a minute or so Kit leaned forward, gasping and shivering. Then he began to carefully feel what he had encountered.

Definitely a rock fall, he decided.

Most of the rocks felt to be about the size of a football but they were rough and jagged, not smooth. Worse still, they were coated in slimy feeling stuff—mud or moss or something, which made them very slippery. Very slowly he crawled up onto the rocks and clear of the water. That was a huge relief, but he was now consumed by excitement and hope so, rather than resting, he kept feeling his way upwards. As he did, the water drained noisily off him. Once again he was thankful for his father insisting he wear long trousers and long sleeves as the rocks were quite jagged and sharp.

Soon there was no doubt—it was a huge pile of rubble and could only be the result of a roof collapse. Heartened, Kit continued to slowly grope his way up towards the top. As he did, his eyes kept flicking from side to side, searching for any sign of light or a gap. To his intense disappointment, he could not detect even the slightest glimmer or lightening. This brought him to a stop for another short period before anxiety and hope again drove him upwards.

A sharp blow to the top of his head caused him to cry out and brought him to a crouch. Rubbing the top of his head he stared around and then reached carefully up. His fingers encountered rock. It was what he had feared.

I've reached the top and hit the roof, he told himself.

The bump on his head had hurt and he stopped for a few moments to allow the pain to ease and to gather his thoughts. First, he very gingerly felt around the top of his head. There was some pain, and he winced, but he was then sure nothing was actually broken. He could not be sure about bleeding as his hair was still wet and plastered to his scalp

Next, he began to carefully explore the gap between roof and rockpile with his fingers, each move taking its emotional toll on his nerves. To his surprise, he found that the roof was actually a large single slab that seemed to slope downwards. His questing fingers found the slab was resting on a large rock with a fair-sized gap beneath it.

After swinging his head to and fro trying to detect any light, Kit lowered himself until his chest was on the rock pile. Then he began pushing himself forward into the gap. But his fingers encountered nothing but rock. The only gaps were tiny ones between the stones. Kit tried to crawl into a gap but quickly discovered that the gap just ended. In the process he bumped his head again and he backed out, shaking his head and feeling dizzy.

For a minute or so he crouched there, trembling with anxiety. No matter which way he looked there was nothing; not a single lightening of the dark.

Stygian dark, he thought, remembering a phrase his English teacher had used.

Some sort of classical or ancient myth, but he had not been paying attention and could not remember the details. The only ancient myth that came to mind had the river of death in the underworld in it.

The River Styx, he thought. Then he remembered that coins were needed to pay the ferryman or his soul would be damned eternally. *And I haven't got a single coin on me!*

That notion got him shivering with mortal dread, and it took a mental effort to get control of his imagination and to calm down sufficiently to think what to do next. To test if there was a gap somewhere, he sniffed at the air and then wet his finger and held it up to try to detect any flow of air. That was now his hope, that fresh air might be coming in from somewhere. But there was no hint of any breeze or even a waft of air. Again he wet his finger and held it up but still felt none of the cooling evaporation on only one side of his finger that he was hoping for. Disappointed, he clung there, sobbing and terrified.

Perhaps there is a gap somewhere else? Kit considered.

That stood to reason. The tunnel was at least 15 metres to 20 metres wide. Slowly but carefully he began moving sideways along the top of the rock pile. His only other choice was to give up and go back to the entrance. But that was a dismaying concept too.

Jellman and his mate will surely have discovered my escape by now and they will be waiting for me, he thought. He was sure their meeting would be painful! It was enough to make him groan with despair. *All my options seem bad.*

Stubbornly determined not to give up, he resumed his search for a gap in the rocks. But his hopes kept going down and he frequently stopped to calm himself and to rest. By then he was feeling battered and upset. His thoughts seemed to whirl and his headache felt worse.

But doggedly he kept on exploring, almost inch by inch, until he came to where the roof obviously curved down on the other side of the tunnel. Defeated in that plan, he gritted his teeth and began probing his way back again to check some of the large gaps a second time. At the same time he kept looking for light and feeling for any air flow.

Then one of the rocks he touched moved and fell a few centimetres and the one above slid lower with a loud grating sound.

Can I dig my way out? Kit thought.

He lay painfully on the rock pile and used both hands to reach in and feel. He was very wary, not wanting to have a loose rock fall on his head.

"I've had enough bumps on the head already," he muttered, very conscious now of his throbbing headache.

There was another rock that felt loose and he gripped it with both hands and pulled. To his dismay, there was a loud cracking sound just above him and then a rumble and several large rocks obviously moved. A surge of panic made Kit let go and put his hands up to protect himself. But the noises stopped and left him shivering there in fright.

Into his mind came more images from the previous year's visit to Undara. The group had walked along a foot track in open savannah to a line of dark green vegetation. In the middle of it they had been shown several places where the roof had collapsed but no opening had occurred. They just looked like huge craters; massive depressions of black and grey rocks with trees and bushes growing around where the plants had been able to access the water below.

The thought that he had almost started a cave-in set him shuddering.

If the roof collapses I will be buried under tons of rock, he thought. *Nobody will ever find my body then.*

That conjured up more ghastly images, of dying slowly, crushed by the rocks and then… He could not face the ideas that followed and just lay there sobbing.

"Keep looking!" Kit snarled at himself, ashamed he was a coward.

So he resumed feeling his way back across the top of the rock pile, but suspecting now that there probably was no exit. Suddenly, something moved under his left hand as he put it down. He felt a tiny shape wriggling and then a sharp, stinging pain in the flesh on the side of his hand near his little finger. His first thought was another snake but then the scuttling feeling in the millisecond before he snatched his hand back brought other horrors to mind: scorpions and centipedes.

And it hurt! The stinging sensation grew rather than faded and terror stabbed at Kit's heart.

"Oh help! I've been stung by something," he cried aloud. But was it a snake or a scorpion, or a centipede?

Whatever it was it scuttled rather than slithered, he decided.

And again images from the tourist trip caused him to blanch with anxiety. There were both scorpions and centipedes living in the tunnels. The ranger had shown them several, the biggest centipede being nearly 20 centimetres long!

Now the pain was extending up his hand into the wrist and arm and with it came fear of death.

"Help me!" he shouted.

But the sound just echoed away and seemed muffled. And the only people who might hear were the men—who might kill him anyway! As the pain got worse, Kit knelt on the rocks and sobbed. He gripped his left hand with his right and was aware that his left hand was not only hurting but that it was puffing up. Whatever the creature had been it had a poisonous sting and it was having a rapid effect on him.

"I'm going to die in here!" he cried aloud.

Gripping his wrist tightly, Kit crouched uncomfortably in the darkness and began to cry and then pray. The pain kept pulsing up his arm and reached his armpit and he let go of the wrist and felt up under his armpit at the lymph node. He knew well enough from Navy Cadets how to treat such a bite but other than pulling off his shirt and attempting to tear into strips to make a compression bandage he lacked the means. But he did at least remember that it was important to reassure the patient and to keep them from moving.

"Calm down!' he ordered himself, aware that he was not acting very rationally.

His thoughts went over the First Aid lessons; about restricting the flow of blood back towards the heart through the lymphatic system. But all he could do was grip his wrist and that obviously wasn't working. His whole left hand was now pulsating and throbbing with pain and felt twice its normal size. And a definite lump had developed under his left armpit.

That means the lymph gland is trying to block the poison, he thought.

But knowing that the next part of his body after that was his chest and in that was his heart did nothing to reassure him. He felt panic growing until it seemed his chest would inflate and explode.

Kit began to gasp and felt dizzy and collapsed onto the rocks. That scratched his face and chest and hurt so much it shocked him. Awkwardly on the uneven rock pile, he levered himself to a sitting position and sat there sobbing, praying to God and gripping his left wrist. His thoughts moved to death and then to the Hereafter. Up till now Kit had not been particularly religious, and had not thought much about death and dying, but now the concept was thrust into his consciousness. He began to wonder if there was a God and if He would forgive him for all his sins.

But after a few moments thought Kit shrugged. "What sins? I'm only a kid. I haven't done anything bad," he muttered.

He did not think being rude with a few girls counted as much of a sin, not when compared on the scale of possible crimes. And then more rational thoughts came to him.

If it was a scorpion I won't die, not unless I have a particular allergy, he reasoned. He knew that Australian scorpions had a painful sting but that this was rarely lethal. *Not like those scorpions in Africa and Asia that you read about or see in the movies.*

And he remembered someone saying that centipede stings were only dangerous if the person had a particular allergy.

Am I one of them? Kit fretted.

He was suddenly overwhelmed by emotions: fear of dying, exhaustion and despair. He began to cry, real crying this time, with tears running down his cheeks while he sat there in that terrible darkness all alone.

But another sort of pain came to his aid. The rocks he was sitting on hurt his backside too much and he had to shift to a more comfortable position. Having done so, he so carefully felt his left hand again. To his dismay, it definitely felt puffy and soft and his anxiety increased. He realised he was panting and feeling dizzy and disoriented. Once again his heart rate increased with apprehension.

The poison must be working fast! he thought.

Then have a memory of something the ranger on the tour the previous year had said struck him like the proverbial thunderclap.

My headache might not be from bumps on the head, he thought. *It might be from poisonous air.* He amended that to mean air that was lacking in oxygen. *The ranger explained how nitrogen sometimes built up in the tunnels to dangerous levels and he showed us the skeleton of a wallaby that had died.*

Fear suddenly stabbed through him at this possible new peril. Kit took a deep sniff to test the idea, but then realised that possibly wasn't a good idea.

That will just draw more bad air into my lungs, he reasoned. Something the ranger had said about the same problem that afflicted deep sea divers flitted across his mind. *Nitrogen narcosis? Making bad decisions because the nitrogen affects the mind?* Kit worried.

And was that exactly what he was doing now? The thought caused him a little sob of near despair. Into his mind came more images: the canary in the coalmine for exactly this danger and the story that his teacher had read in primary school about the miners in the old days whose light was provided by candles and who knew there was danger when the candle flame changed colour.

Was it to blue? Kit puzzled.

Then he shook his head. It didn't matter. He didn't have a candle anyway!

And then another horrifying idea took firm root in his thoughts: *Those crooks have been running diesel engines in this tunnel. Has there also been a build-up of carbon monoxide?*

That concept got him feeling really anxious, his chest tightening up and exacerbating his feeling of dizziness. He knew from Chemistry at school that carbon monoxide was colourless and odourless but he was sure he could now smell diesel fumes. Again he looked around almost frantically for any hint of a light or the feel of any fresh airflow.

None. Kit realised he was faced with a real 'Devil and the deep blue sea' situation.

"If I stay here, I will die. I have to go back!"

But fear held him there for another couple of minutes during which he experienced a flow of morbid and terrifying thoughts.

If I die here nobody will ever find my bones. Poor Mum and Dad! They will be devastated. Then he thought about his friends and who else might be upset by his passing. *There is Diana—no, not Diana. It is poor little Elise who will miss me the most.*

And then another dismaying thought came to him: he must go back through that water!

Terrifying memories of that ghastly encounter with the snake caused him to tremble with apprehension. He sobbed and wondered how he could possibly summon up the courage to face that situation again.

But his head now felt like it was spinning. He did not know if it was from the snake bite, the centipede sting, or the poisoned air. But what was crystal clear to him was that he had to make a decision—and make it quickly.

Chapter 28

THE DEVIL AND…

For a few more seconds Kit dithered, but he knew he had to make himself move.

"I can't stay here. I need to move fast before I collapse from the poisoned air," he muttered.

Across the window of his mind flitted the horrors of going back through that black water in total darkness.

Oh, this is going to be a test of courage! he told himself. Then he gave a wry grin. *Come on O Ghost Who Walks! The Phantom would not hesitate like this.*

By an effort of sheer will power he forced himself to move. He began lowering himself slowly down the rock pile, careful that his rubber-soled gym boots did not slip and very aware of the sharp edges—except on his left hand which felt puffy and numb. When he realised that, he paused to test it and then to use his right hand to gently feel and squeeze. The left hand was definitely not as swollen as he had thought. And the pain had subsided. There were no longer shooting pains up his arm and a careful probe determined that the lump in his armpit was still there but not as noticeable.

Maybe I am not going to die from the sting, he told himself.

His hopes went up and he resumed his careful movement downwards. He reached the water sooner than he had expected, only realising it when he felt his gym boots getting wet. Here he paused for a few seconds to think.

Which wall should I follow back? he wondered.

He knew he had to follow one of the cave walls or he would possibly swim in circles. He also knew that the one on his left was closer and he that knew the route. But that was the one where he had been attacked by the snake!

But I know that I can walk most of the way back with no difficulty, he reasoned. *I don't know what the other wall is like, or how deep the water might be.*

It was another of those cruel dilemmas that he felt were all too much. He just wanted it all to end; he wanted to just sit down. But he had to move. After spending another couple of seconds dithering in self-pity, he knew that he really didn't have a choice.

Better the Devil you know! he told himself.

But the possibility of another battle with that snake was very daunting. Then another poetic notion came to him: the old saying of being caught between the Devil and the deep blue sea.

Well, I wish it was the deep blue sea. I could cope with that better.

But there was nothing to be gained by waiting and he was again reminded of his peril by a bout of coughing. The pressure from the coughing pushed at the back of his eyes with each cough in such a painful way he was afraid it would harm them. Only then did he realise his eyes had a burning sensation around them and he wondered if that was caused by the fumes.

Torn between being frightened to stay and afraid to go, he forced himself to start crawling to his left along the edge of the water across to the wall of the tunnel. Several times he slipped and that resulted in a few painful whacks on knees and elbows and fingers. And then he reached the cave wall and really had to force himself to go on.

With a sob he began to carefully edge down into the water. Nothing bad happened and he found he was standing on firm sand in knee deep water. Then he started walking, sliding his boots along the bottom so as not to trip and keeping his fingers against the wall for balance. To his dismay, he found he was reeling and unsteady on his feet. That was the scariest bit. And his headache seemed worse, reaching the 'splitting' stage.

Oh my God! If I faint, I might drown, he worried.

That fear kept his left hand against the rough stone of the cave wall. Wading in the dark was horrible.

That snake is somewhere ahead. Oh my God! God help me! he thought, his body trembling with anxiety.

He had to fight down the temptation to scream and shout for help. Angrily he lectured himself.

"Forget the snake! It's only a python. If it was a poisonous snake you would be collapsing and dying now. Now get out of here before the gas kills you!"

So he continued to wade slowly along, his numb hand scraping along the rock wall. The water became deeper, as he knew it would, and soon he came to the deeper part and had to swim. That got him sobbing with fear and then coughing from foul air. As he tried to control the coughing, he swallowed water and choked. For a few seconds he had to tread water, terrified of losing contact with the wall and of drowning in that inky blackness. Luckily his fingers encountered a rocky outcrop and he was able to grip it while he spluttered and coughed. As his breathing returned to normal, he clung on to the rock and allowed himself a minute or so to slowly recover. Then he resumed swimming.

To his enormous relief, he felt his boots hit the bottom again and he was able to rest and then wade, his head just clear of the water.

Oh God, is there no end to this? his mind cried.

The whole time his ears were straining for any sound that might warn him of the approach of the snake. He knew he must be in the vicinity of where it had attacked him and he began to softly whimper and sob with anxiety.

But nothing struck at him and he found the water was now only chest deep and getting steadily shallower. He tried not to allow hope to blossom too soon but it was an emotion he found hard to control. When the water was only waist deep, he gave several long sighs and felt sure that the worst was now behind him.

Except those men are still ahead of me!

Kit plodded on, still cautiously sliding his boots to avoid stepping unexpectedly into a deep hole or tripping. Several times his boots encountered rocks but he was expecting that so avoided falling. Despite his headache, he was able to keep his wits about him to that extent. And he found that his fingers were starting to tingle at the tips. That awareness brought him to a stumbling standstill and he carefully felt his hand.

No doubt about it! The hand was starting to lose its swelling and feeling was returning. Only then did he realise that there was blood.

I've scraped them raw on the rough stone! Kit thought in astonishment.

But it didn't hurt much, and it only felt like only a trickle of blood, so he sucked at them and then shook his head and resumed walking.

The water grew steadily shallower and that sent Kit's spirits up.

Not far to go to dry land, he told himself.

He began counting his slow steps and at 50 stopped to get his breath.

A bout of dizziness almost sent him reeling but he managed to lean on the wall and steady himself. The worry that the air in that part of the tunnel might also have too much nitrogen or carbon monoxide for safety got his feet moving again.

And then he detected a lightness, a glow. Kit blinked and stared then rubbed at his sore eyes.

Yes! I can see the shape of the tunnel. I've made it back.

After another 25 paces he was wading in water that barely covered his boots and then he found his boots padding on dry mud. He was clear of the water! That was such a relief that all he wanted to do was throw himself down and sob. But he knew he must keep moving, and after another 50 paces Kit was sure.

That is the electric light at the workshop area, he told himself. *But are the men there? Have they discovered that I got free? Are they waiting for me? Talk about between the Devil and the Deep Blue Sea!*

By then Kit's head was pounding to the rapid beat of his heart. His eyes kept going in and out of focus and he realised he was staggering. He tried to lean on the wall but found he had stumbled away from it. When he tried to change direction he reeled unsteadily and then fell to his knees. Dismayed and worried in case he blacked out and then died of poisonous gas, he made the effort to get back to his feet. He immediately felt like he was losing his balance and staggered forward.

Once again he tried to get back to the wall but after a few faltering steps realised that he really needed to cross the tunnel to follow the other wall.

That will keep me in shadow longer and it is the side I need to be on to get back to where they had me tied up, he rationalised.

For a few seconds he stood there swaying and blinking and then remembered what he was trying to do. With an effort he focused and managed to turn to face the wall to his right.

Still feeling woozy and unsteady, he walked across the 20 or so paces to the other wall. On reaching it he leaned on it and found his head spinning and his throat and lungs feeling as though he was breathing sand. To his horror, he felt a cough start tickling the back of his throat.

Don't cough! Don't cough! The men are just around there, he told himself.

In desperation he fell to his knees and used both hands to cover his mouth and nose. The result was a few painful but muffled grunts, each one sending a painful stab through his skull. But he managed to avoid a bout of coughing. For perhaps a minute he knelt there, dry retching and gasping, his consciousness swirling in and out.

"Come on, move!" he ordered himself.

By what seemed like a massive effort he got to his feet, still leaning on the rough rock face. Then he turned left and began groping and stumbling towards the light. This turned out to be harder than he imagined as he kept stubbing his boots on rocks, even though his eyes had noted them. For some reason his boots felt like they were made of lead and he had extreme difficulty lifting them. But he was cheered by noting that the mud had given way to dry sand.

Twice he tripped and had to painfully get to his feet, but after another minute or so he finally staggered around the bend, the backs of the vehicles slowly coming into view with each painful step. Kit kept blinking and trying to focus his eyes, searching for any sign of the men.

Where are they? he fretted, afraid they were hiding and ready to pounce out and catch him. He was sure a kicking or a bashing would then result.

Fear brought him to a standstill on the edge of the bright lights. He found he was trembling and gasping for breath. And still no sign of the men! Then he jumped with fright at the sound of steel being hit by steel. Kit flinched and looked anxiously around and then the sound of banging on steel came again, along with the murmur of voices.

Then Kit quite clearly heard Jones say, "Hold the bloody thing tighter!" and then the banging began again. That puzzled Kit.

That must be Jones and Jellman working on something. Surely they have discovered that I have escaped?

Kit frowned and edged forward, keeping in the shadow of his father's trailer as much as he could.

Is that Snake bloke back? Is one of them waiting for me? he wondered.

But the sound of working went on and there did not seem to be any alarm or anxiety in the tone of the men's voices. It gave Kit the impression that they were not searching for him. That surprised him and he wondered how long he had been away. It had seemed like hours, but he realised that it may have been much less than that.

It just seemed like a long time, he told himself.

He reached the back of his father's trailer and reached out to steady himself. To his surprise, he got the sensation of cold metal through the fingers of his left hand. Glancing at it he noted that it was still a bit swollen but had definitely gone down. At that he shrugged and told himself he obviously wasn't going to die from the bite or sting of whatever it had been.

Or not immediately anyway!

Every nerve alert Kit continued moving back towards where he had been tied up, alternately crouching to look under the vehicle and forward. Reaching the front he paused and peeked around.

There is Jellman's bunk but he's not in it, Kit noted.

So where was the man called Snake? Was he back yet or not?

Kit clung to the front fender for a few seconds as a wave of dizziness almost made him collapse and then he stealthily crept forward, head spinning and eyes going in and out of focus. Now he was beside the refrigerated container and the noise of its motor blanked out any sound the men might be making. There, only about 25 paces ahead, were the ropes he had left in an untidy tangle when he had escaped.

Do I go back there, or do I keep looking for another way out? he wondered. *How the hell do I get out of this place?*

Chapter 29

WORK EXPERIENCE HELPS

Kit realised with some dismay that he was right back where he had been an hour or so before. Still thinking hard about how to escape he made his way forward beside the refrigerated container until he reached the back of the prime mover.

Just as he did, he heard footsteps and Jellman say, "I'll just check."

Oh no! Here he comes! Kit thought.

At the same moment it came to him that his escape must not have been noticed or such a comment would not have been made. If that was so then bluff seemed to be the best option again. Quickly he scuttled to where he had left the ropes. Sitting down he reached down and began to try to arrange coils of rope around his ankles.

But the sound of boots was close and Kit had to give it up. With a little sob of despair he lay down and gripped the remainder of the rope up out of sight behind his back—and just in time! Jellman came wheezing around the front of the prime mover. This time Kit twisted his head up to look at Jellman with a mixture of hate and anger. Thinking it was the best policy made him glare at the man. Jellman saw this and curled his lip in a return sneer. He strode over and Kit feared he would bend down and check the knots.

To his enormous relief, Jellman did not. He just walked over and kicked him hard in the stomach.

"You little shit! You'll get yours when the big boss arrives," he snarled.

Kit made no reply, partly because he was now half-winded by the blow and partly because he did not want the man to stay and look carefully. To his great relief, Jellman didn't check his bonds and just turned and walked away.

Kit lay there, gasping and curled up in pain but seething with anger until he heard Jellman speak to Jones. He could not determine the actual words other than 'yes' but it seemed that Jellman was reporting that he was still there.

Then Kit heard Jones say, "Now grab onto that end again."

Kit was amazed. *They did not check that I had escaped the whole time I was in that awful tunnel,* he thought.

Which got him again trying to calculate how long he had been away. At the time it had seemed like hours—just forever emotionally—but now he decided it must have only been half an hour to an hour.

And that Snake bloke must not be back yet. And Jellman just said something about the Big Boss. I wonder when he will get here? Which got all those dark fears swilling up again until he felt like fainting. *I need to get out before the Big Boss arrives,* he told himself. *Now, how do I get out of here?*

His first move was to get free of the ropes again. But this time he lay the rope in neat coils so he could quickly pull them back into position. Then he crouched and looked around. Deciding to see if there was some other entrance on the far side of the tunnel, Kit crept under the truck and across to the other side. Here he looked in all directions and then did a stealthy creep around behind and under the next prime mover. From there he could study the closest part of the workshop where the two men were working on some sort of steel framework. He carefully scrutinised the 'office' with computer, printer, and folders on a table, the small kitchen set up; and the other way, the bunks along the cave wall. To his great disappointment, there was no sign of any other tunnel or entrance.

Kit was left feeling defeated and frustrated. *How the hell do I get out?* he thought.

For a while he considered trying to steal one of the prime movers and simply driving up the ramp to smash his way out. But that depended on getting the key to that vehicle.

Where are the keys kept? Kit wondered, eyeing the office table. But then he shook his head. *I doubt if I can do it. That concrete floor will probably be too heavy and might be locked and the truck won't get up enough speed anyway,* he brooded.

He rolled back to the other side of the truck and studied the steel frame below the concrete floor. He shook his head. It looked strong and heavy.

And the only prime mover in position has our heavy lift trailer hooked on and that container full of prawns on it. That will weigh too much to get much speed going up that steep ramp, he thought. It was all dispiriting.

And then suddenly the steel trapdoor clanged open. Kit froze in fright and then moved to look up. To his added dismay he saw Snake's boots and lower legs appear.

Oh bugger! He's back. He will be more thorough, he thought.

That got him moving. As Snake came down the ladder, Kit crawled and scurried on hands and knees back to the ropes. Once there he began to carefully wind the rope around his ankles and then set to work to try to make it look like his hands were also secure. That was all nervous fluster and he kept experiencing the 'fingers-and-thumbs' fumbling that goes with anxiety. As he did, he saw the two lines of teeth marks from the snake bite on the side and top of his right hand. They were very obvious but had stopped bleeding and did not hurt.

As he did this, he heard the men talking but not clearly enough over the noise of the refrigerator unit to actually understand what they were saying. Then things suddenly began to happen and Kit was left lying there, heart racing and mouth dry with fear.

What are they doing? What's happening? he wondered.

Snake's voice called loudly. "Be quick after I open the shed floor."

Jellman replied something and then came tramping around the front of the prime mover beside Kit. He looked down at Kit and then kicked him again, this time in the upper thigh.

"You little shit! I oughta run you over."

Despite the pain, Kit said, "What's going on? Let me go!"

Jellman was a few steps past him by then and just laughed. "Big Boss and Snake will sort you out, you little runt. I reckon you are for the high jump," he called as he turned and stepped up onto the steps of the cab.

That is the stolen XRT. He's going to drive that truck, Kit thought.

A stab of concern added to a good dose of conscience made him shake his head and worry about possible consequences. As Jellman opened the cab door to climb in, Kit hesitated to say anything but a shard of guilt made him speak.

"Jellman, don't drive that truck. It's got damaged steering," he called.

Jellman paused, glancing down at him. "Shut up you little know-all!"

Then he climbed in and slammed the door. Kit lay back, shaking his head but now very aware of how close those big tyres were to him. The truck's engine burst into life. At the same moment, light flooded in and Kit saw that the concrete floor of the shed had begun to lift.

There is the way out, he thought. His mind raced with options, the simplest being to just run up the ramp. *Now! Get up and go now!* he told himself, very aware that Snake and Jones were both somewhere nearby.

But there was Jones! Sharp banging on the front mudguard of the prime mover right near Kit made him jump with fright and then turn his head to look. Jones was trying to attract Jellman's attention by hammering a spanner on the steel. He banged again and then shouted and pointed.

"Jello! Jello! Stop!"

The truck's engine, which had just given a couple of surges of power, eased back and Kit glimpsed Jellman's face as he leaned forward to look down through the windshield. "What?" he called.

Jones pointed back past Kit. "The power cord! Unplug the power cord and pass it to me. I'll roll it up," he yelled.

A surge of contempt went through Kit. *Bloody idiot! He was going to drive off with the power still plugged in!*

Jellman swore and Kit heard the gears clash as he put them into neutral. Then the cab door opened and Jellman clambered out and dropped to the ground, muttering and swearing but leaving the door open. He ignored Kit and strode back along between the trailer and the tunnel.

Kit looked up at where the cab door was swinging half open. *The engine is going! I can drive this truck.*

For a second or two he debated whether to just get up and run, a glance showing that the concrete floor of the shed was now half up and rising fast. But he wasn't sure where Snake was or how long it would take him to follow. Underneath the vehicle he could just see Jones's legs near the middle of the trailer.

No, use the truck! Kit decided.

Even as he did he rose to a sitting position, thankful now for all those sit-ups that allowed him to do it. As he did, he saw that Jellman had his back to him while he tugged at the plug of the power cord near the back of the refrigerator unit.

Yes, I can do it! Kit told himself.

Slipping his feet out of the coils and tossing the ropes aside he stood up. As he did, he kept his eyes on Jellman, ready to turn and bolt if the movement was seen. But Jellman was focused on the task and had his back to him. Jellman bent over to toss the coiled-up power cord back underneath to where Jones was waiting.

With a half-sob, half-gasp of apprehension, Kit stepped across to the steps to the cab. Reaching up he gripped the hand-hold half way up and then stepped up off the mud. Careful to make no sound he placed his boot on the first step and levered himself up, eyes still half on Jellman. Three more steps and he was up and sliding through the doorway into the seat.

As he settled in the seat, Kit went to close the door but then shook his head.

Don't make a noise, he cautioned himself.

Gripping the steering wheel with his right hand he automatically placed his left on the gear lever. Only to discover that his feet did not reach the pedals!

"Bugger!" Kit swore.

He glanced to see in the rear-view mirror what Jellman was doing— only to be frustrated because the door was still half open.

Not knowing whether Jellman was on his way back gave a sharp edge to Kit's anxiety. Letting go of the gear lever, he reached under the seat and fumbled to grip the lever to adjust it. And now those many sessions of work experience at his dad's workshop paid off. His hand closed on it immediately and he was able to pull the seat as far forward as it would go.

The sound of a loud gasp of surprise next to him caused Kit to swivel his head around and his heart leapt into his mouth with fear. Jellman! He was right there beside the vehicle, staring down at the tangle of ropes. His back was to the truck and Kit knew he must move instantly. Later he would marvel at the speed at which his mind considered options. Close the door or not? He was already reaching out when he shook his head.

No! The door will close as I accelerate up the ramp, he thought, noting as he did that the band of light in front indicated that the concrete entrance was almost fully up.

Too bad if it isn't. Go! Kit told himself, pressing hard on the accelerator as he did.

Having driven this truck he knew roughly what to expect but even so, was almost caught by surprise as the vehicle seemed to leap up and forward. The engine roared, drowning out a shout from Jellman. But Kit had no time for him as things started happening far too fast. As he had anticipated, the door swung shut with a loud bang, cutting out much of Jellman's angry yells.

The cab bounced and Kit bounced with it as it surged forward. Despite a convulsive grip on the steering wheel, his face slammed forward and the wheel struck him a hard blow on the forehead, half stunning him. But he was now terribly afraid and desperate so he clung on and kept his boot jammed hard down on the accelerator. The motor screamed and whole rig lurched and bounced as it changed from going forward to going up the steep ramp.

To his dismay, Kit found himself sliding backwards on the seat and only by gripping tightly with both hands and hauling himself up could he maintain pressure on the accelerator. As he did, he cursed his small size but equally knew that he was only able to hang on because of the physical exercise he had done at home.

His next problem was seeing where to steer. Because of his small stature he could not see over the bonnet from where he had slid to and panic began to surge as he saw the band of light and the steel beams under the concrete floor getting rapidly closer. His mind registered that the floor was still being raised and he gritted his teeth in anticipation of a crash.

It will hit the top of the container, if not the roof of the cab, he thought.

The ramp seemed impossibly steep and Kit did not dare touch the gears. To stall now would be fatal! He was vaguely conscious of the screaming noise of engine and gears, the clanking and growling from the pintle and the trailer as the front wheels came up onto the change of slope. Then the whole weight of prime mover and container came on the transmission and the rig perceptibly slowed. In desperation Kit gripped the wheel and pushed his foot down as hard as he could.

Bam!

There was a sharp metallic clang and the whole rig jerked and almost stopped. Wheels spun and the smell of burning rubber came to Kit's nostrils. For a moment he feared he had failed and he gritted his teeth and held on. The wheels obviously spun again and then gripped and the rig leapt forwards.

Directly in front was a steel girder supporting the base of the concrete floor. Kit flinched and flung up his arm to protect his face as the bonnet seemed to lunge up at it. But then the front fell downwards hard. Just in time Kit realised why and managed a grip that kept his face from again slamming into the steering wheel. The front wheels hit the gravel floor of the shed and then bounced. At the same time there were horrible, expensive noises from the towing pintle and trailer.

Oh, I hope I haven't wrecked dad's new rig, Kit thought as he struggled to keep his grip on the wildly bouncing and shuddering wheel.

But his brain noted that the whole windshield was now filled with daylight and a quick glance showed that the prime mover was up the ramp and heading out of the front of the shed. A steel post loomed up on the left and Kit jerked at the wheel in a frantic attempt to keep control.

He managed this—almost. A massive bang of steel on steel told him that part of the container or trailer had struck the post. But by then the nose of the prime mover was out of the shed and heading across the yard.

The gate! Where's the gate? Kit thought, flustering.

Things were happening too fast and seemingly out of control. His eyes noted steel cattle yards and even some brown cattle scattering away from the roar of the over-driven motor. And then he saw the gate—and it was closed.

It came to him instantly that there would be no time to stop, dismount, open the gate and then get back in the cab before some very angry crooks had caught up.

That Snake will be after me now, he thought. *And he will be ropeable!*

That left only one unpalatable option—ram the gates. So Kit did. Only just managing to get control of the steering in time, his flustered being all in a dither, he drove straight into the closed steel gates.

Oh, I hope I don't smash dad's truck too much! Kit thought as the front of the rig slammed into the steel posts and rails of the gate.

Kabam! Cruunch!

The rig came to a sudden crunching stop. Kit was again flung forward and only just managed to hang on enough to make the blow to his face merely a painful whack. The entire rig came to a shuddering standstill and the engine stalled. Dust suddenly enveloped the cab, just as Kit remembered to glance at the rear vision mirror. But he did get a glimpse of twisted steel pipes poking out from under the back of the rig and it came to him in a flash that he could not hope to use the truck to escape in.

"I have to get out. Get out and run for it!" he told himself, panic so close to the surface of his emotions that he was choked up and gasping.

But where were the men? How close were they?

Doesn't matter. I've got to try! Kit thought, reaching for the handle.

Chapter 30

RUN!

K it swung the door open and was immediately engulfed by a cloud of dust.

He was surprised that the rig had stirred up so much in such a short distance and he started to cough and wave a hand to clear it away. But fear was stronger than discomfort and he looked back, glimpsing the shed through the rapidly clearing dust cloud. No-one was in sight but he had no doubt that the crooks would be on their way.

Hastily he scrambled down, his rubber soled joggers slipping on the steel steps as he did. Only a quick grab at the door prevented a nasty fall. Fear now driving his movements, Kit jumped the last metre to the ground. He landed with puffs of powdery dust among the ruins of the steel gate and at once began to clamber over it to his left. As he did, he heard a shout and glanced back. Through the remnants of the dust he saw Jellman appear at the top of the ramp.

"Oh help!" Kit gasped.

A spike of terror-driven adrenalin surged through him and he sprang over the last twisted steel rail caught under the front of the prime mover. In front of him was the larger yard with cattle in it, and beyond that another steel fence. Beyond that was the large open area and then the ridge of black stones that ran along to his left and off behind the shed. His consciousness vaguely registered that everything was an odd reddish colour with lots of shadows.

By then he was running, his boots thudding in thick dust and cow pats. From behind he heard Jellman yell to stop, but that only spurred him to run faster. He was sure he could expect no mercy from the crooks now. A glimpse of where the vehicle track went left up over the long ridge gave him both an objective and hope. But it was a long way off, a hundred metres or more!

More shouts behind added to the terror now gripping Kit's straining chest. He sprinted across the yard, his boots kicking up little spurts of dust. Frightened beef cattle scattered ahead of him, running off in both directions. One of the beasts panicked and ran back and then propped almost directly in front of Kit. He saw its eyes dilate in fear and its feet slithered in the dust, just as his own did as he skidded to standstill. The beast then swung its head from side to side, its eyes rolling up in fright before it sprang around and bolted away to his left. Kit gasped and resumed running, dust making him cough as he did.

It was Snake who Kit was really frightened of, and he glanced back several times but saw no sign of him. And now the steel fence was there, blocking his path. It looked to be a typical cattle yard fence—vertical posts and horizontal rails, steel pipes in this case. As Kit pounded towards it, his eye measured the size of the gaps and distances and his mind did rapid calculations. Climb over or go through?

Kit opted for going through, but this turned out to be almost a mistake as the horizontal steel rails were so close together that he had trouble squeezing through. Fear helped. Stopping amid a small cloud of dust he slid his right leg through and held the rail with his hands while bending to lie on it. When he found his head just fitted through he was a bit concerned, but when he tried to slide his body through and it wedged there, a real stab of concern, bordering on panic, struck him. Fearing he had made a possibly fatal mistake, he sucked in his stomach and pushed harder. To his immense relief, he slid out the other side, almost sprawling in the dust.

More angry shouts got him glancing back as he sprang to his feet. It was Jellman. He was now clambering across the remains of the gate beside the prime mover.

Still no sign of Snake, Kit thought.

A tiny spark of hope helped to overcome his pain and the fact that he was quickly becoming winded. Turning his back on the fence, he ran.

Now he had to cross the wide, dusty flat where the truck had first stopped when he had arrived there. Ahead, and growing rapidly closer at every running pace, was the place where the vehicle track turned left and went up over the long, low ridge of black rocks. Kit pushed himself to run as fast as he had ever run in his life.

As he did, he noted that everything was looking red, and he feared that meant he was going to collapse from overexertion. Until the reason struck him.

That is the sunset on the trees across the clearing, he thought.

Now he consciously noted that only the tops of the trees were touched by the rays of the setting sun. The fact that it was nearly dusk surprised and worried him until he realised that it might be a good thing.

It will be easier to hide in the bush in the dark, he reasoned.

More shouts from behind him got him glancing fearfully back. And this time his fears were reinforced. There was Snake climbing over the remains of the crushed gate. Jellman was now at the fence 75 metres behind Kit, but when he tried to slide through as Kit had done it was instantly obvious that he was too fat. Jellman had to waste valuable seconds backing out and then clambering up and over the rails. He jumped down and was obviously no athlete as he went sprawling in the dust. Swearing and spitting angrily he got up and dusted his hands and then started lumbering after Kit.

Another glance showed Kit that Jellman was really no direct threat. The man was running at a hobbling trot and obviously gasping for breath.

He is too fat and unfit, Kit thought with malicious satisfaction.

No, it was Snake who was the real danger. And Snake was now approaching the second fence at the run. To Kit's horror, Snake just sprang up onto the rails and then vaulted over, landing on his feet and immediately breaking into a run again.

By then Kit was also gasping and winded and the beginnings of a 'stitch' was starting to hurt in his right side. But he had reached the upslope over the long, low ridge and he went racing up it, his boots landing heavily now as his strength drained away. It was not much of a slope, the ridge being only about five metres high and 25 metres wide, but it was enough to make him really puff. As he went up the slope, his mind raced with what to do next to get away.

Do I go right, or left, or straight on? he fretted.

A half-formed idea crystalized as he reached the top and a single glance confirmed it: appear to obviously go left but then, once he was out of sight of the crooks, turn back and go right. Kit reasoned that running on along the vehicle track would not be a good plan.

Snake is fitter and will just run me down, he thought.

So, as he went over the top, he turned sharply left, glancing towards the crooks as he did to check on their positions. Jellman was puffing and panting halfway across the big open space but Snake was almost up with him and taking a course slightly to his left.

Snake is the clever one. He is running to cut me off rather than taking two sides of the triangle, Kit reasoned.

So as soon as his head was below the long ridge, Kit swerved back around to his right and dashed down along in the grass on the left-hand verge of the road. He then turned right again and leapt across the dirt vehicle track, his brain warning him to try not to leave tracks as he did. He landed just on the edge of a wheel rut and then raced into the knee-high long grass. Ahead of him stretched a huge flat area of savannah woodland with no obvious hiding places, not a single dip or gully or even a big log, and his hopes went crashing down.

And then so did he. Kit tripped on a rock in the long grass and went down hard. In the process he almost smashed his face into another football sized rock and got several bruising knocks on knees, elbows and forearms from other rocks.

"Ouch! Oh bugger!" he cried.

Smarting with pain and sobbing with fear, he pushed himself up and started running again—only to trip on yet another rock hidden in the grass. Scrambling painfully to his feet, he sucked at bleeding knuckles and began hobbling away from the road. As he did, he kicked or saw more rocks and it dawned on him that the whole area was probably studded with them. The only way to progress without tripping was not to run!

But the men were just there! Kit felt he had to run, but knew he couldn't. The only other option was to hide, but where? In every direction except back towards the long rocky ridge on his right was just flat savannah woodland—knee-high grass amid an open forest of black-trunked iron barks. Knowing that Snake must appear on top of the rocky ridge at any second sent pulses of fear through Kit and got his brain racing.

The same hard options came up—go right, left or straight ahead? Kit swept a frantic gaze around and then decided. Left was now parallel to the vehicle track he was 20 paces from, and right was parallel to the rocky ridge which was 30 or forty 40 away. The rocky ridge extended off into the far distance with a few dark green bushes or clumps of scrub on it amid the long grass and obvious piles of rocks. Diagonally ahead of him was just flat bush.

Now desperate, Kit looked back to try to catch the first glimpse of Snake as he came up onto the skyline. For a fleeting moment he considered running back across the road, but then discarded it as no good. In the distance that way he got a glimpse of the rocky hill beyond the shed. It was only visible because the last of the sunlight was now on the tops of the trees on it.

Movement on the skyline of the ridge decided Kit. He threw himself flat in the long grass, landing heavily on a dozen rocks of various sizes. The pain and discomfort he ignored. No other option seemed possible, and his hammering heart was now in his mouth with near despair.

They will find me in ten seconds flat, he thought.

Staring back over his right shoulder through a tuft of grass with eyes that seemed to be all dancing black dots and blurry focus, Kit saw Snake come to a standstill on the crest of the ridge. The man swung his head back and forth, obviously looking for him. Kit pressed himself lower and experienced spasms of pure terror that set his already hammering heart thudding and his entire body trembling.

Then Jellman came to a gasping stop on the vehicle track on top of the ridge, only about 40 metres away. He also looked around and then called, "Where did the little mongrel go?"

Kit quivered with fear and bit his lip, tensing to spring up and run.

They will find me easily in this short grass, he thought, actually surprised he had not already been detected.

Snake swore and answered. "Litte weed must be hiding. Start looking. He can't be far away."

Kit now gritted his teeth and tried to steady his breathing, determined to play it out to the bitter end. He carefully groped in the grass and found a cricket ball sized rock that fitted well into his hand. It was not much of a weapon but heartened him a tiny fraction.

Slow your breathing! Stop gasping! They will hear you, he told himself, aware that the beating of his heart sounded as loud as jungle drums.

"Which way did he go?" Jellman queried.

"I thought I saw him go this way," Snake said, pointing to his left.

Kit nodded agreement and stared hard at the man, noting that the sunlight had gone off the trees on the hill and that Snake now stood out against a pale pink sky as a black silhouette.

Both men stood and stared for a minute or so and then Snake said loudly, "Jellman, go and check if there are any tracks on the road. I'll look in this long grass."

Snake then began picking his way down the rocky slope. Jellman grunted and then walked down the vehicle track, his head bent forward as he stared hard at the dusty road surface. Once he paused and Kit guessed it might be where he had deviated off onto the grassy verge. Then Jellman grunted again and moved down onto the flat only 20 or 30 metres behind Kit.

As he did, Jones appeared on the road at the crest of the ridge. "Where is he? Where did the little mongrel go?" he called.

Both Snake and Jellman answered. Snake repeated himself, staring off into the distance along the dirt vehicle track as he did.

"I think the little rat is hiding here in the grass. He couldn't have run along the road out of sight. He didn't have time. Are then any tracks, Jellman?"

Jellmand shook his head. "Nope. None that I can see," he replied, leaning forward and squinting down in the gloom.

Kit realised with a thrill of hope that dusk was setting in fast.

So did Jones. "Geez, it's gettin' dark fast. We'd better find him before it does."

Jellman straightened up and looked around, his gaze sweeping right across where Kit lay, sending a shiver of apprehension through him.

"It shouldn't be too hard. There's no real cover. He must be just lyin' in the grass."

Snake came over to the road, the rustling sound of his progress through the grass seeming loud to Kit. It also warned him that any attempt to move might make similar noises.

Snake now spoke. "Spread out and let's search this area. He can't have gotten far," he ordered.

I haven't. Oh, bloody hell! Kit thought.

He heard the men spread along the road. Jones stayed near the ridge, Jellman sounded as though he was almost directly behind Kit, and Snake was 20 paces to his left rear.

The men began walking side by side slowly into the long grass, their heads swivelling from side to side. Kit's hopes plummeted and he braced ready to run, wondering how he could avoid tripping on those hidden rocks. But he was grimly determined and clenched his rock as he braced ready to spring up and bolt.

When Jellman is ten metres away, he decided.

Chapter 31

FIELDCRAFT

K it tensed his muscles preparatory to springing to his feet. Fear gripped him.

Get ready! he told himself.

And as he went to move, a yell of pain and the sound of Jellman falling in the grass made him pause, seemingly every muscle quivering.

Jellman had tripped on a rock. The other two men stopped and Snake called, "What's the problem?"

"Ow! I bloody tripped. This grass is full of bloody rocks!" Jellman snapped. He struggled to a kneeling position, rubbing his left knee. "Ouch! And this bloody grass is spear grass and full of prickles."

It was too! Kit was suddenly conscious of all the grass seeds that were embedded in his shirt and trousers and prickling his skin. Once again he was thankful for his father insisting he wear long trousers and long sleeves.

Snake was not amused and swore and then Jones stumbled. "Bloody hell! Jello's right. I nearly fell over when that rock rolled under me boot," he called.

Jellman got to his feet and began to cautiously walk forward. "We could just set fire to this grass and burn the little turd out," he suggested, sending chills of apprehension through Kit.

Snake vetoed that at once. "No! The little germ would be able to hide in the smoke and a bushfire would attract attention. We don't want the cops and the bloody Rural Fire Brigade turning up, not with that rig stuck on the gate."

The men began moving cautiously forward, feeling for the rocks in the grass. Kit again tensed ready to run. And then another problem arose—he realised he was going to sneeze! A comment he had heard one of the army cadets at school make came to him—Peter Bronsky he thought it might have been—and he acted on it instantly.

Place your thumb under your nose and your finger on the outside and press up till your eyes water, that army cadet said, Kit remembered.

So he did. And it hurt—but worked. Lying there scared and itching from prickles and also worried about snakes and spiders he had the inconsequential thought that he was glad he was a navy cadet.

The army cadets can have this crawling around in the grass stuff!

Jellman again stumbled and then stood there muttering. Jones also stopped moving forward.

"It's gettin' bloody dark fast. We need torches or a light," he commented.

"Get the Land Rover," Jellman suggested.

Jones snorted. "Good idea, but first we gotta get that rig orf the gate."

Snake, who was now only about ten paces to Kit's left, stopped and spoke. "Good idea. We gotta stop this little rat reaching the highway. Jonesy, you come with me and we will get the Rover and a couple of torches. Jellman, you wait here. And stay still and quiet so you can use your ears. Come on."

The three all turned and began stumbling and rustling their way back to the vehicle track. As they did, Jones said, "How we gunna get that rig off the gate?"

Kit was moving by then, crawling around the big rock that was blocking his chest and using the noise of the crook's movement to cloak his own.

He heard Snake say, "Later. First we will just unbolt a panel in the fence and move it aside. Later you can get the oxy torch and cut those pipes off under the prime mover."

He's the clever one alright, Kit thought.

He came to a stop five metres further from the road. Even that small move made him dislike crawling in the grass intensely. It had prickled and scratched his face and arms and he was terrified of encountering a snake or spider.

Once bitten, twice shy, eh? he told himself. And then he realised his left hand was hurting from the rocks and sharp grass and twigs. *I've got feeling back in it. Good!*

By then all three crooks were back on the road. Kit heard the thud of footsteps heading back towards the ridge, and Jellman call out as they did, "Don't you blokes take too long."

Jones called back, "What's the matter, scared of the kid are ya?"

"Get stuffed!" Jellman snarled.

"Scared of the dark more like," Snake added as he and Jones went up the slope.

Kit gave a sardonic grin at that. He disliked Jellman intensely and it was good to know that the enemy were not a united team. Twisting his head around, he glimpsed the two men against the rapidly darkening sky as they went over the crest. That got him looking up and he noted that the sky went from reddish pink over to the west to pale blue overhead and then to darker blue. The first star was already visible. That cheered him.

I might make it, he thought.

But could he creep away without making any noise? Jellman was now a good 30 to 40 metres away, barely visible in the twilight. He was more audible because he stamped his feet a couple of times and was wheezing and grunting as he breathed.

Kit knew that this was a chance he had to take. *I must get well away before they come back with a vehicle or torches,* he reasoned.

He decided that even if Jellman heard him and tried to chase him he could probably outrun him. The risk of a bad fall that might injure him would just have to be taken. So he very slowly did a body-press to lift himself to his hands and knees. He suspected he was risking his back becoming visible above the grass but thanked his lucky stars that his shirt was a dark colour.

Very cautiously he felt the ground ahead with his left hand and found a few leaves and a dry stick. These he gently moved aside and then gingerly lifted his left knee and edged it forward about ten centimetres to the place he had just cleared. Then he tried to do the same with his right hand but found he had to let go of his rock. Reluctantly he did so. His right knee was moved forward.

Kit paused to look back and listen. It was so dark now that he could just glimpse Jellman, but he could hear the man moving about and muttering to himself.

If the idiot stood still, he would have a better chance of hearing me, he thought.

Very slowly and carefully Kit repeated the movements. It took real willpower as every instinct was to get up and hurry away, knowing that the other two crooks could come back at any minute. He really had no idea how long it would take them to find tools and unbolt a panel of the cattle yard fence, and that got him shivering with apprehension.

The whole process of crawling was painful and took the conscious application of will power. The rocks hurt his knees and hands and the prickles and spear grass seeds stuck into his clothing and he even got one in the corner of his eye and had to stop and carefully scrape it out with a finger nail. Feeling with his fingers and moving any deadfall that might crinkle or rustle took time, and each short move was an effort. But minute by minute he slowly gained distance.

Kit estimated that he was crawling at about three metres a minute but without a watch he realised that could be a wildly inaccurate estimate.

It is only getting dark now so must be about 6 o'clock, he thought. As he knew the truck had been stolen in Mount Surprise at about 3 o'clock that meant only about three hours had elapsed since the rig was stolen. *It seems like days!* he mentally moaned. *That means I was only free in that tunnel somewhere between an hour and an hour and a half.* It had seemed much longer!

Very carefully he continued his slow crawl. After a time he developed a technique that kept the spear grass away from his eyes and which made things easier. He found that it was the basalt rocks that were the real problem—he knew they were basalt from the field trip the previous year. The whole place was studded with them. Many were about the size of a football, but some were so big he could not crawl over them but had to go around them. And he was hating every moment of it. Never in his life had he ever even walked through the bush, let alone crawled in it in the dark! Fear of snakes and spiders and other creepy crawlies slowed his movements.

Every time he moved Kit paused to glance back and to listen. He also noted that he was leaving a fairly obvious trail.

If the crooks find that they can just hurry along it and catch me, he worried.

But there was no help for it so he continued on. Five metres, ten metres, fifteen metres. He was now so far from the road he had trouble detecting Jellman in the gloom.

Is he still there? Kit worried, pausing to peer into the darkness and to listen. And then Jellman farted and Kit had to suppress the urge to laugh. *You gross slug!* he thought.

Knowing his enemy's location boosted Kit's morale considerably. He resumed his slow crawl.

And then Kit got a shock. For several minutes he had been vaguely aware of a sort of change of light off to his left front. Now he frowned and stared in that direction and then shook his head. There was a distinct yellowish glow showing among the trees. Then realisation hit him.

The moon! That is the moon coming up! he told himself.

A memory from the boat trip at Karumba the previous evening—was it really only last night!—came to him. As they had headed back from the sand island towards the land, the moon had come up from behind the lights of the town.

A big, bright full moon, Kit remembered. It had bathed the water with a wonderful silvery glow. *So this will also be a full moon—or nearly,* Kit reasoned.

For a moment he felt embarrassed as a navy cadet not having the moon and tides in his mind, but now he remembered that the moon came up about 45 to 50 minutes later each day.

But it will be a full moon and it will make it nearly as bright as day! I need to get away from here before it does, he told himself.

And that meant standing up to go faster—which was a real risk. So, another set of poor options: stay and risk getting caught, or stand up and walk and risk being seen!

But Kit knew which it had to be. *I can outrun Jellman. If I wait, then it is that Snake mongrel I have to worry about.*

And they would have a vehicle with its headlights and probably a spotlight as well. The notion of the spotlight added another whole new level of fear. He had heard that people went hunting at night using spotlights. An absolutely chilling thought came to him:

What if these crooks have a gun?

Now that was a truly terrifying idea! Kit shuddered and understood that the sooner he was well out of the area the better. So after another careful pause to listen, he crawled over behind one of the black-trunked Ironbarks and then slowly stood up, leaning on the rough bark for support as he did. Then he paused again and looked back to see if he could see Jellman. There was no sign of him in the darkness and no sound.

Nothing for it but to take the risk, Kit thought.

So he turned around and began carefully moving one foot at a time, feeling for dry sticks and twigs that might snap and warn his enemy. Unfortunately there were plenty of those, so many Kit began to wonder if it would not be quicker and safer to continue on hands and knees. But the memory of that spear grass in his face and eyes made him shake his head and persevere. He tried to keep the tree trunk between him and Jellman, but uncertainty about the man's position made that a matter of guesswork.

It was actually the rocks that were more of a problem. Kit's boots encountered one or two with every step and he had to be very careful not to trip or twist an ankle. Understanding that such an injury might lead to fatal consequences made him concentrate on being both careful and silent.

Now he estimated he was moving ten metres a minute. Which was good progress but still very slow. He knew that the speed of the 'Quick March' was a hundred metres in one minute. And there was the first glimmer of the moon showing through the trees ahead!

I must get away from here fast, he told himself, fear again gripping his chest.

And then more worrying thoughts came to him. He realised he was walking directly towards the moon.

But is that good thing or a bad thing? he wondered.

Images from evenings standing on the Esplanade in Cairns with the moon rising from behind the mountains across Trinity Inlet gave him the answer. He clearly remembered watching the black silhouettes of boats and a destroyer crossing that band of rippling silver moonlight.

So I need to not have the moon between me and the enemy, he decided.

Immediately he swung right, then wondered if he had done the correct thing.

That ridge of rocks is somewhere in this direction. Should I follow it or cross it? he worried.

He decided that crossing to the other side might not be a bad idea as it would confuse the crooks and place a physical barrier between him and any headlights or spotlights. So, continually glancing to his right, he angled off through the bush. To keep direction he kept the rising moon on his left front, walking a diagonal which steadily took him both further from Jellman and out of the moon's direct path.

Rather sooner than he expected he came to the ridge. He saw it as a long, dark rise before he reached it. By then the moon was fully up and casting bright beams of light through the trees. Luckily this also meant lots of shadows, which increased as the moon rose and shone through the tree canopies.

Kit began very carefully climbing up the rocky side of the long ridge. The rocks were all piled roughly on top of each other, some very unstable. After his experiences of bites and stings during the afternoon, he had to make himself reach down and bend forward to grip the next big rock so that he had a firm handhold before moving either foot up onto another rock. Fear of snakes and scorpions caused his mouth to go dry and his nerves to tingle.

He was almost at the top, climbing in a patch of moonlight, when a sharp metallic sound to his right caused him to jump with fright and then freeze. His heart rate shot up again and he lowered himself onto the rocks even as another *ting!* noise came to him. Now he realised he could see a distinct glow and by edging a bit higher he saw that it was coming from a vehicle's headlights.

Snake and Jones must be using that Land Rover's headlights so they can see what they are doing, he decided. Which also meant that they would be working faster. *By the sound of it they have undone one of the fence panels. They will be through in a few minutes.*

That was a real worry. Kit lifted himself to keep on going, noting that the area on the other side of the ridge was also lit up by the moon but not by the vehicle's headlight beams. He deduced there must be a slight drop in the ground.

The moon was directly on his left and Kit glanced towards it. It was now rising above the tree tops and casting long shadows. Then, as he moved his right foot and felt for a stable rock to put his weight on, another thunderbolt thought came to him.

The moon comes up in the east. I am now going south. The highway is to the north. I am going the wrong way!

That made him pause again while he puzzled over which way to go. He knew that there was also another highway somewhere to the east, the one that ran south from the Forty Mile Scrub to Lynd Junction where it split, the righthand road going to Hughenden and the left to Charters Towers. But how far to that road? He felt sure that the Savannah Way was closer.

Still undecided he half rose, ready to move. As he did, the sound of the vehicle's motor reached him, and suddenly the headlight beams swung around. Just in time he lay flat on the sharp jumble of rocks, closing his eyes and burying his face in a small hollow between several larger rocks. The headlights swept over him and then steadied for a few moments.

Kit kept his face turned away from the vehicle, a Land Rover for sure, and looked to his left. He was just in time to see the flat area on the south side of the ridge lit up momentarily before the vehicle swung left and went up over the ridge behind him. As it did, he swung his head to watch. To his surprise, it came to a stop just over the crest and he saw that it had been turned so that the headlight beams lit up the area to the left of the road, where he had initially run. The vehicle moved very slowly, causing the beams to traverse slowly across that area.

That sent another chill of apprehension through Kit. *That Snake is definitely a clever mongrel!* he decided.

Snake (He presumed it was him and not Jones driving) then reversed the vehicle a few metres back onto the crest and then moved it to make the beams sweep across the area where he had gone to ground. Jellman was briefly lit up and then silhouetted by this. Kit looked anxiously to see if his movements had left any obvious trail of crushed grass. To his relief, there did not appear to be, and he now decided he would go down onto the flat ground on the south side of the ridge.

I will go east beside it so I can just switch back to the other side if I need to, he decided.

He lifted himself up with his arm and thigh muscles and started to crab across the top of the rocks. As he did, another bright light came on over at the cattle yards. Kit froze and looked that way and then heard sounds of metal on metal, but only a sort of clanking, chinking noise.

Jones doing something to the rig? he wondered.

Satisfied he was not being observed, Kit continued on and was soon down the other side of the rocks and out of sight of the Land Rover on the crest. As soon as he was, he turned left and began walking carefully but quickly through the rock-studded long grass towards the rising moon.

He had only gone about 20 paces when a sharp hissing noise behind him made him halt. Goosebumps prickled the back of his neck and head. His first thought was a snake. But then his brain told him that the noise was quite distant. That made him look back and he saw a shower of bright sparks fly out from beside the rig. That puzzled him for a moment and then he shook his head and knew what he was looking at.

Oxy torch! Jones is cutting up the pieces of the gate to clear the prime mover. They are clever with stuff these guys.

His concern about the efficiency of the crooks then went up another notch when he heard voices on the other side of the ridge. They were too far away for him to catch the actual words but he was sure it was Snake telling Jellman what to do. Then a flickering of light attracted his attention. Looking back he sucked in his breath and experienced yet another stab of fear.

Torches. They are really searching for me now, he thought. And he was at most only 75 to a hundred metres from them. *I must get away from here fast!*

Chapter 32

LAVA PLAIN

But it couldn't be fast!

It was like one so those horrible nightmares where you want to run but you can't. Your boots are too heavy or you are wading in treacle. In this case it was all the rocks in the grass.

After a couple of banged shins and stumbles, Kit had to move at a walk. His anxiety level shot right up and he kept looking back. Seeing the torch beams flicking on the trees on the other side of the ridge kept the adrenaline pumping.

Just in case Snake climbed up onto the ridge, Kit began angling away from it. He knew that was taking him southeast, but it seemed the best option. The walking was easy except for the rocks. The moonlight made it simple to avoid any logs, trees or larger rocks. It was only the small rocks hidden in the long grass that were a problem.

With every step his hopes climbed up another notch. By looking back continually he was able to keep track of the flickering torch beams on the tree canopies. To his intense satisfaction, the glow of the vehicle headlights grew more distant all the time. And then he got another scare. As he glanced back, he suddenly glimpsed movement against that glow and he at once dropped flat in the grass behind the trunk of a large gum tree.

The flicker of moving light warned him and he stayed down until it moved away. Then he carefully raised his head and peeked around the side of the trunk. It was Snake shining his torch out on the flat on the southside of the ridge. The man was starkly silhouetted against the glow of the headlights. Kit noted with satisfaction that he was now so far from where Snake stood that the beam of the man's torch barely reached where he was.

There was even more satisfaction when Snake clicked off his torch and went back down the northside of the ridge. Kit waited only a few seconds before rising to his feet and starting to walk. As before, he angled away from the ridge—was already a good 50 metres from it. He tried to keep the big tree between himself and where Snake had appeared but soon realised that he wasn't sure. So he just kept the moon on his left front and the glow of the headlights behind him.

Some metallic hammering behind him made him duck behind another tree and look back. It was coming from the cattle yards, now several hundred metres away. There was more hammering and then the flicker of more tiny, golden coloured sparks as Jones resumed cutting the wrecked fence and gate away from under the prime mover with an oxyacetylene torch or an angle grinder. Nodding with satisfaction at that Kit resumed walking.

After another 50 or so paces, Kit began to think he had a good chance of escaping. He started to relax, only to get a sudden fright. A bird of some sort took off from almost under his feet with a loud whir of wings. Kit jumped back and clutched his chest as his heart went into his mouth. Then he stood and gasped with relief and calmed himself.

Only a bird! But what bird? he wondered. *Never mind birds! Get moving! Get to safety,* he told himself.

Once again he started walking, and this time he became conscious of sounds. Far back behind him was the sound of banging on metal and the purr of the Land Rover's engine, but now he realised there were normal, natural night noises: insects, bats, and the sigh of a faint breeze in the leaves.

He also found that the further he got from the ridge the fewer rocks there were. This got him striding through the long grass in his anxious desire to get as far away as he could quickly—until he suddenly stood on a cricket ball sized rock which rolled under his boot. His left foot shot forward and he almost did 'The splits', the muscles in the back of his calves and thighs getting a sharp and painful wrench. With difficulty he avoided a fall, but his face and upper body ended up down in the spear grass. He was just in time to shut his eyes but the prickly grass scratched his face and dozens of sharp seeds stuck through his shirt and embedded themselves.

As he struggled to get his legs back in their normal relationship, Kit had to endure the grass on his face and arms. Spitting and muttering swear words, he got to his feet and brushed himself down. Then he stood for a minute shaking, plucking at the seeds and telling himself to be more careful.

If I injure myself out here and nobody finds me, I will just die of thirst, he thought.

From that came horrible notions of the crows pecking out his eyes and of his body being devoured by hawks, wild pigs and dingoes, and of his bones being scattered. The images made him shudder until he got a grip on his thoughts.

Stop that! he told himself sharply. *The Phantom doesn't think like that. You are free, now get to safety.*

He resumed walking but much more slowly. He had only gone ten paces when the sound of the Land Rover's engine revving came to him. Alarmed, he turned to look back. He was just able to make out that the vehicle's headlights were no longer directed into the bush eastwards. Instead they were facing north. Puzzled but relieved he watched as the headlights headed off, obviously going north along the road. The sounds of the vehicle's motor and movement died away.

Now, where is that going? And is there anyone still back there looking for me and listening? Kit wondered.

The most obvious answer was that the crooks were checking that he wasn't walking towards the highway along the vehicle track.

And they may be going to the junction to try to catch me if I go that way, he reasoned, knowing that was what he would make happen if he was their boss.

Which meant that there was almost certainly one still back searching; as well as Jones working at clearing the rig.

Which also meant there was nobody close to him. Kit now estimated he was a good 200 metres from the place where he had first left the road. He decided to walk east for another 500 paces before changing course to go north.

With the bright moonlight and the flat ground it was relatively easy going. Only the hidden rocks were a cause of concern—until he thought of snakes. The moment he did he wished he hadn't. But he could not help it.

There will be brown snakes in this dry open savannah, he thought, remembering a tourist sign with illustrations that he had read. That got him worrying in case he encountered a Taipan. *They can be big, aggressive snakes, and their poison is deadly. One bite can kill what is it? Two hundred sheep or something?*

He found he had come to a sobbing, trembling stop. *Oh, stop scaring yourself! What sort of Ghost Who Walks are you?* he berated himself.

With difficulty he made himself start stepping forward through the knee-high grass. Only to get another shock. A grunting noise stopped him with his heart racing.

Was that a wild pig? he wondered. He had heard stories from his uncles about wild pigs and how dangerous they were. But then a bellow came from the direction of the sound. *That's a beast,* he told himself, unsure if it was a cow or a bull. *Oh, I hope it isn't a bull!* he thought.

He looked wildly around for a tree that might be easier to climb than one of the straight trunked ironbarks. There were none and his anxiety went up even more.

Thudding and trampling noises and more cattle noises told him that there were several beasts and that they were moving away from him to his right. He stopped beside a tree and peered into the night, just managing to see bobbing dark objects moving away, silhouetted by the moonlight.

This is a cattle station after all, he reasoned.

Then he gave a wry smile, remembering a comment by his father when they had visited a cattle property near Georgetown the year before: *'They are scared of us son. Remember, we eat them, they don't eat us!'*

Satisfied that the cattle were not going to attack him, but worried that the men might have heard them, Kit resumed walking, angling a bit more to the east to be sure of avoiding the cattle.

But it was not cattle that sent his heart leaping in fright next. It was the swoop of some night bird that flew by close by his head, the flapping of its wings very audible.

Owl? Or a big bat? Kit wondered, calming the sudden gulping breaths he had started taking.

Kit had never walked through the bush except for a few metres on a couple of holidays and that had been in daylight. He had certainly never walked through it in the dark and he found it a terrifying experience. All those imagined horrors kept occurring to him: snakes, spiders, centipedes, scorpions, wild pigs. He found it took a mental effort to force each foot to move forward and despite the coolness of the night air he realised he was perspiring. But he was even more scared of the men and that gave him motivation. He was also aware that army cadets did it all the time on night navigation exercises and patrols and that induced a feeling of shame. Not wanting to let the ANC down, he gritted his teeth and kept moving.

On he walked, or rather plodded, as he was getting tired and was starting to feel his aches and pains. Then he stopped and swore. He had forgotten to keep counting his paces after the owl. He thought he might be up around three hundred so he started from that and resumed walking.

Then another fright—dark shapes leaping up from the grass ten metres in front of him and bounding away with a thud-thud-thud noise.

Oh! Bloody kangaroos! he thought, and then swore again.

He glimpsed at least four, a family he presumed. He wasn't really scared of them, even though he had heard and read of big male kangaroos attacking people. These looked smaller and he suspected they were just wallabies.

Walking once again, now directly towards the moon. The terrain stayed flat and the trees appeared to have a sameness about them that made it look like he was getting nowhere. Only the odd rock in the grass now to stumble over or kick.

It is a lava plain, he told himself.

That meant that all the dips and creek lines had probably been filled in by the oozing lava to make the area very flat—or was it very gently sloping level ground. He wasn't sure and he was now so tired that in the moonlight he found his focus going from time to time.

More cattle, further away this time but visible as whitish shapes in the moonlight. *Brahmans or something like that,* Kit told himself.

And another group of wallabies or kangaroos. Kit came to a stop. He had just counted 555. *I've gone too far.* Then he shrugged. It didn't matter.

Better to be further away from the junction at the highway where that Land Rover might be waiting.

Kit trekked slowly on, his boots brushing through the long grass, with each step taking its little toll of his nervous energy and reserves of courage. His mind was on the slithering and creepy-crawly things that lived or lurked in that long grass—but the next assault on his nerves hit him right in the face. It was a spider's web, strung between two trees. As soon as he felt the web on his face, Kit knew what it was and the adrenalin pumped. And the repulsive thing actually scuttled over his skin. He felt its feet on his cheek and nearly fainted with horror. Kit only just managed to suppress a scream as he sprang back and scraped at his face with both hands. His fingers encountered the spindly legs of the creature and he panicked and flicked it away and then scrabbled to get the sticky mess off his skin.

Where did it go? Where is it? his mind cried in near hysteria.

For a few seconds he jumped around, clawing at his face and neck and beating at his clothes, close to hysteria.

Did it bite me? Where is it? Oh! he thought, fear causing him to brush and beat at his front.

So overwrought was he that he could only stand there and sob, his whole body shaking from reaction. He found that his breathing had shot right up and realised that he was gasping for air as though he had run a race. A wave of dizziness made him stagger. Still anxious about the location of the spider, he started walking away from the area, brushing at his face, neck and arms.

Slowly he regained control of himself. It took him a deliberate effort of will. Thinking about spiders helped.

Here I was worrying about things like trapdoor spiders that live in holes in the ground, and I forgot about the ones that catch birds and insects.

He came to a standstill and thought about the types of spiders, wondering if it had been a St Andrews Cross spider or a Golden Orb Weaver.

Both make big webs between trees that can catch a small bird, he considered.

In a deliberate attempt to calm his nerves he now told himself that neither had a sting that was known to be fatal to human beings.

And I can't feel anything that feels like a spider bite. So I don't think it bit me, he reasoned.

As he stood there, he became aware of how much he hurt. Every part of him seemed to have its own ache or pain. His left hand and arm throbbed, his right hand ached, his knees hurt, his head throbbed, his eyes felt hot and his skin was all itches and smarting from the numerous scratches and scrapes. For a minute or so he stood and looked around and listened. Apart from the usual natural night noises of wind and insects and birds and so on, he could not hear anything to alarm him.

I'll just rest for a few minutes, he decided.

Rationalising that he had all night to walk to the highway, he looked around and noted an area of bare ground. Deciding that would do to sit on he moved to it and, with a groan at the many aches and sore muscles, lowered himself onto it.

Only to spring up and yelp a minute later. Ants! Big ants he could even see in the moonlight.

Red meat ants? Or bull ants? he thought while angrily scraping and hitting at the creatures that were nipping hard at his hand and ankle.

Quickly moving away from the nest, he stood and muttered and plucked off a couple that were now inflicting painful little nips.

Bloody things! Why aren't you in bed asleep? he grumbled.

Walking another ten paces Kit stopped and did a pee. There wasn't much liquid to be pumped out and the smell of the urine was strong. That made him think of a Cadet Instructor's warning that they should be drinking enough to have almost clear urine or they were in danger of dehydrating. That made Kit aware that he was thirsty and that the dry air was starting to crack his lips. For the first time finding water became a worry.

After another 25 paces, Kit selected an area of grass free of rocks and spent a minute or so trampling it flat to chase away any scorpions or… or other things that might be there. Very cautiously he lowered himself to a sitting position and then leaned his back against the truck of an ironbark.

Now he became more aware of his battered physical state, the bruises where he had been kicked, or where he had fallen on rocks, his skin tingling from the grass scratches and so on. He was also aware that he was shivering with over-exertion and nervous exhaustion.

But I am safe for the moment, he told himself. *The crooks won't find me here, not out in the middle of nowhere.*

Closing his hot and blurry eyes he deliberately tried to calm himself and to think out his next move.

And promptly fell asleep.

Chapter 33

THE MOON

K it woke up from the intense pain of a cramp in his left thigh. The agony was so acute he cried out before realising the need for silence. Urgently he pummelled and massaged at his locked muscles. The onset had been so sudden and so painful that he was shocked. It took him a couple of minutes to wake up properly, all the while tensing in anticipation of another cramp while trying not to. With wakefulness came awareness of his predicament. Panting and fearful of another sudden attack, he sat there and rubbed at his gummed-up eyes and then looked around.

Still bright moonlight, he noted.

It occurred to him that he should be up and walking while the moon was up, so he struggled to his feet. For a while he stood there, swaying from fatigue and pain. The air was now cool enough for him to attribute that to his shivering. But he also understood he was feeling both hungry and thirsty—particularly thirsty. He ran his tongue around lips that were now definitely dry and cracked.

Then he began walking before realising that he wasn't navigating. *Am I going the right way?* he wondered.

Stopping to get his senses working and to check he looked up at the moon. It was almost directly overhead and he had to 'crick' his neck right back to see it.

Now, which way is east? he asked. And then shook his head as another mental thunderbolt flashed across his mind. *I can't tell! The moon is too close to vertical.* The notion that he could not use the moon to find direction staggered him. *Or did I just sway because I am exhausted?*

To steady himself he leaned on the tree beside him, then plucked it away as fear of spiders reminded him to be careful. Again he checked the moon. Looking at the shadows of the tree trunks was not much help either. He could see they were all going out in the same direction, but not very far.

If I start walking now I could end up like those people who you hear about who walk in circles when they are lost.

That notion of being lost bothered him. Part of his private 'Navy Cadet' pride was somehow offended.

I'm not lost. I know roughly where I am. I am just not quite sure which way to walk at the moment. After another glance at the moon he resigned himself to waiting for an hour or so until the moon was clearly past its highest point. *Is that the zenith?* he wondered, annoyed at his own ignorance.

He badly wanted to keep walking, to put as much distance between him and the crooks as he could. Getting to the highway by dawn seemed like a very desirable aim.

After carefully selecting another area of grass free of stones, Kit lowered himself down, but not without a few groans as his sore muscles made themselves felt. Again he looked up at the moon, except this time his eyes noted a few bright stars. He knew that on nights of bright moonlight most of the stars were not visible but the really important constellations and individual stars and planets still shone though.

Can I navigate by the stars? he wondered, swivelling his head to study the sky.

He was instantly rewarded by recognising the Southern Cross. It was almost behind him and low in the sky, lying on its side. Just seeing it and being able to name it gave his hopes a real lift. But then he shook his head and the hopes became ashes of defeat.

I don't know how to use the Southern Cross to find north or south, he thought.

Once again, he berated himself for his ignorance. There was double shame in that he knew that boy scouts were taught that skill.

And so are the Army Cadets.

Now that rankled his pride again and he silently vowed to fill those gaps in his knowledge.

He recognised and could name a few other constellations: the Milky Way, the Saucepan, the Scorpion, and Orion, but the same problem applied. He did not know how to use them. All he was sure of was that they moved continually across the sky so using them might be tricky.

Feeling quite down, he shook his head and sat there brooding, waiting for the moon to move sufficiently far across the sky so as to make west clear. He at least knew that.

And he fell asleep again.

* * *

This time his sleep was more disturbed. After a time he slumped down and lay flat but kept half waking as his mind conjured up frightening images of snakes slithering through the grass towards him. Each time he dropped back into an uneasy slumber, punctuated by a few more cramps.

It was one of them that jerked him awake at about 04:00am—although he did not know the actual time.

Oh, bloody hell! I fell asleep! he berated himself. *Where is that bloody moon?*

Rubbing at his sore calf muscles he looked around and was horrified to see that the moon was now well down in the west. Anxious and annoyed that he had been asleep when he should have been walking, he got to his feet—not without difficulty as he was all aches and pains and trembling. For a few moments he stood there leaning on the tree—tired, sore, hungry and thirsty. Then, having checked which way was north by the moon, he started walking.

The moon was setting in the west, he reasoned. *So if I want to walk north I must still have it on my left side.*

So that is what he did. It was easy going except for the occasional stone, log or termite nest in the grass. He was able to proceed at a steady plod. As he walked, he kept listening and looking around. One of the things he was expecting to encounter was the long, rocky ridge he had crossed but he saw no sign of any such feature. That bothered him and set him worrying lest he be going the wrong way.

Or did it just peter out and come to an end?

Not knowing made him anxious but his tired mind told him that as long as the moon was shining on his left side he must be going north.

And the Savannah Way is somewhere to the north, he thought.

Clinging to that notion he kept going. But he was aware that he was feeling very worn out and thirsty. After what he thought was about a quarter of an hour, he stopped to rest for a few minutes. He reasoned that he could have walked about a kilometre. By his estimate the crook's lava tube was only about ten kilometres south of the highway.

If I just plod on slowly, I should make it in a couple of hours, he told himself.

Then he told himself he was just being unrealistic and amended it to three or four hours. Groaning at his stiff muscles, he resumed walking. There were more frights and little alarms, including another spider's web. But this time he only caught one strand on the edge of it and did not have a fit of hysterics. He was ashamed of that earlier loss of control now. This time he brushed the sticky strand aside and went on, wishing he had a walking stick to hold in front of his face. But there was no way he was going to start groping around on the ground to find a stick.

With my luck I will pick up a snake!

There were more cattle and kangaroos and once some big night bird called in the distance. Then curlews began their mournful cries. That did not bother him so much as he liked curlews. A family of them had been nesting in his front garden at home all his life and he thought them interesting birds.

I love the way they hide by just lying still when an enemy is near, he thought. That made him feel a small pulse of pride. *It was by being like a curlew and just lying still in the grass that I evaded those men.*

And he wished he owned a watch. *I must ask dad for one for my birthday,* Kit thought as he counted his steps. After two more walks, each of a thousand steps, he had another longer rest. He assumed that it was about 05:00am but wasn't sure.

The moon is right down among the treetops. It will set soon, he told himself. That meant daylight was not far away. And then he detected a distinct grey paleness to the sky to his right. *Definitely dawn,* he decided.

It was. Fifteen minutes later there was no doubt, with pink and red lighting up the eastern sky. Despite feeling utterly exhausted he did not stop, but continued to walk and stumble on at a slow plod. By the time the first glimmer of the actual sun glinted through the trees to his right, he thought he had walked at least three or four kilometres since waking up.

He came to a large open area and walked on. It was fully light by then. After a few minutes his tired mind at last noted that there were no trees for about a kilometre ahead or to right and left. The change puzzled him slightly and only after walking another hundred metres or so did he realise that there were no rocks and that it was a different type of grass, stiffer and waist high. Then the reason came to him.

This is a swamp!

But it was a very dry swamp. He kept looking down, hoping to find some water but the ground was a sort of grey clay or dust that grew under clumps of stiff reeds or grass. Disappointed, he stopped and looked around. Thus he noted a small hill a kilometre or so away to his right front. It poked up among the trees on the far side of the open area.

Should I go to that? Kit wondered. His reasoning suggested that it might give him a good view of the area. *It's not far out of my way. I'll go there,* he decided.

So he changed direction towards it. And then he did find water, but not in any form he could stomach. The ground was all churned up and in the hollows was a sludge of grey-brown liquid.

What did this? he wondered.

And then it came to him as a chilling image: wild pigs! Straightening up and panting with anxiety, Kit looked in all directions. Then he swore.

What an idiot I am! I have walked right out into the middle of this big open area where there is no cover and I can be seen for miles!

And there was no tree nearby to try to climb if pigs did appear and attack him!

That got him walking quickly, his eyes scanning in all directions as the full force of the sun came onto him, making him sweat. Movement! No just a bird—hawk or something—off to his left front. And there were some brown cattle among the trees to his left rear. Anxious now to be off that open ground, Kit strode forwards as quickly as he could—until he saw the snake.

It was a red-bellied black and as thick as his arm. The reptile was curled up in a clump of grass and at his approach began uncoiling hastily. Kit spotted the movement just in time to not step on the creature. He sprang back, heart hammering as the snake suddenly uncoiled and slid off out of sight. Watching that glistening metre or so of black scales slither out of sight sent a shudder through him.

Bloody hell! Nearly stepped on that! he told himself.

For a few moments he was too scared to resume walking, and now he went very slowly, peering anxiously down among the stalks and tufts before moving each foot. And now the sun was above the trees and shining directly on him and he could feel its heat. He soon felt very hot and knew he was getting sunburnt but there was no help for it. Only by walking with his back to the sun could he avoid that—and that would be back towards the vehicle track the crooks used.

Kit was more than three quarters across the swamp when he saw more movement. This time it was among the trees to his right rear. Squinting and shielding his eyes against the sun he stared, then felt his pulses quicken with fear. Wild pigs! At least a dozen of all sizes. They were walking out of the savannah woodland into the open and mostly vanishing from sight in the longer swamp grass!

There are piglets there, Kit thought. *And that means sows.*

Another spasm of pure fear coursed through him. The notion of mothers defending their young crossed his mind and he bit his lip and studied the line of pigs. After a few anxious moments he decided they were not heading towards him.

Maybe they are making for that place they dug up?

Fear got him moving—his emotions in conflicting turmoil. He wanted to go slow to watch for snakes, but really wanted to be away from those pigs! His speed was a compromise and he spent more time looking down and ahead than behind. And it was as well that he did because there was another snake!

It was some sort of indeterminate olive, greeny-browny thing and it reared up and hissed. Kit didn't linger. He fled, back and then sideways and then towards the edge of the swamp, now only about a hundred metres away. As he ran, he told himself he was going too fast for any other snake to have time to strike at him. He was sure it had been a dangerous snake because it had risen into the striking 'S' and hissed but also knew that what type it was could only be determined by counting its belly scales and the scales diagonally around its body.

Could have been a common brown or eastern brown or a taipan, he thought as he slowed to a gasping walk.

This was from necessity as he was so worn out and winded that he could not keep running. A glance back to check if the pigs had seen him showed a couple of black humps moving back in the middle of the swamp. They did not appear to have noticed him. Kit sighed with relief and then stopped to lean on the trunk of the first tree he came to.

While resting, he placed his right hand on the tree trunk to steady himself and then got a shock. He now saw in daylight the teeth marks from the python bite. There were in two curved rows that went around to the flesh of his palm and were about 3 centimetres apart (It had felt much bigger at the time!) and he noted with concern that the puncture wounds were red and inflamed.

I suppose I shouldn't grumble, he told himself. *It could have been a poisonous snake.*

After resting until he had normal breathing and his eyes had stopped going in and out of focus, he started walking again, aiming for the small hill that was now only a few hundred metres away.

It still took him nearly ten minutes to reach it and another five to plod up it. It was topped by a cluster of big boulders and dark green bushes among a stand of trees. By the time he reached the boulders, Kit was so puffed he had to stop. Leaning on a rock he experienced a wave of dizziness and for a few minutes could not do anything but pant.

Having restored his breathing and sight Kit carefully climbed up onto the rock pile and sat down in a tiny bar of shade cast by the bushes and a tree trunk. Then he looked out. The top of the hill was just above the tops of the tree canopies on the lava plain and Kit stared at what he realised was an amazing sight.

Bloody hell! What an unusual landscape, he thought.

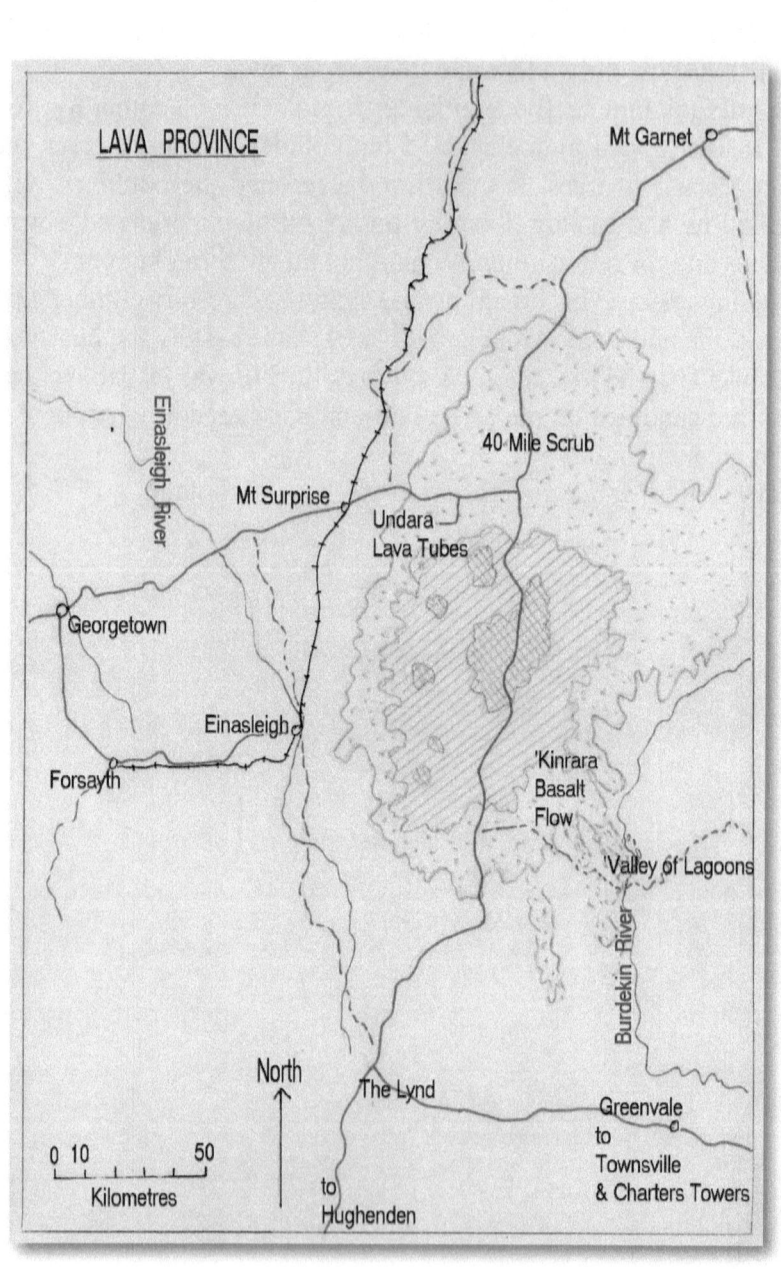

Chapter 34

SHIELD VOLCANOES

From where he sat, Kit had a view that he estimated went for over a hundred kilometres. His foreground was just a level mass of treetops, mostly eucalypts, In the middle distance, slightly to his right (*Southeast*, he calculated) was another hill. It was obviously bigger and he guessed it was the remnant of a volcanic cone. Several other cone-shaped hills and knolls stood out in the distance.

Beyond that the curve of the earth seemed to show and Kit experienced a most peculiar sensation, as though he could not tell up from down. In the far distance, seemingly beyond the curved line of the horizon of bush, was a line of mountains, half-hidden in haze. He had to blink and then rub his eyes and stare before he worked out what the problem was.

It is some sort of optical illusion, he decided. *I am on a huge shield volcano and it is sloping down and away from that hill or cone or whatever. So the ground is not completely flat but actually sloping very gently away. I am looking downhill but those mountains that look like they are up in the air are actually just on the next upslope.*

Kit shook his head and moved his gaze around. As he did, he tried to remember what Mr (Captain) Conkey had taught them in Geography. His simile had been of a giant boil on the surface of the earth with puss oozing out and spreading slowly in all directions.

Or a saucepan of chocolate or custard boiling over and oozing out in all directions. That's how the lava tubes form, the lava flows down the creek lines and fills them up. Then the lava spreads across the landscape. It levels everything out. Then it cools on top but keeps flowing underneath. And a lava tube only forms if gas or steam then push the remaining hot magma out of the tube.

What that meant was an almost flat landscape, except where ridges of rocks were pushed up by two flows meeting or where a lava flow spread and then cooled, leaving a distinct 'wall' or rise. Mr Conkey had shown them lots of slides of surface lava flows further south in the Charters Towers area and also some of a huge lava flow in that area that had gone cold to form The Great Basalt Wall, a feature about 50 kilometres long.

That's why there are no creeks or much surface water in shield volcanos, Kit thought.

He remembered the dry swamp and looked around to see if there was another one. As a typical teenager, he did not pay much attention to the weather, unless it was spoiling a day at the beach, but he did have a reasonable understanding of the climate. He knew that in North Queensland the 'wet' season usually ended in April, and there might be no rain at all west of the coastal ranges along the east coast until summer storms in December.

There was no sign of any open area with its lighter coloured grass to indicate a swamp to the north, and that worried him. He ran the tip of his tongue over his cracked lips and then pressed them together.

I'm bloody thirsty. I had better find water soon or I will get heat exhaustion.

He actually meant heatstroke, but that was a potentially fatal medical condition and he did not want to face that reality. Carefully he studied the country around him, hoping to see a tree line indicating a creek, or even a building.

Swivelling to face north again, he studied the terrain in that direction. To his dismay, it just looked to be another mostly flat plain covered with savannah woodland. Only a couple of small hills poked up, none in his direct line of proposed march. More dispiriting was that in all that vast area, hundreds of square kilometres he thought, there was not a single sign of human existence—not a house, road, or open paddock. The sheer vastness and emptiness of Australia was forced on his consciousness, resulting in little talons of fear clutching at his heart again.

"I'd better get moving and get to the highway before I collapse from… Ow! Ouch!"

Kit stopped muttering to himself and snatched his left hand up. At first he thought he had been bitten by another centipede or scorpion but now the culprits were obvious.

"Ow! Bloody green ants!" he cried.

He saw several nipping at the soft flesh on the outside of his palm and he quickly brushed them off or plucked them off. Then he realised that there were dozens more on the rock and on the bushes beside him.

Springing up, swearing as he did, he quickly retreated, sliding down off the rock and moving away. After crushing a couple more that were giving him nips whose pain was quite disproportionate to their size, he moved further down the slope away from the bushes and rocks.

Here he paused for a moment to check that he had removed all the attackers and then to orientate himself. This time he used the sun. Having determined which way was north he resumed walking, taking care as he went down to the level ground again.

Within ten minutes he got another scare. A small head on a long neck suddenly poked up out of the long grass about 50 metres to his left front. He stopped and experienced a pulse of fright before recognising the creature as it stood up.

Oh, a bloody emu! he told himself.

The huge bird looked at him with beady blue-black eyes even as it began running away from him. He found it fascinating to see how its head was kept swivelled to look at him as the emu went off westwards

There were more cattle and kangaroos or wallabies and a couple of small birds, but otherwise it was just more of the rock-studded lava plain. It was also very hot. Kit realised he should have been perspiring, sweating even, but wasn't.

That's a worry. I must be dehydrating fast, he thought. He estimated that it was now 18 or 19 hours since he had a drink. *Or food,* he added as his stomach grumbled.

He began to consider just sitting in the shade rather than walking in the blazing sunlight but then shook his head.

"I will still be hot and sweating even just sitting," he told himself, so he kept walking.

And then he got another shock. An area with more rock than grass lay in his path but it was only when he was crossing it that he saw the hole. With something of a shock he saw that the hole was about a metre in diameter and looked to be quite deep. Just in time he stopped himself stepping into it.

Bloody hell, what's this? he wondered.

Carefully, and anxiously aware that he was unsteady on his feet, he leaned over to look in. No bottom was visible—just darkness.

Is it a well, or a mineshaft? he wondered, looking around for signs of human effort, vehicle tracks, mullock heaps and so on.

But there was nothing. To check the depth he picked up a loose stone and tossed it in. The rock landed with a faint thud and that told Kit the hole was quite deep. He repeated the experiment, wishing he had paid more attention in school so he could do the maths to calculate the distance by the time of flight.

"Bloody deep anyway," he muttered. But what was it? Then it came to him.

That's a lava tube down there! Part of the roof has fallen in. Bloody hell! I nearly stepped into that.

A shudder ran through him as he thought of how badly he might have been injured. Then it occurred to him that he could have encountered it during the night.

I wouldn't have noticed it in the dark.

He shuddered again and had gloomy thoughts about lying injured there in the darkness till he died, in a place where his body would never be found. Then he remembered the water in the other lava tunnel. To check if there was any down there, he tossed in more stones but there was no splash. He gave a wry smile.

Even if there is, I have no way of getting at it, he mused.

Shaking his head and shivering at his close call he resumed walking, scanning the grass and rocks ahead of him even more carefully.

An area of dark green vegetation appeared a few hundred metres to his left front. Thinking it might be the entrance to another tunnel that might have water in it, he deviated from his course and walked to it. The dark green was trees and bushes and, with memories of the green ants in mind, Kit avoided them and stayed on the black rocks. These now became so abundant that there was almost no grass. He detoured around a clump of bushes and came to a standstill, gaping in surprise.

In front of him was a huge crater at least a hundred metres across and 30 or 40 deep, the surface of it entirely a massive jumble of the black rocks.

"What the?" he muttered. Then he understood what he was looking at.

This is where the roof of a lava tunnel has collapsed.

It was what he had been hoping to find when he had escaped along the other tunnel. But he could not see any entrance, just a mass of rocks of all sizes. And it was fearfully hot. The morning sun was reflected in it and without any breeze it was a stifling environment. Kit decided to detour around and keep going. This necessitated a hundred metre detour to his right before he found a gap in the rocks. He checked north and set off again.

More cattle and kangaroos. And an annoying crow that 'caarked' from time to time from the trees nearby.

Those cattle are a good sign, he told himself. *There must be water not too far away.*

And there was. Away off to his right he sighted a fence line, a typical three strand barbed wire fence with steel 'star' pickets. It was angling in and he saw that if he kept going he would come to it. So he hurried on, hoping now to find help. Away ahead of him he detected cattle. Most were whitish Brahman types and most were lying down. And beyond them, among the trees, was a large dark green water tank on a low stand.

Water! Kit mentally cried, his lips too cracked and sore to want to open.

He hurried forward, noting that the water tank had a black steel water trough out beside it and that it was against the fence. The water tank and trough did not stand in a clearing as he had expected but in among the trees. But the cattle had eaten all the grass so the ground cover gave way to a dusty area dotted with cow pats of various ages.

As Kit approached them, the cattle got to their feet, all their heads turned in his direction. Then, when he was about 50 metres from the nearest, one turned and bolted. Immediately all the others did too, stampeding off away from him into the scrub along the fence line. Kit swore as he hadn't wanted to make that happen and he noted the rising dust and vanishing cattle with annoyance.

But it was the water trough he was most interested in. By this time he was very thirsty and badly needed a drink. As he approached the trough, wending his way through the dung splatterings and droppings, he noted that beside the water tank stood the remains of what he guessed had once been a windmill. Only the steel tower remained but on top it had a radio mast and some sort of antennae that looked like a radar scanner. A large solar panel under that obviously provided the electricity. Kit understood what he was looking at. The windmill had been replaced by a solar-powered electric pump and the system could be turned on and off by radio from the station homestead.

That got him looking to check if there was a camera there but he could not see one. He came to a stop at the tough and looked with distaste at the dirty water in in it. The water had lots of small floating 'stuff' in it. The sight of them, and knowing they must include a lot of cow poo, made him grimace.

"If I drink that I might get sick," he muttered.

That got him studying the pipes and the valve and tap arrangements where water obviously came out of the tank to flow into the trough. To his annoyance, it was all in a sealed unit and obviously worked by radio signal, not by hand. That got him studying the water tank and he clambered up and lifted himself to look on the top, hoping to find an access. Careful not to slip, Kit climbed up onto the tank stand and hoisted himself up to look on top. There was an opening but it had a closed cover. Using his arms, Kit hoisted himself up, once again thanking all those chin-ups he had been doing to give him that strength. He then knelt on top of the tank, noting that it was thick plastic and very hot in the sunlight.

But he could not open the cover. Muttering with annoyance, he lowered himself back over the side feet first, then hung by his fingertips before getting his boots on the tank stand again. Carefully he jumped down, very conscious of a sharp twinge in the ankle he had turned the night before as he landed.

Don't injure your ankle, Dumbo, he told himself. *You have to walk a few more kilometres yet to get to the highway.*

He wasn't sure how many but put the figure of 5 on it. Once again, he stood and studied the dirty water. But there was nothing for it but to take the risk.

"If I don't get liquid into me, I will get heat exhaustion and collapse," he told himself, conscious that he was already suffering many of the symptoms: headaches, dizziness, blurry vision, rapid heartbeat, unsteady on his feet. "And I've stopped sweating, so my body is running out of fluid."

From First Aid courses he knew that heatstroke followed. The body concentrated the remaining liquid to try to maintain the blood flow for the heart to pump. That left the extremities without fluid to cool it. It also meant that the flow of blood to cool the brain was reduced.

That's what causes the strokes, and can also cause heart attacks, he remembered. It was a worrying concept and when he felt his skin and noted that it was dry and hot he knew he had to drink. *I am on the edge of heatstroke,* he decided, adding, *and it doesn't matter if it makes me sick tomorrow. You have to be alive to be sick.*

So Kit carefully cupped his hands and bent forward to slip them slowly into the clearest piece of water he could see. Very slowly he then lifted them up to his lips. Despite being careful the movement still set up small swirls in the water and the bits of dark matter began to move around. The smell was enough to put him off but he shut his mind to it and sucked in as much water as he could. It was heavenly. Almost at once he felt better.

Carefully and slowly he repeated the process, drinking amid grimaces at the taste and then the gritty feel of 'things' going into his mouth. It took will power to drink slowly to try to keep the water clean but after each mouthful he felt better. After a few more mouthfuls he was suddenly conscious of a prickling in his skin and to his intense delight he began to perspire.

"Aah! That's better!" he told himself.

After a few more drinks he began to feel bloated, so he changed to carefully rinsing his face and neck, very aware of how sunburnt he was. Then he began to splash water on his shirt. That was wonderful, cooling and refreshing! He washed his hands, noting unhappily that the teeth marks in his right hand were now looking angry and red and some had pus forming and crusting. All he could do was shrug, feeling sure it would all be treated when he got to safety.

The crow 'caarked'. Kit splashed more water over his head and shoulders. Then he stiffened.

What's that sound?

He stood there, water dribbling off as he listened. It was a vehicle— and it was approaching fast!

And there it was! His eyes were drawn first to trail of dust among the trees less than a hundred metres away. His brain registered the meaning, and his heart skipped a beat.

"It's that Land Rover! Oh bloody hell! It's the men," Kit cried.

Through the trees he could see the vehicle approaching along the two wheel ruts that he now noted went west among the trees.

But what to do? Run, or try to hide?

Chapter 35

COLD!

K it stood there for another couple of seconds, his mind racing. No good trying to hide. A glance showed there was nowhere.

So run! he told himself.

Suiting actions to the thought he turned and dashed around the side of the water tank away from the approaching vehicle and threw himself down in the dust to roll and wriggle under the bottom strand of the barbed wire fence. In the process his wet skin and clothes became coated in dust.

Spitting grit and now on the edge of panic, he scrambled to his feet and started sprinting away across another area of dusty bare ground littered with cow manure. Behind him he heard the Land Rover arrive and skid to a stop, and that spurred him to run faster. But that was hard to do. He was exhausted and not very fit and his sore ankle began to really bother him.

Behind him he heard doors open and then slam shut followed by yelling. It was Snake.

"Stop you little bastard or I'll shoot!" he shouted.

Oh my God! He's got a gun this time, Kit thought. But did he really?

Kit risked a glance over his shoulder and glimpsed Snake run to the fence and stop—and he definitely had a gun, a rifle or shotgun. The man shouted again. Kit was now labouring and winded and nearly at the start of the grass. Fear rose up to grip him and he dithered in indecision, not wanting to believe that the situation was real but knowing it was.

He looked ahead and there was nothing but a long, gentle downslope through a forest of amazing similar trees with black trunks, and quite short grass. Gasping now from effort but he still did not want to give up.

Crack!

The bullet threw up a spurt of dust ten paces ahead and to one side and then skittered along until it hit a rock and went screeching off to hit a tree trunk with a very audible *thunk*. Kit nearly wet himself. He had never been shot at before but knew exactly what the noise was. And at that moment his boot stepped on a small stone in the grass. The stone rolled and Kit went down hard, his left ankle getting another savage wrench as it did. Half stunned he lay there, spitting dirt and hurting, fear and a sick feeling of defeat swirling nauseously in his empty stomach.

Snake yelled again. "Stay down, kid. I won't miss next time."

Kit twisted his neck to look back and saw Snake crawling under the fence and Jellman standing at it. There was a moment of malicious satisfaction when Snake snagged his shirt on the barbs but that was quickly overwhelmed by the fear. Kit began to shake but whether from over-exertion or the growing terror he could not tell—did not want to admit. Bitterly understanding he had no choice, Kit lay there, nursing his sore ankle and shaking his head.

Snake ran over to him, rifle held in both hands. The man stopped next to him and pointed the muzzle at him.

"You little shit! I should shoot you now, after all the trouble you've caused. I've been up all bloody night lookin' fer you," he snarled.

Then he gave Kit a savage kick on his left buttock and another in the kidneys. Kit cried out and then gasped as he was winded. Pain shot through him and he stared up at that rifle muzzle, which was now only a few centimetres from his eyes. Fear of death swamped his emotions for a few moments and then anger at being kicked while he was down.

"Well why don't you?" he gasped back.

Snake's answer was to kick him again and then step back. Keeping the rifle aimed at Kit, he curled his lip. "Because the grounds too bloody hard to dig a grave and we don't have any tools. Besides, the Big Boss want to question you, so get up!"

"I can't. I've hurt my ankle," Kit replied, now genuinely in pain.

"Get up or I'll bloody well drag you!" Snake snarled.

Sensing that this was exactly what would happen, Kit made the effort. With some difficulty he rolled onto his hands and knees and then got to his feet. Sharp little stabs of pain shot up his lower leg and he several times cried out with involuntary gasps and little whimpers.

Snake gestured with the rifle towards the Land Rover. "Get going, kid. Any trouble and I will shoot you, and it will hurt. Now move!"

Kit eyed the man, his own anger now near boiling point. His eyes flicked to the rifle and then back to Snake's face.

That's only a bolt action sporting rifle and he hasn't re-cocked it, he noted.

He had done one lesson at Navy Cadets with .22" bolt action, target rifle and one 'shoot' at the range, so he had at least some idea. For a second or so he considered whether he could catch the man off guard enough to throw him and disarm him.

But Snake was wary and stepped away, gesturing angrily. Kit was left with no choice but do as he was told. Limping at every step, he made his way back across to the fence. Jellman jeering at him and laughing did nothing to ease his feelings. By now he was not only feeling battered and bruised but the sheer bitterness of failure and defeat was galling.

It took a real effort to get down and crawl back under the fence, and as he struggled to his feet Jellman grabbed him by the shirt front and punched him in the face with his other hand. Kit was half-stunned and would have fallen but for that. Snake also crawled under and then got up.

"Stop that, Jellman!" he snapped. "Just get some of those cable ties and tie him up; and make a better job of it than your last effort."

Jellman looked surly at the insult but turned and led the way to the Land Rover. Kit was pushed by Snake and he reeled for a few steps then steadied himself. Although terrified, he was consumed by curiosity.

"How did you know I was here?" he queried.

Snake laughed and pointed past the back of the Land Rover to a large tree. "There's a camera up there that is activated by motion sensors. It transmits to our base station by radio."

Kit looked up and saw the camouflage-coloured camera strapped five metres up the tree and pointing at the water trough.

Damn! he thought. He was annoyed with himself. *I looked for a camera but didn't think to look behind me.*

Snake laughed and Jellman ordered Kit to turn around and put his hands behind his back. That was the last thing Kit wanted to do but he had to obey, fear surging back in. He saw that Jellman had white nylon cable ties and then felt one pulled tight around both wrists.

"Ow! That hurts!" Kit protested.

Jellman laughed and pulled it even tighter. "Tough! Let's see ya get outa that one," he jeered. "Now get up on the tray."

The tailgate of the Land Rover had been let down by Snake who then reached into the cab and took out a small radio.

"Got him. We'll back in a few minutes," he said.

Kit had no choice but to sit up on the tailgate. He went to lie back but Jellman was too quick, giving him a hard shove. Kit went down on the tools and junk in the tray so hard he went numb in his right shoulder. Jellman grabbed Kit's sore right ankle, causing him to cry out in pain.

Jellman smacked at him. "Shut up kid and stop makin' a fuss or I'll give ya sumthin' to really cry about," he snarled. "Now put yer feet together."

Reluctantly Kit did so and felt a cable tie go around both his ankles. It was also pulled tight. His attempt to keep it loose by placing one ankle bone on the other so it could move slightly afterwards was defeated by Snake reaching in and shoving.

"Pull it really tight, Jellman," he ordered.

Kit was then roughly bundled in and the tailgate was slammed up and locked. The tray was open and there was no canopy so Kit could see out. The two men got in the front and the engine was started. After reversing, the vehicle did a sharp turn and went back along the track that wound through the trees. Dust billowed in and Kit began coughing. He had to shut his eyes and only opened them for quick glimpses.

What was bothering him was how far they might have to go. *These guys arrived within ten or fifteen minutes of me reaching that water trough,* he thought. *So they must have been close by.*

The Land Rover drove fast along the dirt track, Kit being bruised and bounced around at every bump and pothole. He tried to follow where they were going and to keep track of time, and was appalled to find the vehicle slowing to do a left turn onto a dirt road after only a few minute's drive—only a couple of kilometres or so.

Is this the road into the crook's secret base? he wondered.

It was. It took only another ten minutes at most before they drove up over the long rocky ridge. The Land Rover came to a stop out in the open area between the cattle yards and the ridge. Kit experienced such a wave of bitter defeat that he began to sob.

I walked all that way, and I only got about ten or twelve kilometres, he thought.

Jones was standing there beside a semi. Kit lifted his head and through his gritty tears saw that the prime mover looked like XRT. But it no longer had the low loader trailer with the container on it. Instead, a normal refrigerated box trailer was hooked on. The truck's engine was going and so was the refrigerator unit in the trailer.

"Get him in there and get going," Jones said to Jellman.

Jellman scowled. "I hope it's safe," he said.

Jones gave him a surly look and shook his head. "Doesn't matter if it isn't. The Big Boss said do it, so you do it!"

"Open the back then and help me carry this little shit," Jellman retorted.

Snake joined them. "Why the hurry?" he asked Jones.

"Boss doesn't want those prawns to go orf. He's got a buyer apparently and they need to be in Townsville tonight," Jones replied.

He then walked to the rear of the trailer and began unlocking the doors. Snake and Jellman got either side of Kit and hoisted him up. Kit wanted to protest as it really hurt but the angry looks on the men's faces kept him quiet. The embarrassment of being carried so easily added to his hurt feelings.

Until he saw that the prime mover really was XRT. "You aren't going to drive this truck are you?" he gasped.

"Yeah, why?" Jellman asked.

"That's my dad's rig, XRT. It's the one you damaged the steering on and it hasn't been fixed. It's not safe," Kit cried.

"Crap kid! I drove it here with no problems," Jellman retorted.

"But I just crashed it into the gate as well," Kit said. A new sort of apprehension started to grip him.

Jellman grunted. "Yeah, ya little shit! Jonesy should give you a real beltin' for that. It took him hours to clear that. Now shut up and enjoy the ride."

They had reached the rear of the trailer by then and Kit felt a wave of chilled air flow over him. He looked in and saw that the whole floor of the box trailer was covered with cardboard boxes of frozen prawns. These had completely filled the container on the low loader trailer but this trailer was longer and he guessed that the cargo had been transferred by hand. Then he realised that he was going to be placed on the frozen cargo.

This is a refrigerator trailer. I will freeze to death! Panic began to surge.

"Hey! You can't put me in there. I will die! Stop!" he shouted, struggling violently as he did.

This earned him a sharp slap to the side of the face and then a punch.

"Shut up kid," Jellman snarled. "You won't feel a thing. Now enjoy yer ride. Ready Snake? One, two, three!"

Kit found himself flying up into the back, tossed like a sack of potatoes by the two strong men. He landed hard on the icy cardboard boxes and instantly felt the nip of the thin rime of ice which had formed on their outside. The boxes were so cold his skin felt like it was sticking to the frozen surface. Another pulse of fear set him shouting in near panic.

"Stop! Get me out! Stop! You can't do this."

Jellman's response was to chuckle and grin. "Enjoy the ride, kid," he called as he swung the first half of the back door shut.

Now real panic gripped Kit and he squirmed and struggled until his eyes bulged.

"Help! Stop! Let me out!" he screamed, his voice quavering in a way that later embarrassed him.

Slam!

The other half of the door was closed and Kit screamed again. He heard the locking bars pushed into position and then the clash of the handles being locked in their brackets. Now he was in total darkness and absolutely terrified. He yelled again but now it was muffled and he quickly subsided to gasping and whimpering. He felt the trailer shake and deduced that was from Jellman climbing into the cab of the prime mover.

"They can't do this! This is murder," he told himself. But they had and he was stunned by the absolute reality and callousness of the situation.

They said the Big Boss wanted to question me. How can he do that if I die from the cold? Kit asked himself, still half hoping.

Then the engine roared and the rig jerked into motion. Kit was half-rolled over by the sudden movement. Now he lay on his right side on the freezing boxes and could feel his body heat melting the thin layer of ice.

Bloody hell! This is cold! I won't last long in this, he thought, already feeling the chill striking into his flesh.

The rig suddenly went sharply up and then, with no warning, went suddenly down again, the towing pintle grinding loudly and protesting at the sudden changes of attitude. Kit guessed they were going over the rocky ridge again and were heading north towards the highway.

Maybe the police are out on the highway with roadblocks, he thought, hoping with quiet desperation to be rescued.

The rig was now travelling very fast on the flat, the trailer bouncing around so much that he was being bounced into the air on the bigger bumps and some of the boxes of prawns were even bounced out of the neat top layer they had been stowed in.

Jellman driving in his usual style, Kit thought.

Despite his fear of dying and wondering what death by freezing might feel like, his mind did the calculation that it would be at least a four- or five-hour trip to Townsville.

"But will I last that long?" he worried.

At that moment, the rig hit a bigger pothole or rut than usual and everything bounced. Then the truck began a sharp swerve to the left. There was a loud bang somewhere ahead and just as Kit's heart leapt in alarm he felt the whole trailer rumble and bounce.

Bloody hell! We've left the road! he thought.

There were more bangs and the trailer and its cargo continued bouncing, and from the noises underneath Kit assumed it was running over very rough ground.

More of those bloody rocks, he thought, now thoroughly scared.

In the total darkness he had no reference to which was up or down other than from gravity but it all felt wrong.

And then he was certain something serious had happened. First he was rolled roughly over by the extreme motion. There was such a violent movement he was flung up and then came back down with a crash that felt like it had broken an arm or dislocated a shoulder. He screamed with fright but was unable to grab hold of anything as he was again flung up. This time he struck what he thought was the side or roof of the trailer and real fear gushed in.

Then the world seemed to rotate and he was struck by flying boxes of frozen prawns and bounced and banged against the walls or roof. His head struck something and he blacked out—just as daylight flooded in.

Chapter 36

ICE AND FIRE

Cold! Bloody cold! And wet! Kit thought.

His head was throbbing and felt ready to split open. He was vaguely aware that he was really hurting, but it was the cold that was bothering him—and the very bright light. With an effort of willpower he managed to open one eye a tiny bit. That got him squinting as he tried to work out what was what. Then it came to him. The very bright light was the sun shining directly down on him. And he was cold and wet because he was lying on and half-covered by blocks of frozen prawns that were melting.

Blinking and opening both eyes, Kit gasped and saw that he was lying among wreckage and long grass on a steep, rocky hillside.

Am I badly hurt? he wondered.

He now understood that the truck and trailer had crashed and rolled. Very gingerly he moved his head and was relieved to find that he could look in both directions. But his back and whole right side felt completely numb.

The horrible possibility of his spine being damaged sent a chill of fear through him and he made the effort to try to move his legs. To his intense relief, he was able to move his left leg slightly, but it hurt to do so. But the right leg did not want to move, felt crushed or broken. Kit experienced more stabs of anxiety and then realised he was shivering violently. Right close to his face was a block of frozen uncooked prawns. Their dead, black but beady eyes appeared to be staring straight into his. Their legs and whiskers were prickling his face and drips of ice water were coming off them onto his neck and cheek.

They are melting, he told himself, already detecting a smell of rotting prawns.

Blinking again to clear his eyes, he tried to lift his left hand and found it trapped behind his back. Then memory came to him in a rush and he realised that his wrists were still secured by the cable tie. Now urgently wanting to be free, he squirmed and pushed the block of frozen prawns off his chest by wriggling around. Then he looked around as well as he could while lying on his back. He saw that he was halfway down the hillside, a rock studded slope now covered in pieces of wreckage and boxes of prawns. Many of the boxes had split open or been torn apart in the crash, so there seemed to be prawns everywhere amid the glitter of melting ice.

Uphill to his left he saw a huge flat piece of wreckage that he recognised as either a side or the roof of the box trailer. Other pieces lay scattered nearby, including a door which had been torn off its hinges and buckled badly. Between him and the large piece, amid the piles and slew of boxes and prawns, was the shattered remains of a tree. Obviously the rolling truck had smashed into it and splintered it so that leaves and branches lay amid the wreckage.

Turning to look downhill to his right, Kit saw that about ten metres down the slope was the base of the trailer. That was bent and warped so that the front end was on its side held up by a large tree. The rear end of the trailer was bent and twisted so that the rear wheels were pointing at the sky. He could see all of the underside, the steel framework and pipes and cables, all coated with dust and grime. Some of the steel framework had snapped, leaving jagged ends poking up or out.

Shifting his gaze to the front of the rig, Kit saw that the prime mover was still attached but was lying on its side with the underside towards him.

Oh, poor old Dad's truck! Poor old Dad! Kit thought.

He knew the vehicle was insured but wasn't sure if it was covered against the type of accident it had just suffered. A stabbing pain lanced through his skull and he closed his eyes and tried to put his right hand up to his face. Frustrated and angry, he had to give that up. But he did realise that being able to move his right arm and hand even a bit was good news.

Once again he realised he was shivering violently and wasn't sure if it was because he was in shock or because he was half buried in boxes and blocks of frozen prawns. In the process he discovered that he was lying on another of the large rectangular panels that was probably one of the sides of the box trailer. Then his eyes detected something that really concentrated his thinking and galvanised him into action. There was smoke rising on the other side of the prime mover—and not just smoke! The glow of flames became visible. They were coming from the front of the rig.

Bloody hell! The wreck is on fire and I am stuck here, tied up in this long grass! he thought. His instinct for self-preservation kicked in and sent the adrenaline pumping through his blood stream. *I must get up, must get away before the flames reach the fuel tanks,* he thought.

There were at least 300 litres of fuel there and if they blew up, he would be engulfed in the flames!

But how to move with his arms and legs tied by cable ties! That thought sent more urgent spasms of fear to his mind and he began to wriggle violently. He realised one of the reasons he could not move his legs was because they were trapped under a pile of heavy boxes and an avalanche of defrosting prawns. He began to frantically push and squirm and several boxes slid aside and then he was able to pull his legs free. Ice and prawns cascaded off.

I have to get my legs and arms free, or I am dead, Kit told himself.

But how to cut or remove the cable ties? He had once been secured by them by his brother, much thinner black nylon ones during a game, and he knew they were too strong for a person to break. But how to cut them?

Kit rolled on his side and looked around but saw nothing that might help. So he rolled the other way and studied the crashed trailer and prime mover. By then his heart was hammering with anxiety and he just wanted to flee—but couldn't. His eyes flicked along the wreck, and then seemed to just focus. There was a steel girder under the trailer base which had snapped. That gave him two jagged ends. Knowing he might have only seconds to act, he began squirming across the litter or boxes and prawns like a seal, jerking up and down with his hands up in the air behind his back. That hurt and he kept getting winded when boxes or rocks cut into his stomach and diaphragm, but he was now desperate so he ignored the pain.

The last few metres were the worst. Another big, flat panel was lying on the slope with a mess of ice, prawns and boxes on it and he slid down it easily—until he realised he was going to slam face first into the bottom of the trailer. Just in time he did a giant twitch and got his feet around to stop his slide. Thoroughly soaked in icy water, Kit reached the first jagged end. To his satisfaction, the steel had snapped, leaving quite a sharp edge, with grey metallic grit showing inside the fracture. But which first—feet or legs?

"I can run with my hands tied behind my back," Kit told himself.

So he rolled on his back and used his stomach muscles to lift his bound feet up to the jagged piece of steel. Once again he thanked himself for having developed those muscles.

It took him two goes, but once he had the nylon cord firmly on the sharp steel edge he only had to saw it back and forth a couple of times before it parted. His feet dropped either side and Kit sighed with relief. To his great relief, his legs were obviously working even though they felt numb and sore. Using his now freed feet to help, he rolled onto his front in the slush and then stood up and felt behind him for the jagged steel.

But his rubber boot soles slipped on the smooth panel and he fell heavily, unbale to break his fall because his hands were behind him. That hurt and winded him. His face had taken another hammering and his chest hurt even more. Trembling from fright and over-exertion and cold, he struggled up again, this time wedging his boots against the wreckage. Then he felt behind him again and, having found the sharp edge with his hands, carefully positioned the cable tie on it.

A sudden *whoof!* and a flare of flame off to his right near the cab sent another pulse of fear through him and he began to saw with all his might. His hands came free so suddenly that he fell again. But this time he was quick enough to use them to cushion the fall. But his boots sank in the slush and slid under the piled-up cargo.

Sitting up and using his arms, Kit grabbed a box of prawns off his lower legs and tossed it down the slope. Then another, and another and his feet were clear. As he did, this he was very aware of those flames now flaring up on the other side of the wreck.

That prime mover is where the fuel tanks are. I need to get going, he told himself.

From where he sat, he could see the two silver 100 litre nearside fuel tanks. They were up in the air and he hoped the flames weren't too close to the ones on the other side as they had to be down in the grass.

Kit struggled amid the slush of wet grass, prawns and melting ice and got to his hands and knees. When he tried to stand up again, his boots slipped in the slush and mess on the smooth panel. But this time he was ready and did not fall hard. Crying out in fear and swearing, Kit scrabbled back to his hands and knees and crawled across the panel and over boxes of half-thawed prawns to reach the grass of the hillside at the rear of the trailer. Except it was not just grass.

Ow! More of those bloody basalt rocks! he thought as he skinned his knuckles and then hurt his knees on them.

But he was able to get to his feet and start picking his way through the wreckage, litter of cargo and rocks to get away from the growing flames. Fearing that the fuel tank might blow at any moment, he wanted to be well away before it did!

On reaching the far edge of the debris, Kit stopped and leaned on a large rock. He was gasping and shaking but needed a pause. Carefully he examined himself for injuries. His whole right side felt cold and numb but his arm was obviously working so he just shrugged. With his fingertips he explored his battered face and head. He discovered a huge, egg-sized lump on his left forehead.

"Ow! That hurts!" he muttered.

As he gingerly explored his skull and sucked in deep breaths, Kit looked back. The flames were still showing along with a column of thick black smoke. That sent another fearful idea through his mind.

That smoke might attract the crooks to come and investigate. I'd better get away from here fast.

He turned and began climbing up the slope, thinking to follow the road out to the highway. Another glance back showed the smoke even denser. And then he had another sickening thought.

Where is Jellman? What's happened to the driver?

Kit stopped and looked back. His eyes scanned the hillside and the underside of the cab. Was Jellman still in there?

Is he trapped, or injured?

As his gaze once more searched the wreckage and nearby hillside, Kit was torn between his fears and his conscience.

Chapter 37

CONSCIENCE

K it stood there swaying and frightened and torn by his conscience. *If Jellman is trapped in the wreck I can't just walk away and leave him to be burnt to death,* he thought. But staying meant he was again at risk of being caught by Snake or Jones! *Should I just hurry out to the highway and get help instead,* he thought.

But he knew that was a cowardly compromise and felt bad about even thinking it.

Oh bugger it! I have to take the risk, he told himself. *If I just leave him to die I will never sleep soundly again for the rest of my life.*

And he knew he had to move fast. The flames were increasing and so was the column of smoke. The fire and fear of being caught in an explosion were one thing; the moral consequences of allowing another human being to be burnt to death were quite another! So Kit turned and began angling down the hillslope. Several times he stumbled on the rocks and steep slope and forced himself to go slow and take care.

As he approached the front of the prime mover, he looked at the underside and his gaze was immediately drawn to the steering. Plain to see was a snapped steering arm.

The bloody fool! I warned him, Kit thought.

He was now sure that Jellman had been driving much too fast for the road and either a sudden big jolt from a rock or pothole or a sudden swerve had caused steering failure, sending the rig off the road and over the side of the hill.

Passing quickly around the front of the vehicle, Kit at once looked through the windscreen.

Jellman, there he is! he told himself, noting that the driver was crumpled down in the lower side of the cab. Somewhat to Kit's surprise, the windscreen was not broken. *Not even cracked.*

And now grabbing his attention was the fire. He saw that the flames were steadily burning at the off-side front wheel of the prime mover. The grass had caught fire as well and the fire was slowly spreading.

But not very quickly. The grass must be too wet, Kit deduced. The fire wasn't close to the fuel tank yet but he could see it could easily spread along in the grass. *Especially if there is any spilled diesel.*

He sniffed and thought he could smell spilled fuel but then shrugged. Big trucks always had a diesel odour about them. That was bad news.

I need to move fast! he thought.

But, as always, there seemed to be two difficult courses of action to choose from: Try to rescue Jellman, or try to put out the fire.

As he stood there dithering, Jellman's eyes opened. The man blinked and stared and then obviously smelt the smoke. He stared at Kit and then at the flames, then opened his mouth and screamed.

"Help, help! Get me out of here!"

Try to save him, Kit decided.

So he scrambled up onto the bonnet, having some difficulty with the whole vehicle lying on its side and needing to keep well clear of the flames. From there he moved to the passenger door and leaned across to unlock it. Because he had to then hoist it upwards at an awkward angle, he had difficulty getting it open—then more difficulty to get it to stay open. Twice it banged shut again, and only by standing on the side of the cab and using both hands could he open the door properly and then jam it to stay upright. As he did, smoke swirled around him and he felt the lick of the flames.

He bent and leaned in. "Can you climb out?" he called to Jellman.

Jellman shook his head. "No! Broken leg. Get me out, this rig's on fire," he shouted back. The man was obviously terrified and in real pain.

"Say please," Kit snapped back as smoke eddied around him, now feeling all his pent-up anger and other emotions welling up.

"Get me out! Save me!" Jellman shrieked.

"Say please I said, you fat slug!" Kit retorted.

'Save me, save me… please," Jellman replied, his face contorting with pain.

"Why should I? You were quite happy to bash me and you kicked me when I was down, you bastard! And you thought it was funny to freeze me to death. I should leave you to be barbequed," Kit snarled angrily back.

"I'm sorry. Nothin' personal. Just business. Please get me out," Jellman said. Then he curled up and gripped his right leg and groaned.

Oh well, nothing for it but to try and from the feel of those flames I'd better be quick, Kit thought.

He understood very clearly that, if the fuel tank exploded while he was in the cab, he would die a horrible death. He was scared but also becoming emotionally numb. He moved to climb in.

Then he made a silly mistake. Bending down to climb down inside Kit put his right hand on the side of the cab and immediately cried out in pain and pulled his hand away.

"Yow! Aargh! Bloody hell, that's hot," he cried.

Changing his grip, he lowered himself inside, worrying as he did that Jellman might grab him or hit him. But it was instantly obvious that the man was so terrified and in so much pain that all he wanted was to be rescued. Kit braced his left foot on the dashboard and his right on the back of Jellman's seat and then reached down to grab the man's shirt.

"When I lift you, try to push up," he ordered.

Jellman groaned an affirmative. Kit took a tight hold and braced himself, then lifted. Jellman's shirt strained and then buttons began to pop. The cloth suddenly tore. Kit changed his grip and tried again.

"Try to help with your good leg, you fat slug!" Kit snapped.

Jellman scowled his resentment but did so and then, as Kit strained, he let out a sharp cry of pain and his head lolled into unconsciousness. Kit was stumped. He released his grip and looked down.

I'm not strong enough and he's caught somewhere down there, he thought. It was plainly obvious to him that on his own he could not lift an unconscious man of Jellman's weight. *God, what'll I do?*

At that moment, a lick of flame swirled around the front of the cab and the windscreen cracked right across. Kit blanched and experienced such a gulp of feat that he was left paralysed for a second or two. But it also gave him some ideas.

Get out and try to fight the fire, he thought, *and maybe try to break the windshield and drag him out through that?*

As quickly as he could, Kit straightened up and then looked around. Now his work experience came to his aid again. There was a fire extinguisher clamped in behind the side of the passenger seat and he grabbed that and then hoisted himself back up and out. Once on the side of the cab he cast a quick, appraising look around, then scrambled down onto the side of the engine cover and then down to the ground. As he did, his mind raced with ideas on how to break that windshield. He knew that kicking with his gym boots would be no use.

Truck windscreens are too strong. I need a tool of some sort.

That meant getting access to a tool box and he knew they had all been padlocked. He cast a quick look around to see if there was a piece of wreckage he could use and then even considered picking up a rock. As he thought this, he saw Jellman regain consciousness, his eyes rolling around. The man began to cough and then scream to be rescued.

Fight the fire then, Kit decided.

Quickly taking out the safety pin on the fire extinguisher, he changed his grip so as to hold it correctly and then advanced around the side (actually the roof) of the cab. He was instantly assailed by fierce heat and had to shield himself, but to his surprise the fire had not gotten much bigger, except the circle of burning grass was expanding slowly. But the flames were licking around the front of the vehicle. That was where the black smoke was coming from, and the acrid reek of burning rubber set Kit coughing.

Pausing for a second, Kit studied what to do next and saw that the flames were actually coming from the grease and oil around the brake drum and from the front wheel that lay on the ground.

That explains all this black smoke, he thought, *and the smell of burning rubber.*

Using the fire extinguisher as he had been trained to do, both by Navy Cadets and by his father, Kit pressed the trigger and directed the cloud of white foam onto the base of the flames nearest to the cab. This had an instant effect, which quite surprised him. He was able to step around from behind the shelter of the cab and get closer. Now he directed the foam onto the engine compartment and was both pleased and surprised to see that the flames were instantly extinguished.

More carefully directed squirts of foam quickly doused the flames among the wheels and then on the grass under the rig. Kit was very pleased and stepped closer. The heat had gone out of the fire and the remaining flames were in the slowly spreading circle of grass and not from anything on the rig. He began walking around clockwise, spraying the burning grass from on the burnt area. He started with the flames beside the cab and ended up near the trailer. But the extinguisher ran out of foam and he was left with the choice of leaving the remaining flames as a risk or of beating them out. As the burning grass near the trailer was wet from the melting ice and was not flaring up much, he opted to do this and soon had the whole circle of flames out.

Wiping sweat from his face and panting from the effort, Kit looked around, a bit incredulous that he had managed to put the fire apparently completely out. Only wisps of smoke rose from various places. There were very strong odours of burnt paint, burnt plastic and burnt rubber and he was sure he could still detect wafts of diesel fumes. That was a worry.

So, what do I do now? Kit asked himself. Again two choices came up and with that apprehension amounting to fear. *I can try to get Jellman out or I can go for help. If I stay here and the crooks arrive I am back in trouble. Time to save myself I think and Jellman will just have to take his chances of a fire breaking out again.*

Having decided that, Kit first looked in at Jellman through the cracked windscreen. Jellman was looking back and still pleading to be rescued in between groans. Resentment fuelled by fear and hatred suddenly welled up and Kit swung the extinguisher savagely at the glass. Jellman flinched back and covered his face while emitting a genuine scream of fear. But the fire extinguisher wasn't heavy enough to shatter the glass and just bounced back, hurting Kit's fingers as it did. He changed his grip and threw the thing at the windshield, causing Jellman to scream again.

Kit shook his fist at him. "Shut up, Jellman, you rotten slug!" he shouted.

"Help! Get me out!" Jellman called, and then when he saw Kit turn and start walking uphill, "Where are you going? What are you doing? Don't leave me!"

"I can't lift you out. You are too big and fat. I'm going to get help. So, while I'm gone you start preparing what you are going to say to the coppers when they arrive," Kit spat back at him.

"No! Help me out! Help!" Jellman shouted.

But Kit ignored him and set himself to plod up the hill, barely glancing at the wreckage and scattered prawns and boxes strewn across the hillside. As he did, he seethed with emotion. To begin with, it was hatred of Jellman and all he stood for. And then Kit was ashamed of having such thoughts.

But it's hard not to have negative thoughts about people like that, he told himself.

He reached the top of the slope, an old lava flow, he decided, and saw that the dirt road did a sharp turn at that point.

"This is the turn Jellman nearly turned the rig over on when he first stole it. The man's an idiot!" Kit decided.

For a few seconds he stood there orientating himself, then he turned north and began walking that way as fast as he could go. He realised he was leaving boot prints in the dust, but he had had enough of trying to make his way through that long grass and rocks!

I just need to keep my ears open and a good watch behind me so that the other crooks don't come driving along and catch me in the middle of the road, he cautioned himself.

He did not know how far it was to the highway, but he estimated it could not be much more than about 5 kilometres.

"I can walk that in one hour if I step it out," he muttered.

But he couldn't. He was too footsore and exhausted and it was also hot. There wasn't a cloud in the sky and the sun blazed down with no breeze to relieve it. When he started he guessed that the sun was just past midday. After half an hour he was chafed, developing blisters and sore feet and very thirsty again.

He really just wanted to stop and have a rest but the image of the truck burning with Jellman trapped in it tormented his conscience, so he forced himself to keep walking. The sun slid a bit more over to the west and Kit stopped perspiring. Once again he began worrying about heat exhaustion. And he knew he was hungry! His stomach kept reminding him of that!

And then he rounded a curve and saw the flicker of a moving car a hundred metres ahead through the trees. Twenty more paces brought him to an area where he could see the fence and cattle grid at the highway. Kit sighed with relief.

Nearly there. Now all I have to do is flag down a car. Then an awful thought came to him. *I'd better make sure I don't flag down the crooks.* From that came another even more worrying notion—did the crooks have another camera watching this entrance? *It would be the sensible thing to do, and it would explain why those men were out ready to open gates for Jellman when he brought the stolen rig in.*

With that worrying notion, Kit became very cautious. He moved off the road to his right and stood behind a tree and then carefully studied the fence line, the cattle grid area and then all of the trees facing towards the opening. And there it was! A camouflaged camera was taped on the north side of the next tree to his left, about ten metres up!

Bloody hell! I was right!

Shaken more than he wanted to admit, Kit backed away, hoping he was outside the area covered by the camera. Once he was about 50 metres back in the bush beside the road, he turned right and started walking east, parallel with the fence and highway.

They can't have cameras watching it all, he reasoned.

The sound of a big engine out on the highway made him stop and crouch under cover. It was from a big road-train heading west. As he watched it go past, Kit gave a wry grin. There was no way he was going to try to stop any big truck. He stood up and continued walking, ignoring a car that went racing past eastwards. He was sure the driver wouldn't see him that far out in the bush.

But God he was tired! And sore! But now a burning determination was building to see the crooks brought to justice. So he gritted his teeth and endured more sore muscles and bruised feet from walking across yet more lava plain with its endless rocks, seemingly identical trees and bloody spear grass!

After ten minutes of walking, during which two trucks went past west and one truck and a 4WD went east, he angled left towards the highway, going slower all the time and hotly conscious that the sun was now nearly half way down the sky in the west. There was a fence parallel to the highway with a fire break track beside it. That gave him pause. Were there cameras aimed along the clearing of the firebreak?

I'm getting paranoid now, Kit told himself. *But better be sure than sorry. I'll just go another couple of hundred metres away from the entrance.*

So he turned right again and continued plodding along through the bush. It was hard going as there will still lots of rocks but then he came to a slight dip and a change of soil and tree types, some sort of gum tree with reddish bark. The ground had more leaf litter than tufts of grass and these were mostly spikey stuff. It was easy going for the next hundred paces.

Then it dawned on him that a camera near the gate could not see anyone crossing the clearing in the shallow dip.

Here, I will get through the fence here, he decided.

Looking both ways, eyes searching, Kit walked slowly towards the fence. A minute later he was on the ground and crawling under the bottom strand of the barbed wire. And then he was out and standing beside a big tree beside the highway.

Now, flag down a car and get to the cops.

There had been a vehicle every few minutes while he was walking, but now the highway was empty. Kit stood there in the shade, hopping impatiently from one foot to the other and afraid to sit down in case he had trouble getting up in time. Minutes ticked slowly by. His apprehension crept up. Was Jellman alright? Have the crooks discovered the wreck? Are they on their way here to look for him?

Then the sound of an approaching big truck came to him from the west. But that just made him shake his head.

I don't want a vehicle going east. They will be going to Cairns or Townsville and there may not be a police roadblock at the Forty Mile Junction.

It was a road-train with beef cattle in four double deck trailers. Kit stayed behind the tree and shook his head. Leaning on the tree he sighed with exhaustion—until he felt something sting his neck.

"Yaargh! What's that? he cried, scraping at his neck.

That, he saw with annoyance, was a hairy caterpillar and it left a big, itchy welt on his neck and on the fingers and palm of his right hand.

"Bloody thing!" he muttered, moving away from under the tree while still trying to stay in the shade.

An RV and caravan combination went past next, also going east. Two elderly people, a man and a woman, were in it and they did not see him and he made no attempt to flag them down. Then a big rig came from the east, pulled by a lovely new silver prime mover. Kit moved behind the tree. It was a road-train hauling fuel and the driver did not see him.

This looks better, Kit decided, seeing a normal car heading west. But he knew it was a real risk. If it was the crooks! *I have to take the risk. I must get the emergency services to Jellman,* Kit told himself.

Taking a deep breath to stiffen his wavering courage he stepped out and began waving his arms. The car began obviously slowing.

Chapter 38

SWEET REVENGE

The car had two people in it and Kit found his heart hammering with anxiety as it slowed and pulled off the bitumen near him. Then his eyes took in that it had a Queensland Government number plate (His dad had taught him to notice such things) and he felt an easing of tension.

Should be alright, he decided.

He did not think that two people in a government car would be part of the gang. Anyway, it was too late.

The car stopped beside him and he saw that it contained a middle-aged man as passenger and a younger woman, who was driving. The passenger window went down and the man looked him up and down and frowned.

"You alright, son? You look like you've been in the wars."

Kit had not thought through what explanation he might give so stammered and again shook his head.

"Yes, I have been," he agreed. "Please, can you take me to the police in Mount Surprise."

"Police! You look like you need an ambulance more," the man commented, running his gaze up and down Kit as he did.

"I do, but police first. There's been a road accident," Kit agreed.

The man looked serious and then opened the door and got out. He opened the rear passenger door and quickly moved a bag to the other side to clear a seat.

"Get in," he instructed.

Kit could not see any option, so nodded and did as he was told, still apprehensive that the people might be part of the gang, despite their dress and manner. He did up the seat belt, now very conscious of his filthy clothes and bruised and scratched hands. The man closed the door and resumed his seat in the front. The car started moving.

The man then introduced himself. "I'm Mr Carpenter and this is Miss Mulrooney. We are teachers doing workshops on Indigenous Education in remote area schools," he explained.

That made sense to Kit. He nodded and said, "My name's Kit Walker, Christopher really."

Mr Carpenter nodded and spoke over his shoulder. "So, what's the story?" he queried.

Kit shook his head. Coming up on the left was the entrance to the crook's hideout and he stiffened with anxiety lest the car slow and turn in. But it was now travelling at the 110kph of the speed limit and the lady teacher driving did not even glance at the side road.

Kit sighed with relief and then replied, "It's too hard to explain quickly. Please, if you have a mobile phone, can you call the police and tell them you have Christopher Walker. They are looking for me."

That caused both the adults to half-turn their heads and the man immediately took out his mobile phone and tried to call. Then he shook his head.

"No service."

Damn! Kit thought.

Now that he believed himself to be safe, he really wanted the crooks to be caught and every minute the police did not know made it more likely the crooks might escape.

Except Jellman. He's going nowhere fast, Kit thought.

The drive now became a frustrating period of waiting till they came into mobile phone coverage. Kit was so exhausted that he just felt like collapsing but his desire to see justice done, and to save Jellman, kept him sitting up and awake. He began recounting his adventures to an increasingly incredulous pair.

They passed the turn-off to the Undara Lava Tunnels Tourist facility and Kit nodded with satisfaction. He had enjoyed going there.

And it gave me some knowledge that really helped.

The car raced on westwards along the highway. And then Mr Carpenter's mobile phone pinged and they were in coverage. He at once called 000 and asked for the police. There followed a three-way conversation while he explained and then asked Kit for more facts. Kit stressed the need for armed police and for an ambulance—or the emergency services helicopter.

By then they were driving in to Mount Surprise. They drove directly to the police station to be met by a sergeant and Kit's father and mother. Kit could not help himself. He burst into tears and rushed to his mother's embrace. Nobody else saw anything odd about that but it embarrassed him when he realised what he had done.

"How did you get here, Mum?" he queried.

"When your father phoned yesterday to say that both you and the truck had vanished I packed a bag and drove here at once," his mother explained.

Was it only yesterday! Kit thought. "Dad, what did you think had happened?"

His father shook his head and looked baffled. "I had no idea. I heard the rig drive off while I was still in the dunny, but as I had the key in my pocket I could not believe it, not till I came out and found it really had gone, and you with it."

The police sergeant interrupted now. "This young fella looks like he's taken a bit of a beating. The ambulance will be here soon and he can get some doctoring."

"Oh no!" Kit replied. "We must hurry to cut the crooks off, if they are still there."

"What about this man trapped in the wreck?" the sergeant asked.

Kit blushed at not thinking of him first. "Yes, and him. He is on the same road so we can go there first," he said.

"You don't have to go. You need to be have these injuries looked at," his mother insisted.

But Kit was adamant. "I am not stopping till Jellman is rescued and I have shown you the crook's hideout. I can take you straight to them. So let's get going," he replied.

They relented at that. The teachers were thanked and went on their way to book in at the hotel, and Kit and his parents were placed in the back of the sergeant's police car. A second policeman followed, driving a police Landcruiser.

Finding the side road was easy—there weren't many to choose from. And finding the wreck site was even easier as Kit recognised the bend as soon as they approached it. And even before he got out of the car he was sure it was the right place as the stench of rotting prawns was the dominant feature. This really hit them when they walked to the edge of the slope and looked down and saw the wreckage strewn across the hillside.

"Oh pswaw! Phew!" was the common comment.

To Kit's relief, there had been no fire and Jellman was still alive and swearing when Kit grinned at him through the windscreen and pointed to the policemen. They were able to lift him out, assisted by Kit and his father. And by then the Emergency Services helicopter had arrived from Cairns and landed in a clearing on the road. A stretcher was carried down and a cursing Jellman carried up on it to be transported to Cairns Hospital.

Jellman scowled at Kit who scowled back. "You could say thanks, you fat toad!" he snapped.

They wanted Kit to go in the helicopter but he refused. "I will show you how to get into the secret tunnel," he insisted. "I'm not hurt (He lied). I'm just a bit tired and worn out."

He really wanted to be there when the crooks got captured and also had that secret desire to reveal a genuine secret.

So they climbed back into the car and drove on, followed by the Landcruiser and a second one with two more armed police from Mt Garnet who had now arrived. As they drove slowly along the dirt road, Kit described how he had escaped and then walked through the bush.

That bush I am looking at out on the left! he observed. *And was it only last night and this morning!* It seemed like days ago.

When they crested the rocky ridge near the cattle yards, Kit's gaze immediately travelled to the shed and he experienced a spurt of satisfaction to note that the Land Rover was still parked there. He then got even more emotional reward when he led the police and his parents across to the far end of the shed and pointed to the small room in the back corner.

The police opened the door in approved style and then moved a cupboard on wheels to reveal the trapdoor. This was lifted and rifles pointed down. Kit wanted to see the crook's faces when the police called out to surrender, but he and his parents were kept well back. But he did get to see them when the concrete floor was lifted up to reveal the entrance and they were led out handcuffed.

Snake saw him first and scowled, then snarled, "You, you little runt! How did you get away?"

Kit could not resist teasing him. "I warned you that Jellman was bad driver. He crashed the truck and broke his leg and I got out. You need to pick better cronies if you are going to be a success as a crook."

Snake swore and Jones looked annoyed and muttered, but Kit could only laugh. "Snake's a good nickname for you, you low, slimy reptile!"

His mother was shocked and his father amazed. His mother told him to stop talking like that, but Kit could only grin at his dad.

"They thought they were so clever, Dad, but they couldn't even tie a proper knot."

"Yes, well done, son!" his father replied, patting his shoulder. "You've solved a mystery that has been bugging the trucking industry for months."

The police sergeant came back from seeing the prisoners into the back of the second police Landcruiser. "So how did you do it lad?" he queried.

Kit shrugged. "Between what my dad taught me about trucks and the Navy Cadets taught me, I had enough knowledge."

"And grit," his father added.

"Did you have any help from anyone?" the police sergeant asked.

Kit shook his head but then replied, "Just from reading the *Phantom.* I kept thinking what would the Ghost Who Walks do."

That got him a laugh, mostly disbelieving. But Kit knew better and just smiled. Inside, he just knew he would never be the same, that he had passed some sort of invisible psychological barrier or test and that he now had a confidence in himself that had not been there before.

And that showed when he went back to school three days later, on the Thursday. But there were a few of life's hard little lessons to go with it. The first one was that nobody appeared to have even noticed that he had been away. The only person who did notice and hurried over to greet him was Little Pixie Elise, and he just put his arms out to her. She smiled and took them and snuggled in against him. Noting the quality of her smile and the look in her eyes, Kit moved to kiss her, in blatant defiance of the school rules. She responded, closing her eyes and bringing her lips to his. When they 'came up for air' after a minute or so he studied the delight on her face and kissed her again, then hugged her. As he did, he noted a sour look on Diana Carstair's face and that pleased him too.

But the real pay-off was during the lunch break when he and Elise strolled side by side through the playground and he saw Ricardo, Piper, and the Drew brothers coming the other way—and all they did was scowl and step around.

Not even a jibe or insult, Kit thought.

What he did not then appreciate was that his body language subconsciously radiated his new-found confidence and that his reputation now preceded him.

He thought it was really good to be alive. So he kissed Elise again.

Author's Note

This novel is a work of fiction. The names, characters and incidents portrayed in it are the work of the author's imagination. Any resemblance to actual persons, living or dead or events is entirely coincidental. The locations, except for the crook's hideout, are real and are described as during the author's most recent trip to the area. The location of the crook's hideout is fictional and placed in that area for convenience. As far as the author is aware no person who has lived, or is living, in that area has ever carried out any illegal activity.

It is strongly recommended that readers who have not visited the area do so. In particular make a point of doing a couple of tours at the Undara Lava Tunnels. They are truly amazing natural features. A trip to the Gulf Country should be made slower than Kit's drive as time is needed to visit the towns of Georgetown (The Terrestrial Gem Museum), Croydon (As a wonderful old historical place), Normanton (Especially the railway station) and Karumba. A couple of days is needed to see each. As a side trip visit the Cobbold Gorge and the 'End-of-the-line' town of Forsayth.

For Fossickers there is the O'Brien's Creek Gem Field north of Mount Surprise and the Agate Creek Fossicking area south of Cobbold.

Enjoy more C.R. Cummings stories

  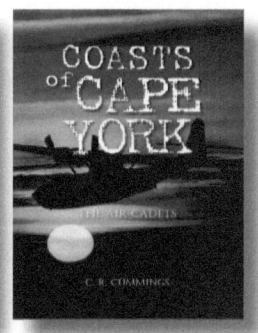

www.ingramcontent.com/pod-product-compliance
Lightning Source LLC
Chambersburg PA
CBHW030937260626
47169CB00002B/513